T0372970

The Island Getaway

Lucy Diamond

The Island Getaway

QUERCUS

First published in Great Britain in 2025 by

QUERCUS

Quercus Editions Ltd
Carmelite House
50 Victoria Embankment
London EC4Y 0DZ

An Hachette UK company

The authorised representative in the EEA is Hachette Ireland,
8 Castlecourt Centre, Dublin 15, D15 XTP3, Ireland
(email: info@hbgi.ie)

A CIP catalogue record for this book is available
from the British Library

HB ISBN 978 1 52943 298 5
TPB ISBN 978 1 52943 299 2
EBOOK ISBN 978 1 52943 300 5

1

Typeset by CC Book Production
Printed and bound in Great Britain by Clays Ltd, Elcograf S.p.A.

Papers used by Quercus are from well-managed forests and other responsible sources.

For Tom, with lots of love

Prologue

Have you ever dreamed of getting away from it all? The Ionian Escape is a luxurious, family-run hotel on the beautiful island of Kefalonia, and it might be the very place you're looking for. Imagine waking up in a light-filled, spacious suite, fully rested after a night on one of our king-sized beds. Step out onto the balcony and take in the view of the bay below – a magnificent sweep of golden sand, the sea a breathtaking shade of teal. We have a well-stocked bar and an award-winning restaurant on our verdant garden terrace, and it's a glorious spot to watch the sun go down in the evening, a cocktail clinking with ice in your hand. A short walk away is our lagoon pool, complete with sunloungers, perfect for taking it easy. There's also our indulgent spa with a wide range of treatments, plus our airy fitness studio with daily classes, and we offer a huge variety of activities for guests, from wine tasting to surfing lessons to day trips around the island.

The office manager lifts her fingers from the keyboard and reads over her words, absent-mindedly twisting the small gold evil eye charm she always wears on a necklace. In truth, the hotel has been an escape for her too, having fled to the island three years ago, pale with stress, a broken doll of a person. Since then, she has slowly rebuilt her life here, piece by piece, day by day. The sunshine has helped, as have her great colleagues, plus those faithful old healers, time and distance. She's a different woman now, stronger if still somewhat wary, and experience has taught her two things: one, that sometimes a person just needs to pack a case and leave everything behind. And two, that everyone – absolutely everyone – has a story to tell.

She returns to the website copy she's updating. *Tempted?* she types. *Then you know what to do. You're sure of a warm welcome at The Ionian Escape hotel – your perfect island getaway.*

Chapter One

Miranda

Miranda is not exactly in a holiday mood as she throws clothes and toiletries into a suitcase with the surliness of a woman defeated. *Disgraced Miranda Faces the Axe*, the tabloids crowed last week when the news broke that she would be stepping back temporarily from the show. Since then, every time she looks in the mirror it's as if she can see that axe hanging over her head, poised on a hair-trigger to fall at any moment. Meanwhile, her inner monologue insists on chanting the sinister end of an old nursery rhyme, just to heighten the sense of doom:

> *Here is a candle to light you to bed*
> *And here is a chopper to CHOP! OFF! YOUR! HEAD!*

'The directors feel very strongly that it would be wise for you to take a complete break,' Helen, her agent, had said. 'Get away from everything, remove yourself from the public eye until the fuss dies down.' In the meantime, Miranda has been written out of the next few episodes of *Amberley*

Emergency – and potentially, warns Helen, the rest of the season if she doesn't get her act together.

'Fancy being told to go on *holiday!*' her grandad had marvelled on the phone when Miranda glumly told him the latest. 'I wish someone would tell *me* to pack a suitcase and head off on a jolly, I really do. Soon as I get my car back from the garage, I'm out of here.'

'Gramps . . .' Miranda never has the heart to remind him that he no longer has a car, nor a driving licence for that matter, since the dementia diagnosis. 'The thing is, I just want to do my job, and get on with my life again. But instead it's like everyone hates me.'

'Well, *I* don't,' he'd said, loyal as ever. 'I couldn't!'

'Everyone apart from you, then. Imogen still won't speak to me. Everyone's slagging me off online too, saying awful things. I was walking down the street today and a woman actually ran out of Greggs specifically to yell at me that I should be ashamed of myself.'

'She never did! Crikey, love, I hope you told her to shove her sausage roll where the sun doesn't shine.'

Despite everything, the idea had made Miranda snort. 'I didn't,' she replied. 'Because my agent will kill me if I get in any more trouble. I'm supposed to be keeping my head down, remember?' She's been on the receiving end of quite enough bollockings lately.

'Miranda. I don't know how much more plainly I can say this,' Helen's parting words had been. 'You're no good to me – or anyone – when you're in this state. Take a break somewhere restful. Have a long hard think about whether you want to stay in the industry – and if you do, try to figure out how you can turn this around. Because you're starting to get a bad name for yourself, darling, do you hear me? We're not quite in Last Chance Saloon yet, but we're walking up to the door. Am I making myself clear?'

Yes, was the short and bad-tempered answer. Since then, Miranda has heard nothing from her agent, who seems to be devoting all her time to a new client, the sick-makingly handsome and posh Giles Shelby. He's currently starring in a Sunday evening BBC World War Two drama, and if Miranda has to see one more rave review for his performance, one more picture of his smug face, she might actually self-combust with envy. Maybe it's as well she's leaving the country.

It has been a trying time, in short. Imogen, her sister, never wants to see her again. Her co-stars have mostly gone quiet on her, presumably thinking the worst. Helen is always too busy to take her calls, palming her off on Greta, the pink-haired assistant, who makes spelling mistakes in emails and says 'expresso' rather than 'espresso'. Then there was the moment last week when Miranda stumbled out of a Kensington wine bar the worse for wear, only to have some obnoxious girls sniggering and filming her – 'Oi, Miranda! Don't slap us!' In hindsight, she probably *shouldn't* have responded by snarling expletives and giving them the finger, but there you go. You can only push a woman so far before she loses her shit. The footage swept through social media, getting such widespread traction that even her own mother came across it on Facebook. ('Honestly, Miranda, I thought I'd brought you up better than that,' she'd tutted on the phone. Clearly not.)

Now Miranda's packing for her exile: bikinis, sun cream, flip-flops. She's booked in at a hotel called The Ionian Escape on Kefalonia, plucked drunkenly from the internet after watching *Mamma Mia!* with a bottle of Pinot Grigio, mostly because the website pictures reminded her of Meryl Streep's house, with those blue shutters and all that frothing pink bougainvillea. It's probably not advisable to make expensive decisions based on this sort of a whim but whatever, she's done worse, as the whole country now knows.

Still, the pool looks all right in the photos, the reviews are glowing ('Heaven!' they say. 'Bliss!' 'Paradise!'), and she got a reduction for booking last minute, too. She'll disguise herself with massive sunglasses and a face-shading sunhat to avoid the stares, and she'll keep her head down, see out the fortnight in dignified silence. Maybe, just maybe, she'll even come up with a way to put everything right with Imogen.

The thought of her sister's white, distraught face is enough to give her pause, though, and she sinks onto the bed, with a fresh wave of despair. Oh God. Everything has gone so catastrophically wrong. Will she ever be able to wake up in the morning without feeling like the worst person in the world? Without glancing around for the axe that is surely waiting to CHOP! OFF! HER! HEAD?

Chapter Two

Nelly's Diary

Corfu, 30 June 1983

An astonishing day! Oh my God, I still can't believe it. I am giddy and whirling and slightly hysterical with what I have done — but I wouldn't change a thing!!

Let me start from the beginning: Lorraine and I schlepped out to the airport horribly early this morning to catch our flights home . . . and then, as we queued up with our tickets and suitcases, I found myself thinking about all of the dreary things that awaited us there — work, bills, Mrs flipping Thatcher — and this terrible sense of doom took hold. 'I wish we weren't going back,' I said, and then, in the very next moment, an outrageous thought came to me.

'Lorraine,' I said, grabbing her arm. 'We could just . . . stay. Why don't we stay?'

She burst out laughing. 'Oh yeah, sure,' she replied, assuming I was joking. 'I can't see Mr Standwick taking that very well, can you? And what about my Jim?'

Like anyone cares what Mr Standwick thinks! And who gives a monkey's about Jim One-Joke Heathersage? (Lorraine, obviously, even though she could do SO MUCH BETTER.)

'I mean it,' I said, this mad sort of determination setting in. 'I'm going to stay here in Greece, for as long as I can. Mr Standwick can jolly well find someone else. He hates me anyway. And—'

'You're not serious, Nelly, are you? What about your room in the flat? Mrs Bartlett will be spitting feathers if you duck out like that. And what about Michael? I thought you and he were—' She broke off before she could finish her sentence. 'No, you're teasing me, I can tell. Very funny! I almost believed you for a minute there.'

The thing was, I wasn't teasing her. Not in the slightest. We were almost at the front of the queue by this point and the couple ahead of us were getting their tags fastened on their suitcases. Now or never, I thought. Now or never! 'I'm not teasing,' I said, stepping out of the line and rummaging in my bag for my keys. 'I'm serious. Give these to my brother,' I went on, dumping them in her hand, 'and I'll get him to pack up my stuff; he'll sweet-talk Mrs B, no problem. As for Michael, I know he's Jim's friend but honestly, we have nothing in common. I don't fancy him, Loz.' She still had that disbelieving look on her face, so I decided to spell it out for her, plain and simple. 'You go back if you want to, but I'm staying.'

'But . . .' Lorraine's eyes boggled so wildly I could actually imagine them plopping out of her head. 'But . . . our flights are booked, Nell, and . . .'

'Looks like my seat's going empty then,' I said, my decision hardening like concrete. 'I'll be fine – I'll pick up a job here for the rest of the summer, then do some travelling. Think of all those beautiful beaches and ancient ruins I'll discover! I can learn to dive and get the best tan of my life!'

8

'*Next, please,*' *called the woman behind the desk. She was wearing one of those silly little red hats, and had ferociously dark eyebrows, plus cheekbones you could peel a carrot on.*

'*Bye, Lorraine,*' *I said.* '*Give my regards to Mr Standwick. Tell him he was the worst boss I've ever had, and—*'

'*Nelly, no, come on. Joke's over. You're being ridiculous! You've had too much sun. You can't just—*'

'*And you can tell Michael he was a terrible kisser, and the thought of his clammy hands ever touching me again makes me want to scream,*' *I added cheerfully.*

'*Ladies!*' *snapped the woman behind the desk, eyes like daggers.* '*You're next. May I see your tickets, please?*'

I made a sort of shooing gesture to Lorraine. '*You heard her. She wants to see your ticket.*'

'*But—*'

'*Bye, Lorraine,*' *I said again, giving her a hug. Then I walked away. And kept on walking, even though she was calling after me (Nelly!* Nelly. *NELLYYYYYY!) I walked all the way out of the terminal and got on the first bus heading back to Kontokali. The whole time I felt jittery, as if I was expecting the police to turn up – or my mum, or Mr Standwick, or my landlady – and force me to turn round again and get on the plane. But nobody stopped me. And so here I am! Still in Corfu!!!!*

I spent the afternoon asking around hotels and guest-houses to see if they needed staff, and have wangled myself a cleaning job at the Aphrodite Hotel. I have a tiny bedroom up in the attic that doubles as storage space for the bedlinen – but that's fine. I'm so happy! I'm free! Today is the start of the rest of my life – and I vow here and now that I'm absolutely going to make it an exciting one!

Chapter Three

The Receptionist

It's Saturday, and the busiest day at The Ionian Escape as guests arrive and leave, and the sky is cross-hatched with aeroplane vapour trails. It's also the first weekend that the receptionist has had to work since returning from maternity leave, and she's already had sixteen panicked messages from her husband, who is minding the baby today. *She won't stop crying. I think she misses you. Do we have any more wipes? I can't find the pink elephant.*

Her husband is not a stupid man by any means – he's a good man, kind and honest – but he can become overanxious at times. However, the receptionist needs to be able to get on with her job without worrying about him *and* their baby all day. She's good at what she does, she likes it here at the hotel and they need the money, more to the point. Somehow or other, they have to make this work between them.

She puts her phone away as a taxi pulls up outside, then watches expectantly as a tall, well-dressed man with salt-and-pepper hair gets out, followed by a small, slight woman with a shingled silvery bob. The driver opens the boot for them and hauls out first one case then another. The woman stops to thank him, pressing some money into his hand, but the man is already hauling the biggest suitcase along and into the hotel as if he's in a hurry. Only when he is two steps away from the desk does he turn round, belatedly realising that his wife is lagging behind.

'*Kalispera,*' says the receptionist with a warm smile as they approach. In all of her years working in hospitality, she has perfected that smile, and can flick it on at will like a lamp, whatever she thinks of people. *It is our job, our duty to treat every guest as if we are delighted to see them,* her boss Dimitris is fond of saying. *To make them feel special, welcomed. First impressions count.*

'Afternoon,' the man says, as he and his wife reach the desk together. First impressions cut both ways, of course, and he is quite a presence, the receptionist registers; in his early sixties, by her estimate, and still very handsome with his aquiline nose, grey eyes and strong jaw. A full head of hair too, and the sort of body that signals a man who knows his way around the gym. Imagine having the energy, she thinks to herself, as the man puts a hand into his jacket pocket to withdraw two passports. She and her husband both went regularly to the gym before the baby arrived but these days her flesh feels soft and slack, and the thought of squeezing herself into Lycra in order to run on a machine or lift weights seems incomprehensible. The scant free time she gets she would rather spend horizontal in bed, fast asleep, than do anything that involves exertion.

'Frank and Leonora Neale,' says the man tersely, slapping the passports – British – down on the counter.

'What a lovely place this is,' the woman adds, perhaps to soften his brusqueness. Working in a hotel means that you encounter new people every day, sometimes every few minutes, and you can't help but become an expert in decoding relationship dynamics. These two are not in a good place, the receptionist decides, picking up their passports and tapping her computer back into life. They are standing a little distance apart, both somewhat stiffly, and the woman's eyes are red, as if she is tired.

'Thank you,' the receptionist says, searching up their names on the system. 'Welcome to The Ionian Escape, Mr and Mrs Neale.' Ahh yes – they are staying in one of the finest suites here, she sees, with a request having been made for flowers and a fruit basket to be awaiting them. Very nice. 'If you could just sign a few documents for me ...' she says, handing over a sheaf of printed forms and a pen. Mr Neale takes them, as she knew he would, and signs with a large flourish. 'Wonderful. And here are your room keys. Would you like any help with your cases?'

They would not, says Mr Neale, although his wife opens her mouth as if she was about to say yes, only to close it once more, her words unspoken. The receptionist pretends not to have seen the flash of resignation on her face – sometimes guests don't like it if you catch their eye, attempting solidarity – then directs them to their suite. From below the desk she hears her phone ping again but there's no time to look at whatever her husband is fretting about now, because in comes a group of six animated young women, who perhaps have had a glass or two of something on the plane over. This must be the German group who have booked two triple rooms; the receptionist makes a quick mental note not to allocate the neighbouring rooms to the family with two toddlers who are arriving later today.

Checking them all in takes some time, and afterwards the receptionist has a brief moment to see the latest update from home – *She still hasn't gone to sleep* – before a young couple arrive, holding hands and leaning against each other as they announce their names. You can tell that the very second they get into their bedroom and close the door they will be ripping each other's clothes off and having sex, the receptionist thinks, with a small pang for the days when she and her husband used to be like that too. She couldn't get enough of him back then – nor he her. Nowadays they stumble blearily into bed and hold one another in silence, like survivors from a natural disaster, clinging on for dear life. This is what parenthood has reduced them to: hollowed-out shells of their old selves, feeble from exhaustion. But she's made it back here at least, she reminds herself. She is reclaiming her old life incrementally, extricating herself from the confines of the motherhood bubble. Which is why she needs her husband to persevere, to learn how to look after their daughter, just as she has had to.

The young couple head off to their room, trailing a cloud of pheromones, and the receptionist picks up her phone to reply to her husband. But his most recent message stops her short:

I don't know if I can do this. I'm sorry. I don't think I'm very good at it.

The receptionist's husband is a proud person, who will not have enjoyed typing those words. As she reads his admission of defeat, her own body lets her know that *it* feels compelled to step in now, her breasts tingling with a familiar fullness in her unsexy maternity bra, aching to feed her baby into milky submission. But she's here, far from home, where her little one is crying and her husband is in despair. All of a sudden, it feels as if she has made a bad mistake, that her priorities are wrong. Giddy in her excitement to be working again, has she let down her own little family?

She gulps some water as two new taxis arrive, wishing she could sneak off and use her breast pump, but that's impossible on arrivals day when the guests keep on coming. Please don't leak, she thinks, glancing down at her clean white blouse in alarm, praying that the milk won't flood through the fabric. She doesn't want to have to scuttle off to Housekeeping to see if there is a spare white top she can borrow.

Just then a woman wearing enormous dark glasses and a floppy sunhat walks in with a huge Samsonite suitcase. 'Miranda Vallance,' she says curtly. 'Staying for two weeks.'

'*Kalispera*,' says the receptionist. 'Welcome to The Ionian Escape. Do you have your passport, please?'

Ms Vallance heaves a massive handbag onto the desk and starts rummaging around inside it, although the receptionist is surprised she can see anything much in there with those sunglasses. Meanwhile, another two taxis have pulled up outside, and her phone is pinging again, presumably with another anguished update from her husband. Something tightens inside her, the feeling that her reserves are being stretched thin. Might she have romanticised working here while under the sleep-deprived cosh of maternity leave? With a rush of guilt, she remembers her eagerness that morning to wear smart clothes and make-up once more, to step back into the old outline of herself rather than being Mama around the clock.

'There,' says Ms Vallance eventually, pushing her passport across the desk.

'Thank you,' says the receptionist, finding her booking. Ahh – she's in the Serenity Suite, the most expensive and luxurious one in the hotel, with a double-aspect room, huge bathroom and a private sun terrace. Well, if anyone needs serenity it's Miranda Vallance, who stalks off with her luggage and room key without so much as a thank-you.

For the rest of the afternoon, the receptionist is so busy she barely has time to think about her baby or husband. Then comes a short lull, and she is about to rush off to find her breast pump when an older woman walks through the door, slowly hauling along a case. '*Kalispera,*' she says when she reaches the desk, passport in hand. 'I'm afraid that's about the limit of my Greek, but I'm Evelyn Chambers and I'm booked in for ten days here.'

'*Kalispera,*' the receptionist replies, typing in the woman's name. Gosh, she's eighty-two, she realises as she adds the passport details. Eighty-two, and still very dapper in a dusky pink tunic top and parchment-coloured loose trousers, her white hair in a neat crop. Good – she's been allocated a lovely room

15

with a sea view and a spacious balcony; a nice, quiet space at the end of the corridor, so she shouldn't be disturbed. 'Here's your key,' she says, retrieving it.

'Thank you, Duska,' says the lady, with a quick glance at the receptionist's name badge. 'Am I pronouncing that right? What a pretty name.'

'It's Dush-ka,' Duska replies, smiling as she hands over the key. 'But you were close.' She glances around for the porter but her colleague Julia has just collared him to escort a middle-aged couple to their room. 'Let me show you to your suite,' she says, getting up from her seat.

'Are you sure? I don't want to be any bother.'

'No bother in the slightest,' Duska assures her. The woman reminds her of her own grandmother, Anna, who died a few weeks before the baby was born. They named their daughter Anna in tribute but Duska has missed her kind, twinkly-eyed *yaya* very much. 'It will be my pleasure.'

She walks Evelyn through the hotel and out onto a path that curves around the bar's outdoor seating area. Guests are settling in with cocktails and bar snacks – there are the German women, getting stuck into large Aperol spritzes filled with ice and orange slices, she notices with a smile. There are the two blonde ladies – sisters, from the Netherlands – who arrived after the Neales, already sharing a bottle of white wine on the next table, one of them having kicked off her shoes to wiggle her bare toes in the late afternoon sunshine. Good. This is what a holiday should be about, Duska thinks, feeling her own spirits rise at the sight.

'So, as you can see, this is the bar,' she tells Evelyn as they proceed along the path. 'Konstantinos and Christos there make great cocktails, but we have a wide range of other drinks, including some delicious Greek wines. Your room has a balcony, by the way, so if you ever fancy a sunset drink just call reception and we will send someone up with it, okay?'

'Now you're talking, Duska,' says Evelyn. 'A sunset tipple — that does sound nice. And why not? I am on holiday.'

'Absolutely!' Duska tells her. It is her favourite part of working at the hotel, seeing people enjoy themselves. Especially the ones whose eyes light up in appreciation, like this lady. 'You can order food here too,' she goes on, gesturing to the tables set up on the terrace. 'Breakfast is from seven in the morning until eleven, and we serve snacks, lunch and evening meals.'

'Wonderful,' says Evelyn happily. 'Gosh, and look at that view. The sort you could never grow tired of, I imagine.'

'I've been here four years in total, and no, not yet,' Duska tells her as they slow their pace to gaze out at the bay below — the stretch of golden sand, the azure sea seeming to meld into the bright sky on the far horizon. The beachgoers will be packing up soon, returning to their guest-houses and hotels to shower off the salt and sand. Seagulls skim across the sky high above them, banking and rolling like stunt pilots.

They're nearly at Evelyn's room now, the path leading them through the garden area, cicadas chirping all around. The path is lined with great banks of gauras, their white starry heads bobbing as the bees cruise between the stems, and there's flowering rosemary too, its fragrance hanging in the warm air.

'Are those myrtles I see blossoming?' Evelyn asks. 'They

smell divine. And lime trees too ... Oh, this is perfect. I feel as if I've had a holiday already, simply walking along here with you.'

'I am glad to hear that,' Duska says. 'And now this is your room, number seven.' She comes to a halt outside the single-storey block, opens the door and holds it for Evelyn to step inside, then follows behind with the case.

'Heavens above! This is too perfect for words,' says the older woman as she takes in the calm, unfussy room with its large olivewood bed and spotless white bedlinen. A couple of comfortable rattan armchairs are visible on the balcony through the double doors, with the sea beyond. 'You'd better watch out, I'm not sure I'll ever want to leave again.' She starts fumbling in her purse. 'Now let me find you something ...'

'Oh no – please. There's no need,' Duska tells her. 'Honestly.' And it's true – seeing the older lady's apprecia-tion is reward enough. She *does* love her job. 'Remember, call reception if you need anything. In the meantime – enjoy yourself.'

They say goodbye and Duska walks back to the reception desk, hoping that a queue hasn't built up in her absence. But the lobby area is empty, save for Julia. Finally. 'Do you mind if I just nip to the loo?' she asks.

'Of course not,' says Julia, who's engrossed in her Instagram feed. Duska grabs her phone, heads for the staffroom, where she has stored her breast pump in a locker, then retreats with it into a cubicle for some privacy. Sitting there, releasing the pressure at last, she enjoys an exquisite moment of relief as she exhales. Then, bracing herself, she checks the latest update from home.

Anna's asleep! she reads, thankfully. *Sorry about all the messages. I'll get the hang of this soon, I promise.*

The tension leaves her immediately as Duska pictures her daughter's tiny sleeping face, her beautiful pink lips slightly parted, her body slack. Everything's okay, she tells herself. They can do this. Between them, they're going to make it work.

Chapter Four

Miranda

Miranda isn't quite sure where she is when she surfaces from her post-arrival nap. She'd been so exhausted after the palaver of travelling – the delay at Gatwick, the cramped flight full of parents with screaming infants – that when she eventually made it to her suite, she collapsed onto the bed and fell asleep almost immediately. She's always been a good sleeper, Miranda – it's one of her superpowers, the ability to shut her eyes and nod off, whether on a train or backstage before an evening performance or in noisy digs with paper-thin walls during the tight-budget days of repertory theatre. 'Classic psychopath,' her sister Imogen once joked, back when they were still friends. 'Most of us normals have this thing called a conscience that keeps us awake at night.'

'I think you'll find that's a *guilty* conscience,' Miranda had retaliated. 'Maybe I'm just a nicer person than you?'

Oh, the irony, she thinks, remembering this now and grimacing. Pushing Imogen from her mind, she starfishes on the vast bed, wondering how big a room service bill it's possible to rack up over the next fortnight. It's tempting, after everything she's been through, to keep at a remove from the other holidaymakers and skulk alone for the duration. But one glance through the balcony doors reveals that it's a glorious evening, the blue sky giving way to tones of bronze and pink as the sun begins its slide towards the horizon. *What are you doing, moping about inside on such a lovely day?* she hears her mother's voice in her ear – an outdoorsy person, who can never bear to stay indoors if the sun is even semi-visible. *Come on, up and at 'em!*

She'll probably be hearing her mother's bossy voice on her deathbed, Miranda thinks, rather grumpily, but swings her legs from under the covers nonetheless and sits up, rubbing the sleep from her eyes. *All right, all right. Give me a minute.*

A while later, following a quick wash and change of clothes, Miranda tucks her long blonde hair up into one of the wigs that she has brought with her, a dark brown pixie crop that she wore years ago in a production of *The Seagull*. She has always loved dressing up, completely inhabiting a role, and, as she checks her reflection in the mirror, it feels as if the real Miranda has taken a back seat for the time being. Tonight, she'll play the part of Happy Single Holidaymaker; far less stressful than being her usual messy self. After putting on some jewellery and perfume – Happy Single Holidaymaker always makes the effort – she sets out to find the well-reviewed taverna that Google Maps assures her is a mere eight minutes' walk away.

The restaurant is down a steep hill towards the beach. It's eight o'clock and the sun has set, but the evening air is still pleasantly warm, which is cheering, given that it was lashing down with rain when she left the UK this morning. A bird swoops silently past her – an owl? she wonders with a thrill – and there is jasmine flowering fragrantly along the fence on her left, as well as the briny tang of the sea beyond. Maybe this will be okay after all, she thinks, as she rounds the corner and sees the lights of the taverna ahead. Her sister's hurt face, Helen's cold disapproval, the paparazzi frenzy ... they all seem mercifully far away now that she's here. Her shoulders are already lowering. Perhaps she needed this more than she realised.

The taverna is a simple structure, built into the side of the hill, and opens right onto the beach at the front. Even in this dusky light the view is gorgeous, with a silvery cast to the sand, and the sea deepening from mid-blue through to inky midnight on the horizon. Inside, it's busy, with pretty candle-lit lanterns on each table, and bouzouki music playing, and the waiting staff shoulder large platters of delicious-smelling food. Oh *yes*, thinks Miranda, suddenly appreciating the liberation of not having to be filmed and shown on television any time soon. There's so much pressure to keep up appearances when you are broadcast into people's living rooms week in, week out; God help you if you dare put on a few pounds, or leave the house without a full face of make-up, because it will be noted and commented on and shared. It's bad enough in print or online, but it's so much worse when people say terrible things to your face, as if you're not an actual human being with feelings. 'Oh! You look much fatter on television than you do in real life,' she's been told before. How are you supposed to respond to that?

A handsome young waiter with dark, gelled-back hair and exactly the right amount of stubble notices her and gestures for her to take a table on the far side of the room. 'Thank you,' she says, as he brings her a menu, a wine list, a basket of rustic-looking bread. Then she undertakes a precautionary sweep of the place, hoping that the wig will be enough to afford her some privacy. Funny that she used to long for recognition, back in the day. Astonishing, to remember the buzz she'd experienced, the frisson, the first time someone approached her in a pub, shyly asking, 'Are you in that cereal ad on the telly?' How ecstatic she had been to say yes! To sign a beer mat, to pose for a photo!

A burst of laughter erupts nearby and she instantly goes cold, convinced that the sound is directed at her. *Oh God, is it her, do you think?* she imagines people giggling to one another, clutching their phones in readiness. *The one who went viral on TikTok?*

She risks a glance behind, only to see that the group she heard laughing aren't looking her way and, in fact, appear to be speaking in a foreign language, so probably don't even know who she is. Okay, stand down, she orders herself. It's not about you. This is what fame does to a person, though – the paranoia, the constant feeling that you might be torn apart on a stranger's whim. *Is it just me,* she'd once read in the comments section of the *Amberley Emergency* Facebook page, *or does anyone else feel like smashing in Miranda Vallance's head with a lump hammer whenever she's in a scene? UGGGHHHHH!* She'd closed down the laptop the moment she saw it, hands shaking, but the comment has lived permanently in her brain ever since. A *lump hammer?* They hadn't been warned about that at drama school.

Good news anyway: at a first glance, she can't detect anyone staring at her or, worse, trying to take covert photos. As well as the table in fits of laughter (five or six young women seemingly having a whale of a time), there are a lot of middle-aged couples with sunburnt noses chatting companionably. A large extended family with a small child slumped asleep in a highchair. A young couple smiling adoringly at one another over the table – eyes only for each other. Safe, safe, safe. Then her gaze shifts to the table nearest hers and she jerks in her seat with surprise. No *way*. Is that really Frank Neale sitting there, mere metres away? Yes, it's definitely him, the celebrity chef and restaurateur whose bestselling cookbooks have found their way even to Miranda 'Microwave Dinner' Vallance's kitchen. Not that he or the woman beside him look particularly overjoyed to be here, she notes, intrigued.

As if reading Miranda's mind, the woman in question swings her head round, catches her staring and gives her a sharp look. Cheeks burning at being caught out, Miranda buries her face in the menu, feeling a hypocrite for gawking. She can't get away with a 'We're both famous' smile of acknowledgement either, because Frank Neale probably wouldn't recognise her, even without the wig. There's this weird fame hierarchy where other celebrities – even fellow actors! – tend to look down on soap stars, when, take it from Miranda, they are the hardest-working people in show business.

The group of young women explode into laughter again and, although the sound is one of exuberance, it sets Miranda's teeth on edge. It makes her feel as if she's back at school, friendless and alone, ousted by the other girls for being too weird, too nonconformist. *You're unique, that's all,* her dad once told her, his kind way of acknowledging her outsider status and trying to put a positive spin on it. But who wants to be unique aged fourteen? It feels like an effort even now, in her thirties. Sometimes she wishes she'd been born with the gene that other women seem to possess, the innate ability to gel with others, to fit in to a pack. Aside from her sister, Bonnie is the only woman she's ever managed that with, she thinks, before remembering that Bonnie Beresford is the worst person in the world.

Sitting straighter in her seat, she tries to channel Happy Single Holidaymaker who has lots of friends back home, thank you, who never feels awkward, and who embraces the chance to dine solo for a change. It's always been easier for her to adopt a role as camouflage rather than sit with her own feelings. But then she's reminded of Patrick, one of her exes, who'd once said to her, exasperated, 'Who *are* you though, underneath all of the roles and the acting? What bit is actually you, Miranda? Because – forgive me, but I'm looking, and I can't see anything there.'

Forgive me, he'd said, like that was possible when he'd basically told her she was nothing. He was a set designer at the National when she was understudying there for a season, ten years ago, and they'd dated for a few months. She'd dumped him soon afterwards though, not quite able to move beyond his damning remarks. *Who* are *you, Miranda?* A failure, Patrick. Exiled here like Circe in the Greek myths, a witch alone in the wilderness.

25

'Madam? You are ready to order?' says her waiter, and Miranda is catapulted from her reverie.

'Oh! Yes, please. I'll have the ... um ... prawns to start, then the sea bream,' she says. 'Thank you.'

'And to drink, madam?'

'I'd like the ...' Miranda opens the wine list and finds the first white wine she has heard of. 'The Assyrtiko.'

'A small glass? A large?' the waiter asks, pencil poised above his little notepad.

Miranda pauses as if she's deliberating, but she already knows her answer. Fuck it, she's on holiday. Even Circe deserved a treat now and then. 'A bottle, please,' she says. Bring on sweet oblivion. After the few weeks she's just had, she's more than ready to fall into the soothing embrace of Dionysus.

Chapter Five

Nelly

Corfu, July, 1983

After Nelly had walked out of Corfu airport that day, her best friend's voice ringing in her ears, it was as if her life split into two and she'd landed on the fun side. It spooled alongside her, that parallel life where she'd boarded the plane with Lorraine and returned to her dreary job and dingy Camberwell flat with the creepy neighbour, and she would feel like laughing at her sheer good fortune whenever she imagined that mirror existence. Because here she was, still in beautiful, blue-sky Corfu, and with a bit of luck she'd never have to type up another letter for her old boss, Mr Standwick, who smelled of cheese and onion crisps, and never cracked a smile.

'What do you mean, you're not coming back?' her mum had spluttered when Nelly broke the news that first evening. 'What are you talking about? Have you gone mad? Derek, come here, Nelly's saying all sorts on the phone. And she's still in flaming Greece!'

'I've got a job and somewhere to stay, don't worry, I'm fine,' Nelly had said, but it was to deaf ears because her mum was still squawking to her dad, who, moments later, grabbed the receiver from his wife.

'Are you in trouble, is that what's going on here?' he'd asked. Straight to the point, as ever.

'No, Dad, it's nothing like that. I just fancied a change. An adventure! And I love it here. So—'

'People like us don't have *adventures*,' he'd told her scathingly. 'If I find out some dodgy fella's got you in the family way, I'll—'

Thankfully Nelly never had to hear the rest of the sentence, because her money ran out and the line went dead. Which was maybe just as well. If her parents knew that her new job was scrubbing toilets and making beds at the Aphrodite Hotel in the Old Town, they'd have been more certain than ever that she'd lost her mind. But it was somewhere to stay at least while she figured out her next move, and she was usually finished by two in the afternoon, after which time she was free to do whatever she pleased. One of the cooks, Dino, let her borrow his bike and she loved cycling around the island, stopping at whichever pretty cove caught her eye and plunging into the sea to cool down.

'People like us don't have *adventures*,' her dad had said, but he was wrong, because here she was, living proof that you didn't always have to do what others expected of you. And even if, so far, her adventure involved her in rubber gloves, with a mop and bucket, heaving endless laundry into the machine, hoovering and ironing, it was all worth it.

A few days later, down at the marina, she was wandering aimlessly along the boardwalk, before she slowed to a stop in front of a gleaming white yacht. Imagine the freedom that must come from owning such a thing, she thought enviously; the joy of being able to travel wherever the mood took you. Then came the sound of footsteps approaching and she turned to see a glamorous couple, ten or so years older than her, walking towards her.

'*Posso aiutarla?*' the woman asked. She was wearing a chic white halterneck minidress and cat-eye sunglasses, her dark hair swept up in a perfect beehive. 'Can we help you?' she added, seeing Nelly's blank look.

'Oh. Sorry. I was just admiring your boat,' Nelly said, blushing. 'And thinking how nice it must be to sail away, wherever you want to.'

A sigh of longing escaped with her words, and the woman smiled in understanding. 'Ahh, yes,' she said. 'It is the best. We are from Italy but we have sailed . . .' She started to count on her fingers, then laughed, her hands flying up in the air. 'Many, many countries now,' she said.

'And we still want to see many, many more,' the man said. He was wearing sand-coloured long shorts and a navy polo shirt, and carried a shopping bag of groceries, a bottle of wine poking out of the top. He manoeuvred a gangplank into place and stepped onto it. 'Come – you want to look around?'

Nelly had heard about swingers, and her dad's dark words about 'dodgy fellas' echoed briefly in the back of her mind, but she had a good feeling about the Italian couple. Besides, how was an adventure meant to start if you said no to every opportunity that came your way? 'Yes, please,' she replied.

As a little girl, Nelly had had a beloved dolls' house and had spent many hours immersed in its miniature world. Seeing the yacht's pleasingly compact galley kitchen with its tiny stove and sink, the salon with its secret storage areas and table that folded out, gave her the same joy. 'Oh, I love it,' she kept saying. 'It must be such fun, living like this!'

The woman, Giovanna, nudged her, an encouraging glint in her eye. 'You don't need to *own* a boat to live this life, *mia cara*,' she said. 'Plenty of boat owners need staff here and there, you know. You can earn your passage if that is what your heart desires.'

Hope soared immediately. 'Tell me more!' Nelly replied eagerly. 'Are you saying that the two of you need . . . ?'

No, unfortunately, Giovanna was not. 'But we will listen out for you, and if we hear of anyone looking for deck-hands we will give them your name,' she promised. 'Right, Paolo? And we'll tell them . . . where can they find you?'

'I'm working at the Aphrodite, do you know it? Ten minutes' walk from here, on the main street,' Nelly said, excited at the idea of working a passage and where that might take her. 'Thank you so much!'

A short while later, having said goodbye, she headed back along the marina, asking everyone she saw if they knew anyone who could give her some work. The answers were all a variation of the word 'no', but her enthusiasm could not be dimmed. Being on board Paolo and Giovanna's yacht had lit something inside her, a spark that burned brightly the entire way back to the Aphrodite.

Whatever her dad might think, there *was* an adventure out there with her name on it, she was certain. All she had to do now was find it.

Chapter Six

Miranda

Leaving her suite with a towel, book and sun cream late Sunday morning, Miranda acknowledges that her role as Happy Single Holidaymaker will have to take a back seat today, after she vomited in the loo twice last night, then woke up dry-mouthed and hungover to shit. Even actors have their limits. She's never drinking again, and that is a stone-cold *fact*.

As she heads down the steps to the pool, her billowing white kaftan brushes against the abundantly planted lavender bushes and she's immediately transported back to Le Manoir aux Quat'Saisons, early summer, and the night that has since haunted her. It was Imogen's birthday, the whole family were gathered there for a celebratory dinner, and Miranda had nipped out for a quick vape in the garden after the main course. Amidst the mingled dusk scents of lavender and rosemary, she'd exhaled vapour into the gauzy evening air, feeling stylish in a midnight-blue column dress, with her hair pinned and sprayed in an up-do. (She's really going to miss calling in favours from the *Amberley Emergency* hair and make-up team if she ends up being chucked off the show for good.) She was also feeling pleasantly squiffy on all the champagne when Felix had appeared behind her, stealthy as a lynx. 'Look at you, Sexy Miranda, star of the fucking show, as ever,' he'd said, husky-voiced, into her ear. 'I can't take my eyes off you.'

Her stomach turns now and she stumbles on the last step, her foot landing heavily on the terrace. She shouldn't think about Felix; she refuses to give him any more time in her head. Nonetheless, she's flustered, as always, by the memory. Damn him.

'Morning,' comes a voice, and it takes a second for Miranda to reorient herself and realise that the greeting was intended for her. There's an elderly woman swimming a slow breast-stroke in the pool, her short white hair gleaming in the sunlight.

'Good morning,' says Miranda in clipped tones. Possibly with an edge of don't-talk-to-me hungover sourness. She's here for herself, after all, and if she doesn't want to be bored to tears by an old grandma's witterings, then that's absolutely her prerogative.

The pool is a decent size, at least twenty metres square, she reckons, with a fenced-off corner for little ones. A striped beachball drifts along the surface in a breeze, with an inflatable dolphin and a couple of floats elsewhere. Having draped her towel over a lounger, Miranda lies down on it, the canvas tightening beneath her. She's already plastered herself in sun cream back in her room – an actress must protect her face – so now there's nothing to do but settle her limbs, feel the warm sun on her body, close her eyes and breathe. Mind empty. Problems far away. Don't think about the way she started chatting up the handsome bartender last night when she returned from the taverna, three sheets to the wind. Don't dwell on her dreadful flirting attempts, all that cleavage-hoisting and doe eyes (cross-eyes, more likely, given how pissed she was). Definitely don't think about how politely he turned down her advances, how he probably went back to his girlfriend or wife, complaining about what a bunch of cougars the hotel clientele are.

Ugh. Stop it, Miranda. You're meant to be emptying your mind, not torturing yourself. She breathes deeply, doing her best to banish his chiselled face from her thoughts. Let there be blankness. Nothingness. Let everything just . . . drift away. Maybe if she can immerse herself in this kind of mindfulness, she'll stop caring so much about her chaotic life. Just inhale . . . and exhale. Inhale . . . and—

'Gorgeous here, isn't it? Aren't we lucky?' comes the white-haired woman's voice again, ruining Miranda's moment of spiritual enlightenment. There's a sound of swooshing water, and Miranda gives a small yelp and opens her eyes as a few tiny droplets splash her. The woman is hauling herself out of the pool nearby and the sun is momentarily blotted out as she stands before Miranda, beaming.

'Mmm,' says Miranda, then reaches down, rather point-edly, to brush the water from her leg. She ends up making something of a meal of it, wiping off imaginary splashes as well as the three or four minuscule droplets, but she *is* an actress, she can't help herself. Also because an apology – or even some self-awareness, some acknowledgement! – would

34

be nice. But no. Annoyingly, the elderly woman doesn't seem to have noticed Miranda's performance, because she's already lowering herself into the neighbouring sun lounger. Damn it.

'I'm Evelyn, by the way,' she says, still smiling. 'You've just arrived like me, haven't you? How are you finding the place? Do you know Kefalonia at all?'

For crying out loud. Take a hint, Evelyn! What part of Miranda's body language and facial expression is *not* saying 'Do Not Disturb'? 'Miranda,' she replies, jaw clenched. 'No, never been before.'

There – the bare minimum. But apparently that's not enough to deter Evelyn. 'Wonderful, isn't it? We came a few times over the years, although we never stayed anywhere *quite* so luxurious as this, I have to say!' Her laugh is rich and throaty, and she's well-spoken, a voice that conjures up National Trust tea rooms and garden fetes. Maybe she's a vicar's wife, Miranda thinks, despite her self-avowed non-interest. She's always prided herself on her ability to get into a character's backstory; it's something that's hard to switch off. Evelyn would be a minor character in a detective series, she imagines: classic granny, the sort who wears a pinny and always has a Victoria sponge on hand, a proper one with jam and cream, in case visitors drop round. She knits baby clothes for the local hospital, and all the kids in the street knock at her house when it's Halloween, because she never forgets to stock up with treats.

'My other half was an archaeology professor, so we often stayed on digs in various parts of Greece,' she goes on though, dispelling Miranda's vicar theory. 'And of course, the work was absolutely fascinating if you were into that sort of thing, but staying in tents with scant facilities ... you know, you considered yourself lucky if you had a bucket to pee into, sometimes! I can't say *that* was my idea of a relaxing holiday.'

Miranda gives a polite laugh, more an amused 'Hm' than anything resembling genuine humour. Why does this woman think she – or anyone – wants to hear her peeing-in-a-bucket stories? Now her mindful serenity has been shattered by images of Evelyn squatting over a— No. Stop. Just ignore her, she orders herself. If only people came with an off switch.

'*This* place, on the other hand ... my word. I don't remember the last time I slept in such a comfortable bed. Delicious food, too. Astonishing views! And everyone seems so friendly, don't they?'

Miranda opens one eye suspiciously. Is Evelyn having a go at her? She remembers seeing the older woman chatting away to the waitress at breakfast earlier. Perhaps she regaled *her* with her bucket stories too.

'SO friendly!' Evelyn repeats. 'I don't know about you but I find travelling alone to be rather fraught with stress at times – all those decisions to make oneself, having to be constantly vigilant through airports and stations, nobody to hold your bag while you go to the loo ... I'm glad I bothered, though. Especially as ... well, for me, this will almost certainly be the last time I'm on Greek soil. You get to my age, unfortunately, and realise how short life is. And how we all need to get over ourselves and make the most of what we've got! Don't you agree?'

Ahh – has she ditched the boring professor husband, then?

Maybe she's rocked up here on the back of some steamy *Shirley Valentine* fantasies. That good-looking bartender had better watch out, if so. 'Absolutely,' Miranda replies. 'Good for you.'

Evelyn squirts sun cream into the palm of her hand, the tube making an accompanying fart noise. 'Oops!' she says, laughing. 'I promise that wasn't me.' Then Miranda can hear her rubbing the cream into her legs and arms with horrible squelching sounds.

Gross, thinks Miranda, who finds bodies in general rather revolting. She has reached a grudging stand-off with her own one after years of hatred followed by some intensive therapy, but still feels a faint repulsion around the smells, noises and clamminess of others. Which can be a problem when you play the character of a doctor on a fictional A&E ward, having to examine patients. She once actually fainted in a scene where there were gallons of fake blood on set, and frequently has to disguise her gag reflex. Still, chances are she won't have to put up with that much longer.

'So Miranda,' Evelyn goes on, 'what brings you here?'

Oh God. How is she supposed to answer that? A jumbled series of images flash up in her mind – Bonnie Beresford's sobbing face ('I swear I never said a word!'); Felix's hand on her waist, turning her towards him amidst the smell of lavender ('Here she is, star of the fucking show'); Grant yelling at her in front of the crew, a vein bulging in his neck ('What is *wrong* with you, Miranda?'); Imogen slamming the door on her ('I can't believe you've done this to me!').

Her throat feels thick with the effort of holding back all the things she could say but won't. 'Um . . .' she says. 'I just . . .'

She swallows hard. 'I just needed to get away. You know?'

'Oh, I do,' says Evelyn, her sun-cream applications merci-fully over. She settles herself back on the lounger, hands folded across her belly. 'I do indeed, Miranda.'

You don't, Miranda feels like telling her. *Take it from me, Evelyn: you have absolutely no fucking idea.*

Chapter Seven

Evelyn

Evelyn is having a splendid day. A slow awakening after a deep dreamless sleep, a delicious breakfast, and then a quiet morning by the pool. For lunch she enjoyed a Greek salad with a side of warm pitta bread and taramasalata, plus a chilled glass of white wine, so fresh and delicious that she savoured every mouthful. Why not? She's on holiday and she's determined to make the most of being here. Tomorrow she will start thinking in earnest about her last task but, after yesterday's tiring journey, she fully intends to take it easy today.

With that in mind, she's come to the so-called 'sanctuary shed', tucked away in the hotel grounds, which offers all sorts of indulgent treats. Forget the throat-clearing consultants who struggled to look her in the eye back in London, this is the only kind of 'treatment' she's interested in now. She'd rather shuffle off her mortal coil moisturised and scented, her old limbs having been blissfully kneaded, than undergo another round of experimental medication. Waiting for her appointment in the small reception area, where a wooden fan spins slowly above her head, she finds herself thinking of the ancient Greek funeral rites Rose once described to her: the anointing with perfumed oils, the adorning of the body with wreaths or other tokens, sometimes a gold coin placed between the lips as an offering to the rulers of the underworld. 'Like paying for a bus fare?' Evelyn had joked, and Rose had pulled a face. 'I won't even dignify that with a proper reply,' she'd tutted.

'Evelyn?' A pretty young woman in a flowing white dress stands before her. She has dark hair plaited around her head and large brown eyes. 'I'm Jasmine. You're here for a full body massage today, yes?'

'Yes, please,' says Evelyn, heaving herself to her feet. She follows the woman into a quiet, dimly lit room with a towel-draped bed. There is a wicker armchair in one corner, and a small unit holding a collection of lotions and potions. A drift of artfully placed tea-lights burn in rounded stone holders, and Evelyn immediately feels her breathing slow.

'Any health issues I should know about?' Jasmine asks, closing the door behind them. Her English is faultless, her manner calm. 'Any allergies?'

'No allergies,' Evelyn says, opting not to answer the first question. Will it make any difference now anyway, other than to trigger an awkward hushed-tone conversation? Jasmine might even decide that Evelyn is too frail, and that the hotel can't be held responsible if she takes a turn for the worse mid-massage. She remembers the nurse gently telling her last week that she had now reached what they termed 'end-of-life care'. Evelyn can't recall the other phraseology used, only that there was quite a lot about her 'pathway', the subtext being, of course, that it was a short pathway, unfortunately, in one direction only, and that she'd be reaching her final destination without much delay. No, she can't face mentioning any of that to sweet-faced Jasmine.

The girl leaves the room while Evelyn removes her sundress and sandals, her bra and her watch. The latter was a present from Rose nearly twenty-five years ago and, although it has seen out several batteries and changes of strap since then, it still keeps perfect time, ticking away faithfully like her own heart. Sometimes she holds it up to her ear and remembers how she loved to hear Rose's quiet rhythmic breathing at night in bed. How, the first time they kissed, there had been that shocking blood-roaring moment afterwards when they had looked at one another, eyes wide, as if to say, *Did we really just do that?* Then Rose had smiled, taking Evelyn's hand and placing it against her own chest. 'Can you feel how fast my heart is pounding?' she'd asked.

There's a soft knock at the door, and Evelyn clambers inelegantly onto the bed, pulling the towels over her. 'Ready,' she calls. Not the word she would have used at the time of that kiss, by any means. She'd been married to a man, then – they both were (their poor unsuspecting husbands) – and although Evelyn wouldn't have said the earth had ever *moved* during her and Charles's lovemaking, she had been very fond of him, nonetheless. (Still is.) Prior to that kiss, had she been ready to embark on a relationship with another woman? In truth, it had never so much as crossed her mind. But when Rose's lips met hers, the universe had turned itself inside out, in a way she hadn't even known was possible.

Jasmine comes back into the room and turns on some music – it's that ambient stuff, pan-flutes and birdsong. Evelyn doesn't mind it, as long as it doesn't become sounds of waterfalls or rain; her bladder is not what it was, and she doesn't want to be lying here the whole time listening to rushing water and wishing she could nip out to the loo. Stop thinking about that, she admonishes herself, and murmurs 'Lovely, thank you,' when Jasmine asks if she is comfortable.

Jasmine tucks the towels around her, presses gently between Evelyn's shoulders and tells her to take three deep breaths. Lying there, warm and cosy, Evelyn finds her thoughts travelling back through the decades to when she had first met Rose, at her and Jonathan's house-warming party. At the time, Evelyn and Charles lived in a quiet road in Harrow on the Hill, pleasant houses full of pleasant people, and Rose and Jonathan were their gregarious new neighbours. They'd moved in one Saturday and promptly invited everyone in the street round for drinks the following Friday. In hindsight, this was a very Rose and Jonathan thing to do, compared to Evelyn and Charles, who'd been there three years and still only knew a handful of people.

'You must be the cello player,' Rose said by way of introduction that evening. It was the mid-seventies and Evelyn, like many of the women present, was wearing a cheesecloth peasant dress with large hoop earrings. Getting ready in her bedroom earlier, she had felt as if she was pushing the boat out by daringly tying a rust-coloured scarf in her long hair to complete her look. When glamorous Rose appeared in her orbit, however, she found herself wondering regretfully if the scarf in fact made her look like a little girl with an Alice band. Her new neighbour was a traffic-stopping vision in jeans that moulded her tiny waist and bottom, flaring out around silver ankle boots. Her tight blouse was black and white satin, striped in a chevron-like design so that the points guided the eye towards her crotch. Her lipstick was juicy red, and her dark hair fell loose and free in cascades around her animated face, as if it would defy any scarf that tried to hold it back. 'It *is* you, isn't it? I've heard you playing when the windows are open. You're smashing.'

'Oh!' Evelyn, never very good at accepting compliments, had blushed a delighted pink. They were in Rose and Jonathan's living room at the time; the walls were hung with paintings she would politely have described as 'experimental', and there was a large empty space where the sofa and armchair had been dragged out into the garden. In one corner of the room teetered a stack of boxes yet to be unpacked, all of which were labelled 'Rose – Books'. A record player was balanced on top of them, and Fleetwood Mac blasted from the speakers. 'That's very kind of you to say so,' Evelyn went on. 'I hope the sound doesn't disturb you.'

'God, no, not at all. It's nice to listen to you while I'm marking the hundredth uninspiring essay on the ancient Greeks.' Rose bent down to stub out her cigarette in the soil of a large cheese plant nearby. She had freckles and a gap between her front teeth, and there was something cool and bohemian about her, something wild, that Evelyn, with her sensible husband and their neatly kept home, knew was beyond her own remit. Later, as Rose made her way around the room, chatting easily to one person after another, Evelyn found that her gaze was repeatedly drawn back towards her in fascination. Then came a moment when Rose glanced in her direction, saw her looking, and winked. Evelyn had blushed so deeply, Charles had asked if she would like a glass of water. 'It *is* hot in here, isn't it?' he'd said.

'Yes,' Evelyn had replied, mortified at having been caught staring. It was like having a pash on a prefect at school or something, she chastised herself as Charles went off to get her the drink she didn't even want.

'Is the pressure okay for you?' Jasmine asks just then, her soft voice returning Evelyn to the room. The massage has begun, without her really noticing – sweeping strokes with honey-scented oil up and down the length of her back. Birdsong twittering away in the background.

'Yes, it's wonderful,' she says, shutting her eyes drowsily. Gosh, it is heavenly to be touched again, she thinks, tuning in to the nerve endings responding beneath her skin, the warmth that spreads through her body. How she has missed it in the eight years since she lost the love of her life. Oh, she fills her time as best she can, with concerts and matinees and get-togethers, but it's rare that anyone ever touches her any more, other than a quick friendly hug, a peck on the cheek. A cashier's hand brushing against hers as a receipt is handed over. The washing of her hair at the hairdresser's, the stylist's thumbs circling her scalp as the suds are rinsed clean.

On the plane over here, the tired-looking woman seated next to her had fallen asleep mid-flight, slumping against Evelyn's shoulder. 'I'm so sorry!' she cried in embarrassment upon waking, jerking herself upright. But in truth, Evelyn had appreciated that small human contact, the press of another body against hers, however fleeting. These are the things nobody warns you about when you are bereaved.

A tear spills from her eye and leaks into the towel beneath her face, because she wishes that she could spool back through time for real: click her fingers and find herself there at Rose and Jonathan's party all over again. The new Led Zeppelin album playing. The women drinking White Russians and chit-chatting about their children, the weather, each other's outfits; the men with cans of Harp discussing West Ham's recent FA Cup win. She and Rose exchanging that secret look; the wink, the blush. The frisson that kept her tossing and turning all night long afterwards.

She wouldn't change any of what happened, not a thing. She has been the luckiest woman alive, merely to move in Rose's orbit. If only she was there still.

The massage comes to a halt suddenly, Jasmine's hand resting lightly on Evelyn's shoulder. 'Am I hurting you? Are you all right?' the younger woman asks in concern.

It's only then that Evelyn realises her emotions have got the better of her, and the single tear of a moment ago has increased to a deluge. 'I'm …' She sniffs, gulps in air, gets a grip on herself. 'Sorry, darling. I'm just …' She searches for a way to explain, to give some context, but the words elude her. What words *are* there to convey something so seismic?

'Honestly, I'm fine,' is all she can come up with. 'Do please carry on; I'm enjoying it, I promise. Thank you.'

Jasmine hesitates for a further moment but then continues pressing and kneading.

Evelyn breathes in and breathes out, in and then out, until she's over her emotional glitch. She'll try her best not to think about anything at all for the rest of the session, she decides. Sometimes it's easier that way.

Chapter Eight

Nelly

Corfu, July 1983

'Nelly? Is that you? Come here, please.'

Her arms full of warm, just-ironed bed-linen, Nelly tensed as she heard the voice of Annalena, the boss's daughter at the Aphrodite, calling from the small office. Oh dear. What had she done now? Had there been a complaint from the man in room five? He shouldn't have tried it on with her like that, she will say to Annalena. The toilet brush was already in her hand; she hadn't meant to swing round at him so abruptly, practically thrusting the thing in his face, but to be fair he shouldn't have undone his trousers and grabbed her from behind. What was she supposed to do?

'Nelly! I need to talk to you.'

'Coming,' she mumbled, setting the bed-linen back down in the laundry room and tramping unwillingly towards what she thought would probably be her dismissal. She remembered the look of horror on Room-Five-Man's face when a drop of – well, she's not sure, exactly, but it came from the toilet brush – splattered across his cheek. Still, he had stopped pawing at her at least, long enough for her to throw the brush at him and skedaddle out of there. Thank God, too, because a scream of shock had frozen in her throat; she hadn't been able to make a sound. She didn't want to think about what might have happened next.

'Hi Annalena,' she said unhappily, leaning against the office doorway.

Annalena's jolly outfit, a short turquoise dress with a lace Peter Pan collar, was at odds with her stern expression. 'So,' she said, raising an eyebrow. 'You want to tell me what you have been up to, hmm? Behind my back?'

Nelly gulped. Annalena was in her late twenties and generally a sassy sort of person, giggling on the phone to her boyfriend half the day and ignoring her dad whenever he tried to tell her to do anything, but now she looked distinctly formidable. 'The thing is ...' Nelly began, crossing her fingers.

'This man who come here looking for you? You are going to tell me about him, eh?'

'I can explain,' Nelly said humbly, staring down at the scuffed lino, no longer able to cope with the terrifying eyebrow-waggling.

'A very handsome man, I am thinking,' Annalena went on, which immediately brought Nelly up short. Wait ... *Handsome?* Room-Five-Man was definitely not what she would call handsome, with his greasy hair, podgy belly and pungent body odour. So who was Annalena talking about?

48

'Ahh. Now you are interested, yes?' Annalena chuckled, patting around on the cluttered desk in front of her and eventually retrieving a piece of paper. 'Here. This is his boat.'

'His ...' Nelly repeated dumbly, before her heart lurched into full gallop. 'His *boat*, did you say?' She stared down at the paper, which had MIAOULIS written on it in capital letters. *His boat.* Oh my God. Was this ...? Might this be ...?

'He also say,' Annalena went on, her brown eyes boring into Nelly's, 'that there is a chob on his boat?'

A moment passed when Nelly swallowed – out of excitement, primarily (thank you, Giovanna!) but also because, as the boss's daughter, they both knew Annalena could make things tricky for Nelly if she wanted.

'You are looking for a *chob*, Nelly?' she asked severely. 'You don't like working for my papa, no?'

Nelly bit her lip. 'Um ... Well ...' she stuttered, only to then notice that Annalena was fluttering her eyelashes teasingly.

'I am *choking*,' she said, making Nelly think for a moment she'd have to vault over the desk and attempt the Heimlich manoeuvre, until Annalena burst out laughing. Keep up, brain, Nelly told herself, laughing too. 'I am choking, my God, Nelly! Your face!' Annalena cried, putting a hand to her chest in mirth. Then she tapped her nose and winked. 'I tell nobody. Go and find your handsome man, Nelly. And good luck!'

Nelly did not need telling twice. Laundry forgotten, she rushed straight down to the marina in search of the *Miaoulis*. Having started with great optimism at the fancier end, where all the grandest yachts were moored, gleaming and swanky, she gradually moved down the line towards the boats that were smaller and somewhat scruffier. Then she stopped, her breath catching in her lungs. There she was – the *Miaoulis*, with a white-painted hull and the Greek flag flapping cheerfully from the main mast. A good feeling spread through Nelly as she looked the boat over, from the wood-panelled upper salon to the big canvas sign on the side advertising day trips and longer cruises to Zakynthos, Kefalonia, Lefkada 'and beyond'. Yes, she thought giddily, she would like to go to all of those places, especially the 'beyond'.

'Hello?' she called as she spotted a sulky-looking dark-haired man, his skinny legs poking out from baggy jean shorts that he wore teamed with a torn mustard T-shirt. He was cleaning one of the salon windows in a half-hearted sort of way, and Nelly's heart sank a little because he definitely did not fit her criteria of 'handsome man', not in the slightest. Still, she told herself, a job was a job, or even a chob. 'Hello,' she tried again when he didn't respond. 'I think maybe you were looking for me? At the Aphrodite?'

This time he glanced round, a sneer on his face, and rattled off something she couldn't understand. By now, Nelly had picked up a smattering of Greek vocabulary, but she was still very much at the hello, thank you, two beers please stage, rather than anything more advanced. 'Er . . . Do you . . . speak English?' she tried, but his response was merely to mutter something and turn his back on her.

Talk about a disappointment! She could almost hear the mocking laughter of everyone who had ever previously teased her for her big dreams, her romantic ideals. *Isn't it time you stopped all of this nonsense and came home again?* her mum tutted in her head. But then she heard the sound of footsteps behind her and another man's voice, deep and commanding, that had old Sulky Mustard suddenly scrubbing with ten times more effort.

Nelly turned and felt a delicious shiver ripple through her. This had to be the handsome man Annalena was talking about: tall, muscular and sexy as hell with his tousled dark hair and big nose (Nelly did love a big nose), wearing a white shirt and jeans, with a gold chain glinting round his neck. It was hard, all of a sudden, to stop herself from beaming. Thank you, Giovanna, thank you, Greek gods (especially you, Eros). Good work, Greece!

The handsome one dispatched Sulky Mustard with a curt phrase, then looked at her. 'You are Nelly, I think?' he asked in what she would later describe in a letter to Lorraine as 'the most knicker-loosening sexy accent I have ever heard'.

'Yes,' she replied faintly, trying not to stare. 'That's me.'

'Alexander,' he said, thrusting out a great big hand. 'Good to meet you. And I hear you are looking for work?'

'Yes,' she said again, her hand feeling like a doll's within his as they shook. Then she pulled herself together, remembering that she needed to make a good impression. 'I'm a very hard worker.'

'Come,' he said, gesturing for her to follow him up the gangplank and on board.

It was on the tip of her tongue to reply *I think I'm about to, Alexander,* but she bit back her smutty thoughts and walked after him, stepping down onto the deck.

'Lovely boat,' she said brightly, as if she was an expert. There was a sudden swell of water as a speedboat zoomed into the harbour and she staggered momentarily, her hand shooting out to clutch for something but finding nothing there.

'You think? I am glad you approve,' he replied as she straightened up, blushing. His lips twitched briefly as if he was teasing her and she had to look away. Oh no. Did he think she was an idiot already? An idiot with no sea legs? 'Sit, please,' he said, much to her relief, indicating the padded seating area.

'So, Nelly,' he went on as they both sat down, 'I need someone to help me in many jobs. You can clean good?'

'Very good,' she replied promptly. 'Definitely better than that guy anyway,' she added, pointing to the smears that Sulky Mustard had left on the nearest windows. She shook her head, purse-lipped, as if such poor cleaning was an affront to her. 'I absolutely love cleaning,' she went on. 'Best you've ever seen. Ask Annalena if you don't believe me.' (This was, admittedly, a high-stakes claim. Just the day before, a guest had complained about finding her asleep in his bedroom after she'd overdone it on the retsina the night before. 'You are here to clean, not sleep!' Annalena's dad had roared, shaking her awake.)

Alexander didn't have to know that, though. 'And you can cook good?' he asked.

'Yes,' she replied enthusiastically, even though back in London she lived pretty much on cheese on toast. She could learn though, couldn't she? How hard could cooking be? 'I love to cook,' she added for good measure, crossing her fingers down by her side where he couldn't see them.

'So you love cleaning, you love cooking ... okay,' he said, his eyes narrowing as if he could see right through so much hyperbole. 'And you speak English – yes,' he said, miming ticking the air. 'But also Greek?'

'Um ... *Kalimera!*' she replied hopefully.

'German? French?' he asked, before speaking in a language she didn't recognise.

This, she reflected, would be harder to blag. 'Er ... I can learn,' she replied, trying not to think about quite how much rapid learning she was committing herself to. 'And I *will* learn! Because I absolutely l—'

'Love learning?' he asked, mouth twitching again, as she said those exact words. 'How did I guess?'

She bit her lip, feeling as if her big chance was swinging in the balance. 'I just really want the job,' she admitted. 'The sense of freedom – going to new places from one day to the next, I can't think of anything more exciting. And I promise I'm a hard worker. I'll cook and clean, I'll be so polite to your passengers.' She thought about Room-Five-Man and vowed silently that she definitely wouldn't thrust toilet brushes into any of their faces. 'You wouldn't even have to pay me – well, not much, anyway, and—'

He put his hands up in the air and laughed. 'Okay! Thank you, Nelly. You have the job.'

'I do? I have?' She felt like flinging her arms around him in excitement, and had to pin them to her sides, not least because he was so good-looking that if she *did* hug him she might not be able to let go again.

'Yes. Start tomorrow? Come to the dock at eight in the morning. We are taking ten German tourists to Paxos for the day. Don't be late. And Nelly ...?'

'Yes?'

'It will be hard work,' he said. 'Every day, hard work. Don't let me down.'

'I won't, Alexander,' she assured him, crossing her fingers again, a little tighter. 'I swear I won't.'

Chapter Nine

The Office Manager

StarMyStay: The Ionian Escape, Kefalonia ★★★★★
What a wonderful sanctuary this hotel is — we just enjoyed a week of sheer bliss staying here. The pool, the fitness studio, the room, the breakfast — everything was perfect. Lovely staff too — special thanks to the reception team who organised a couple of day trips for us (a visit to the Melissani Cave is a must!) And we all fell in love with Konstantinos' cocktails at the bar — amazing!

Jude and Brandon, Ohio, USA

StarMyStay: The Ionian Escape, Kefalonia ★★
Hotel was nice but we couldn't get over how many stray cats there were hanging around the streets nearby, begging at all the local restaurants. There was even a mangy dog going from table to table at one taverna. Why can't anyone do something for these poor animals?

Mrs M. Naylor, Essex, UK

It's Monday morning, and the office manager has started her week with the usual batch of online reviews to read through and, if necessary, follow up, although she has no idea how she will respond to the low-star review about the local cat population of all things. First, though, is the more pressing task of messaging her mum, Barb, back home in Melbourne, along with the photo she sneakily took, rather unprofessionally, of Frank Neale having breakfast with his wife in the hotel garden.

Look who's dropped in to stay this week! she writes, along with a string of heart-eye emojis. *How soon can you get over here?!* Barb is a big fan of Frank Neale, and even took time off work to see him when he last did a book tour in Australia seven or eight years ago. ('I am relieved to report that your mother did not, I repeat, did not, throw her knickers at him on stage, contrary to expectations,' the office manager's father, Jerry, had said drily afterwards. 'Nor did she manage to persuade him to replace me as her husband, so there's that too.')

It's early evening in Melbourne right now and she pictures her mum standing barefoot in the kitchen, bringing out a tray of fragrant lamb kleftiko from the oven, and yelling to Jerry and whichever other family members are there that grub's up, and could somebody lift a finger to knock up a salad, or does she have to do everything herself around here?

The office manager closes her eyes briefly as she is hit by a sudden wrench of homesickness. She's hoping to go back for Christmas this year and can't wait, although her joy at seeing her family and friends is always tempered by the dread that she might accidentally bump into Marcus, her awful ex-husband. Her fingers fly automatically to her throat, seeking out the small gold evil eye charm she always wears, only to realise that her neck is bare. The charm was a gift from her friend Duska a few years ago, to 'protect you from bad luck, bad people,' as she'd said. 'Especially bad men.' This was after a night when they had proceeded to get very drunk together, when secrets had been shared. Since then, the office manager has worn it every single day, and the knowledge of it strung between her collarbones, shining like armour, has always made her feel a tiny bit stronger, as if her friend is with her throughout. But today, in her rush to get to work, she must have forgotten to put it on.

It's only a necklace, a pretty object that has no real power, she reminds herself, trying to quell the spiral of panic now blooming, stupidly, inside her. She mustn't get superstitious about a piece of jewellery that cannot protect her from anything, least of all her ex-husband. Nonetheless, it's as if her armour is down, her guard lowered. Because what if . . . ?

Don't think about him, she orders her imagination. Do not go there. The next second her phone pings and it's her mum, predictably, with an *OMG!!!!!* plus a flurry of colourful heart emojis. Then a further message pops up: *He doesn't look very happy, does he? What have you done to my future second husband??*

Smiling to herself, the office manager looks again at the photo, agreeing with her mum that actually, Frank Neale doesn't look exactly enraptured. Neither does his wife, whose gaze is faraway and strained. Trouble in paradise? she wonders. They have lots of rich and successful people coming to stay at the hotel and, of course, they are only human beings at the end of the day, but nonetheless it still takes her by surprise when the lives of these people are not wholly gilded and gleaming. They'd had a famous American singer staying the other week who'd suffered dreadfully with mosquito bites, bless her. A Danish TV presenter whose sunburn was so severe he'd ended up in the local hospital. Then there was that British film star, young and gorgeous, who had wet the bed three nights running, according to housekeeping.

What, she wonders, is the deal with Frank Neale? She's sure they'll all know by the end of his stay. You can't keep anything a secret from hotel staff.

She turns her attention to the new bookings that have come in, one of which is from a family who were only here two weeks ago, now reserving rooms for the following summer. She makes a mental note to tell Dimitris, her boss, who always loves to hear about returning guests. 'Rock and roll, Claudia!' he says, pretending to play a power chord on an imaginary guitar.

It's funny how things work out. Her mother's family, the Gatakis, originally came from Kefalonia, but almost all of them emigrated to Australia following the terrible earthquake of 1953. They've kept close ties with the island in the years since though, and stocky, bald-headed Dimitris, as well as managing The Ionian Escape, also happens to be the son of her uncle Kostas' best schoolfriend, Spiro. 'Dimitris is as decent and solid as ... well, a hand-made oak wardrobe,' Claudia had described him to Barb soon after starting work at the hotel. 'But better-looking, obviously. And funnier. And ... okay, a wardrobe wasn't the best simile, thinking about it, but he's a good person anyway. I'm glad I'm here.'

58

'Me too, darl,' Barb had told her. 'And hey, show me a woman who doesn't love a great wardrobe! We all need one of those in our lives.'

Say what you like about her big, loud, interfering family, but they hadn't half excelled at pulling together in a crisis. As soon as they had got it out of her, three and a half years ago, that her marriage was utterly toxic, they'd stepped up immediately, en masse; her squad. Her parents, having brought her home, treated her like an invalid, reinstalling her in her old bedroom and waiting on her hand and foot. Her sisters screened her calls and let her cry on them for hours at a time. Her beefiest cousins went to the house and boxed up all her belongings, casually giving Marcus a bloody nose in the process ('He fell,' said the oldest cousin with a shrug). Come the Sunday, her devout grandma even had the local church congregation praying for her future wellbeing.

Then her Uncle Kostas got in on the act with a practical suggestion: for her to get right away from Australia and the ruins of her relationship, with a three-month break at the hotel. 'You'll have to earn your keep, mind; Dimitris is a businessman, not a charity,' he'd told her. 'But it's a great place – and if you ask me, just the escape you need, my darling.' The rest of the family agreed, unanimously, that Kostas had hit upon the perfect solution. With no better ideas of her own, Claudia was dazedly packing a suitcase and checking in to her flight before she knew it. Little could any of them have predicted that Covid-19 was about to sweep around the world, and that the Australian borders would soon be closed for almost two years.

The phone rings and she answers it in Greek, remembering how scared she had been to take any calls during her first few weeks at the hotel, terrified that Marcus might have discovered where she had run to. It was almost a relief when lockdowns were announced, aeroplanes were grounded and she could let out her breath, knowing that he was stuck in place for the time being, and she was safe. The hotel had to shut, but Dimitris permitted her, and a couple of other staff members, to stay on the premises for the duration. She still has a fondness for room seventeen, which was her bedroom in that period; a small, high-end bolthole while the rest of the world fell apart. She and the other members of staff became a family for each other, painting and decorating the hotel from top to bottom to keep themselves busy, taking it in turns to cook and eat dinner in the restaurant. Over the weeks, her Greek rapidly improved, her confidence crept up once more, and Marcus began to feel like a bad dream from which she had now awoken. These days, Kefalonia is home; she has forged a proper life for herself here. She has her own apartment in the nearby town, complete with the stray ginger cat that has adopted her; she has bought houseplants, a bike, saucepans. She is on chatting terms with all her local shopkeepers, and has friends among the staff, not least Duska, whose adorable baby Anna she is the godmother of.

'When are you coming back, Claudie?' Barb is always asking, though. 'Not just for Christmas, for good?' These are difficult questions to answer. Working here, living here, has been to exist behind a protective shield, preserving her from having to make decisions about the rest of her life. And it's pretty great behind that shield! For one thing, she's never had a job where the feedback is almost unanimously positive. She is astonished how many people get in touch after a holiday to thank the hotel staff for a wonderful stay. *Can't wait to come back again,* they say. *Best holiday of my life.* One British woman actually emailed last week saying that she'd had such a fantastic time holidaying with her girlfriends, it had made her re-evaluate her entire life. *I've left my moaning husband and I'm renting a flat in my old hometown, nearer friends and family,* she'd written, or words to that effect. *Thank you for opening my eyes to what really matters!* Another woman, this one Canadian, had recently sent a photo of a bonny baby girl, with a note saying *Thought you might like to see our new arrival . . . who was conceived at The Ionian Escape! We've called her Iona, and can't wait to bring her to Kefalonia when she's older.*

The office manager firmly believes that hotels can change people's lives for the better – this one certainly changed hers. Job satisfaction? Tick.

'I don't know,' she tells her mum, because there's also the fact that, the minute she leaves the island for a permanent return to Australia, she'll be starting from scratch again – staying with her parents or one of her sisters until she can find a flat she can afford, applying for new jobs. And what will she even do? Before she came here, she'd worked for a small office supplies company in Melbourne, doing their marketing, but it's not as if she's really missed churning out press releases about their new range of gel pens or Post-it notes. Sure, her experience here means that she could walk into a hospitality job back home no problem, but it wouldn't be the same as being here in Kefalonia, with—

She stops herself before she can finish her own sentence. No. Been there, done that, fled the bastard, she reminds herself. She is not about to lose her head *or* her heart again.

Now then – while the phone is quiet once more, she should tackle some of the emails that have come in over the weekend, she decides, opening the hotel inbox. Let's see ...

She barely gets through the opening line of the first email though before she gulps in a breath, her brain freezing in sudden panic. Her mouth opens but no sound comes out. It's as if she can see the little world she has built for herself being smashed in slow motion. A brick shattering her bedroom window. Her sweet stray ginger cat fleeing in fright as the door is kicked in. Her fingers reach for the comfort of her necklace but it's not there, it's not there. Her heart thunders as she reads the email again. He's found her. Somehow or other, he's found her. So what the hell does she do now?

Chapter Ten

Miranda

It was a January afternoon, earlier in the year, when Bonnie first popped her head round Miranda's dressing room door to introduce herself. 'Hello,' she'd said cheerfully. 'I'm Bonnie.' They'd been in the midst of a bleak spell, with sub-zero temperatures at night and brilliant glittering frost every morning, and Miranda's first impression was of how wholesome Bonnie appeared, with her nose red from the cold, her cheeks flushed, a damson-coloured woolly hat flattening her hair. A sweet little chipmunk in human form, she'd thought as she smiled back politely.

'Miranda,' she replied. 'Nice to meet you.' As *Amberley Emergency* was a drama set in a hospital, there were new actors coming and going in each episode of the show and, although Miranda tried to be professionally pleasant to everyone, their names and faces tended to get dumped from her brain the second shooting was over.

The chipmunk had a dimple in one cheek when she smiled,

and neat white teeth. 'I'm soon to be your – or rather, Doctor Kelly's – new worst enemy on the ward, gobby little Nurse Bell,' she went on. 'I thought I'd drop by and say hi before we start tearing chunks out of each other in rehearsal tomorrow.'

Miranda laughed. She could always get on with women on a surface level, after all; it was just that none of them seemed to view her as best-friend material. ('You can be quite . . . cold?' her sister Imogen had once ventured after a few too many mulled wines one Christmas when Miranda drunkenly voiced her fears. 'No, not cold,' she'd amended rapidly, as Miranda blanched. 'Brusque. Just a tiny bit brusque.' Was it brusque to refuse to put up with people who annoyed her, though, or did that merely indicate high standards?) Whatever, Bonnie seemed inoffensive. Not a diva, not a whinger, not obsessive about weird things – and God knew the cast already had its fair share of that sort. (She had learned the hard way, for instance, always to steer clear of Sienna during Mercury retrogrades because she never shut up about it. Ditto Jason whenever a new series of *Real Housewives* dropped.)

As the weeks went by, Bonnie proved to be a step up from merely inoffensive. She was patient with Geoff's perfectionist directing; collaborative and unstarry amidst her fellow actors, and fun to gossip with while they waited around backstage with vapes and coffees. The two of them were in page after page of scenes together, with Bonnie playing a new nurse who frequently clashed with Miranda's doctor character, and Miranda was soon looking forward to their two-handers as being the best part of the week. When the episodes were broadcast, the public responded well to the chemistry between them too, and viewing figures rose steadily. Devotees of the show started to proclaim themselves tribally for TeamKelly or TeamBell on social media, and even neurotic Geoff managed an occasional 'Well done' or 'Good work'.

Winter rolled into spring, and a friendship developed that saw the pair of them close out the long days on set with a glass or two of wine in one of the nearby bars after work. They messaged each other stupid jokes and cat gifs, formed in-jokes about their colleagues and took to confiding in one another. Bonnie would turn to Miranda for advice about her on-off boyfriend Harry and her scarily overbearing agent Stella, while Miranda poured her heart out, first about Ryan, the YouTuber she was seeing (loaded but loved himself), then Max the Championship footballer (sexy and fit but not the sharpest knife in the block). Then, when that fizzled out, she made the mistake of telling Bonnie about Felix, which was where everything started to go wrong. How could she have been so dumb?

'Hi,' comes a voice just then, and Miranda is dragged back into the present: Monday, Kefalonia; a quiet beach, far from prying eyes. That was what she'd hoped anyhow, but when she turns her head, it is to see that a woman with a jaunty blonde ponytail has appeared, seemingly from nowhere, and is now leaning over her sunlounger. They can find you anywhere, these people, she thinks, heart sinking.

'It *is* you, isn't it?' the woman goes on. 'I'm such a fan of the show! I'm like SO in love with Todd Collins! Can I have a selfie with you?'

'Oh,' says Miranda, who is wearing a bright orange bikini,

and suddenly feels all too conscious of her pale rounded tummy and the amount of feta and wine she's put away in there recently. 'I'd rather you didn't, to be honest, if—'

'It'll only take a minute,' the woman says, already crouching down beside the sunlounger and holding up her phone. 'My mum is going to be *psyched* about this!' she goes on, seemingly oblivious to Miranda's tense unwillingness to co-operate. 'She absolutely loves Todd as well. Have you and Nurse Charlotte made up yet, by the way? What did she do anyway?'

'Really – please – I just want some priv—'

Too late. No privacy allowed. The woman is tilting her head towards Miranda, so close that Miranda can smell her coconut sun oil, then she's pouting into the camera, click click click, done. For fuck's sake, thinks Miranda as the woman thanks her effusively then scuttles away to a cluster of sunloungers nearby, where a group of other women fall on her like jackals, wanting to see the results. She feels like pulling her towel over her head and leaving it there for the rest of the day. She should have worn the bloody wig, but it's so hot today, and she was hoping to swim later, and ... oh God. All she can think about is the images now on the woman's phone and what she might do with them. Miranda really doesn't want pictures of her frowning, arguing, looking a bit bulgy and sweaty in her bikini, popping up in social media feeds, being passed around, commented on, laughed at. It's all a big joke to them, a bit of fun, but for Miranda it's like having someone tear off yet another piece of her flesh. Now she can't even get up and go for a swim for fear of the woman and her friends filming her getting in or out of the water in her bikini.

I didn't know you could see whales in Kefalonia lol, she imagines them captioning gleefully with cry-laughing emojis. Is there nowhere she can hide?

She puts her earbuds in but swears she can still hear distant high-pitched laughter. Sometimes it feels as if she's been on the outside of a cackling female group her entire life, paranoid that the joke is on her. *I'm just not much of a girly girl,* she would say loftily in the past, pre-empting anyone noticing that she didn't have a squad of BFFs on speed-dial. Who needs them anyway, she'd told herself, when she was always so busy bouncing between one boyfriend and the next throughout university and her twenties. Besides, she always had her sister, Imogen, as number one confidante and cheerleader. Until Felix came between them, anyway, and then Bonnie made everything a million times worse.

She's been trying not to think about Imogen, but it's impossible to cut a sister out of your mind when your whole lives have been bound up together, from the small pink bedroom they once shared as little girls to the in-jokes that have built up between them, layer after layer, like sedimentary rock, over the decades. It's as if their lives have been one long conversation, pinging back and forth until now, when she no longer knows what to say. How many times can you tell a person you're sorry before you give up?

She'll come round, Seb, their younger brother, messaged the other day, but he's always been on the outside of their close bond, he can't possibly understand what the loss means to her. She'd feel sorry for him but of the three of them he's the one who's most together, with his diamond league job in Silicon

Valley, his ranch, his icily beautiful partner Gabrielle (not Gabby, never Gabby), who always buys Miranda and Imogen expensive skincare sets for Christmas. ('How long before she cracks and just gives us Botox vouchers, do you think?' they have sniggered in private before now.)

There are two blonde women staying at the hotel, Dutch at a guess, and you can tell they are sisters – from their similar appearances, but also from their body language, so natural and easy with one another. She misses that. 'What are you two giggling about now?' their mum, Tracey, was always saying throughout their childhoods, often in exasperation, when Miranda and Imogen were whispering and tittering about their parents. They called their mum 'Trufflepig Tracey' or 'Truffs' for short (it was to do with how loudly she breathed whenever her reading glasses had slid down her nose). They called their dad 'The Pun-Gent' (later 'The Punge') because of his penchant for terrible jokes. Then, when Tracey gave him some awful (in their opinion) new aftershave for his birthday one year, he became 'The Pungent Pun-Gent', which was quickly shortened to 'PP' and then 'Peeps'.

'Maybe you shouldn't have called *us* such stupid names, then,' Miranda would retaliate if either of them dared complain. Imagine being so into Shakespeare that you christened your poor children Miranda, Imogen and Sebastian! It had been particularly hard being a Miranda in secondary school, when the boys started calling her 'Randy'; an ironic, mocking nickname that couldn't have been less appropriate for virginal, awkward, heavy-period-suffering Miranda. 'Miranda is a beautiful name!' her mum would cry whenever she moaned about it. 'Yes, and it could have been worse, we nearly christened you Swanhilda,' her dad would add, with a secret wink at her mum. God knew what that was about.

Anyway. This is all irrelevant, seeing as she and Imogen will probably never make up stupid nicknames for anyone again, and her parents probably secretly hate her now too for ruining Imogen's life. 'We're not taking sides!' Tracey had cried when Miranda had all but accused her of this. 'I can't bear for you both to be so unhappy. Imogen's very upset, you know.' Oh, Miranda knows, all right. Not an hour goes by without her dwelling on just how upset Imogen is.

Hold your head up high kiddo, her grandad messaged her this morning. *PS you look smashing in that airport photo on the* Sun *website! Super dress!!* It's very sweet that he has taken it upon himself to send Miranda these daily pep talks but kind of dispiriting, too, that the one and only person in her corner is an 87-year-old dementia-sufferer in a retirement facility in Devon.

'Excuse me,' comes a breathless voice just then. Trying not to groan in irritation, Miranda turns her gaze wearily, to see a tall middle-aged woman in a navy one-piece looming over her, beaming. Then the beam slides away. 'Oh – sorry,' says the woman, who then laughs self-consciously. 'I was going to ask if you were Miranda Vallance, you know, the actor, but you're not, of course. My bad! Sorry to bother you.'

It's all Miranda can do to muster the thinnest of smiles. 'No worries,' she says through gritted teeth.

The woman lingers, apparently in no hurry to move on. 'I should be glad really,' she goes on conspiratorially. 'That you're *not* her, I mean. She comes across as such a bitch, doesn't she? Nasty cow, she probably would have slapped *me* too!'

'Probably,' Miranda agrees, a hysterical laugh building inside her. The woman trudges off across the sand, her words reverberating in Miranda's head. *Nasty cow. Bitch.* The exchange has left her feeling on a knife-edge, as if it'll only take one more unkind comment, one further intrusion, and she'll lose it. 'Watch out, world,' she mutters under her breath, rolling resignedly onto her front.

Chapter Eleven

Evelyn

As soon as Evelyn wakes up on Tuesday, she knows it's going to be a difficult day. There's a queasiness in her belly and a tight pinching band round her forehead that her cocktail of medications and painkillers isn't likely to change. Today would have been Rose's birthday had she still been alive, a day when the enormity of her loss seems to swell within Evelyn's body, so that it's harder to breathe than usual.

'Happy birthday, my darling,' she says aloud into the quietness of her hotel bedroom, her voice cracking on the last word. Rose always celebrated a birthday so splendidly. She was typically generous with the occasion too – it was never a day about herself, more an excuse to gather loved ones closer around, in a candle-lit restaurant, an elegant wine bar, the gastro-pub round the corner from their flat. They'd fill a long table, with Rose at the centre wearing something sparkly, laughing with her head thrown back, her hair escaping whatever up-do she'd wrestled it into, her eyes so bright and welcoming, so interested in what everyone else had to say. God, she was a peach of a woman. A gorgeous, juicy peach.

Her phone buzzes with a message from Charles. *Dear E, thinking about you today. Hope you are well x*

It's sweet of him to remember – even though in truth it is probably down to Hazel, his second wife, reminding him. Good old Hazel, who swept in to take Evelyn's place following her flit to Rose, thus blotting up some of the guilt she'd felt about leaving. It's thanks also to Hazel that Charles became a father to two boys, and eventually a grandfather to six youngsters, with the first great-grandchild now on the way. Evelyn is glad for them both and grateful for the open hearts they have always shown her when she knows that, back in those more inhibited, unimaginative times, many an ex-husband would have washed his hands of her.

There had certainly been plenty of head-shaking and lip-pursing about the affair from other quarters; plenty of 'Well, it's not natural, is it? It's disgusting!' comments. Former neighbours blanked Evelyn and Rose if their paths crossed in the supermarket or post office. Even some so-called friends were icily disapproving, rallying around Charles and Jonathan, saying how lucky it was that there were no children involved at least, then angrily demanding of Evelyn and Rose, 'What on earth are you playing at?'

'We're not playing at anything!' Evelyn had retaliated, stung. 'This is not a *game*. We love each other!' And they had done, blissfully, passionately, devotedly, for years and years and years, through the best of times and the worst. The world has changed since then, at least – in fact, one of Charles and

Hazel's grandsons is gay, another grandchild non-binary, and it has barely been an issue for anyone. Quite right too.

Other messages are appearing from friends who also loved Rose, who know how hard this day always is for her. *Thinking of you,* they say. *We still miss her too. We'll raise a glass to her tonight.*

So will Evelyn, she decides, putting her phone down with a small sigh. But before then she must start thinking about how she can fulfil the last remaining part of her final promise to Rose. This is why she's here in the first place, however much she's dressed the trip up as a holiday. She has a task to complete.

'We need to have a horrible but important conversation, I'm afraid,' Evelyn had announced to her, heart in mouth, once it became obvious that Rose's time was running out. She was in the hospice by then, her cheerful little room belying the dreadful sadness of the situation. 'And not about which restaurant menu I'm going to look up for you next,' she added, trying to soften her words. Rose was having trouble keeping anything down by this point and, having loved food all her life, she missed tasting it so desperately that she'd been getting Evelyn to read her Greek and Lebanese restaurant menus aloud, item by item, so that she could longingly imagine their flavours.

'Turkish,' Rose said immediately, and Evelyn laughed, a sound close to a sob, as she squeezed Rose's hand, so thin by then that it felt like a bundle of sticks.

'We can get to that later,' she'd replied, 'but first, I really need to ask you about – well, what you want to happen at the end. Or rather, after the end.' She'd gulped in a breath, hating her own words but aware that she had put them off long enough. Two days ago, Rose had seemed so confused and befogged by her new painkillers that Evelyn had been jolted into vowing that she had to tackle the subject the next chance she got. This was her moment. 'I know you want to be cremated, but is there anything else you'd like to add to that? Is there somewhere special you want me to scatter your ashes? Any particular requests for the funeral?'

'Well,' said Rose in the faint scratchy voice that had replaced her formerly lovely rich tones, 'I hope you will play something beautiful that has everyone bawling their eyes out.'

Evelyn made another of her laugh/sob noises, a lump in her throat. 'Of course I will,' she replied. 'I'll rustle up an entire orchestra for you, my love.'

'Excellent,' Rose said, smiling up at her. 'And about my ashes . . . I can't decide, Evie. There are so many special places. Would you take me to the Acropolis again, do you think? I love the thought of being there, maybe at the Temple of Athena.'

'Of course,' Evelyn assured her. 'In a heartbeat. Even if I have to queue all the way up there.'

'Or Pompeii . . . do you remember that trip we took there together? Wasn't it the best?'

'I'll never forget it,' Evelyn said, and in the next instant the overheated hospice room seemed to vanish, replaced by dusty Pompeiian back streets. The sound of cicadas, Vesuvius looming ahead of them, and Rose clutching her hand, thrilled to be showing Evelyn around the place.

'Rome, of course,' Rose went on, her eyes half-closing with the exertion of remembering. 'Istanbul. Trier – I was so happy when we went there, Evie. That perfect day!'

'I was too. I couldn't have been happier, my darling.'

'And oh – Kefalonia. Definitely Kefalonia.'

Evelyn had nodded, even though Rose's eyes were shut and there was nobody else present to see her. The lump in her throat swelled to such a size that she didn't trust herself to speak immediately. They had honeymooned in Kefalonia after their civil partnership ceremony, when both of them were in their sixties, and it had been one of the most romantic, blissful weeks of Evelyn's entire life.

But this wasn't getting them anywhere in terms of decision making. 'So – what are you saying, you want me to go on some kind of extended pilgrimage across Europe?' she joked, trying to lighten the mood, for herself as much as for Rose. 'Scattering your ashes here, there and everywhere, like the Rose Farleigh Greatest Hits tour?'

She had been rewarded by a weak chuckle, a sound as precious as gold. 'Would you do that for me, Evie? Because … well, you'll need something to keep you busy, won't you, when I'm not around? Can't have you getting bored without me there chivvying you about.'

It was no good, Evelyn was simply not brave enough to maintain her poker face, because they both knew she was going to miss Rose unbearably, and that she'd have given anything for the so-called chivvying to continue for years longer yet. A sob had burst out of her despite her best efforts to hold it back. 'Sorry,' she gulped miserably. The last thing she wanted was for Rose to feel bad for her.

Rose, who had seemed close to sleep moments earlier, tightened her grip on Evelyn's hand, her eyes fluttering open again. 'Oh, darling,' she said. 'I'm being silly. You don't have to go anywhere to scatter my ashes. Just dump me in the nearest park, that'll do me. It doesn't mean anything anyway.'

'No,' Evelyn told her stubbornly. 'I want to take you to those places. I would love to do that for you.' She imagined being in Pompeii and Athens and Istanbul without Rose's animated eager face, without her usual running commentary every time they wandered round a ruin, and felt something tear inside her at the prospect. Could she really do that? Even though she had basically just promised as much? 'I'll do it,' she vowed. 'Whatever you ask of me.'

When Rose died, less than a month later, a terrible moroseness had weighed Evelyn down; a sadness so crushing and dreadful that it had been hard to see the point in going on at all, without her. But then she'd finally got round to sorting through the belongings the hospice had bagged up, and she found a note in unfamiliar handwriting, which presumably had been dictated to one of the nurses in Evelyn's absence.

Where to take my ashes (please) (only if you can face it) (absolutely fine to go with the park option), she read, and smiled, imagining Rose's precise instructions around the bracketing of all these phrases. Then she studied the list below:

The Acropolis

Knossos

Pompeii

Rome

Trier

Istanbul

Sicily

Kefalonia

And a tiny pinch in Russell Square so that you can still go there and be with me.

Or – of course – none of the above!

It was exactly what Evelyn needed: a plan, a project, a roadmap to help her through the grief. And so she'd set about booking flights and hotels, organising the trips that Rose's final request would require. The easiest one first: she'd put a teaspoon of Rose's ashes into a sandwich bag and taken her down the road to Russell Square, the site of many of their clandestine early meetings when Rose was lecturing at UCL. She found the bench where, once upon a time, they would meet for lunch and kiss one another, then discreetly tipped the ashes behind it. 'There you are,' she said under her breath. 'Rest easy. I'll visit you all the time here.'

After that, there was no stopping her. She'd sprinkled Rose at the foot of the olive tree in the Temple of Athena at the Acropolis before taking another flight on to Crete, where she'd bid farewell to her at the Palace of Knossos. The following year, she took her to Istanbul, booking herself onto the same Byzantine Empire walking tour she and Rose had undertaken together five years earlier, and surreptitiously shaking out another scoop of ashes as the group ambled along the Constantinople Walls. Then came her most ambitious solo trip, to Pompeii and Rome and Sicily in one particularly tiring fortnight, after which Evelyn had been so wiped out she seemed to pick up every virus London could offer her. And then, just as she was nearing the end of the list, the pandemic had hit, scuppering everything, including Evelyn's own health.

That had been a lonely, trying few years all right, but last autumn she'd taken the Eurostar to Brussels, then caught another train to Luxembourg and on to Trier, the beautiful medieval city in Germany. The first summer after leaving their husbands, she and Rose had travelled all over Germany together, partly because Evelyn had always wanted to go to the annual Bach festival in Leipzig, and also because it was a country neither of them had spent much time in. They fell in love with Trier, for its Roman ruins (Rose), the Karl Marx house and museum (Evelyn) and the Moselle wine (both of them). On returning this time, Evelyn had discovered the Queergarten, apparently the first queer beer garden in Germany, and decided Rose would be tickled to have some of her ashes left there.

Kefalonia is the last place on the list and she is finally here, with the remainder of Rose's ashes to scatter somewhere on the island. It has been an epic slog, a true pilgrimage, to obey Rose's dying wishes, and, now that Evelyn is dying herself, the impetus to complete her task has at times felt like the only thing keeping her alive. And yet, coming to the end will mean the very last goodbye, the shift into a new era, when she no longer has Rose with her at all. She's still not sure she's ready.

That said, in other ways she *is* ready, she concedes: ready to let go herself, mission accomplished. She's so tired now. Her body aches all the time. She dreams of Rose every night, as if the boundaries between them are melting, falling away; as if their reunion is at last approaching. Back at their Bloomsbury home, the townhouse that has always felt too empty with only one person living there, she has left her will on her desk, along with a neatly typed list of passwords for various accounts, all the practical tasks that will need to be ticked off by her nephews when the day comes. She suspects it won't be too long. Her neighbour has her front door key. Everything is clean and tidy, bills paid. Before leaving for the airport, she wiped the dust from her cello and tuned it for the first time in years, before taking up her bow. Then, with trembling fingers, she had done her best to play the refrain from Bach's Cello Suite No.1 Prelude one last time. It was always Rose's favourite piece in her repertoire, and Evelyn has found the music a solace in her darkest times. Her technique is poor these days, her hands too stiff to do the passages justice, but all the same, hearing the notes swell and soar through the apartment once more felt like a fitting goodbye. The closing of a door.

She can feel the disease eating away at her from the inside; she pictures it as a spreading blackness moving stealthily through her cells with deadly intent, silently increasing its hold. Who knew dying was so bloody gruelling? Maybe she will rest another day, she decides, catching sight of herself in the mirror – still in her nightdress, hair unkempt, her face crumpled from the pillow. She will take herself down to the pool again, lie in the shade with a book, snoozing occasionally, swimming now and then, perhaps even ordering herself a cocktail, just for the hell of it. What harm could it do now?

'Tomorrow, I will take you somewhere wonderful,' she says aloud, certain that Rose is with her here. 'Don't worry, I'm going to keep my promise. Even if it's the last thing I do.'

Chapter Twelve

Nelly

Athens, July 1983

Nelly took to boat life like … well, like a boat to water. The freedom of travelling, albeit while shepherding groups of tourists from one island to another, made her feel alive, right in the moment, with each day full of discoveries. She had learned, for instance, that waking up every morning in her bunk, feeling the boat gently rocking beneath her, was her favourite way to start a day. She now knew that it was impossible to tire of seeing a Greek sunset, with the sky a different abstract painting of bronze, pink and russet tones each night. And she had also discovered that working in close proximity, day in, day out, to a man you had the most gigantic crush on felt by turns impossible, glorious and devastating. Oh, Alexander. Whenever he glanced over at her and they shared a secret smile about whatever stupid thing their tourist passengers were doing now, it was as if her heart leapt inside her.

The work was hard and constant; from the moment she was up, she had one task or another ahead of her. Buying and preparing food for that day's trip. Washing and changing laundry after overnight excursions. Serving food and drink to their passengers with a polite smile, even when the women made rude comments about her cooking, or the men tried to look down her top. And of course the never-ending cleaning, from mopping decks to scrubbing the tiny loo to washing up.

It was all worth it, though, for the brief interludes when she and Alexander had some downtime. When they arrived on an island – Kefalonia, Zakynthos, Lefkada – and he gave her time off to explore, so that she could climb up to the headland and smell the wild thyme as she gazed out to sea, or rent a bike and cycle around the coastal paths, charmed by the population of wild goats that would stare at her mid-graze as she skimmed by. *I'm having such a good time I might never go home again!* she wrote on postcards to Lorraine. *I'm alive and well, don't worry about me!* she assured her parents on theirs.

Best of all were the moments at the end of the day, once their work was done, when she and Alexander would sometimes hang out together. He taught her how to play backgammon. She taught him how to play Old Maid. She learned that he had grown up on Ithaca with a brother and a sister; that his dad was a fisherman and had taken him out on the boat as soon as he could walk. She teased him with descriptions of London life in comparison – the grimy Tube carriages where you were crushed in with hundreds of people, the traffic and smoke, the gaudy lights of Piccadilly Circus – and he would shake his head and laugh, saying it sounded like another planet to him. 'And – sorry, London – not a planet where I would like to live.'

Then, at the end of July, a group of Norwegian holiday-makers booked Alexander to take them on a week-long cruise around the Peloponnese all the way to Athens, with plenty of stops en route. Their guests were charming (and very generous with their tips) but the days were long – often Nelly and Alexander would work sixteen hours straight – and by the last evening of the trip, docked at the beautiful, unspoilt island of Hydra, they were both glad when their passengers went out to a restaurant, leaving them in peace. Out came a few cold and well-deserved bottles of Alfa beer, out came the backgammon once more, the games becoming increasingly competitive. As the sun sank slowly behind them, the water gently sloshing against the side of the boat, Nelly felt overwhelmed by a rush of pure happiness. 'I love this,' she blurted out, no longer able to keep her feelings to herself. 'Living on a boat, all of this . . .' She swung her arm around, taking in the harbour, the sea, the boat. Him, obviously. 'I'm so enjoying being here. Thank you for taking a chance on me.'

She had never kidded herself that he saw her as anything other than his scruffy little colleague, someone chopping watermelon in the tiny galley kitchen, someone he could laugh with about the most obnoxious tourists when they were exhausted at the end of a long day. An idiot who punched the air and did a victory lap of the deck, singing 'The Winner Takes It All' at the top of her voice, the one and only time she won a game of backgammon. But when she confessed her feelings, something in his face softened and he smiled back at her with real warmth. 'I love it too,' he said. 'It is the only life I have ever wanted to lead. True freedom – the joy of being at sea. There's nothing better.'

As they sat there, looking into each other's eyes, the mood suddenly seemed to shift into a whole other territory. Uncharted waters. The night was still but Nelly felt goosebumps prickling all over. She was convinced that something was about to happen between them. That he might try to kiss her, or take her hand, or—

No. In the next second they heard the cheerful-sounding voices of the Norwegians returning from their evening in Hydra, and the spell broke. Alexander and Nelly smiled ruefully at one another as if they both knew that the moment – whatever it might have become – had been snatched away. At least, that was Nelly's conclusion. Was he thinking the same? she wondered, replaying the scene in bed that night. Perhaps it was for the best, she told herself, feeling shivery when she thought about the way his body had turned fractionally towards hers, the intensity of his gaze. Nonetheless, it was almost impossible to get to sleep wondering what it might have felt like to kiss him, to feel his arms around her. What might have happened next?

Chapter Thirteen

Claudia

You stupid pathetic Bitch.

I've been looking at your website. 'Get away from it all,' you say. 'Leave your cares behind at The Ionian Escape'. HOW FUCKING IRONIC, wouldn't you say??? Is that supposed to be funny? Shame on you. You have destroyed my life, Bitch, and I'll never rest until I get my revenge. Wouldn't it be a shame if your precious hotel burned to the ground? If everything was destroyed, including you? I would love to see that. Maybe I will?

Ares

Claudia still hasn't replied to the aggressive email that appeared in her inbox on Monday, but it's been impossible to ignore. She's no expert on Greek mythology but she knows that Ares was the god of war, and a cold terror sweeps through her body whenever she thinks about the last person who called her a stupid pathetic bitch. What's more, she's certain that this message is merely the opening shot fired. She once saw Marcus tearing the legs off a spider, one by one, for amusement. That's nothing compared to what he'll do to an ex-wife.

With her system flooded by adrenalin, she has barely been able to think about anything else since reading the email. But she must, because this is how she copes: busying herself with her tick-list, working through her jobs, keeping on top of everything. This is how she originally rebuilt the broken walls around herself, she remembers, valiantly checking over the upcoming staffing rotas (tick) and replying to the new reviews on the StarMyStay travel website (tick). This is how she will continue functioning as a human being.

It's no good though. She can't help returning to the vile email and what it might mean. Even the scandalous news this morning about Frank Neale can't distract her. *I am heartbroken, livid and deeply disappointed. Those poor women!!!* Barb WhatsApped her, along with a crying emoji, an angry face emoji and a knife emoji. No wonder he and his wife Leonora have been looking so strained and unhappy; they must have known this was on the horizon. The stories that have been leaked in advance of a BBC documentary are damning, to say the least. At least a dozen women have come forward with historical allegations of abuse, bullying and assault. Social media is awash with videos of women setting fire to their Frank Neale cookbooks in revulsion. His upcoming UK TV show *Frank's Family Favourites* has been shelved. His management team are, apparently, 'taking these allegations very seriously', which presumably means they're drawing up severance papers right now. Bye-bye, Frank, you dirty old scuzzball.

Normally Claudia would be gripped by the unfolding saga, especially with the key player currently under the hotel roof, but she's still so consumed by her own fears it's hard to engage with much else. She's so worked up, in fact, imagining scenarios where Marcus appears at the hotel, bent on vengeance, that when Dimitris knocks at her office door around one o'clock that day she gives a startled cry and finds herself grabbing the nearest implement – a stapler – on instinct. Then there's a moment where they both freeze, staring at one another, and Claudia puts a hand to her chest, her heart thumping like that of a frightened rabbit. How has Marcus found her? Who would have told him?

'Sorry,' she says, embarrassed, putting the stapler back on the desk. Dimitris' eyes are hooded with concern as they follow the movement, then return to her face. 'I'm a bit jumpy today.'

She tends to speak Greek at work, like the other staff members, but she's so agitated now that the words come out in English. Luckily he's fluent himself, having spent a year studying in the US as part of his degree, and he follows suit. 'Is everything okay, Claudia?' he asks, glancing at the computer, and she hesitates, embarrassed that she has brought her tawdry mistakes to this beautiful calm place. Dimitris is in his mid-forties, only eight years older than her, but right now she feels like a teenager, still floundering about in screw-ups, compared to him.

'Well ...' she stalls, but he has walked over to the desk before she can think up a convincing lie, and is peering at her screen. He squints, leaning closer to it, before looking up and gesturing to her reading glasses, currently perched on the end of her nose. 'Can I?'

'Sure.' She passes them over, hoping he won't notice how her hands are trembling. Marcus's face flashes into her mind and she is transported back to the final months of their marriage; how terrified she'd been of stepping out of line. 'Must be some random lunatic, I guess,' she adds, reflecting miserably that she's covering for him even now. But what choice does she have?

Dimitris shakes his head as he reads the message. Even with her jags of adrenalin, it does amuse her to see her delicate purple-framed glasses balanced on his considerably larger nose. 'Ares, eh?' His lip curls. 'This is a bad person, not any kind of god,' he says scornfully. 'A coward too, hiding behind the computer rather than coming here and taking action, I think. If he was really going to burn this place down, he would just do that, yes? Not try to scare you – us – with his ... how do you say it? Threats.' He passes the glasses back to her and straightens up, folding his arms across his chest. 'What do you want me to do about him?' he asks, before picking up the stapler and brandishing it in the air. 'Staple him to death, yes?'

She's so grateful for the chance to laugh at his joke that in the same minute she almost wants to cry. Thank goodness she has him as an ally, she thinks, imagining him drawing back his fist and smacking Marcus in the face. She hates violence, but it's a pretty satisfying image. 'That's one option,' she replies with a small smile, then glances back at the screen, only for the words 'stupid pathetic Bitch' to leap out at her again.

She must have inadvertently shuddered, because Dimitris is eyeing her strangely, as if he can tell there's more to the story.

'I will ask my son to help,' he announces. 'He will tell us the place where this message was sent. The IP address, I think? If it comes from somewhere in Greece – okay, we can take action, we will go to the police, we report this person. But if the message is from another country, somewhere far from here ...' He makes shooing motions with his hands. 'Then we know this man is weak. He is all talking and not wearing the trousers, or whatever you say. Yes?'

'Yes,' she says faintly, appreciating his practical suggestion, the fact that he is taking her seriously rather than dismissing her fearful response as an over-reaction. When she agreed to her Uncle Kostas' suggestion of leaving Australia, she had begged him not to blab to Dimitris – or anyone – what a mess she had ended up in. Dimitris is no idiot, he probably figured out the broader brushstrokes himself long ago, but she has always been glad of him respecting her privacy and not trying to weasel out any details. 'Thank you.'

'He won't hurt you, this ... this *kakos anthropos*,' Dimitris goes on contemptuously. 'Okay? Nobody will, while you are here. This so-called Ares, he is probably a sad ugly little person with a tiny penis, angry at all the women who won't sleep with him.'

She bursts out laughing despite herself, and his eyes twinkle at her. 'And now I am saying to you, it is time to take a break, that this computer must go off, because you are going to have lunch with me, yes? We can sit outside with a cold drink and something delicious to eat, and we will talk about so many other important things, you will not be able to think about this person. Okay?'

'Okay,' she says, grateful for the intervention. 'Thanks.'

She powers down the computer, switches off the light and locks the office door behind her (tick, tick, tick), then follows him out into the sunshine. He's right, it's good to step away, she thinks gladly as they take up a table on the patio and Zoe, the waitress, comes to take their lunch order. Despite the warmth of the day and the holiday buzz in the air though, a tension remains in her body. She loves the life she has built for herself here, but how strong are the foundations, really, if Marcus wants to smash it all to pieces? She bites her lip as she watches Dimitris animatedly discussing today's menu with Zoe, and it feels as if her heart is cracking at the thought of her boss finding out the truth about her. He'll think she's such a loser, won't he? Every bit the stupid pathetic bitch of the email.

'And Claudia? What would you like?' he asks her now, and she has to paste a quick smile on her face and rattle off an answer before he can see the terror lurking inside. Keep it together, she orders herself fiercely. Whatever problems she has, she'll deal with them alone, and that's just the way it has to be.

Chapter Fourteen

Evelyn

Evelyn still hasn't decided exactly where on the island she will scatter Rose's ashes, but has booked a taxi for tomorrow morning to take her to Fiskardo. She remembers the two of them visiting the sweet little town on their honeymoon, how they'd enjoyed pottering about the harbour, having lunch, seeing some Roman ruins (a cemetery, perhaps?) and wandering along to the old Venetian lighthouse. But is that the right spot to leave her? She wants this final resting place to be somewhere truly fitting, and still isn't sure where that might be. She'll figure everything out tomorrow, she tells herself. There's no rush.

For now, she's having a pleasant time by the hotel pool. Before her health deteriorated, Evelyn was a busy, active person, but there's something about the sunnier weather that has always brought out the lizard in her, content to stretch out on a lounger, unmoving, for long periods. Lying there now, she luxuriates in the sensation of warmth sinking into her bones. It's become decidedly autumnal back in London since her departure, apparently, with misty mornings and cooler nights. Knowing this makes the Greek sunshine against her skin feel even more of a treat.

She's immersed in her book, tuned out from the other guests on nearby loungers, but nevertheless she can't help but pick up on the excited twitter that sweeps about the pool all of a sudden. 'Look, it *is* her,' she hears a young blonde woman nearby whisper to a woman Evelyn assumes is her mother. 'She's just wearing a dodgy wig, that's all. But I swear it's her. On my life.'

Evelyn gazes around curiously. She can only assume they mean the sulky-faced woman in the big sunhat who has just arrived. Miranda, that's it, the one who made it quite clear she did not want to chat the other morning, despite Evelyn's best efforts. Everyone else seems to be looking at her too, with nudges and mutters.

What on earth . . . ? thinks Evelyn, bemused. Is this *the* hotel for famous people or something? She's already noticed that celebrity chef and his wife a couple of times at breakfast – him glowering when anyone so much as glances his way, her looking thoroughly miserable, as if this holiday is nothing but an endurance exercise. Now she's wondering if this Miranda is a Somebody too. It would explain the haughty attitude and the constant wearing of those huge sunglasses and sunhat, she supposes. In her own career, Evelyn never reached a point of success where she could have been considered a Somebody herself, but she met plenty of famous conductors and orchestral soloists along the way. She knows the type.

The young blonde woman is now manoeuvring her phone surreptitiously in Miranda's direction as if she's trying to take a photo.

'Darling, leave her in peace, come on, she's on holiday,' the mother chides in a low voice when she notices.

'Yeah, but this is gold, Mum,' the blonde replies, watching Miranda, who has taken a seat on the other side of the pool and is currently adjusting her bikini top. 'Anyway, why be an actress in the first place if you don't want to be filmed? Part of her job, isn't it?'

Poor woman, thinks Evelyn in disapproval, her eye flicking from the blonde girl to her prey. It's not the most flattering angle for Miranda to be recorded at, either – although perhaps that's the point.

'Come on, really, I don't think you should do this,' the mum says, reaching over to try to stop her daughter.

Perhaps Miranda has a sixth sense for such things, because suddenly she is peering across the pool at them, her body language rigid. 'Are you filming me?' she snaps, her voice carrying through the air like a whip-crack. She stands up, her fists clenched. 'Seriously? Are you actually fucking filming me? On my *holiday*?'

'Florence, switch it off,' the mother says unhappily, but the blonde – Florence – merely raises her phone in defiance so as to better capture Miranda's angry response. And angry it is – she's now marching round the pool towards them, bristling with rage, which has Florence looking even more delighted. Evelyn tuts, very unhappy about how this is unfolding. Whatever happened to sisterhood? Honestly!

Miranda stalks past Evelyn in a waft of perfume and begins wrestling – actually *grappling* – to get the phone out of Florence's hand. But Florence is no match for Miranda's fury, and yelps, 'This is assault! Give that back!' as her phone is ripped away.

Florence leaps up from her lounger but Miranda, holding the phone out of reach, has already jabbed a swift, practised finger at the screen. 'Deleted. So fuck you,' she says, then hurls the phone into the pool, where it begins sinking dreamily through the water.

'What the hell? You maniac!' Florence yells, aggrieved, and for a second Evelyn thinks she's about to go for the other woman and there will be an actual fight. But Florence's priority is to jump into the pool after her phone with a great splash. She dives beneath the surface, then re-emerges, spluttering and (rather pointlessly) holding it up out of the water. 'If this is damaged . . .' she shouts at Miranda, who has returned to her lounger and is now furiously gathering up her belongings. 'If you've ruined my phone, I'll . . .'

'You'll what? Write a bitchy little post on Instagram?' Miranda interrupts, unmoved. She hauls her tote bag up onto her shoulder and turns. 'People like you make me *sick*,' she goes on, marching away. 'Have a bit of respect!'

There is a stunned silence as she departs, everyone left agog by the public soap opera. 'Oh my God, *drama*!' someone says with unpleasant glee. 'What a psycho,' comments a very sun-burnt woman, who really should get in the shade (and keep her nasty thoughts to herself, in Evelyn's opinion). Several people grab their phones and immediately start typing into them, as if compelled to excitedly report back to their friends what just happened. *You'll never guess what!*

A beefy bald man – the manager, Evelyn thinks – comes down the steps to the patio, no doubt having heard the commotion. 'Is everybody all right?' he addresses the group at large.

'I wouldn't say so, no,' the blonde girl growls, ineffectually wiping her sodden phone with her towel.

'We're fine,' her mother answers in the same breath.

The manager says he'll bring the girl a bowl of rice for her phone, and the moment passes. But even as the atmosphere settles once more, Evelyn still feels jarred by the whole ugly business. Her father was something of a bully to the rest of the family and she's been left with a lifelong unease around raised voices. Plus she can't help but feel sympathy towards Miranda, however grumpy she might have been yesterday. It's one of the few things in life that make her glad to be of an older generation – all of this constant filming and photo-taking of one's self, the loss of privacy, and the seeming lack of compassion towards others, too. What is wrong with people?

It's no good. She can't slide back into the relaxed lull she was enjoying before that little scene erupted. Her swimming costume is still too damp to put her clothes back on, so she stuffs them and her book under one arm. Her trusty Birkenstocks on her feet, she heads up the lavender-edged steps and back to the terrace. Miranda is long gone, and Evelyn hesitates for a moment, catching her breath and wondering what, if anything, she should do now.

She is on the verge of returning to her room to dry off and

maybe have a snooze when she catches sight of Miranda on a first-floor balcony nearby, scowling as she puffs on a vape. Aha.

Evelyn walks over so that she is standing within view. 'Are you all right?' she calls.

Miranda looks quite different without her sunglasses and sunhat, Evelyn registers, gazing up at her. She seems smaller, somehow. Younger. (And *is* that a wig she's wearing? Evelyn wonders, remembering the comment by the pool.)

'I've had better days,' she says shortly.

'Do you want to talk about it? I was just going to get a cold drink,' Evelyn improvises. 'I could pick one up for you too, if you'd like.'

She's braced for an outright no, perhaps a Mind Your Own Business, given the fury she witnessed two minutes earlier. Miranda's anger must have burned itself out though, because after a momentary hesitation she leans a hip against the balcony railing and nods. 'That's very kind of you,' she says. There's a wary note in her voice nonetheless, a guardedness. Maybe she's wondering why Evelyn is poking her nose in, and is reluctant to trust her. Who can blame her?

Evelyn drops her belongings, puts her hands in the air and turns round slowly as if she's a criminal under suspicion of carrying a weapon rather than an 82-year-old pensioner clad only in an ancient swimming costume. 'I'm not filming you,' she says. 'And even if I did, I wouldn't have a clue about how to put it on YouTube or anything like that. I only use my phone for listening to music, most of the time. I'll be dead soon anyway. You can trust me.'

Miranda blinks at this needlessly dramatic closing statement, but clearly it piques her interest because her lips suddenly quirk in what could almost be called a smile. 'Well … that's pretty hard to argue with,' she remarks, deadpan. 'Thank you. Just a Diet Coke or something would be lovely, if you don't mind.'

'Give me two minutes to put some clothes on, then,' Evelyn says. 'I don't want to frighten anyone with this bod.'

That's definitely a smile now. 'You won't—' Miranda begins, then laughs. 'Okay,' she goes on. 'Thanks.'

A short while later, having made herself decent, Evelyn heads to the bar. The burly manager is sitting at one of the restaurant tables nearby, having lunch in a shady spot with a pretty dark-haired woman with a smart white dress and excellent lipstick. His wife? Evelyn wonders with interest. His girlfriend? Or merely a colleague? They like each other, she can tell, but there's a weird tension about the woman, who is holding herself rigidly in her chair. Interesting. Evelyn prides herself on her ability to spot such things, although Rose would always tease her for it. 'You and your bloody hunches!' she'd groan. 'It's like living with Miss Marple.' 'Yes, and look how often *she* was right,' Evelyn would retort.

The barman turns to her. '*Kalispera*,' he says. 'What can I get you?'

Evelyn orders a Diet Coke for Miranda and a lime cordial for herself, 'with lots of ice, please'. Then, because she's had a stressful few hours, what with it being Rose's birthday plus all of that drama, she orders two glasses of ouzo as well. What the hell, Miranda looked as if she could do with a pick-me-up, she figures, and Rose would certainly approve. 'Could I have a tray as well, please?' she asks, suddenly realising that carrying four drinks up the stairs to Miranda's room might be a recipe for disaster.

'No need, madam, I can bring the drinks over for you,' the barman assures her. 'Where are you sitting?'

'Thank you! Actually I was going to take this up to another guest's room but I don't know the number, I'm afraid. It's Miranda though – the famous Miranda?' She says this low-voiced, as a punt – yes, another of her hunches – and is intrigued to see a tightening around the barman's eyes at the mention of Miranda's name, a fleeting expression of . . . well, it's hard to tell, actually. Dislike? Amusement? Scorn? He didn't dispute the 'famous Miranda' tag, though, she registers. So who is she?

'Yes,' he says. 'I know the person you mean.' He is too much of a pro to give anything else away, and merely flashes her a smile and promises to bring the drinks up shortly.

'*Efcharisto*, Konstantinos,' she says, having peered at his name badge. 'You'll probably catch me up, I'm such a slow walker these days,' she adds, before setting off towards Miranda's room. The famous Miranda's room, rather. Evelyn's more eager than ever to have a proper chat with the woman now.

Chapter Fifteen

Miranda

Miranda is already slightly regretting having said yes to the offer of a drink from over-friendly Evelyn (clearly her Diet Coke addiction got the better of her in a weak moment). Then, when the woman herself knocks on the door accompanied by none other than the handsome bartender, he of her embarrassing failed seduction, she almost shuts the door in both of their faces. Is this a wind-up? Some kind of joke? Apparently not.

If the bartender is one to bear a grudge, he doesn't show it, at least, merely greeting her politely and asking where she would like the tray of drinks. (Christ, are those *shots*? she notices, eyebrows jerking upwards. Is Evelyn trying to get them both hammered or something?) 'Just here, please,' she says stiffly, indicating her chest of drawers, then hurriedly closing one of the drawers where a froth of underwear and bikinis is spilling out. 'Thank you,' she mutters as he sets down the tray, trying not to think about how politely he rejected her abysmal flirting. Cringe.

'*Efcharisto*, Konstantinos,' says Evelyn, fumbling in her purse to give him a couple of euros. 'For your trouble,' she says, putting them into his palm.

He makes a little bow. 'My pleasure,' he says and then, while Evelyn is putting her purse away, he winks at Miranda as if this whole awkward situation is hilarious.

She blushes bright red and turns her face away, but not before catching his smile. Thankfully he departs, leaving Miranda feeling unusually hot and bothered. To mask her fluster, she picks up the tray and leads the way through her suite. As well as the wicker loungers on her balcony, she has an indoor seating area with two comfortable sofas and a large coffee table. With the air-conditioning running, it's pleasantly cool, and more private than it will be sitting outside, she decides. 'Is this okay for you?' she asks, placing the tray on the table and gesturing to the sofa nearest to Evelyn. 'Have a seat. What are we drinking anyway?'

'Well, you have your Diet Coke, as requested,' Evelyn replies, lowering herself carefully into the cushions. She's changed into a long pale-blue dress and white pumps, and looks surprisingly youthful as she crosses one leg over the other. Maybe that thing she said about dying was a joke, after all. 'But I took the executive decision to order a couple of ouzos as well, because ... well, you know. It seems to be turning into that sort of day. Although don't feel you have to have yours, obviously, if you'd rather – oh ...' She trails off, looking amused, as Miranda promptly takes hers and knocks it back in a single gulp. 'Okay,' she goes on. 'Well, in the spirit of fairness, I should do the same, right? Bottoms up!' She tips her own shot similarly down her throat, then sets the empty glass down and blinks a few times. 'Oof,' she says with a little shudder. 'Now that's what I call a sharpener. But anyway. Are you all right? That looked rather an unpleasant experience for you, down by the pool.'

'Yes,' said Miranda. She screws up her face, already wishing she hadn't reacted quite so dramatically as to hurl the young woman's phone in the pool. If this gets back to Helen, she'll be toast. 'I wish I could say it was a one-off, but I've had a lot of that sort of thing lately, unfortunately.'

'Oh gosh, how awful,' Evelyn says, clasping her gnarled old hands together. Her bare arms are brown and freckled, Miranda notes, and her eyes, when Miranda raises her gaze to them, are periwinkle-blue and full of compassion. Miranda has to look away; she isn't always that good with people being nice to her.

'Do you want to talk about it?' Evelyn continues after a moment. 'I promise it will go no further. Sometimes it's good to speak an experience aloud, if only so that you're not hanging on to it inside your body.'

Miranda doubts that this theory would survive any scientific examination, but she knows what the woman means. *Does* she want to talk about what happened? Not particularly. But the ouzo feels as if it's already roiling through her bloodstream, taking the edge off her inhibitions. 'Well,' she stalls, then, in the next moment, finds herself confessing, 'Everything's gone wrong for me lately. Like – catastrophically wrong.'

Evelyn nods in understanding but doesn't comment further, and there's something about her sitting there so still and calm that prompts Miranda to keep talking. 'I've been sort of banished here, in disgrace. Exiled, to reflect on all of the terrible things I've done,' she goes on.

'Good heavens,' Evelyn says. 'I don't know whether to be more intrigued, impressed or scared for my life. Do carry on.'

Is she being facetious? It certainly feels as if she isn't taking the situation – or Miranda – seriously. Rather haughtily, she replies, 'Oh. Well, I'm an actor. Miranda Vallance?' There's not a flicker of recognition on the older woman's face. 'I'm in *Amberley Emergency*? Doctor Kelly?' Still nothing. It's always a pin-scratch against Miranda's ego, that kind of blank response, but – silver lining – she won't be in for a flurry of questions about her co-stars, at least. 'Anyway,' she continues. 'I'm on a sort of hiatus after . . .' She stares down at her knees. 'Well, I basically got into a fight with one of the other actors.'

'Gosh.' Evelyn puts her drink down. 'An actual fight?'

'Yeah. I'm not proud of it, but I . . . pushed her around a bit.' There's a long pause. 'Hit her.'

MIRANDA'S 'MOMENT OF MADNESS' the tabloids had shrieked when the photos surfaced the next day, along with blurry but identifiable CCTV stills of Miranda shoving Bonnie against a Soho door front, grabbing her by the throat, slapping her face.

'Mirrie! Are you all right?' her dad had asked on the phone when the story broke. 'What's going on? We've had Imogen round, saying all sorts, she's very upset. And now this in the papers . . . ?'

'That sounds pretty ghastly,' Evelyn says. 'I'm not surprised you needed to get away from it all.'

Her kindness is almost harder to take than the judgement and fury Miranda has had heaped on her by others, and their voices jangle in her head like a disapproving Greek chorus in counterpoint. ('Never speak to me again!' – that's Imogen. 'This is not acceptable behaviour, Miranda!' – there's good old Geoff. 'Greta's going to put you in touch with a counsellor specialising in anger management strategy; I strongly advise you to book some sessions' – thanks, Helen but fuck off. And you too, Greta, for that matter.) The thing that nobody has taken on board, when they're all shouting at her and telling her how dreadful she is, is how upset and hurt *she* is about it. Yes, and how bloody angry too. How could Bonnie have been such a snake?

'Mmm,' is all Miranda mutters now though, sipping her Coke.

'And then for that woman to try and film you like that . . . well, I can see how it must have felt like the last straw,' Evelyn goes on.

Miranda stares glumly down into her drink. There have been a lot of last straws recently, even she has to admit. Maybe she should actually have looked into the email Greta sent about anger management rather than furiously deleting it as soon as it arrived. Her rage keeps boiling up from out of nowhere; it's like being in charge of a massive flame-thrower. As a result, she's been starting one bonfire after another around her life. With a shudder, she finds herself thinking of the video of herself, shouting and incoherent, that went all over TikTok; and, worse, the thousand-plus comments that accumulated underneath.

God, she's proper minging without TV make-up, isn't she?

Absolutely lost it 😄

Imagine waking up and being Miranda Vallance.

Yeah, imagine. Right now, it's not great. She really hopes there won't be further repercussions from what she did down at the pool – that nobody else was filming her, that some other wannabe won't take it upon themselves to juice up the anecdote and hold it out to the press vultures like a hunk of fresh meat. Usually in posh restaurants or hotels you get left alone; people don't want to appear uncool by hassling you. She'd complain to the management about the lack of privacy she's been afforded if she hadn't made such a scene herself with the other woman's phone. The last thing she wants is to draw any more attention to her own burst of temper.

Evelyn seems to be taking her reticence for suspicion. 'Don't worry,' she says. 'I meant what I said earlier – that your secrets are safe with me. Chances are I'll be dead soon, so if you want to get anything off your chest feel free to let rip.'

Miranda winces at her phrasing. The last time they had spoken to one another, down by the pool, she had pegged Evelyn as a sweet, cake-baking grandmother, she remembers; a far cry from such macabre talk. 'Um ... are you okay?' she asks. 'I've never known anyone be so candid about ... well, about death before. Or so accepting. But maybe I'm wrong?'

Evelyn sips her drink, considering. 'I was not remotely "accepting", as you put it, when my wife died,' she says, and Miranda must have shown her surprise at the word 'wife' because Evelyn's mouth twists in a sudden smile. 'Ahh, you weren't expecting that, were you?' she asks, looking pleased.

'You'd written me off as some benign old nana, hadn't you, baking scones and helping out at church fetes? I can see it all over your face, don't deny it.'

Even Miranda can't act her way out of this one. 'You got me there,' she admits, putting her hands up. 'Guilty as charged.'

'Good. I love confounding people's expectations,' Evelyn replies. 'Although I say "wife" but, with ours being a civil partnership, we were technically supposed to call one another "civil partners". Sod that, we decided, we're each other's wives and that's that. But anyway, she died eight years ago, and I was devastated. Went off the rails myself, actually, got arrested for throwing a brick through a shop window one night when I . . . well, lost my shit, as young people say.'

'Evelyn!'

'I know! What a hoodlum! I was off my head for a while,' she says with a meaningful look at Miranda, 'so I know all about overreacting in a moment of rage; you can become completely consumed by your feelings, can't you?' Then she looks faraway, emotions passing fleetingly across her face. 'But I'll tell you what really helps afterwards,' she goes on. 'Saying sorry.'

Miranda snorts. Oh, here we go. And now for the moral of the story, she thinks. 'It's not that simple,' she replies.

'Well—' Evelyn begins, but Miranda cuts her straight off.

'And I'm not sorry anyway,' she says stubbornly. Well . . . not entirely, she amends in her head. She's sorry for her thuggish behaviour, and regrets losing her temper so spectacularly, yes. But after what Bonnie did, she actually wishes she had smacked her a bit harder. She's not sorry about that at all.

This time it's Evelyn who looks away first. 'Ahh,' she says, then she shrugs. 'Fair enough.' There's a moment's silence, and then she finishes her drink before hauling herself up to her feet. 'Oof,' she says, standing still for a moment as if the blood has rushed to her head. 'Well, I'll leave you to it,' she goes on. 'Very nice to talk to you, Miranda. Don't let the bastards get you down, as they say. For what it's worth, I'm glad you threw that girl's phone in the pool, served her jolly well right.'

'Thank you,' says Miranda, following on as Evelyn proceeds slowly towards the door. 'And thanks again for the drinks. That ouzo really hit the spot.'

'Didn't it just? I need a lie-down now to recover.' Evelyn opens the door. 'And after that, I'm going to look up the programme you said you were in, give it a whirl.'

'That'll have you dozing back off in no time,' Miranda says, but she's pleased, nevertheless; her fragile ego appreciates the thought. 'Bye, Evelyn.'

She closes the door, smiling to herself because, duff advice about saying sorry aside, her self-invited guest has somehow taken the sting out of the pool incident. *And* she's had to rethink her image of Evelyn being a pinny-wearing grand-mother too – make that an ouzo-necking, brick-throwing, death-prepping lesbian. And do you know what? Good on her.

Drifting back through her spotless empty suite, she wonders what to do now. She can't plod sheepishly back down to the pool, that's for sure. In fact, she'll probably never go there again after today's shenanigans. What with that, and her failed flirtation coming back to bite her, the hotel is starting to feel as if it's closing in around her, like a net. She came here to get away from everything, and she definitely hasn't achieved that. Although the holiday is still young, she reminds herself, grabbing her phone and opening up the browser. Plus she has plenty of money at her disposal. Perching on the end of the bed, she taps away at the screen. Time to make some plans.

Chapter Sixteen

Nelly

August 1983

The *Miaoulis* had been booked back-to-back with one cruise after another throughout July and August, and Nelly and Alexander fell into a collaborative groove on board, working seamlessly alongside each other. Tickets issued, customers on, transported, fed, photos taken, then off – again and again, day after day. It was non-stop, it was fast-paced, and Nelly had never slept so deeply at night before, but it was fun, so much fun. She and Alexander got on well, mostly taking the mick out of one another, but he looked out for her too. He noticed, for instance, the time when one of the male guests kept pestering her, constantly trying to put his hands on her, and then later on, when this same male guest was showing off to his friends by clambering up to balance on the edge of the yacht, it just so happened that Alexander accidentally revved the engine, sending him toppling off and into the sea below. 'I don't know what you mean,' he'd said later on when Nelly thanked him. 'I'm a professional sailor, I take my work very seriously.'

Nelly had raised an eyebrow at him. 'Coincidence, was it? Right.'

'One of the Greek gods decided to punish him, perhaps,' Alexander mused, a smile twitching on his lips.

'That's how you see yourself now, is it? A Greek god? Not modest, are you, Alexander?' she'd teased, but the episode made her glow inside all the same. He cared about her. He was looking out for her. She'd been so caught up in how well she was managing out here, all on her own, that she'd almost forgotten how good it felt to occasionally lean on another person.

Towards the end of the month they moored up at Fiskardo, Kefalonia, and, once that day's passengers had disembarked, Alexander announced that they were going to take the next day off together. 'Or rather,' he said, 'it will be YOUR day off. For a change, I will be waiting on you, foot and hand, as you say.'

He looked so pleased with himself, Nelly didn't have the heart to correct him – besides, she was pleased too. She liked the sound of a day off very much. 'Great!' she replied. 'Although I should warn you, I can be very demanding. You might live to regret this idea.'

He laughed. 'I have three demanding sisters and a demanding mother,' he replied. 'Don't worry, Nelly, I am used to being told what to do by women.'

Nelly laughed too, although she couldn't help but feel a

pinch of disappointment at being bracketed with his sisters and mum. She didn't want him to regard her in a *brotherly* way! But then again, having lived and worked with her in such close quarters all of this time, he had only ever seen her with her hair scraped back in a sweaty ponytail, wearing vest tops, shorts and flip-flops. It was nigh on impossible for anyone to look sexy or glamorous when they were cleaning the bathroom, stinking of bleach or tearfully chopping onions. Mind you, you wouldn't think it was possible to look attractive when unblocking a toilet or changing the fuel filter either, but he seemed to manage it just fine.

'Anyway,' he went on, 'time off starts now. Do you have any nice clothes in that suitcase of yours? Because I'd like to take you for dinner tonight. You've worked really hard – and so have I. Tonight we celebrate.'

'I've got nice clothes,' she assured him, feeling a sudden thrill at the chance to doll herself up for a change. It seemed so long since she and Lorraine had been out on the town in Corfu in dresses and heels, the idea was like looking back at somebody else's life. 'Dinner would be lovely.'

With that, she vanished into her cabin and set to work. She washed her hair, painted her nails, and then spent some time deliberating over what to wear. Was it too vampy to put on her clingy black dress? She might have thought yes, had he not made that remark likening her to his sisters and mum. She just wanted him to see her as a *woman*, rather than the sisterly type, she thought, slinking herself into it before she could change her mind. It was a pleasant surprise to realise that all of the hard physical work had toned her up; the dress, formerly a little tight on the tummy, now skimmed her body in a perfect fit.

This'll show him, she thought, turning from side to side in front of the small bathroom mirror. Then she dug out some lipstick and mascara, put her hair up in a loose twist with a few wispy tendrils softening around her face, and retrieved her black wedge sandals, rather squashed from having lain unworn at the bottom of her case this whole time.

'Da-dah!' she cried cheerfully, clonking out onto the main deck, where Alexander was waiting. He was dressed in a short-sleeved white shirt and jeans, his hair still damp from the shower, and he smelled good. Correction, she thought, because he always smelled good to her: he smelled of soap and aftershave, rather than engine oil, or fresh sweat.

His double-take was almost comical. 'Wow,' he said. 'Nelly, you look ...' He seemed dazed, as if he were seeing her for the first time. Maybe he was. 'You look beautiful,' he said.

It was quite disarming, having him compliment her when she was used to him joking around all the time. 'Thank you,' she said, blushing immediately. 'You don't look so bad yourself. So where are you taking me?'

They went to a fish restaurant on the waterfront, the sort with a three-page wine menu and heavy cutlery, and candles flickering in glass jars on every table. The sun was going down, the food was delicious, and they talked and talked, the rest of the world seeming to fall silently away as the shadows deepened around them. They'd developed a good working relationship and always got on well, but this felt different – more personal, more intimate. A man and a woman getting to know each other in a decidedly romantic setting. Nelly spoke about her family, and told funny stories about her old job in London, and he confessed how little he would enjoy a job like that, indoors, at a desk, constrained by an ironed shirt and uncomfortable shoes. 'I can't imagine you in an office,' she said, amused. 'No offence, but ... no. You'd hate it!'

He laughed. 'I wish all women thought like you,' he said, pulling a face. Reading between the lines, Nelly got the impression that his last girlfriend, Sofia, had pressed him to work for her dad's shipping company rather than wasting his life messing about on a boat (her words) and that his dogged refusal was why they had eventually broken up. *Big mistake, Sofia*, Nelly thought indignantly. Why couldn't she have accepted Alexander as he was? Talk about small-minded! 'Nobody should tell someone they love what to do,' she said hotly before she could stop herself. 'The whole point is that you love them for who they already *are*, not an idea of the person you want to turn them into! I wouldn't dream of insisting you—' She broke off abruptly, her brain catching up too late on how her words sounded. 'Well, I mean ...' she blustered, appalled at her own big mouth. The wine was talking for her; she had to get a grip on herself. 'I wasn't saying that I ...'

He looked as if he was trying not to laugh at her. 'Yes?'

'I mean, if we were in love, like you and she were, then— Oh God.' She was making it worse by the second. She put her face in her hands. 'I think I'm going to shut up now.'

He did laugh, then. 'Maybe that's a good idea,' he said, 'And I think I'm going to get the bill and take you home.'

'That's another good idea,' she replied gratefully.

Back at the boat, the night was still balmy, so he lit a paraffin lamp and cracked open a couple of beers, then they put a load of cushions on the deck and sat against them, side by side. Nelly unpinned her hair so that it cascaded loose around her shoulders, and took off her sandals with some relief, having found them uncomfortable after so long wearing flip-flops. The stars were bright silvery beads against the black velvet sky, and there was only the faint shushing of water around the boat to be heard. She was very conscious of his body so close to hers, how breathless it was making her feel.

'So,' he said, 'what was it you were saying back at the restaurant? Something about being in love with me . . . ?'

'Alexander!' she yelped, glad of the darkness to hide her blushes. He had no idea how right he was. 'I wasn't saying—' Then she noticed his wicked smile. 'Oh shut up,' she groaned, swatting at him.

He grabbed hold of her hand mid-swat. 'Actually, I was glad you said that,' he went on, but all she could think about was the warmth of his hand round hers. Oh God, she thought. Don't make a fool of yourself now, Nell.

'Really?' she asked, trying to sound nonchalant even though her heart was thundering a tattoo. 'Why, because you can give me a hard time for it?'

'No,' he said. 'Because I actually think that I . . .' And then he leaned towards her until their faces were almost touching. She held her breath, her pulse racing. 'I think that I . . .' he repeated, then kissed her, oh so gently. 'Might be falling in love . . .' he went on. Another kiss, this one lasting a few seconds longer. 'With you.'

The air seized in her lungs and her heart pounded in a sudden wild gallop. 'D-do you mean that?' she stuttered, feeling shivery all over as she stared into his beautiful eyes, his face silvered by moonlight. Was he just saying this because he'd had a few glasses of Robola and felt horny? She wasn't sure she could bear it if he didn't feel the way she did. 'Seriously?'

His gaze was steady as he looked back at her. 'I have never been so happy,' he said, 'as I have been the last few weeks with you. I've never smiled so much or laughed so much or ...' He kissed her again. '... Wanted to kiss anybody as much as you. What have you done to me, Nelly?'

There was no time to answer because she kissed him back and the kiss went on and on, her body feeling as if it was melting against his. It was the sort of kiss you never want to end, so passionate, so tender, so euphoric. But then, as their hands started to slide beneath the other's clothes, he broke away. 'Nelly,' he said thickly. 'Is this ... okay?'

'Yes,' she told him, and then, just in case he still had any doubts, she pulled her dress off over her head in one swift movement and threw it across the deck. 'Is *that* okay?' she asked, half-joking, half-serious, but he didn't reply because they were kissing again, and everything had stepped up a gear, becoming urgent and intense.

Afterwards, the two of them lay entwined beneath the glittering night sky, and she felt as if she was the happiest person in the entire world as the blood rushed around her body, her heartbeat finally slowing. 'Well,' he said, his arms still around her. 'That was definitely okay.'

She smiled, her face against his shoulder, one arm flung

114

across his chest. 'Yeah,' she agreed. 'Very, very okay. Good start to the day off.'

'The day off, yes!' he said, his laugh rumbling beneath her. 'What will we find to do with ourselves for a whole day off, do you think?'

It felt so right, she thought joyfully, as the night breeze stroked their cooling bodies. So *good*. She already liked him so much, she knew what a great man he was. This, she told herself, was going to be the most epic love story of her life. The night that changed everything.

Except it turned out to be the next *day* that was to change everything. The next day, that would throw the most epic love story one enormous, no-way-back curveball, shattering her heart into a million pieces.

Chapter Seventeen

Evelyn

Waiting in reception for her taxi the next morning, Evelyn feels her insides knotting up with agitation. Today's the day, Rose, she thinks, clutching her handbag, in which nestles the sandwich bag containing her late wife's final scoop of ashes. It's taken her eight years, but she's got to say goodbye now. Let go for ever, with only an emptiness stretching ahead. Oh Lord. She still isn't sure if she'll be able to do it, when the moment comes. Is that dreadfully weak of her? She suspects as much.

She checks her watch again – ten past nine – and wonders what's happened to her cab. She'll give it another five minutes before asking someone to check the booking, she decides, trying to quell her feelings of impatience. It's not as if she's in a rush.

The weather outside looks glorious, at least – blue sky and sunshine, the temperature forecast to be in the high twenties again. Only the faintest breeze, too; a bonus when one is scattering ashes. In Sicily, where she had chosen to leave part of Rose's ashes in Petralia, a sudden gust of wind had rushed in at the worst possible moment, sending the gritty grey dust of her wife straight into Evelyn's face. Typical Rose, who had loved a practical joke, Evelyn had thought, wiping her eyes, unsure whether to laugh or cry.

A large black car pulls up outside just then. Aha. Is this her ride at last? She rises expectantly as the driver gets out and enters the lobby, keys in hand and a clipboard under one arm. Here we go, she thinks, but when the man goes up to one of the receptionists and speaks to her in Greek, the receptionist – it's that nice Duska, Evelyn notices – doesn't look over in Evelyn's direction, instead nodding and picking up her phone. 'Good morning, madam,' she hears her say into the receiver. 'Your car hire is here. Could you come down to reception and sign for it, please?'

Feeling rather self-conscious for having stood up, and unable to wait any longer, Evelyn approaches the other receptionist. '*Kalimera,*' she greets her. 'I booked a taxi for nine, but it hasn't arrived. My name is Evelyn Chambers, and I was hoping to go to Fiskardo. Would you mind checking for me that a car is still coming, please?'

'Of course,' says the woman, whose name badge reads Julia. She has long dark hair that falls, poker-straight, either side of her face, and a millimetre-perfect fringe. Dialling a number on her phone, she then speaks quickly into it, her expression gradually becoming more exasperated. 'I'm sorry,' she says to Evelyn after a few moments, 'there has been some kind of mix-up. Their booking system, it . . .' She mimes an explosion, complete with sound effects. 'They apologise and have offered a half-price fare for your journey, but won't be able to get a car here for perhaps thirty minutes.' She rolls her eyes apologetically. 'Are you happy to wait?'

'Oh dear.' Evelyn doesn't know whether to feel more annoyed or relieved that she's been given extra time with her bag of ashes. Then she hears footsteps behind her, followed by a familiar voice. 'Miranda Vallance for the car?' the voice says.

She turns her head to see a woman with a shoulder-length chestnut bob – goodness, that must be another wig, if it really is Miranda. Then her brain catches up. 'Actually,' she says to Julia, 'let me see if I can come up with an alternative. One minute.'

As well as the new wig, Miranda's wearing taupe-coloured cigarette pants and a sleeveless gauzy black top; quite the transformation from the kaftan-and-swimwear look Evelyn has previously seen her in. Hovering at a polite distance, she watches as Miranda signs something contractual on the man's clipboard, then follows them when they go out to inspect the car together. No harm in asking, she tells herself, as the man points out a dent in the passenger door and a scratch on the front left bumper. 'I hope this isn't cheeky of me,' Evelyn puts in when this business seems to have concluded, 'but you're not going to Fiskardo by any chance today, are you? Only I've had a bit of a taxi mix-up and . . . Well, I find myself rather stranded, unfortunately.'

It's an exaggeration, yes – technically she's only stranded for thirty minutes, but Miranda doesn't have to know that. Just for good measure, Evelyn puts a hand on her chest and glances worriedly at the sun. 'I wouldn't ask, only I was hoping to get away as early as possible, rather than spend too long out in the heat,' she goes on. 'Given my condition, and everything.'

Miranda has donned a pair of fifties-style cat-eye sunglasses but, even so, Evelyn can feel the suspicion in her stare. The man with the clipboard wants her to sign something else now, presumably acknowledging the dent and scratch, and she scrawls her signature with a flourish and gives the clipboard back to him. Then she asks, 'You're not one of those annoying back-seat drivers, are you, Evelyn?'

'Definitely not,' Evelyn assures her. 'I pride myself on being a respectful passenger at all times.'

'I like to listen to loud music while I'm driving,' Miranda goes on, poker-faced. 'Maybe too loud for someone like you.'

'Oh good, I love a bit of loud music,' Evelyn replies. 'Especially if it's Bach.'

'It won't be B—'

'And if I decide your taste is too awful, I can simply pop my hearing aid out,' Evelyn goes on, demonstrating. 'So it won't be a problem.'

A small laugh splutters out of Miranda. 'Oh, well, that's very good of you,' she says sarcastically. There's a beat, and then she adds, 'Fiskardo, did you say? Sure, we can go there.'

'Thank you *so* much,' Evelyn says. 'That's very kind. I can chip in for petrol if you like—'

'It's fine, I can afford it,' Miranda tells her drily.

'Or maybe I could treat us both to lunch then? Anyway, let me just cancel my taxi, and I'll be right with you.' She's smiling all of a sudden, feeling better about the journey now that she won't be alone. 'Road trip, here we come!'

Five minutes later, Miranda is familiarising herself with the car's controls and muttering, 'Stay on the right, stay on the right,' under her breath as she starts the engine. There are a few jerky bunny-hops while she adjusts to the unfamiliar clutch, but then she settles in and drives them smoothly off the hotel premises. Evelyn, who would have pegged the younger woman as a headstrong, brash kind of driver, is relieved to discover her chauffeur is actually comparatively calm behind the wheel. The car is a four-by-four, a Hyundai, she thinks, and has tinted windows and comfortable seats. Far posher than the old Mini she and Rose used to bomb around in, that's for sure.

'So, what's happening in Fiskardo then?' Miranda asks as they head out of town. 'Have you been before?'

'Yes, with Rose – my other half,' Evelyn says, nudging her handbag down in the footwell with her sandal. She isn't sure whether or not to mention what she's planning to do when they arrive. Some people get very weird when you mention a loved one's ashes, as if you are actually toting a dead body around with you. 'We had our honeymoon here on the island, back in the day.'

'Did you? That's nice.' The road has opened up a little and a vineyard stretches away down the hillside on Evelyn's left, row after row of vines hung with clusters of fat dusty grapes.

There's a pause. Normally, Evelyn would take this as her cue to ask Miranda if she was married herself, or if there was a dashing partner waiting for her back home. But, truth be told, Evelyn spent a nosey half hour last night looking up Miranda online and is pretty certain she already knows the answer to that. She has been unlucky in love, from what Evelyn has read, with a few short-lived relationships with soap stars Evelyn has never heard of, as well as a fling with a YouTuber (absolutely no idea) and a dishy-looking footballer. 'I watched your show, by the way,' she says instead. 'You're wonderful in it.'

Miranda glances at her quickly, possibly disbelievingly. 'Thank you,' she says. Then, in a casual tone, she asks, 'Which episode was it?'

Talk more about how wonderful I am, is what Evelyn hears, so she obliges her driver – she is getting a lift out of her, after all – by praising a scene in which Miranda's character had to deal with an aggressive patient. 'I loved the way you portrayed her humanity,' she says, because she imagines all actors like to hear these words. 'I thought it was a very strong performance.'

'Thank you,' Miranda says. She's sitting a little straighter in her seat now. 'She's a good character to play, Doctor Kelly, exactly because of that,' she goes on. 'I mean, she's a bit of a cow, most of the time, and gives people hell, but every now and then you see her vulnerability. Her depths.' She hesitates, then that casual tone of hers returns. 'I was actually nominated for a TV award this year, for that role.'

'Were you? Wow!' says Evelyn, even though this is something else she knows from her internet trawls. 'Did you win?' She could kick herself as soon as she asks the question, remembering that, no, actually it was Miranda's rival Bonnie who scooped that particular trophy. 'I mean – not that these things are the be-all and end-all,' she adds quickly, then changes the subject before Miranda has to answer. 'By the way, I'm not taking you miles out of your way, am I?' she asks. 'Where were you planning to go today before I stuck my interfering oar in?'

'Oh ... just ... I don't know really,' Miranda replies, eyes flicking up to her mirror to check on the silver BMW that is driving too close behind her – *right up her bum*, as Rose, who hated pushy drivers, would have said. 'Overtake me then if you want, there's plenty of room,' she mutters aloud to it, then, as the BMW does just that, with a great roar of its engine, adds 'Arsehole' under her breath. 'I felt a bit as if the walls were closing in on me, there at the hotel,' she goes on to Evelyn. 'As if everyone was getting in my face, if you know what I mean.'

'I don't, but I can imagine,' says Evelyn, thinking of all those column inches and headlines about the younger woman that popped up on her iPad, page after page, opinion after opinion. How dizzying it must be to feel as if the whole world is gawking at you on the sly. No wonder she lost it yesterday at the pool when that blonde girl was so rude. 'It can't be easy, being constantly gossiped about.'

Miranda's nostrils flare. 'Ahh. Been snooping around, have you?' she asks in an unfriendly way. 'I seem to remember you'd never heard of me last time we spoke.'

'Not *snooping*,' Evelyn says hastily. 'Just—'

'I'm surprised you'd want to get in the car with me, now you apparently know everything about me. Aren't you scared that Mad Miranda' – she deliberately swerves out of her lane and back, her voice rising – 'will drive herself off the nearest cliff? That's what the press all seem to want.'

There are no other cars on the road – the silver BMW is

long gone already – and Miranda isn't driving particularly fast, but all the same Evelyn grabs the handle in her door as they swerve. 'Sorry,' they both say in the next moment.

'Really, I am,' Evelyn adds. 'After I watched the show, I looked you up to see what else you'd been in, that's all. I promise. But some of those stories that came up about you seemed very unkind. And untrue, a lot of them, too, I bet.' She's thinking again of the one that said Miranda was having an affair with her sister's husband, a shady-looking chap called Felix, who has one of those awful thin moustaches. That can't be true, surely? Not least because of the diabolical moustache.

'I'm sorry too,' Miranda says in a quieter voice. 'I'm not a dangerous driver, don't worry. I promise I'll get you to Fiskardo in one piece. I just . . .' She exhales, and the sound is one of pure frustration. 'My temper keeps running away with me. I feel a bit . . . out of control. Partly because I'm just so sick of everybody knowing my business.'

'Of course you are,' Evelyn says. 'Although I hope you didn't mean that about driving yourself off the nearest cliff. Not for my sake but yours. You are . . . okay, aren't you? Well – I can see you're not. But if you feel like you really can't cope, then—'

'Thanks, Evelyn,' Miranda cuts in. 'But I'm okay. Not going to do anything silly.'

There's a pause where it feels as if they both exhale. 'I'm glad to hear it,' Evelyn says. Time to lighten things up around here, she decides. 'If only because a taxi to Fiskardo would have set me back an absolute *fortune*. You're saving me a packet by taking me.'

Miranda's gaze remains on the road, but Evelyn sees some of the tension leave her face. Phew.

'Tell me something about your honeymoon, about – Rose, did you say?' she asks. 'I don't want to talk about me any more.'

'Copy that.' Evelyn glances down at her bag and feels an ache of love in her heart. 'Well, it all started when a new couple moved into the street, over fifty years ago now, and invited us to their housewarming party ...'

Chapter Eighteen

Miranda

Miranda drives in silence while she hears Evelyn's life story, still a bit shocked at herself for deliberately swerving in the road, with an elderly passenger beside her, no less. Back in the day, her dad had taught her to drive (a fairly testing experience for them both), and he'd been so keen to impress upon her the weighty responsibility of a driving licence that on her very first lesson, before she'd so much as heard the words Mirror-Signal-Manoeuvre, he had intoned sternly, 'You are now in charge of a two-tonne killing machine. You need to remember that fact every single time you get behind the wheel.' *Yes, Dad,* she had replied meekly, but later hadn't been able to resist doing stern-faced impressions of him to her siblings that became a running joke between them for months on end. (*You are now in charge of a two-tonne killing machine: your bumhole!*) She can only imagine what he would say about her impulsively wrenching the wheel over like that in a burst of pique, how the blood would drain from his face in appalment.

Sorry, Pops, she thinks, keeping her hands at ten to two on the wheel like he'd first instructed her. She's had a couple of messages from her parents by now, nice chatty ones about the cat, and the neighbours' new granddaughter, which has left her feeling less of a total outcast. *You take care of yourself now,* her mum had signed off last night. *You'll get through this, and we love you.* Miranda can't lie, she'd burst into tears when she read the words; she has been feeling so alone lately. *Thanks, Mum,* she'd replied. *I promise I'm going to sort everything out.*

She puts them out of her mind and tunes back in to Evelyn's stories about the fabulous-sounding Rose. Gosh, she thinks, will anyone ever fall madly in love with me the way that Evelyn and Rose seemed to love one another? She's dated a lot of shallow pretty boys in her time, but there's never been any depth. Never any real love. 'You need to love yourself first, Miranda,' she's been told by every therapist she's ever had, but she hasn't even been able to manage that. It figures that the hotel barman wasn't interested in her either the other night, she remembers mournfully; he was probably able to detect the toxic streak running through her. *One Star, Would Not Recommend,* that's the signal she seems to be giving out.

She sniffs surreptitiously. *Get over yourself, Miranda.* 'So, you coming back here, is this like a tribute to Rose?' she asks.

'Um . . .' Rather uncharacteristically, Evelyn hesitates. 'Yes, you could call it that,' she says. She swings her head away to look out of the window, and Miranda gets the distinct impression there's something she's not being told. 'Anyway,' she goes on, 'enough about my wife. Tell me more about the show you were acting on. Did you like it there?'

126

Miranda slows as she passes a cheerful-looking mutt that appears to be taking itself for a walk. 'Amberley Emergency? Well . . . it's not something I'd have watched in my own free time, put it like that, but it was a regular acting job with decent pay, so in those terms it was pretty good.' She's been in touch sporadically with Todd, but hasn't been able to face asking how they're working around her absence in the script. No doubt her character has suddenly gone on holiday, or perhaps has been taken violently ill. She imagines the writers, some of whom she has clashed with previously, enjoying the task of having to write Miranda's character out altogether. They'll probably give her the most horrific, revolting death, including a scene where the other characters discuss in hushed tones how awful it was to hear that Doctor Kelly died of a freak case of the bubonic plague, covered in suppurating boils, or whatever other ghastly end they dream up.

'Would you go back if they begged you, do you think, or have you got your eye on another project now?' Evelyn wants to know.

Miranda snorts, because it doesn't exactly work like that in her industry. 'Oh yeah, I've got my eye on a leading role in a Hollywood box-office smash, playing a smart, brave, incredibly nuanced heroine,' she replies sarcastically – and probably kind of bitterly too, let's face it. 'But back in the real world,' she adds, in case Evelyn has missed the point, 'there sadly *is* no other project on the horizon. So yeah, if they begged me – and chucked Bonnie Beresford off the cast – then, for the sake of my mortgage, I'd probably have to crawl back on set. Ugh.' It's not a great thought, however badly she needs the money.

'Bonnie Beresford is the one you—' Evelyn begins cautiously, then breaks off, as if she isn't quite sure how to say 'slapped in the face and shoved up against a wall'.

'She's the one,' Miranda confirms, gruff-voiced. 'Although I thought we weren't talking about that any more.'

'Sorry,' Evelyn says meekly. 'Ooh, by the way, have you seen all that stuff in the news about Frank Neale? You know he's staying at our hotel, don't you?'

'What stuff?' asks Miranda, who has been on a self-imposed news and social media blackout for two days, since she saw the sickening press release about that smirky twat, Giles Shelby, landing the lead role in a massive new Netflix thriller. Not now, Satan, she'd thought, and immediately deleted her apps.

'Oh gosh! So much stuff! There's a *Panorama* programme coming out later this month and it's all about what a sex pest he was in the nineties and early . . . I never know what to call that decade,' Evelyn says. 'The noughts? The two-thousands? Then, anyway. Lots of women have come forward with stories of harassment, and other nastiness.'

'God,' says Miranda. 'I hate to say it but it's not a huge surprise.' At least this will send her plunging down the news agenda for a while, she thinks, wrinkling her nose. 'I was wondering why his wife always looks so unhappy whenever I've seen her around the hotel,' she goes on. 'They must have known this was coming.'

'Poor woman, I agree. Did she have any idea he was that kind of man, do you think? Surely she wouldn't have stayed with him and put up with that, if she'd been aware?'

Before Miranda can reply, the navigation app on her phone

pipes up. 'In two hundred yards, turn left at the junction,' it orders.

'Got it,' murmurs Miranda, temporarily shelving Frank Neale for a proper deep-dive chat later.

'Fiskardo two kilometres,' Evelyn comments, pointing at the sign. 'We're nearly there.' She reaches down and picks up her small tan-coloured handbag, then cradles it on her lap. 'Nearly there,' she repeats under her breath.

Miranda shoots her a questioning look, but Evelyn is staring down at the bag and it's hard to tell what's on her mind. 'Everything all right?' she asks as she slows at the junction. 'What are you planning to do when we get to Fiskardo anyway? Is there somewhere in particular you've got lined up to revisit? Evelyn?' she prompts when there's no answer forthcoming.

Evelyn takes a few moments to reply. 'I'm not sure,' she says vaguely, her hands tightening round the bag.

Miranda glances over at her again, before she has to focus on a junction. 'Um ... Are you okay?' she asks once they're through the other side. 'I feel like there's something you're not saying. I mean, you don't have to tell me *anything*, obviously, but if you want to, then ...'

'I'm fine,' Evelyn replies, then gusts a sigh. 'Or rather,' she goes on, 'I'm like you: *trying* to be fine, *pretending* to be fine, not always succeeding. We're a right pair, aren't we?' There's another pause, and then: 'I think today might be ... difficult,' she says, her voice unusually flat. 'And I don't know if I am brave enough to do ... what I'm supposed to be doing.'

Wow, that's all very cryptic, Miranda thinks, but she doesn't push for further details. 'Okay, I hear you,' she says. They're nearly into the town now and she needs to concentrate on finding somewhere to park. 'Let's just get to Fiskardo,' she suggests, 'and then we can take it from there.'

Chapter Nineteen

Nelly

London, 1984

It was well over a year after she'd returned from her adventures in Greece before Nelly felt like smiling again. Nobody had *quite* been unkind enough to say, 'I always thought staying in Greece was a daft idea' when she returned, broken-hearted, to London, but you could tell that everyone thought it – her parents, her brother Richard, Lorraine. *Well, what did she expect? Giving up a perfectly sensible job and a perfectly normal life . . . to mess about on a boat all summer? I tried to tell her from the off that it would never work out, but would she listen?*

'I suppose you want to stay with us now,' her mum had sighed, with a martyrish air, when Nelly appeared at the door with her suitcase, her face puffy from crying the whole way home. 'Just as I've got the spare room set up all nice for visitors, as well!'

It was clear from her mother's tone that Nelly didn't qualify as one of these precious 'visitors'. Previously she might have made some waspish comment about going to sleep in the bus station then, fine, if her mum was going to get her knickers in a twist about a stupid spare room. It was a sign of just how broken she was though that she merely mumbled, 'Sorry, Mum' and 'Thanks, Mum' instead. Then she took to her bed, where she stayed for three solid days, alternately sleeping and crying, with an occasional dreary traipse downstairs to make herself another round of cheese on toast. ('At least have an apple with that,' her mum fussed at her, the closest she ever came to expressing motherly love aloud. 'Get some vitamins down you, Nell, we don't want you getting scurvy on top of everything else.') Who knows how long this might have continued had her dad not had his hours reduced at the factory ('Bloody Maggie Thatcher'). The hit to the family's financial situation meant that any remaining sympathy for weeping Nelly instantly evaporated, to be replaced by a lot of comments about it being time to pay her way now and contribute to the family coffers. Or, as her mum put it, 'For heaven's sake, drag yourself out of that stinking bed, wash your hair and get down the temping agency, will you? The gas bill won't pay itself, do you hear me?'

Nelly heard her, as did most other people in the street, probably. Nonetheless, on Monday morning out she went with smart clothes, neatly brushed hair, and make-up, and dutifully picked up some temporary office work. Day after day, week after week, she typed letters, sat through boring meetings jotting down the minutes, and sweated over temperamental photocopiers in offices around London. Crammed in on the

Tube, navigating unfamiliar streets, being called 'the temp' and 'Oi love, what's your name again?', she clocked in and clocked off like a sad, pale ghost drifting through the capital's business empires. The bright sunshine of Greece, the gloriousness of boat life seemed to slip further away with every pay packet she received; the glittering blue sea remote from the concrete and glass landscape she now found herself in. The miners went on strike, an assassination attempt was made on Gerry Adams, and police officer Yvonne Fletcher was shot dead in the space of a few weeks. Everything was grim and dirty and miserable; she felt as if she were being buried alive.

'Cheer up,' said Lorraine, who had just announced her engagement to Jim and was, according to her, the happiest woman alive. Nelly loved her like a sister but, even so, there was only so much relentless joy anyone with a broken heart could stomach. 'Hey, Michael has been asking about you, by the way, I don't suppose you fancy—'

No, Nelly told her before Lorraine could finish her sentence, she absolutely did *not* fancy going for a drink with Michael Wet-Lips Rothman. Had Lorraine forgotten that she was in love with Alexander? She would *always* be in love with Alexander, for as long as she lived! You didn't just move on from somebody like that, and definitely not for a pillock like Michael Eyes-Too-Close-Together Rothman.

Then in stepped Fate, with his big interfering ideas, plucking her up like a toy and dropping her into a whole new game. 'We've got an exciting little job for you next week,' Janice from the agency told her over the phone during their regular Friday catch-up. By now it was late summer in 1984, almost a year after Nelly's return to England. She was renting a cramped basement flat in Blackheath, where the mice careered around like overlords and the condensation was so bad she had coughed that entire first winter. It was no palace but it was hers, at least, paid for by saying yes to whatever Janice and the agency staff offered her.

'Sure,' she replied, as ever.

'It's in Soho – lovely – and, get this, it's two weeks covering reception and secretarial duties at Guy Drewers Management – you know, the talent agency?'

'Oh great,' said Nelly, even though she'd never heard of them. Soho was easier to get to than her current job all the way over in Plumstead at least, she was thinking.

'Let me know if you hear any showbiz gossip, won't you?' Janice said at the end of the call, once she'd given Nelly the details. 'And hey, don't you go falling in love with anyone famous, now.'

Nelly gave a hollow laugh. 'You don't need to worry about that,' she'd said.

Once the job started, she felt more confident than ever in her own assurances. No way would she fall in love with anyone from the telly when they all seemed so neurotic and self-obsessed. She supposed that 'being dramatic' was basically the job description for actors but, dear God, she wanted to bang their heads together half the time, what with all the whinging and exaggerating that went on. By the end of the first week, she'd been regaled by the most extraordinary excuses regarding lateness to auditions or missed rehearsals – and she, as the receptionist, was tasked with passing on these elaborately crafted tales to the actors' long-suffering agents. Still, she had to hand it to them – they were extremely good at fake-coughing down the line, so those years at drama school hadn't been completely wasted.

The agents were fun to observe, at least – sharp-eyed and fast-talking, forever vanishing off to lunch and then returning triumphantly four hours later in a rush to get contracts out and signed before the important people involved sobered up enough to change their minds. They represented all sorts of creative talents – screenwriters and authors and TV presenters as well as the actors – and there were always tickets going spare to the launch of this, the opening night of that. Plus, it was kind of exciting every morning to open envelopes containing speculative scripts or novels from writers and flick through the pages, wondering which of them, if any, might be rewarded by a nod, a handshake, a great big contract in return.

Then, one slow midweek afternoon, one of the agency's most famous actors, Michael Cranborne, staggered into reception, reeking of booze and weaving around unsteadily. Oh no. She'd heard the agency assistants bitching in the staff kitchen about this particular client, notably about what a liability he was. 'Somebody needs to install a Michael Cranborne panic button for every time he calls up and gives us shit,' she remembered Cath saying while pulling a face. Cath was a die-hard New Romantic who wore frilly shirts and imitation leather trousers and claimed to have kissed two members of Spandau Ballet and one of Duran Duran ('SO FAR,' she liked to add.)

Now here was the man himself, and unfortunately the panic button was still only wishful thinking. Michael Cranborne was in his mid-forties and, according to the newspapers, going through a divorce that was proving both expensive and acrimonious. Perhaps it was taking its toll, because on this occasion, as he made his way towards Nelly he suddenly dropped to his knees, stared into the middle distance and then flung out an arm. 'Doubt thou, the stars are fire,' he cried, his voice ringing in the space like a struck bell. 'Doubt, that the sun doth move!'

'Um . . .' Nelly said uncertainly, glancing around and wondering what she was supposed to do. Cath had complained at length about Cranborne's passive-aggressive phone calls, but Nelly couldn't remember her mentioning unprompted soliloquies before.

'Doubt truth to be a *liar*,' he went on, bellowing this last word with such ferocity that she actually jumped in her seat. What the hell . . . ? 'But never doubt' – here he turned his head slowly towards Nelly and locked his gaze on hers – 'I . . .' – a long dramatic pause for good measure, then – '*love.*'

Cringing in embarrassment on his behalf, Nelly had to swallow back a fit of nervous giggles. What a twat, honestly. Where did the agency find these people? She was already looking forward to telling Lorraine about this absolute knobhead when she saw her tomorrow night, complete with full melodramatic impersonation. 'Hello,' she said politely. 'Can I help you?'

'Help? Ahh, but I am beyond help, they say,' he declaimed, returning his gaze to the middle of the room, perhaps imagining an adoring audience seated there. Apparently he was in no hurry to get up from his knees again, nor, indeed, act like a normal human being.

Nelly bit her lip, uncertain of the correct protocol for dealing with drunk, weird actors. If there had been something in the handover notes, she must have missed it. Should she make a discreet call to George, one of the assistants, who was six foot two and pretty beefy with it? Or even enlist the help of Hilary, Michael Cranborne's agent, who had the quietly terrifying air of a ruler-wielding headteacher? Her crisp, disapproving voice would sober up anyone in a heartbeat, surely – but then again, she might tear a strip off Nelly too, for not having the initiative to handle the situation single-handedly.

'Er ...' she dithered. He didn't look at all well, she registered. Even from where she was sitting she could see the sweat shining on his forehead, the unhealthy pallor of his skin. As for his complexion, it was positively green. Just as she was thinking this, his face spasmed with a startled expression, then he vomited stupendously all over the carpet.

'Oh my God!' Nelly cried, jumping to her feet. 'Mr Cran— Oh *no*.' She hurried round the desk to where he had keeled over on the floor, eyes closed, his face squelching into the rancid pool of his own sick. Yuck. 'Is anyone around to help?' she yelled in the general direction of the office beyond, not daring to leave him in case he started choking.

'I can help,' came a voice, and she swung round to see a tall dark-haired man who'd just walked in through the main door. A delivery driver, she thought in a fluster, or perhaps a tradesman. Whichever, she wasn't about to turn him down.

'Thank you,' she said. 'He just collapsed, I need to—' She knelt down beside him, recoiling from the stench and doing her best to avoid getting her skirt in the pool of puke. (It was dry-clean only and she wasn't made of money.) 'Mr Cranborne, can you hear me?' she said, gingerly patting his arm. 'He's still breathing,' she added in relief.

'Jesus, is that *Michael Cranborne*?' the man asked, with renewed interest, then, before she could reply, knelt alongside her and gave the actor's arm a proper shake. 'Here, Mr Cranborne, can you get up for us now, please? Come on, you can't stay here, mate. Up you get!'

Nelly wondered if she should permit one of the agency's highest-earning stars to be manhandled and called 'mate' like he was on a building site or something, but at least the actor was opening his eyes in bleary response.

'Mr Cranborne?' she repeated, and grimaced as he let out a putrid-smelling belch then closed his eyes once more, settling a little deeper into his own vomit. 'Oh Lord,' she groaned.

'Don't worry,' the dark-haired man said. 'I work in a pub, I've seen it all before. Mr Cranborne!' he added in a louder voice, before glancing back at Nelly. 'Do you want to get him a glass of water and maybe some cleaning stuff while I keep an eye on him here?' He winked at her. 'I promise I won't let him die in your reception area.'

She was too grateful that he was there, unfazed and suggesting a plan, to pay much attention to the wink. 'Are you sure that's okay? That's so kind of you.'

'Not at all,' he said as she got to her feet. 'I'm Frank, by the way. Frank Neale. Nice to meet you.'

'You too,' she replied, so flustered by his dazzling smile that she forgot to tell him her own name. 'I'd better . . .' she gabbled, waving an arm in the direction of the office, before scuttling away, cheeks flaming. She couldn't cope with the attention of a handsome stranger right now, on top of everything else.

Hurrying between desks, she headed to the area where the assistants sat. 'Michael Cranborne has thrown up all over reception,' she gabbled to Cath, George and the others. 'Where can I get a mop and some carpet cleaner?'

There was a flurry of activity as various staff members rallied to help, including scary Hilary herself, whose nearby office had its door open. 'That fucking man, honestly, if he's not already dead I might just kill him myself,' she growled before heading resignedly to reception. By the time Nelly returned with a bucket of hot soapy water, George and Hilary had wrangled Michael Cranborne into a sitting position, where he now sat meekly sipping a paper cup of water. Cath, meanwhile, was behind Nelly's desk, answering the phone. ('I'm sorry but this waistcoat is velvet, and you know what that's like for hanging on to smells,' she reasoned apologetically. 'No way am I getting too close to Sickboy.')

In her new role, Cath had also thought to ask Nelly's dark-haired rescuer who he'd arrived to see. Unfortunately for Nelly, it was none other than the agency boss himself, David Willoughby. Her whole body became hot as he appeared on the scene, looking furious upon realising that Mr Neale had become caught up in events. 'I am extremely sorry that you've been dragged into this . . . this *debacle*,' he said, shooting a glare at Nelly. He steered Frank around the carnage and towards his office, tight-lipped. 'I assure you that this sort of episode is absolutely *not* the norm here at Guy Drewers, and that I will be looking into how on earth you happened to be left there alone.'

Nelly froze, bucket in hand, as dread took hold of her guts. Frank Neale was a *client*? But how could that be when he'd just told her he worked in a pub? Oh hell. David Willoughby's face was thunderous; surely it was only a matter of minutes before she was told in no uncertain terms to leave the premises, they didn't want such a brainless temp working here any more. But thankfully she was still in earshot when Mr Neale replied, 'Are you kidding me? Water off a duck's back! In fact that pretty girl you've got on reception handled everything very well.' This was said with a cheeky look over his shoulder at Nelly, who was still standing there like a muppet.

Eventually Michael was dispatched, calm was restored, and Nelly was able to return to her desk amidst a cloud of strong air freshener. Roll on six o'clock and the chance to get out of here, she thought darkly. Famous people were such dicks. No sooner had her equilibrium returned, though, than her dark-haired rescuer reappeared in the reception area, along with David Willoughby, who – thank goodness – was all smiles. Feeling self-conscious, Nelly pretended to be jotting down a phone message as the two men shook hands.

'I think this could be the start of something extremely promising,' David Willoughby said warmly.

'Cheers, Dave,' Mr Neale replied. 'Good to talk.'

Dave! thought Nelly, trying not to giggle as she stared fixedly down at the notepad in front of her. Nobody ever shortened the boss's name like that. Her phone rang in the next moment and she answered it, feeling not a little disappointed as the mysterious Mr Neale said goodbye to David Willoughby, and left the building. Despite the circumstances of their meeting, despite him being a client and out of bounds to the likes of her, she was intrigued about who he was, why he'd come into the agency and if he really worked at a pub, as he'd claimed. Was he penning soulful poetry between pulling pints, perhaps? Had he written a tub-thumping polemic about the state of the hospitality industry? She was already planning to get chatting to Madeline, David's secretary, and see what she could find out.

But there was no need because, practically the second she replaced the receiver after her phone call, there he was, strolling back into the building. Her heart stepped up a gear as he walked over to her desk and leaned an elbow on it.

'Hi again,' he said. She had time to look at him properly now, taking in his sweep of dark hair, his amused-looking grey eyes, the stubble just starting to show around his jaw. He was about the same height as Alexander, although skinnier and a little gangly with it, and there was an air of mischief about him that was hard to dislike.

'Hello,' she said, trying to keep her cool. 'Here for another meeting with "Dave", are you? I thought you had a pub to run.'

'I'm here for a meeting with you,' he replied, ignoring her question. 'What time do you finish? I'm taking you out for a drink.'

'Oh, are you now?' she asked archly. Despite her best efforts to sound detached and impervious to his charm, she was pretty

141

sure her cheeks were betraying her with a rush of heat. 'You seem very confident about that.'

'That's because I *am* confident. I'm the love of your life,' he told her assuredly, then, imitating David Willoughby's plummy tones, added, 'And I think this could be the start of something extremely promising.'

'Is that so?' she replied deadpan, but his charm must have been working on her nevertheless, because when he added, 'You didn't tell me your name earlier. Let me guess. Angie? Susie?' she found herself answering, 'No, Leonora. Leonora Maguire.' She was drowning in those eyes by that point, she must have been, because then she heard herself say, 'And I finish at six.'

He whistled. 'Leo*nora*! That's posh,' he teased. 'Should I call you Nora for short?'

'Not unless you want me to ig-Nora you,' she told him, and he grinned at her.

'I definitely don't want that,' he replied. 'Go on, then, what should I call you? Princess? Gorgeous One? Future Wife?'

'Give over,' she said, before relenting. 'Everyone calls me Nelly.'

'Nelly Neale! Sounds good, right?' He had dimples when he smiled, she noticed, and it was hard not to smile back.

'It sounds like a cabaret act,' she reproved him, shaking her head.

'Ahh, you'll get used to it. And you can be Leonora Neale for best. So – do you know The Cambridge? Of course you do. I'll see you at six, Nelly Neale. Don't be late.'

Even if she'd wanted to argue, it would have been impossible, because he was already putting up a hand in farewell and walking jauntily away, whistling as if he was pleased with himself.

'Nelly Neale indeed,' she muttered under her breath, but she was smiling nonetheless, and her heart was skittering with the memory of how it felt to experience a burst of attraction for someone. How life could seem . . . interesting again. Fun.

Job done, thought Fate in satisfaction, moving on to interfere with somebody else's life.

Chapter Twenty

The Bartender

The bartender is crating up the empty bottles around the side of the hotel, beside the pungent waste and recycling bins, when a motorbike swings past him and into the nearby staff car park. The bartender narrows his eyes, wondering if this is a guest who has taken the wrong turning – there's a far more salubrious parking area for hotel residents elsewhere, away from the smell of bin-juice – but when the motorcyclist parks up and takes off his helmet he sees that it's Andreas, the boss's son.

'Hi,' says Andreas, striding over, the helmet dangling from one hand. He's in his early twenties and built like Dimitris, with muscular shoulders and a chest as broad as an ox. Just the bartender's type, actually. 'Is my dad around, do you know?'

'I'll see if I can find him,' the bartender replies, abandoning the crates and straightening up. The last time he saw Dimitris, he was in conversation with Yiorgos, one of the groundsmen, and they'd vanished off together. He could be anywhere. 'Let's try his office first,' he says as Andreas falls into step beside him.

They're in luck: Dimitris is in his glass-walled office, having a meeting with a smartly dressed man and woman who are sitting earnest-faced at the large round table there. The bartender hesitates, unsure whether or not to disturb them, but then Dimitris glances up, sees Andreas, and immediately beams broadly and gestures for them to open the door. 'This is my son,' he tells the man and woman as he gets up and claps Andreas on the shoulder. 'Andreas, could you give us another twenty minutes? These very nice people have come in to discuss having their conference here with us next year, and we are not quite finished. Konstantinos, perhaps you could take Andreas to the bar and get him a drink, please? Thank you.'

'Of course,' says Konstantinos, closing the office door, then leading Andreas out to the bar. He is struck, as always, by the easy, warm relationship between Dimitris and his children. *This is my son,* he hears Dimitris say proudly again, with that hand on the shoulder, love emanating like sunbeams from his face, and he can't help but feel a corresponding stab of envy in response. Imagine, he thinks with an inward sigh, how good that must feel. Like a thick blanket around you on a cold night, like a forcefield against the stresses of life. In contrast, Konstantinos' own father, Nico, has never expressed love or pride in him. He wishes he could say that he has given up hope but it's not true. However tough he tries to make his own skin, there will always be a soft vulnerable part of him that can't help holding out for fatherly approval.

'What can I get you?' he asks when they reach the bar.

A dreary ballad is playing, the sort of thing his divorced aunty listens to, and he skips the song and selects 'This Hell' by Rina Sawayama instead to liven things up. *Let's go, Rina,* he thinks, listening to the opening riff. Zoe, one of the waitresses here, loves a bit of melancholy and is frequently trying to sneak Mitski or Taylor Swift tracks into the playlist, but although Konstantinos can see that songs of mournful yearning have their place (in his divorced aunty's living room, for example), that place is not a hotel bar where people are on holiday.

Andreas asks for a Coke and Konstantinos serves it to him with ice and a slice of lime. Not for him a warm glass and a so-what attitude, even when he's pouring a simple Coke. In Konstantinos' bar, every drink can be a party in a glass, something special to be savoured. Get him started on the cocktail-making and he's in his element, absolutely loving the theatre and spectacle. The first rule of hospitality – make everyone feel special, that they are worthy of your time and care. Not that his dad seems to understand. 'Pouring drinks for rich people, is that really what you want to do with your life? When are you going to get a proper job?'

A proper job, like a real man, that's what he means. A man's job in construction, maybe, or farming, or engineering. Work that involves one's hands; rough, tough outdoor work. Konstantinos' dad has spent thirty years on building sites, he can't understand why his son wants to take a so-called woman's job in a bar. The thought of him ever announcing to his colleagues, 'This is my son' with love in his voice like Dimitris just did ... it will never happen.

'A man of your age, you should be settled down with

a wife and family by now, providing for them. You can't mess about with a cocktail shaker for ever, you know,' Nico had pronounced last year when Konstantinos was home for Christmas. He had caught his mum's eye at the words 'wife and family' but she shook her head in a tiny no, a silent gesture that begged, *Don't spoil Christmas.* There's so much Nico doesn't know – and doesn't want to know either.

'Family's not everything,' Zoe tells him, but it's all right for her, training to be a doctor at university; her parents must be crazy with pride for *her.* 'Anyway, I know it's not the same, but you can make your own family, right?' she'd said the other day. 'You're always telling me I've got little-sister energy, so . . .' She'd poked a finger into her cheek and batted her eyelashes at him, and they'd both laughed. He's going to miss her when she goes back to uni.

Two middle-aged women have approached the bar and, after some deliberation over the cocktail list, ask for a Pisco Sour and a Paloma. 'Excellent choices,' Konstantinos says, setting to work on the Pisco Sour. He puts the ingredients together in a cocktail shaker, slaps the lid down and shakes vigorously.

'That looks hard work,' one of the women comments, her eyes on Konstantinos' upper body. 'Who needs the gym, eh?'

'The perfect workout – and a drink afterwards,' her friend says. 'What's not to like?'

'Absolutely,' Konstantinos says, smiling back at them. ('These poor women,' Zoe often teases, when the two of them are having a break together. 'Clustering around you like the wasps to our pastries. And all the while wasting their time. It's a tragedy, Kon. So many hearts shattered.')

Having added ice to the cocktail, Konstantinos shakes the contents again for a solid thirty seconds, before pouring the mixture through a strainer. Then for the garnish – four careful drops of angostura bitters dotted around one side of the foam, and the gentle pull of a cocktail stick through them to create a line of hearts.

'So pretty!' the first woman cries, clapping her hands.

It's only while he's making the Paloma, rolling the glass rim in chilli salt, that he notices that Dimitris has brought the man and woman from his meeting to the bar, and that the three of them are observing the performance. 'Konstantinos here is our very best mixologist,' he hears Dimitris tell them. 'His cocktails are an art form, believe me! So your guests would be well looked after in the evening, with his expertise on hand.'

There's a bursting feeling in Konstantinos' heart as he looks up from the glass he's holding to see his boss's face and the warmth therein. The – dare he say it? – the pride. It's only the smallest moment – Dimitris is already shepherding the two of them away, talking about the menus they could offer at the restaurant, the number they could cater for – but the glow Konstantinos feels burning inside him after his boss's comments will end up lasting for the rest of the day.

I know it's not the same, but you can make your own family, right? he hears Zoe say again in his head as he garnishes the Paloma, and he smiles to himself. That's the thing about little sisters, he supposes. They drive you mad with their musical tastes but, every now and then, they get it right.

Chapter Twenty-One

Claudia

StarMyStay – The Ionian Escape, Kefalonia ★
I can't believe how much this place charges for an average room FULL OF MOSQUITOES AND SPIDERS!!!! The air con didn't work properly and the breakfast was cold and disgusting. There was a leak in the bathroom sink and the room hadn't been hoovered properly. Also the pillows were so uncomfortable, like trying to sleep on concrete blocks. REALLY DISAPPOINTED. Don't waste your money!!!!
Theresa Honeywell, Jersey

StarMyStay – The Ionian Escape, Kefalonia ★★★★★
We came here for our honeymoon and I've never felt so well looked after at a hotel. A beautiful room, the most comfortable bed, a wonderful pool, with a great beach five minutes' walk away. The food is amazing, the staff couldn't have been kinder and more helpful. Thank you to all the staff, especially Claudia and Dimitris who made our stay truly memorable. Dream team!
Rosie and Ned, Aberdeen

For a long time, Claudia had enjoyed being with Marcus, first as his girlfriend, then wife. He was handsome and urbane, with his well-cut suits and gym-toned physique; his whitened teeth that were always (almost always) flashing a broad, confident smile. Before their paths crossed, her life was pretty ordinary, what with her unremarkable marketing job, her shared Collingwood flat, her evenings spent at the pub with friends or with TV and takeaways. But then one evening she came home from work to see a removal van in the street, and found her flatmates clustered excitedly at the front window, all perving over the apparently drop-dead gorgeous man moving in across the road. 'Wait till you *see* him,' they cried, sighing and clapping their hands to their hearts. 'Should we go round and introduce ourselves?' they giggled. 'Invite him over for Wednesday-night takeaway?'

It became something of a running joke between them, the arrival of Hot Neighbour (as he quickly became known), with all sorts of enjoyable musings about his name, his occupation, his proclivities. What his voice sounded like (deep, husky, suggestive, they predicted), his star sign (Madison was certain he'd be a dynamic Aries, Kayla thought he had the heft of a Capricorn, while Claudia's vote was for a sultry Scorpio). What he listened to when he went out running (rock classics? hip-hop?) and if it would be too obvious if they all took up running as well and orchestrated an accidental collision in the nearest park.

So far so fun. Who doesn't love a crush? Then one morning the postie accidentally delivered a letter addressed to Claudia to the Hot Neighbour's house. Answering the door that evening, already in her PJs and big fluffy slippers (it had been a long day), she felt a delicious fluster at seeing him standing there, even more handsome close up than when spied on through bamboo blinds. 'Claudia?' he asked, holding up the letter. WHAM. Straight to the heart.

'Yes,' she said, as an explosion of lust detonated throughout her body. 'That's me. Hi.'

Easy as that. Nice moves, Cupid. She was twenty-nine and conscious of the next decade looming on the horizon. Friends were starting to get engaged or move in with their partners; one couple she knew had just announced that they were having a baby. While Claudia was not by anyone's standards a shy princess waiting for her prince, the boys she'd dated before then had been pretty lame, on the whole. Flakes. Cheaters. Stoners. Woefully immature, the lot of them. Enter Marcus, a proper grown-up with his own car and mortgage, a successful career, someone who knew all the best restaurants in town. He flossed his teeth, he competed in triathlons, he was dynamite in the sack. It was like winning the boyfriend lottery. Too right she said yes when, less than a year later, he got down on one knee in the Grace Darling and proposed.

'It's like a fairy-tale,' Barb sighed the night before the wedding, when Claudia was back home for a family dinner. The white dress was hanging upstairs, she'd packed a honeymoon case full of swimwear and lingerie, and she was looking forward to wife life with all her heart. 'Your happy ever after, Claudie!'

That was what they all thought, anyway. And why wouldn't they? He'd been nothing but charming and generous to

Claudia, and everyone in her immediate circle, from the off. The only person who hadn't fallen under Marcus's spell was Elodie, Claudia's friend from work. 'So what's the catch?' she'd asked, raising a suspicious eyebrow. 'I mean . . . he seems too perfect to be true. There must be a dark side somewhere, right? A few dodgy skeletons clattering around in the old closet. Don't you think?'

Claudia had laughed. 'Not at all! He's just . . . good. Men like that do exist, you know.'

'Hmm,' Elodie said. 'Well, I'm glad for you, Claud. Although if it turns out he's secretly into devil worship and kills old ladies for kicks, then . . .' The eyebrow was lowered again. 'Don't say I didn't warn you.'

Marcus wasn't into devil worship and killing old ladies – as far as Claudia knew – but he was, it turned out, highly skilled at psychological and emotional warfare. It started small, shortly after their marriage, with little put-downs that made her question herself, sudden bursts of temper about things she had apparently done wrong in his eyes. He became very jealous if she went out with friends, or saw her family without him there too, and he would blow up afterwards, accusing her of all sorts, refusing to believe her protestations of innocence. It became simpler, on the whole, to tell other people that she was busy, really busy, sorry, could they meet up some other time? It became easier, also, to leave her job, after he became convinced that she was having an affair with her boss there, a chubby family man called Peter, just because she'd once been foolish enough to comment on how nice he was to work for.

'Are you sure you're okay?' Elodie asked low-voiced at her leaving drinks when Marcus had gone to the bar. He had turned up as a surprise and had been at Claudia's side the entire time until now. 'You don't seem yourself, Claud.' She'd hesitated, glancing around, before asking urgently, 'You would tell me, wouldn't you, if something was wrong?'

'For goodness' sake! I'm fine!' Claudia snapped, so sharply that Elodie's eyes widened and she backed away. Was that another friend lost? Claudia had wondered in resignation that night in bed. Still, Marcus would be glad if so; he'd never liked Elodie anyway, calling her an interfering shit-stirrer and making crude remarks about her sexuality.

Thank goodness though that Elodie was harder to dissuade than some of her other friends. That she had persisted in being a so-called interfering shit-stirrer, doggedly calling and messaging, eventually contacting Claudia's family and expressing her concerns about how controlling Marcus was. Thank goodness, most of all, that Marcus had been away on a business trip to Sydney when her parents and Elodie turned up and basically staged an intervention. 'We're worried about you, darl,' Barb had said on the doorstep, her mouth scrunching up as it did whenever she was emotional. 'We feel like something might have gone a bit wrong. And we want to help you.'

At first Claudia had rejected their help, insisting that everything was fine, she didn't know what they were talking about, but then Barb took her hand, looked into her eyes and said, 'Claudie, it's us. We're on your side. We love you.' Somehow this broke the enchantment, because all of a sudden Claudia started crying and couldn't stop. Her mum sat there holding her tight, while Jerry busied himself making everyone cups of tea and Elodie packed her an overnight bag. 'I can't leave,' Claudia wept, still unconvinced. 'You don't understand. He'll be so angry.'

'You can leave,' they told her. 'And him being angry is exactly why you *should* leave.'

It wasn't until she was back in her old bedroom in Fitzroy, coddled and cared for, that she started to realise just how thoroughly and expertly Marcus had dismantled her life, so that she had virtually nothing left in it other than him. The perfect husband had, in fact, been rotten to the core.

She has only seen him once since then, back in January when she'd gone home for a holiday. She'd been in the Gem with Elodie and her partner Ash, and was waiting to be served at the bar when she heard his voice. 'You stupid pathetic bitch,' he said, and time instantly folded in on itself. There she was, back in their marital home, cringing with fear as he shouted at her, trying not to cry as he shook her and told her how worthless she was. For a moment she thought she might throw up with terror, her system drowning in adrenalin. In the next second Elodie and Ash were flanking her, and they were speaking on her behalf.

'Don't you dare even look at her, you fucking piece of shit,' said Elodie.

'Get away from her this minute,' Ash said, putting a hand on Marcus's chest and shoving him hard.

Marcus did not like being shoved or threatened, and he definitely didn't like feeling as if he'd been bested by his stupid pathetic bitch ex-wife and her so-called weirdo mates. But then the bar manager was on the scene, asking, 'Is there a problem, Elodie?' and when Elodie replied, 'Yes, this person is a problem', Marcus was refused service and asked to leave the premises. 'I'm not finished with you yet,' he spat at Claudia before stalking out in a fury. 'Not by a long shot.'

The words have haunted her ever since, even here on Kefalonia, miles away from the streets of Melbourne. She knows he is the sort to nurse a grudge, to play the long game, and she has been waiting for him to strike out eventually, show his hand. Receiving the aggressive email at work was the moment she has been dreading, the prelude to him smashing his way back into her life.

But perhaps she was wrong. Because when Andreas, Dimitris' computer-wizard son, comes to the hotel to take a look at the message, he's able to trace it back to an IP address not in Melbourne, as she'd predicted, but to a town in England called Leighton Buzzard. 'Are you sure?' Claudia asks, frowning. Has Marcus travelled there on business, maybe? It seems unlikely – the last she'd heard, he was working for a haulage operations company based in Geelong, and it's a stretch to imagine them flying him out to a town in – where was it again? Bedfordshire, wherever that is.

'Absolutely one hundred per cent,' Andreas confirms.

She can feel Dimitris studying her face. 'I think this is good news, yes?' he says. 'That this idiot is not in Greece, we do not have to take him too seriously. And that maybe ...' He hesitates. 'Maybe this is not a person you know, after all?'

She gulps, because the news is still sinking in. The message is almost certainly not from Marcus, she repeats to herself. He hasn't found her. He isn't about to turn up and ruin everything in the name of some petty vengeance. It's only then that she realises just how pent-up she's been feeling. How the stress of his potential reappearance has been like a giant weight on her, pressing her flat. She nods, trying to pull herself together and react professionally, but instead, to her horror, she bursts into tears.

'Hey, hey, come on, now,' Dimitris says. He gestures for Andreas to make himself scarce, then grabs a handful of tissues and holds them out to her. 'Here.'

'Sorry,' she says, taking the tissues and blowing her nose to buy herself some time. *For heaven's sake, Claudia, get a grip!* 'Ignore me,' she says after a moment. 'I'm fine, really.'

'Well, no,' he corrects her. 'You're not fine, Claudia. By the way.'

She laughs, although it sounds a pretty unhinged kind of laugh. 'I will be fine,' she says, as much to herself as to him. 'It's just . . .' It's not Marcus. He hasn't found her. Perhaps it's the relief, but in the next moment she drops her guard. 'Okay, yes, I was a bit scared,' she hears herself admitting. 'Scared it was my ex-husband. He . . .' Then she trails off, because even talking about Marcus is enough to conjure him up in the office, mocking her. 'He was a bad mistake. A bad person,' she says quietly.

They're sitting either side of her desk, the computer screen pulled round so that it faces both of them, and he puts his hand over hers, clasping it momentarily. 'You are safe here,' he says. 'I promise you. Bad people are not allowed in my hotel.'

'I know. Thank you. I just . . .' His hand is warm against her

156

skin and it's enough to ground her again. Back in your box, Marcus, she thinks. You're in the past.

'If it makes you feel better, I too once made a bad mistake with a . . .' He glances towards the doorway, lowers his voice. 'A not-so-great person. Lili and Andreas's mother, Elena. Not a good marriage. And we were far too young, as well. Just twenty! We knew nothing.' He shrugs. 'But we are human beings, we make mistakes. And it's painful when you realise that you married the wrong person, yes?'

She nods, slightly taken aback that he is revealing such personal information to her. He's friendly and kind to everyone at the hotel, but he's also a private sort of man, keeping his cards close to his chest. He mentions his kids frequently – they all know how proud he is of them – but this is the first she's heard of his not-great ex-wife. 'Yes,' she says.

'But I am glad that your wrong person is not' – he gestures at the screen – 'this arsehole who calls himself the god of war. And because of this, I will now reply to him on your behalf, I think.' He grins at her as he pulls the keyboard towards him. 'Let's make *him* sweat for a change, hey? Let's see who's the most pathetic person here now.'

Blowing her nose one last time, Claudia feels a new lightness expand in her body. Dimitris is right – she *is* safe here. She has rebuilt her life on solid foundations, without any input from her ex. Even if Marcus were to burst through the door tomorrow, she has enough good people around her who would have her back, who'd send him packing. He's only as scary as she allows him to be, she realises. Like the bogeyman, like a horror film. She can close the book, shut down the narrative. Stop believing.

'Thanks, Dimitri,' she says as he types furiously. He pauses to read under his breath whatever firm rebuttal he's just concocted, then resumes typing. She'd almost like to be on the scene in Leighton Buzzard when this 'Ares' opens his email and gets the full burst of Greek wrath, she thinks. See how *he* likes it. Then she frowns. *Leighton Buzzard*. The place name is ringing a bell somewhere in her distant memory, but why?

'There,' says Dimitris, jabbing at the Send button with an air of finality. 'You are not welcome at my hotel, you are not even welcome on the *computer* of my hotel.' He turns his gaze on Claudia. 'You are okay now?'

'Yes,' she assures him and he gets up from the desk, pats her on the shoulder and leaves her to it. She slowly lets out her breath then examines her feelings. She wishes now that she had kept her cool, that she had not burst into tears. It has been a point of pride that she has managed to keep a protective shell around her while she's been working here; that she has not let the past ruin her future. But the strange thing just now was that she found herself wanting to confide in Dimitris, that she wanted to be truly honest with him, rather than pretend. He's the sort of man she feels she could trust. The sort of man, even, that she could . . . well, love.

The word startles her and she blinks and closes down the thought immediately. No. That's ridiculous. Has she learned nothing from this email episode? She's his employee, they are colleagues, and she cannot – must not – do anything that would make that awkward. Been there, done that, fled the bastard, she reminds herself sternly, getting back to work.

Chapter Twenty-Two

Evelyn

'Oof. Perfect. Very good,' says Evelyn with an admiring whistle as Miranda squeezes the hire car into a tiny parking place on the edge of Fiskardo.

'For once, the god of parallel parking is on my side,' she says, switching off the engine. 'Whoever that might be.'

'Well, Hermes is the god of travel,' Evelyn says thoughtfully.

'Thank you, Hermes,' says Miranda with a little salute.

'Or maybe it's Tyche, goddess of success, fortune, luck and prosperity,' Evelyn goes on.

'She sounds like someone you want to be on the right side of,' Miranda comments. She unclips her seatbelt, then puts her hands together as if in prayer. 'Thank you, gracious Tyche. Much appreciated.'

The two of them emerge from the car's air-conditioned confines into the warmth of the day. The sun beats down on Evelyn's bare head and she finds herself wishing she'd thought to bring a sunhat like Miranda's. Her white hair has thinned over the years and it's not pleasant to imagine her scalp, pink as a side of bacon, turning crispy with the heat. The last thing she wants is sunstroke when she's saying her final goodbye to Rose, she thinks, her hand tightening round her bag strap. *Are you ready in there? I'm not sure I am, you know.*

They set off down a street of colourfully painted Venetian-style houses. According to the local history website she read the night before, this village was one of the few places on Kefalonia to be unaffected by the terrible earthquake back in the fifties, which makes the houses here some of the oldest on the island. What must it have been like for the local people at that time, she wonders, to have heard about the hundreds of deaths and injuries elsewhere on Kefalonia, as well as reports of so many other islanders having had their livelihoods reduced to rubble, utterly destroyed? If you were one of the few whose home and family remained unscathed, would you feel lucky to have been spared, or plain old guilty?

'This is gorgeous,' Miranda says, and Evelyn decides to keep her dark thoughts to herself. 'So you came here before, on your honeymoon, you said?'

'Yes,' Evelyn replies, remembering how they'd hiked up to the old Venetian lighthouse together through the fragrant pine trees, the sea glinting below. She has an image of Rose walking beside her in a full-skirted summer dress, yellow with a splashy print of red and white flowers, and white trainers. They'd held hands, the rings they'd bought each other for the civil part-nership ceremony glinting whenever they caught the sun. *Oh, Evie, I'm so happy that we're here, that we've done this,* she'd said, and Evelyn had felt as if her heart might overflow with joy.

'Are you all right?' Miranda asks, and Evelyn crashes back into the present day, with Rose mere ashes in a bag. 'You look very faraway.'

'Just reminiscing,' she replies with a sigh. Coming back to a place where she's been with Rose always makes her feel as if time has concertinaed and she's simultaneously experiencing the past and present. It's a dizzying sensation, as if the ghostly figures of their younger selves are still here, trapped in some kind of time echo, and all she has to do is turn her head quick enough and she'll be able to see them. If only.

She and Miranda head down a flight of stone steps to the harbourside, which is lined with restaurants and cafés, while yachts butt up against the quay. There are ice cream stalls and souvenir shops, the smell of coffee and fresh bread, the occasional flap of a sail from a mast whenever there's a breeze. They'd had lunch somewhere along here, Evelyn remembers, and— Oh. She stops walking.

'Are you *sure* you're okay?' she hears Miranda say.

'I just . . .' She's remembered something else: that they had an argument here that day. That their happiness had soured like old milk. What had they argued about? Vague fragments turn in her mind . . . an unpleasant little scene here on the harbour, with Rose squaring up to a man, and Evelyn trying to pull her away. That was it – there had been a homophobic comment thrown at them, perhaps after they'd kissed in public. Evelyn had been upset and dropped Rose's hand immediately, whereas Rose was defiant, snatching it back, gripping it so tightly, in fact, that it had almost been painful. 'Oh dear,' she murmurs under her breath, recalling a miserable lunch in the immediate aftermath, with Rose furiously eating a salad and lecturing Evelyn about standing up for herself, being true to herself. She had completely forgotten that until now but suddenly she is right back there, poking a fork at a bowl of spaghetti and feeling as if she might cry for being such a disappointment to her new wife.

'Evelyn, what is it? You're worrying me,' Miranda says. 'Shall we sit down in the shade and have a cold drink, maybe? You look a bit wobbly.'

'Yes, let's,' Evelyn says faintly, dismay cascading through her. Well, she can't leave Rose here then, she decides. Not when it's the site of an unhappy memory. She hugs her bag close as Miranda steers them into a nearby restaurant, where they take seats under a big umbrella. 'Sorry,' she says, seeing Miranda's look of concern. 'I've brought you here, and I'm already wondering if it was a mistake to come at all. I . . .' She hesitates but can no longer hold back the truth. 'I'm meant to be scattering the last of Rose's ashes somewhere on Kefalonia, you see. I'm on this kind of . . . quest. This is my last stop.'

'Wow,' says Miranda in surprise. 'What a lovely thing to do for her. What, and you're going to scatter them here, in Fiskardo?' Her eyes narrow. 'Or not?' she adds perceptively.

Evelyn sighs. 'Originally, I thought this would be a good spot, but . . .' She trails off as a waiter approaches, and then orders herself a bottle of mineral water, while Miranda opts for a double espresso.

'I just remembered that we had an argument here,' Evelyn continues after the waiter has vanished again. 'Me and Rose,

162

I mean. And I'm just not sure I can bring myself to leave her in a place where she told me I was a wet lettuce.'

Miranda splutters. 'You? A wet lettuce? Never,' she declares.

'Compared to her I was,' Evelyn replies. She remembers arriving at the hotel where they'd stayed, and Rose insisting on them walking up to reception hand in hand, magnificently facing down anyone who so much as gave them an odd look. You could tell that the place was a bit old-fashioned because the twin beds that they pushed together every night would be firmly separated again by the cleaners by day, but nobody questioned them aloud, probably because of that I-dare-you glint in Rose's eye. 'She was always much braver than me,' she continues. 'Much better at standing up for injustice, for civil rights, for the oppressed. She was a proper firebrand, Rose. That was what was so awful about her wasting away at the end, being so … so … weak.' She gives Miranda a rueful smile. 'But when you're married to a firebrand, sometimes you end up getting a bit scorched, I guess. One of the small prices we pay for love.'

Miranda nods, takes off her sunglasses and puts them on the table. Her eyes are a lovely conker brown, beneath delicately arched eyebrows. 'I love hearing you talking about Rose,' she says. 'Even if I disagree profoundly with her wet-lettuce allegation. And from all that you've said, I totally get that you want to find the right place to scatter her ashes. But you don't need to apologise for bringing us here. We can try other places. I've got the car all week; I don't mind driving you around, if that helps.'

'Oh, Miranda,' Evelyn says, touched by the offer. 'You don't have to do that. It's very generous of you but I couldn't possibly impose on your holiday in such a way.'

'Why not? Honestly, I don't have anything better to do. Besides, I could do with carrying out a good deed here and there, to see if I can get karma back on my side.' She pulls a funny face but there's a sadness about her too. 'Might even keep me out of trouble,' she adds, a little forlornly.

To think Evelyn had found Miranda so stand-offish at first when the truth is that, beneath all of the trappings and attitude, she's really just a girl who's lost her way. Not that she'd thank Evelyn for any such pitying observations, mind you. 'Well, if you're absolutely sure and not just being polite, then I would be delighted to take you up on that,' Evelyn tells her. The waiter returns and sets down their drinks, and she sips her water. How can she convince the other woman that she is an ally, to be trusted? *Tell me,* she wants to say. *Confide in me.* She's old enough to know by now that you don't turn your life around by squashing your troubles into dark hidden corners – they need to be brought out and aired, like washing on a line. But you can't force someone to open up to you just because you think they should. 'Don't forget by the way, seeing as you're driving, that I'm paying for these – and for lunch too, when we get to that,' she says instead. 'No arguing!'

Miranda's lips twitch in amusement. 'God, no, I wouldn't dream of arguing with a wet lettuce,' she teases, raising her tiny espresso cup in the air. 'Cheers, Evelyn.'

'And cheers to you too, Miranda. And FYI, as the young people say, I will be writing up an extremely glowing commendation for whoever's in charge of karma.'

'Please do,' Miranda says fervently. 'I need all the help I can get.' She wrinkles her nose. 'Have you ever googled yourself, Evelyn? Because if you google "Miranda Vallance bitch" or "Miranda Vallance ugly" or "Miranda Vallance shit", you'll discover there are literally thousands of people out there who seem to think I'm the worst person alive.'

Evelyn's mouth drops open in disbelief. There's so much of this little speech she simply cannot fathom. 'Why on earth,' she begins, 'would you google "Miranda Vallance bitch"? Please don't do that again. What good can come of it? You're not a bitch, you're not ugly, you're not shit. There – I've saved you the bother of ever having to look those things up again.'

Miranda responds with a smile but it's not a proper one. She shrugs. 'It's just … I don't know. Kind of a self-hatred itch that you need to scratch sometimes, I guess. Everyone famous does it.'

'Do they? I know lots of insecure famous people too, but they never go in for quite such brutal self-flagellation,' Evelyn says. 'Please, Miranda, I'm serious. I know it's a free world and you're entitled to do what you want, but that seems a particularly masochistic path to take. We were always told never to read our reviews. Deliberately seeking out negativity seems to me—'

'Wait a minute,' Miranda interrupts. 'Who's "we"? Are you an actor too?'

'No, not an actor. A musician. I played the cello,' says Evelyn. 'A long time ago now, obviously.'

'But … professionally? Famously?'

'I wouldn't say "famously" but yes, professionally, for lots of orchestras around the world. For the London Symphony Orchestra for many years,' Evelyn says, her thoughts spinning back to some of the more memorable evenings she spent performing: at the wonderful Concert Hall in Lucerne, the Musikverein in Vienna, and of course the concrete unloveliness of the Barbican in London, which will always hold a special place in her heart.

'Wow, Evelyn, you are such a dark horse,' Miranda says. 'What a fantastic career to have had. All those lives you must have touched, all those hearts you must have gladdened ...'

'Well, I don't know about that,' Evelyn demurs, but she's pleased nonetheless. When you get to eighty-two, people tend to look at you and write you off as old and feeble; they can't see that you have decades of vivid, glorious experiences stacked up behind you. Adventures. A career. Audiences in auditoria rising to their feet in applause.

'I bet loads of people have fallen in love, listening to you play,' Miranda goes on, warming to her theme. 'Marriages proposed, babies conceived ...'

'Not at the Barbican, I hope,' Evelyn says severely, but she smiles, amused to imagine how appalled Gregor, their terrifying conductor, would have been at the suggestion.

'Well, you never know,' jokes Miranda. 'If the mood takes you, then the mood takes you, Evelyn ...'

The waiter, arriving at the table to see if everything is okay, seems a bit taken aback to find the two women hooting with laughter. '*Efcharisto*,' Evelyn says, still chuckling. 'We're fine, thanks.' Her lips twitch again. 'Dear me. Babies conceived indeed. There's a thought.'

She's still clutching her handbag, she realises, and sets it down on the ground, looping the strap round her chair leg. It looks like her beloved Rose has a stay of . . . hmm, execution is the wrong word under the circumstances, she thinks, screwing up her face – but they will at least have a little longer together, now that she's ruled out Fiskardo as her final resting place. And that's fine, she decides, exhaling. It's taken her this many years to deliver on the promise she made her, after all; there's no rush to finish the job. She'll know the right place to leave Rose when she finds it. In the meantime . . . well, she has a feeling she's going to rather enjoy herself with Miranda as her companion. Who would have thought?

Chapter Twenty-Three

Nelly

'Our first stop in approximately ten minutes will be the stunning Melissani Cave,' announces the tour guide, an adenoidal woman called Agnes, from the front of the coach. 'It is very very famous place here in Kefalonia, said to be cave of Pan and his nymphs, back in antiquities. Cave roof, he has fallen in, long long time ago, so lake inside is open to the sky. Very beautiful, you will see.'

Following weeks of gossip and speculation, the storm has finally broken over Frank's head, and it's worse than Nelly could ever have imagined. 'It'll blow over,' Emily, Frank's agent, had said when the first rumours surfaced last month. She has been with Frank since David Willoughby retired six years ago, and has a steely air of authority. 'This is all puff-of-smoke stuff, nothing but speculation and fabrication.' Since then, photos have emerged, grainy but damning. Women have been coming forward with unpleasant stories about being harassed by Frank during his so-called 'wilderness years' of drinking and substance abuse. A dossier has apparently been compiled by two journalists. The words 'sexual assault' have been used, and the Metropolitan Police are reported to be investigating a number of allegations. There's a *Panorama* documentary in the offing too, which sounds as if it will be very damaging indeed. Emily, funnily enough, has stopped talking about puffs of smoke and has instead introduced them to a legal team, who are preparing a statement on Frank's behalf.

'It's not true, is it, Dad?' Owen, their eldest son, asked yesterday on FaceTime, after the tabloids had all splashed on a story about the then eighteen-year-old work-experience girl who Frank – allegedly – took to a hotel room, plied with alcohol and drugs and had sex with. He would have been thirty-eight at the time, only six years older than Owen is now. 'Of course it isn't,' Frank had blustered. 'It's complete lies. These women are just trying to get money out of me, and there's nothing more to it than that.'

How Nelly wishes she could trust her husband when he rants on that the whole thing is a conspiracy to bring him down, an absolute confection of lies, and that some people will do anything for publicity. How she wishes, moreover, that she had the guts to ask him Owen's question herself and have him look her in the eye when he answered. No father wants his son to think ill of him, but a husband should be able to tell a wife anything, however shameful, however difficult to confess. Otherwise what does it say about their marriage? *Frank, be honest with me, I really need to know.* But the words remain unsaid, stoppered up inside her like corked wine. Because . . . Well, because what if the allegations are true?

He might be at the centre of the storm, but her world has been violently upended by the stories too. Has she been that gullible, that stupid to have believed in their happy marriage for all this time? It feels as if someone has taken a mallet to her life, battering everything out of recognisable shape. 'Is this why we're here on Kefalonia?' she'd asked him yesterday morning, when they woke up to the blaring headlines and his phone vibrating ceaselessly with notifications. 'Did you know that this was all about to break?'

'Of course not! Can't I treat you to a holiday now without you turning against me as well?' he'd retaliated, turning puce. 'You're supposed to be my *wife*, Nelly! Whose side are you on, anyway?'

Good question, Frank. Really good question.

Take it from Nelly, having both your marriage implode and your husband's reputation blown to smithereens while the two of you are sharing a hotel room is not ideal. It has been hellish, in fact, being trapped with him inside their suite, however luxurious, while the rest of the world clamours at your door. 'I need to get out,' she told him last night when the walls started closing in, when the calls kept coming. 'I can't bear this.'

'*You* can't bear it?' he'd jeered. 'How do you think I feel?'

How do you think those women felt, Frank? she wanted to yell. *I'm not sure you're actually the victim here.* Again, though, the words remained unsaid. Her feelings are all over the place. He is still her husband, however angry she might feel right now. They have been together for decades and, despite everything, the instinct to take his side, protect him, remains hard-wired in her. But how can she take his side on this occasion, given

170

everything that is coming to light? When a grim certainty is starting to take hold: that the man she married might not be the lovable charmer she has always thought?

I don't know what to think, she messaged Lorraine earlier, in reply to one of her supportive texts. It's cowardly, though, to keep backing away from the big awful truth she suspects has sundered their marriage. To hide behind an 'I don't know'. The uncertainty remains a restless energy racing around her body; by yesterday evening, all she wanted was to run, get away, be alone for a while, but where? If they were at home, she'd jump in the car and take herself off for some headspace, knock on Lorraine's door and cry in her kitchen, but that's not possible here. 'I'm going to see if the hotel can sort out a day trip or something, just for a change of scene,' she'd said in the end.

'What, like one of those coach tours?' he'd said, scorn in his voice. 'Count me out then.'

You, she felt like retorting, *are not invited anyway.* She didn't say that either. But now here she is, on a day-long island excursion (yes, Frank, 'one of those coach tours'), and for the first time in ages she feels able to breathe again, away from the strain of being Mrs Frank Neale. It's odd, not having him beside her, but it's a reminder that before she met him she'd been perfectly happy to make her own independent way through life. And so far she's rather enjoying herself, taking pictures through the coach window of the sweet little wild goats munching grass at the roadside, and looking forward to the sights in store. After the caves, they're due to stop at two little towns, Poros and Assos, then pause for a brief photo opportunity up on the headland overlooking Myrtos Beach. According to Agnes, some of *Captain Corelli's Mandolin* was filmed there and it is the prettiest beach in all of Greece. 'Put your pictures on social media,' she advises. 'Everyone will love!'

Nelly presses her lips together as she stares out of the window, doubting very much if she will be looking at social media any time soon. Neither will Frank, if he has any sense.

A lump forms in her throat, because she can be as determinedly independent as the next woman but there's no getting away from the fact that it feels odd to be here without him today. Not least because, until she first got wind of these claims, their marriage had mostly been a good thing. Ever since that first drink, following their chance Michael-Cranborne-related meeting ('We will name our first child after him,' Frank was vowing a week or so later), there had been something sparky and exciting between them – enticing enough that she could finally put Alexander and her Greek odyssey behind her and move on. That night in The Cambridge she'd discovered that he wasn't merely 'working in a pub', as he'd modestly claimed earlier. No, he was head chef at the restaurant of an historic coaching inn in Buckinghamshire. 'More of a hotel, strictly speaking,' he'd admitted. At the tender age of twenty-eight, he'd been nominated for a prestigious culinary award, a fact that had caught the attention of one David Willoughby, who'd happened to be dining there some weeks earlier. Later, at the bar, David had struck up conversation with the charismatic young chef and pronounced himself impressed. 'I'm going to get you on television, Frank,' had been David's parting words. 'Call me.'

'He reckons he can make me famous – and both me and him loads of money,' Frank had told Nelly in the Cambridge, shrugging a little, as if this sort of thing happened to him every day. 'So I reckon you could do worse than sticking with me while we find out if that's true, Nelly Neale – wouldn't you say?'

He could always talk the talk, that was the thing about Frank. Should she have seen this as a red flag at the time? She was too busy rediscovering the giddy flutter of fancying someone again after a year of heartbreak, though, to check too closely exactly what she was getting herself into.

In the early days, when Frank's star first went into orbit with the launch of his TV show, Owen was two and Cameron had just been born, and she had been tucked away with them in their new Sussex farmhouse, blissfully ignorant of any shenanigans that might have been afoot. That was how they split the labour: Frank had gone on to open his own Chelsea restaurant, then written a series of bestselling glossy cookbooks with his face on the cover, while Nelly brought up the boys and made them all a home. She was proud of his hard work, proud of his success – they had a lovely life together, wonderful holidays. Yes, she knew he partied hard as well, yes, she'd become aware of the excess drinking, the drugs and benders. The way he'd occasionally vanish, unseen for days on end, which she found particularly stressful. But if the accusations are to be believed, his behaviour wasn't limited to self-abuse during those periods – he was actually up to far worse. Making a mockery of everything she had held precious.

Had she been part of the problem though? she keeps

fretting. Because a couple of buried memories have come back to her in the past few days, troubling her greatly. She remembers being on set once and noticing a female runner being comforted by some other women in a cluster, over-hearing one of them saying, 'He's such a piece of shit' before hurriedly changing the subject when they noticed Nelly in the vicinity. Other moments – seeing a glance between members of Frank's (female) PR team once when he was making a speech at a publishing party, and realising, with a little shock, that they didn't like him for some reason. The occasional overheard remark, prompting questions she didn't want to hear answered. Each time, she'd felt that same prickle of uncertainty – was *Frank* being called a piece of shit? Was that contempt in the women's faces? Why? – but she'd chosen not to further interrogate these lines of thought, chosen instead to bury them in the depths of her subconscious.

What if she had been braver, she keeps asking herself. What if she had trusted her instincts, asked a few questions? Is this her fault, too, for colluding and keeping quiet?

'Of course it's not your bloody fault!' Lorraine had exploded down the phone when Nelly voiced her concerns. 'You took his side – that's what we do! It would have been a crap kind of marriage if you'd immediately taken the side of complete strangers rather than your own husband, Nell. You trusted him, like we all did. Don't you dare start blaming yourself, do you hear me?'

She closes her eyes miserably, trying to tune back in to the coach trip, and Agnes' potted history of the island as they con-tinue along the winding roads through the rugged mountains.

The only problem is that, with Agnes' strong accent, the mountain she has referred to several times, Aenos, sounds unfortunately like Mount Anus, which makes the two young women in the seats behind convulse with giggles at every repetition.

'Now, let me tell you about Pan,' Agnes goes on. 'He is son of Hermes, and god of shepherds and flocks, wild groves and woodland. He is very sexual, very funny, very ugly.'

The two young women start tittering again. 'Pretty sure I've met him out at Revs,' says one. 'Totally,' says the other. 'I reckon we've all been Panned.'

Nelly meanwhile can't help but think about her husband once more. Apart from the ugliness, he is apparently so Pan-like he regularly had so-called raunchy sex and cocaine parties with girls from the television production company, according to a new story in the *Mirror* this morning. 'It got to the point where some of us actually took the decision to quit our jobs rather than have to work with Frank Neale again,' one of them was quoted as saying. Those poor girls, honestly, Nelly could weep for them. And for herself too, the unsuspecting mug rustling up dinner back home at their cosy family farmhouse, telling him he was working too hard when he eventually made it through the front door, baggy-eyed and exhausted. She's totally been Panned.

Agnes goes on to tell the story of Melissani, a nymph who was so devastated to have been betrayed by Pan that she threw herself into the pool at the bottom of the cave, thus meeting her death. Who'd be a woman – or nymph? thinks Nelly, her hands curling into fists on her lap. We think times have changed, that everything's got better, but the bastards are still betraying us left, right and centre. Oh, what is she *doing*, still here in Greece with Frank, when all the evidence points to a pattern of atrocious, disgusting behaviour? Why hasn't she fled back home already, far away from him? *Come and stay with us when you get back, Mum,* her youngest son Cameron said the other night on the phone, and she is tempted. Stepping out of the story, letting it all swirl on without her, while Cameron and his boyfriend Nate fuss about her in their Twickenham cottage . . . the thought gets more appealing by the day. Lorraine, bless her, has offered Nelly the use of her and Jim's static caravan in Dorset, should she need another option. 'It might not be the luxury you're used to,' she'd warned, 'but it's so windy out there on the headland that nobody can hear you scream, at least.' Good to know.

They have arrived at the caves and the coach parks up. Everyone disembarks into the sun's glare, and Agnes counts out passes for them to show at the ticket desk.

Once through the barriers, and past a replica carving of the lascivious Pan himself (dirty old git, Nelly thinks, curling her lip), the group has to queue down a steep rocky tunnel to the entrance of the cave. As they shuffle forward through the tunnel, the light becomes steadily brighter ahead, until they eventually reach the opening to the cave, and the lake beyond. 'Feels a bit like being born, doesn't it,' quips a woman behind her in the queue to her friend. Nelly's not sure about that but all the same, it's impossible not to gaze up, up, up the steep rocky sides of the large cave to where they eventually reach the cloudless blue sky above without feeling impressed. The light on the water is something else too – the most gorgeous bright cerulean, fading to a deep indigo in the shadows. There are rowing boats lined up at the water's edge, and Nelly and the other day-trippers step wobblingly on board one and find seats. Then a guide stands in the middle, takes up the oars and pushes them away from the jetty, singing an echoing 'O Sole Mio' with great gusto, which raises a few laughs. No doubt he makes the same joke at least twenty times a day, Nelly thinks, as they glide through the clear water, past craggy stalactites and stalagmites.

'Are there eels in there?' a woman asks, pointing into the lake.

'Eels, yes, big eels,' comes the reply. 'Eels in the water, bats up above. Lots of creatures in the caves.'

The splashing of the water against the side of the boat suddenly takes Nelly back to a different time, a different boat, when she was a young woman in Greece, on the *Miaoulis*. She'd found her old diary from that time earlier this year and read through the entries with great nostalgia and fondness. One of the happiest periods of her entire life, she has always thought. Followed, of course, by one of the unhappiest. She thinks of herself back in her mum and dad's house, weeping face-down into the pillow, experiencing her first real heartbreak, and wonders now where she'll go if she and Frank split up. Cameron's a generous host but the cottage isn't large, and she doesn't want to impose on him for too long. Nor does she want either of their sons to feel they have to take a side. She'll have to sort out a flat – or maybe he'd be the one to move out, or . . .

Oh God. It's going to be awful, whatever happens. She never expected that she'd have to go through this again in her sixties. But something has to change, surely? She and Frank can't ignore the huge great fault line that has abruptly cracked open their marriage.

The little boat heads into the far recesses of the cave, where, once out of the sun's heat, the temperature drops noticeably. Here the water is the colour of dark ink, broken by the occasional gull feather or streak of bright white birdshit. It's creepy and quiet in the shadows, with only the sound of the oars splashing. Her thoughts turn to Charon, the mythical ferryman, transporting the dead across the River Styx, and she wraps her arms around herself, pressing her fingers against her bare skin as a reminder that she is still alive.

Just like she got through the awful summer after Alexander, she'll get through this time too, she vows. She picked herself up and figured out a way forward then, didn't she? Somehow or other she needs to channel her old fighting spirit, the same love for life that the younger Nelly had, and find a way to keep going, whichever direction that means she takes. Plunging from a great height like the doomed Melissani is simply not an option.

Chapter Twenty-Four

Miranda

It's going well, this strange little pairing on their strange little road trip, Miranda thinks as she noses the car into a village called Assos. It's Evelyn's next request stop in her quest to find Rose's Kefalonian resting place, but the journey there has not been a sombre one – quite the opposite. In fact, she had forgotten, until now, how enjoyable it is simply to talk without any kind of agenda, without feeling as if you might be walking into a trap. Even though she now despises Bonnie with all her heart, she has been aware of the friendship void inside her since their bust-up. She's missed their silly chats and messages, the companionship.

Assos is picturesque, an Instagrammer's dream with its rows of charming painted cottages, pink, blue and orange, with shuttered windows, and bright flowers growing up their frontage. There's a small pebbly beach with calm, shallow waters; a few boats bobbing in the harbour. They wander along the harbour wall, looking out to sea and stepping over the multitude of snoozing cats sprawled out here and there in the sun. 'Well, this is lovely,' Miranda comments as, having decided to lunch at a beachside taverna, they find seats under one of its big umbrellas. 'Beautiful and tranquil – and hopefully a place with no wet lettuce associations. Good call, Evelyn.'

Evelyn smiles, but it's not one of her full-beam smiles. Is that a regretful look in her eyes? 'It *is* beautiful,' she agrees after a moment, gazing out to sea. 'And you're right: I don't have any bad memories about this spot.'

Oh dear. There's a 'but' coming, Miranda can practically smell it. 'But ...?' she prompts.

'Well ...' Evelyn stares down at the table. 'The thing is, I'm afraid I don't have *any* memories about this place. I mean – I'm sure we had a lovely time. But I can't remember being here at all, which makes me think this probably isn't the spot for Rose either.' Her shoulders sink in a small sigh. 'Because it should be meaningful, don't you agree? All of the other places I've left her, I've felt very close to her there. But here ... I was hoping a memory would flash back into my head, but I'm drawing a complete blank. Nothing.'

'No flashing,' Miranda says, raising a suggestive eyebrow, and Evelyn shakes her head.

'Not the tiniest flash,' she confirms ruefully.

'That's a shame,' says Miranda, 'but I agree it's got to be meaningful. Don't worry, we'll find the right place.'

Evelyn bites her lip, not looking convinced. 'Sorry,' she frets. 'You must be finding this pretty tedious, all my shilly-shallying. I just ...'

'You just want it to be right. I get it, Evelyn, that's fine,'

Miranda says, leaning down to scratch a circlet of mosquito bites on her ankle. The pesky little so-and-so must have got her last night when she was sitting out on her balcony. 'And even if this isn't where you want to leave Rose, it's still a good spot for us to visit and have lunch, isn't it? I think it's absolutely gorgeous here. If I was still posting on Instagram I'd be taking photos left, right and centre. Five stars, would recommend.'

Evelyn smiles. 'I think *you're* five-stars-would-recommend,' she says suddenly. 'I do, Miranda, don't argue,' she pre-empts when Miranda opens her mouth, surprised and touched. 'You're a very nice person, and I'm exceedingly grateful that you're bothering with me and my whims today.'

It's silly, but for a few seconds Miranda can't actually find any words. Her instinct is to joke the moment away, say something glib, but she forces herself to sit and absorb the compliment instead, and it warms her right through. 'That is possibly the nicest thing anyone has said to me for days. Apart from my grandad's uplifting text messages, anyway. Thank you. I think you're pretty bloody marvellous yourself. And I'm honoured to be your chauffeur.' Okay, so 'honoured' is over-egging the pudding, she acknowledges, but all the same she's glad for the company. What would she be doing now, if Evelyn hadn't gate-crashed her day? Driving around crossly, probably, feeling angry with everyone and sorry for herself. Hanging out with Evelyn is turning out to be far more entertaining.

The waiter appears at their table just then. 'Ladies,' he says with a little bow. He is grey-haired and portly, with a bristly-looking beard, a grubby apron tied round his sizeable middle. 'Can I get you something to drink? Something to eat?'

Evelyn asks for a glass of Robola and another five minutes for them to think about food. Miranda orders another double espresso, wishing that she didn't have to drive back along the hair-raising cliff roads so that she too could have a cold glass of wine. Later, she promises herself.

'Actually,' Evelyn goes on, as they pick up their laminated menus, 'on the way over here, I did have another idea for where to leave Rose: Argostoli, the capital of the island. I remember us seeing masses of sea turtles by the harbour there, hanging around for the scraps that the fishermen were throwing overboard from their boats. It was wonderful to watch them, so majestic and graceful in the water. Also, Rose and I once had a conversation about reincarnation, and she said she quite fancied being reincarnated as a sea turtle. She thought that their crinkly little eyes always make them look as if they're smiling. Beautiful creatures.'

'Do you believe in that?' Miranda asks with interest, putting her menu down. 'Reincarnation?'

Evelyn wrinkles her nose. 'Not really,' she admits. 'Nor did Rose with any proper conviction, I don't think. It was one of the awful bedside conversations we had towards the end, when I was trying to make sure I knew exactly what she wanted, when it came to ... well, the actual end itself. If there was anyone she still wanted to say goodbye to who hadn't already visited, if she wanted us to resuscitate her if her body went into arrest, that sort of thing.'

'Gosh,' says Miranda, feeling a bit blindsided by these blunt practicalities. 'There's a lot to consider. A bit like a birth plan, I suppose, only . . .' Her face becomes hot and she leaves the rest of the sentence unsaid. *Idiot,* she thinks.

'Only a death plan,' Evelyn finishes for her. 'Yes. And because of that, I was trying to cheer her up, by talking about afterlife options. Whether she was going to haunt me, what she fancied coming back as if she was reborn, that sort of thing. Which, admittedly, we both knew was not very likely, but it was easier to face, the thought of her still being around *somewhere,* rather than being blotted out for ever.' She puts her menu down too, food forgotten. 'I was actually quite disappointed when she *didn't* haunt me, to be honest. I think I would have liked having her naughty ghostly presence around the place.'

'I can imagine,' Miranda says, thinking back to when her nan had died and her gramps went on speaking to her for weeks and months afterwards, stubbornly refusing to accept that she was no longer there. Then her attention is caught by a crowd of people suddenly swelling into the harbourside – a coach-load of day-trippers, she guesses, newly disgorged into the sunshine – with a familiar figure dawdling along at the back. 'Oh, look,' she says, interest piqued. 'I think that's Frank Neale's wife over there. *Sans* Frank.'

Evelyn immediately swings round to stare, and Miranda can't help but cringe at how obvious she is ('Cringe-atron two thousand,' she hears Imogen say in her head, another of their teenage catchphrases). 'You're right,' Evelyn replies. 'Poor woman. Some holiday she's having. At least she's ditched the sex pest for the day, by the looks of things.'

'She'll have drowned him in their whirlpool bath if she's got any sense,' Miranda says.

Evelyn shakes her head, turning back. 'You do feel for the family and loved ones in these circumstances, don't you? The ones who never wanted the limelight, getting dragged into it like collateral damage.' She hesitates. 'Do you think we should ask her if she wants to join us?'

Miranda feels hot all over at Evelyn's words about family and loved ones, given what's happened with Imogen. A recent headline flashes into her head – *Exclusive: Miranda Vallance – Seduced by My Sister's Husband* – and she has to swallow back a sudden rush of bile as she imagines people discussing Imogen the way she and Evelyn have just discussed Frank Neale's wife. 'Um . . .' she says, Evelyn's final question only belatedly registering. 'No. Let's leave her be.'

The waiter returns with their drinks just then, and they pick up their menus hurriedly. 'Sorry, could we have another five minutes, please?' Evelyn asks as he sets them down.

'No problem, no problem,' he tells them, stepping away.

Miranda sips her espresso, appreciating the jolt of caffeine. 'What were we talking about anyway?' she asks, keen to steer away from the subject of famous people's transgressions.

'Sea turtles,' Evelyn says. 'And death plans. I've written up one for myself, by the way, if you were wondering. I'm hoping I'll just slip away peacefully in my sleep, obviously, but if not . . .' She spreads her palms and smiles. 'No harm in putting a few requests down in writing, I'd say.'

'Gosh,' says Miranda, 'I suppose not. Is it like one of those riders you get from megastars at Glastonbury, asking for a bucket of M&Ms with all the yellow ones taken out, or twelve puppies and a private jet? You might as well, right?' She's finding refuge in flippancy again, she realises, because this is pretty heavy stuff for a sunny lunchtime. 'Sorry,' she adds. 'I don't mean to sound glib, but . . .'

Evelyn laughs, thank goodness. 'No, I think you're making an excellent point,' she says. 'I should update my list, throw in some outlandish requests, shouldn't I? Mine's very basic as it stands: one of Bach's Brandenburg Concertos playing, very strong painkillers and someone kind holding my hand. Pathetic!' She sips her wine. 'Anyway, enough about death. We should think about food.'

'Agreed,' Miranda says. 'But just briefly on the sea turtles – we can go to Argostoli tomorrow, if you want, or even later today if we have time.'

'Thank you,' Evelyn says. 'You're definitely getting an A on this karma report, for putting up with all my dithering. Or – what was it you said? – *Five stars, would recommend.* Yes, that's what I'll be submitting. But lunch first, eh?'

'Sounds good to me,' Miranda replies. 'Especially if you're still offering to pay. Now then, what's the most expensive thing on the menu, I wonder?'

They fall silent, studying their menus, and Evelyn takes another sip of wine. Perhaps it's going to her head because in the next moment, she says, 'Go on, then, I've opened up to you. Why don't you tell me a bit about what happened with you? This Bonnie must have done something pretty terrible to upset you so much.'

Miranda stiffens. The question has caught her off guard.

Images of newspaper headlines instantly flash up in her head; loud, trashy and life-shattering.

Spotted at the Clinic – Did Miranda Vallance Have A Secret Abortion?

Miranda Vallance: I'm A Slut and Proud.

Will there ever come a day when she doesn't think about those damning words? She gets her vape out of her bag and puffs on it to buy herself a few moments. 'If you must know, I confided in her,' she says eventually. 'I spoke to her about ... some stuff that had been on my mind.' She grimaces, picturing the two of them sitting there in Miranda's dressing room sharing a bottle of wine. How Miranda had eventually divulged what had happened with Felix; how impossible she'd found it to think about anything else. *I mean, I know I'm a slut – yeah, and proud of it too,* she'd said, trying to lighten the mood, *but Jesus, I'm not a monster. What should I do?*

This was the problem with so-called friends and making yourself vulnerable. This was why she would never get into such a situation again, ever. That 'I'm a Slut and Proud' head-line had been totally, wilfully, taken out of context – she'd said it offhand as a joke, trying to deflect from her conflicted feelings, rather than making an actual statement. What sort of bitch betrayed another woman by twisting everything so grotesquely, knowing the damage it would cause?

'I'm guessing she didn't keep your confidences to herself?' Evelyn prompts after a moment.

Miranda shakes her head. 'At the time, we were both caught up in this big PR thing that was being pumped out from the show into the media,' she says. 'Both getting a lot of press attention, in terms of me versus her. Two different levels of it, in fact: our characters on the ward, always clashing and trying to outdo each other, and our own selves, in real life, because we were both up for the same award. I can only assume that she must have decided to give herself the edge by making me public enemy number one. A quick phone call to the nearest gossip columnist, job done. Probably earned herself a tidy sum in the process too.'

'How despicable,' Evelyn says, frowning. 'On top of everything else you were going through as well. That must have been the last thing you needed.'

No doubt her words are kindly meant, but Miranda's skin prickles all the same. 'When you say, "on top of everything else ...",' she replies coldly. 'What do you mean?'

Evelyn looks taken aback, probably by the sudden iciness in Miranda's voice. 'Well ... I assumed ... I mean, the papers said you had gone to have a termination, but ...'

Miranda feels winded, as if she's been punched. Not you as well, Evelyn, she thinks, dismayed. 'Yes, they did say that, didn't they?' she replies through gritted teeth. 'But guess what? It was a complete lie. Yes, I was at a sexual health clinic, but that rubbish about me having a secret abortion was exactly that: pure rubbish. I've never been pregnant in my *life*. I was there for a prescription of the pill – I have horrifically heavy periods, so— oh Jesus, why am I even bothering? What business is it of anybody else's? You probably don't believe me anyway. Nobody believes me. Not even my own sister.' She winces as she thinks of Imogen's white face, the hatred blazing from her eyes, and swallows hard. *Oh, Imogen.* How will she ever make this right with her?

'I'm s—' Evelyn says, looking stricken, but Miranda is already speaking over her.

'Let's talk about something else,' she says. 'Or even better, let's just stop talking altogether for a bit. I came on holiday hoping to get away from all of this shit, okay? I don't need to be reminded of it by you!'

'I am so s—' Evelyn starts again, but then the sodding waiter arrives.

'You are ready to order some food now?' he asks.

'Could we have another five minutes, please?' Evelyn says weakly. 'Thank you.' Off he waddles, and then it's the two of them again, with a horrible, charged atmosphere like a miasma between them. Miranda stares down at the menu. *Meatballs, kleftiko, moussaka,* she reads once more, but the words skip about before her eyes and she can't concentrate. She's back there on the morning that the stories about her first blasted into the headlines, with her phone going berserk. She'd had the most debilitating panic attack of her life, feeling unsure whether she was going to vomit with sheer shock or simply stop breathing altogether. Her heart had pounded so fast it felt as if her body was vibrating. She simply could not believe what she was seeing in print.

WHAT THE HELL??? she had messaged Bonnie. *HOW COULD YOU???*

Bonnie's response was immediate, as if she'd anticipated Miranda's hurt. No doubt she'd been looking forward to it all morning, with a great big smirk on her face. *I promise it wasn't me,* came her bleated reply. *I swear, Miranda! I'm as shocked as you are!*

Yeah, right. Save it for when you reach the gates of hell. *I promise it wasn't me,* indeed; like it could have been anyone else, when Bonnie had been the only person she'd told. The single person she'd trusted enough to unburden herself to.

Evelyn breaks the silence. 'I think I'm going to have a Greek salad,' she says. 'How about you?'

Miranda still hasn't been able to read the menu properly. 'Um ... maybe the stuffed vegetables,' she says, forcing herself to look at the food listed. 'Sorry I had a go at you,' she mumbles a moment later. She'll probably have lost her five-star rating for this mythical karma report now, but never mind.

'It's fine. Consider it forgotten,' Evelyn says. 'Just going to the loo,' she adds, heaving herself up from the chair with what looks like a gigantic effort. 'Would you mind ordering for me if our waiter comes back while I'm gone?'

She's so spirited that Miranda keeps forgetting she's an old lady, not well, every bit as wobbly on her feet as her beloved gramps. Shame sinks through her for having been so curt with her just now. 'Of course,' she replies, remembering her agent's words about anger management and vowing to do something about it as soon as she gets home. She's a mess, isn't she? She can pretend all she wants, but she's a churned-up, hot-tempered mess, and she's still getting everything wrong.

Her eye is drawn to a couple of tiny girls squealing as they gleefully race in and out of the water down below. The smallest one stumbles and suddenly bumps down onto her bottom in the sea, then wails in shock as a wave crashes into her little face. The older girl rushes over immediately and hauls her up again before the mother can get there, then they wade back to shore together, holding hands.

There's a pain in Miranda's heart, a tightness in her throat. *Oh, you two*, she thinks. *Keep holding hands for ever. Keep helping one another up. Don't make the same mistakes I did, whatever you do.*

Chapter Twenty-Five

Evelyn

That evening, Evelyn still feels bad about how she upset Miranda earlier; her and her big blabbing mouth. Rose did always say she never knew when to shut up. The rest of their lunch was cordial enough, but nevertheless it felt as if something had been lost between them, as if Evelyn had shown herself to be as untrustworthy as this Bonnie woman. Afterwards, Miranda had looked at her phone and said that the best time to see the sea turtles at Argostoli was first thing in the morning, so they might as well go back to the hotel now. Evelyn couldn't help wondering if she'd changed her mind about being her chauffeur, after what had happened.

It would be a shame if so. Until then, Evelyn had been enjoying talking to her, finding out who she really was, and also having the chance to speak about Rose. Yes, she'd ended up pontificating about death (again), but it had been fun to talk about life, too. And so, with this in mind, she heads down to the bar and asks for a bottle of Robola, the Kefalonian wine she has really rather fallen in love with, and two glasses. She then takes a deep breath and heads up to Miranda's suite.

'Who is it?' Miranda calls through the door without opening it.

'It's Evelyn, and I have wine,' she calls back. 'And an apology to make,' she adds meekly when Miranda opens the door a moment later. 'I'm sorry I spoke out of turn earlier. Can I pour you a drink?'

Miranda is wearing pink shortie pyjamas and has her hair – her real hair for a change, long and blonde – tied back in a loose ponytail. Barefoot and bare-faced, she looks much younger than the groomed, elegant TV star who was at the wheel of the hire car earlier. 'Sure,' she says. 'That's kind of you. Come in.'

'Never go to bed on an argument, that's what my mum always used to say,' Evelyn goes on, following Miranda into the suite. It smells floral, from a nice bath oil or body lotion, perhaps. 'And I was feeling bad about upsetting you. Poking my nose in. If you've had enough of me for one day, I understand – the wine is for you, you don't have to—'

'Evelyn, I'd love to have a glass of wine with you,' Miranda tells her, interrupting before she can get any further. 'And we're all good. I was probably a bit oversensitive anyway.' She gestures at one of the armchairs. 'Have a seat. We could sit out on the balcony if you'd rather, but be warned, I got bitten to shreds by the mozzies last night.'

'Here is fine, thank you,' Evelyn says, easing herself into the armchair, which is splendidly comfortable, with cushions galore. After a day sitting in a car, her body feels seized up and stiff; she's grateful for all the padding she can get.

Miranda's pouring the wine when Evelyn's phone rings. The Godsend, the screen reads, and she smiles. 'Sorry, I'll just get this and tell him I'll call back,' she tells Miranda, swiping a finger to answer. 'Hello, dearest Orrible,' she says. 'How are you?'

'Hi, Evil, just thought I'd check in and say hello,' he replies. 'How's the holiday going? Tearing up the town?'

It's so lovely to hear the voice of her beloved godson. 'Not quite, although I am having a glass of wine poured for me right now by a very famous person,' she says, which has Miranda rolling her eyes. 'So I'm being rather rude, answering my phone, actually. Can I ring you back later?'

'Evil! What, you're not even going to tell me who you're hobnobbing with?' he cries, feigning outrage. 'You and your VIP lifestyle, honestly. Okay, I'll let you go. There's no rush to call back if you're gallivanting.'

'I'm not gallivanting!' she splutters, pulling a face at Miranda. 'All right, darling, I'll speak to you later. Bye.'

She hangs up, to see Miranda looking at her in amusement. 'I couldn't help hearing that person calling you "Evil",' she says, passing over a glass of wine. 'Please tell me that is your actual nickname, Evelyn. If so, I absolutely love it and I am one hundred per cent going to adopt that myself, immediately.'

Evelyn laughs. 'That was my godson, Oliver, who, when he first started talking, couldn't pronounce Evelyn, so called me Aunty Evil for the first few years of his life,' she explains. 'His parents thought it was hilarious and called me that as well and ... well, it kind of stuck for them. By the time he was a teenager and still calling me "Evil", I decided I should redress the balance and give him a nickname back. He campaigned hard for me to call him "The Godsend" – in fact, he often still signs off emails like that, cheeky boy – but I vetoed that, and call him Orrible instead. Even though he *is* actually a godsend, to be honest, and absolutely divine.' A singularly excellent thought occurs to her in the next moment. 'And he's *single* too, Miranda! Can I show you a picture of him? He's really and truly gorgeous! Even I, a decrepit old lesbian, think so.'

Miranda laughs too. 'I'm off men right now, thanks, Evelyn; I'll take your word for it. Anyway' – She holds up her glass – 'Cheers to you, for your wine and excellent company, and cheers to finding the perfect place to say goodbye to Rose tomorrow.'

Evelyn's eyes well with sudden tears. 'Cheers,' she says, clinking her glass gently against Miranda's. 'And to you too, for *your* excellent company and your kindness. I had a really good day with you.'

They both sip their wine – 'Delicious,' says Miranda – then Evelyn's phone beeps with a new message from Oliver. *Intrigued by your famous drinking companion. Do tell!!*

'Sorry,' she says, picking up her phone to unlock it. 'One, two, three, four,' she murmurs under her breath as she punches in the code. 'Your star-crossed lover is asking about you. Do you mind if I tell him I'm having a drink with you? He's not a journalist, he won't do anything with the information, he's just nosey, that's all.'

'I don't mind,' Miranda replies, 'although Evelyn, have you ever thought about changing your phone passcode? Because one-two-three-four is a pretty basic one, you know.'

Evelyn is not paying her any attention, instead typing 'Miranda Vallance – she's an actor' into the screen and sending it. 'Right, sorry about that,' she says, stuffing the phone out of sight. 'Old people today, always on their phones, eh? Tsk tsk.'

They chat for a while, about this and that, Miranda asking her more about her professional life in various orchestras, and then opening up about her love of the theatre and how maybe she'll return to the stage and 'do something a bit more highbrow for a change', as she puts it. 'Being in a soap is brilliant, but it's a bubble,' she says, 'and a really comfortable bubble at that – the sort that stops you from wanting to leave, and maybe challenging yourself in the way you did before.'

Before they know it, it's gone ten o'clock, and Evelyn suddenly feels so shattered she can hardly string a sentence together. Or perhaps that's the wine that they've long since finished off, followed by a decent amount of a new bottle from Miranda's minibar. 'Thank you for a lovely evening,' Evelyn says as she manoeuvres herself out of the chair. 'I've thoroughly enjoyed myself.'

'So have I, Evelyn,' Miranda says, following behind as she makes a wobbly path across the room. 'I'm so glad you came round. And thank you for the wine.'

Evelyn pauses when she reaches the door, wanting to express quite how delightful she thinks Miranda is beneath those tough outer layers of hers. But she's drunk enough that it'll probably come out wrong – patronisingly maybe, or platitudinous. She'll tell her in the morning, she vows, when there's nothing more intoxicating than a coffee in her bloodstream and she's able to summon the right words.

'So – Argostoli tomorrow, then, is that the plan?' Miranda asks. 'You're not too tired for back-to-back road trips?'

'That would be wonderful if you're sure you don't mind,' Evelyn replies. 'And I'll be fine tomorrow, I'm sure. I've been sleeping so well here, I've definitely got more energy than usual.' It's true, she thinks, as she says goodnight and makes her way rather blearily back to her own room. She began the holiday feeling quite depleted, but there's something about the warmth here, the friendliness, the beauty of the island that has reinvigorated her.

It's only when she's back in her room that she thinks to look at her phone again. There, waiting for her, is another message from darling Oliver. *No way! Tell her that I saw her years ago at the Donmar in some Pinter play (I think), she was fantastic!*

Evelyn smiles and is about to screenshot the message and send it on to Miranda (they have swapped numbers so that they can be in touch about Argostoli), but then holds back. Far nicer to pass on a compliment in person, she decides, if only to enjoy the pleasure on the other person's face. *She will be so thrilled to hear that,* she replies. *I will tell her tomorrow once I've sobered up. Goodnight sweetheart, talk to you properly soon x*

Chapter Twenty-Six

Nelly

It's six o'clock on Thursday morning and Nelly has been awake for hours, lying beside her slumbering husband, who is snoring as if he doesn't have a care in the world. Another day in paradise, she thinks grimly, as the golden dawn light seeps around the curtain edges. Another day of skulking around in sunglasses, trying not to catch anyone's eye; another day of the tabloids trumpeting new Frank-related horrors to their avid readers, and Frank's black mood of denial as he holes up in their room and tries to ride out the storm. She returned from her coach trip yesterday to find him downbeat and unwashed, trays of half-finished room-service food stacked up by the door, and barely speaking to her, as if this is somehow all her fault.

Well, it's not, she thinks, sliding out of bed, unable to lie there a second longer. She's been a loyal member of Team Frank for decades, but right now that loyalty is starting to feel misplaced. Consider this the renouncing of her membership, she thinks. Fuck Team Frank.

Retreating to the bathroom, she washes, moisturises, attends to her latest mosquito bites and put some clothes on. They came here together for a holiday, but today she actually needs to take a holiday away from *him*, and the grubby little maelstrom of which he's the centre. What's more, she can't hang around for him to wake up in order to say as much. She can't even stand to be in the same room as him any more.

Woke early – decided to go out for a while, she writes breezily on the hotel notepad. *See you later.* Then she props it up by his favourite place, the enormous mirror, where he can't miss it, grabs her bag and shoes, and eases the door open.

If the sweet-faced young woman down on reception with a massive steaming coffee at her elbow is surprised to see Nelly up and about so early, she doesn't show it. '*Kalimera*,' she says. 'Did you enjoy the coach trip yesterday?'

'Um . . . yes, lovely,' Nelly says politely, even though in truth she had felt as if she was merely going through the motions the whole time, too numb to pay attention to her surroundings. 'This is such a beautiful island,' she adds, suddenly wanting the woman to like her. She feels so alone right now, so desperate for human warmth, she'll take it from a total stranger if she has to.

The woman smiles at her. 'Good! I'm very pleased to hear that,' she says. 'Can I help you with anything this morning? Another trip?'

Nelly comes to a standstill. She's halfway across the reception area, having vaguely planned to go for a walk, but she hadn't thought any further than that. Really, she'd like to be out much longer than the time it'll take her to stroll along the beach and back. She wants to get far, far away from snoring, revolting Frank. 'Well . . . yes, actually,' she says, walking slowly towards the desk. 'If you had a day to yourself, where would you go? What would you recommend for me?'

The woman – Duska, it says on her name badge – picks up a colourful brochure and holds it out to Nelly. 'There are some other nice tours around the island that I could book for you,' she replies. 'When would this be for?'

'Well . . . for today. For now,' Nelly says. 'Is that possible, do you think, or . . . ?'

'Ahh.' Her face drops. 'For today, no,' she replies. 'I can check availability for tomorrow, if you like?'

Nelly shakes her head, already starting to regret her impulsive departure from the bedroom. It's barely seven o'clock, and if she'd just tried a bit harder she might have been able to drift back to sleep. 'No, thanks,' she says. Then her eye is caught by the cover of the brochure, a coach wheeling around a vertiginous cliff path, with a couple of yachts in the turquoise water below. 'How about a boat trip – is there somewhere I could catch a boat out around the island, maybe?' she asks.

She grimaces, aware how vague a question this is. But thankfully Duska is nodding, the light of an idea in her eyes. 'You could take a ferry to Ithaca, spend the day there,' she suggests. 'Have you been before? It's lovely; perfect for a day trip. There is a morning ferry in . . .' She types quickly on her computer. 'Ninety minutes. I can book you a ticket from here if you like? And order you a taxi to Sami, the port?'

Nelly swallows, because of course she has been to Ithaca before. It's the place where her heart was broken nearly forty years ago, never to fully recover. But it would be away from the hotel, where everyone knows her as Frank's wife, she figures; away from prying eyes and difficult questions. Away from Frank too, most importantly.

Bugger it, the past can't hurt her more than the kicking she's been getting from the present, can it? 'Great idea,' she says. 'Yes, please. Thank you very much.'

'And that's for . . .' Duska hesitates. 'One person? Your husband also?'

There's an ache in Nelly's heart. This is going to keep happening, she realises. 'Just me,' she says. 'No husband today.' She's trying to sound casual but her voice cracks traitorously on the word 'husband' and then – oh no – tears spring to her eyes. 'Sorry,' she says, horrified, as Duska glances up at her. 'I'm okay, honestly.'

Duska reaches out and puts a hand on hers, a brief momentary gesture of solidarity that is so welcome, so kind, that Nelly almost breaks down into full-blown sobs. 'I will sort all of this out for you,' she says quietly. 'One trip to Ithaca coming right up.'

Chapter Twenty-Seven

Miranda

Miranda should have known from the start that Felix was trouble. From that first morning, five or so years ago, when Imogen unexpectedly appeared with him at their parents' house for Christmas. 'Everyone, this is Felix!' she'd cried, gazing at him adoringly as if his presence was the greatest of all gifts. By then, the whole family had heard about this mysterious man – the adorable meet-cute of them both staying at the same quirky Lisbon hotel, where she'd been for a hen do, and he for his best mate's stag. They knew how he'd whisked Imogen off her feet, wining and dining her, when she'd returned home; how handsome and funny and dynamic he was; how she had never felt so in love. Then there he was, suddenly in the family hallway, like some kind of hunky catalogue model, wearing a fisherman's jumper and jeans, one arm slung round Imogen's shoulders. Miranda, who was halfway downstairs, still in pyjamas and with atrocious bed-hair (she'd just come off a taxing ten-day-straight shooting schedule, all right?), was unable to escape this ill-timed moment of introduction.

'Felix, this is Mum and Dad – Tracey and Paul to you. Seb, my brother, and his wife, Gabrielle. Miranda, my – oh my God, have you only just got up, or something? My big sister.'

There were several aspects of this phrasing that displeased Miranda, not least the 'big sister' part, when she was swathed in a vast padded dressing gown and probably looked twice the width of sylph-like Imogen. Afterwards, she'd wished that she could have said, 'A week of night shoots takes its toll!' or something equally cool and impressive, instead of blushing hotly, but everyone else was saying hello to Felix, and the moment vanished.

'Greetings, Vallances,' said the man himself, brandishing a Selfridges bag in the direction of Miranda's parents. 'Have some festive gifts; my shameless attempt to bribe you all into liking me.'

'Ooh,' said Tracey, taking it eagerly from him and peering inside. 'Gosh, Felix, you shouldn't have. Well – consider me bribed! It's lovely to meet you. Come in, both of you. There's some gingerbread just out of the oven – do you like ginger-bread, Felix?'

'What sort of a question is that?' he laughed, following her. 'I love gingerbread, especially if it's home-made and still warm. Christmas starts now!'

Miranda had been left to traipse heavy-footed back upstairs, cheeks burning, and dive into the bathroom to make herself presentable. But she couldn't feel awkward for long. Felix slotted right into the family as Imogen's boyfriend – faultlessly charming towards their parents, bonding with Miranda and Seb by affectionately taking the mick out of Imogen over the dinner table. In fact, the first time Miranda felt his foot pressing against hers beneath said table, she assumed it must have been accidental. Because in every other way he seemed the perfect addition to the Vallance clan: funny, confident, comfortable in his own skin. Lucky, lucky Imogen, Miranda thought – until she realised, the second time she felt his foot nudging against hers, that actually, no, the contact between them appeared to be deliberate. As was the way he tended to stand a bit too close to her sometimes, or brush past her unnecessarily when they were in the same space, touching her body with his. Or he'd give her a private smile now and then, one meant only for her, as if they were in on an intimate joke together. Conspirators.

It was all incredibly discomfiting. Because although he was – is – heart-stoppingly gorgeous, and under any other circumstance she'd have flirted right back, he was also – is also – with her sister. What was she supposed to do? Maybe she was reading too much into it, and he was just one of those shamelessly flirty people, winking and giving the eye to everyone. But surely a partner's *sister* should have been off-limits?

Having tied herself in knots over it for ages, Miranda finally broached the subject with Tracey when she was home for the weekend a few months later. 'Mum, have you ever felt there's something a bit . . . off about Felix?' she'd asked. It was a sunny April day and they were both in the garden, pegging out a load of laundry on the line. Her mum had almost dropped the peg-bag with surprise. 'Felix? No, not in the slightest!' she'd cried, looking perplexed. 'I think he's fabulous – and so does your sister. Why do you ask?' The words had turned to dust in Miranda's throat and she'd been unable to come out with her misgivings, especially as each instance of him overstepping the line had been a tiny, blink-and-you'd-miss-it moment, the sort Felix could easily deny with a feigned look of bewilderment. 'No reason,' she'd mumbled in the end, and turned to peg up a wet pillowcase, feeling her mum's baffled gaze on her back.

The next time it happened, she confronted him directly. It was the end of May, Tracey's birthday, and the family had assembled, even Seb and Gabrielle, to celebrate with lunch at her favourite restaurant. Having left the table to go to the loo, Miranda had walked out of the Ladies to find Felix leaning against the wall, apparently waiting for her. 'I think we're alone now,' he'd said, deadpan.

'Is this a joke to you?' she'd asked, glaring at him. 'Because I don't think Imogen would find it very funny if I told her.'

'If you told her what? I don't know what you mean,' he'd replied, wide-eyed.

'If I told her – and I *will* if you don't pack this in – that you're harassing me. Trying it on. You know exactly what I mean.'

He'd burst out laughing and she'd flushed bright red in the face of his mockery. For an awful moment she'd wondered if she'd imagined the whole thing, if she was deluded. 'I think you've had a bit too much to drink, Miranda,' he'd chuckled. 'Trying it on indeed. In your dreams, love!'

'Just leave me alone,' she'd snapped, and barged past him, revolted by his vile power games. Cursing herself too for having said anything in the first place, and dreading him reporting the incident back to Imogen. No doubt he'd only twist the narrative so that it looked as if Miranda was the one at fault; acting weirdly out of some jealous desire, maybe, or merely spite. 'Oh dear, I think your big sister's got a bit of a deranged crush on me,' she imagined him saying, and felt sick.

Nothing seemed to deter him, and she learned, over the years, to avoid being near him at a dinner table, to make sure they weren't ever alone in a room together, to act in a deliberately stiff, formal way around him, rebuffing any friendlier relationship. Surely if she kept ignoring him, refusing to play this game, he'd get bored and stop? In the meantime, as Miranda kept making excuses not to be at birthdays or other get-togethers, a wedge formed between her and Imogen. How she hated this wedge! How she missed having her sister there at the end of the phone, her most loyal confidante, the one person in the world who truly understood her. She threw herself into touring theatre productions that meant she was travelling for months at a time, she busied herself with her own boyfriends too, even if none of them stayed around for very long. But then Felix proposed to Imogen, and preparations for their wedding got under way – preparations that Miranda found herself dragged into, like it or not.

First there was the hen do, a drunken weekend in a Somerset spa hotel, which began with a blow-out boozy afternoon tea. By the time they were emptying the last drops of champagne into their glasses, Imogen was pissed as a fart. 'Here's to me and my happy ever after,' she cried, looking around for a member of staff so that she could order another bottle. 'And my sexy, wonderful husband-to-be. Even if *she* doesn't like him!'

This last was directed at Miranda, and instantly turned what had been a gooey-eyed celebratory 'Aww!' moment into a surprise attack. 'What?' cried the other hens, rallying to Imogen's side. 'How could anyone not love Felix?'

'I do like him!' Miranda had protested. 'What are you on about? Of course I do!'

'We both know you don't,' Imogen retorted, nose in the air, 'but that's okay because I love him. And he loves me.'

'Absolutely!' the hens chorused, some of them flashing accusatory glances at Miranda. 'You two are perfect together, babe! This is going to be the wedding of the year!'

Thankfully, a waiter appeared with more champagne, taking the heat out of the exchange. The moment passed, becoming largely forgotten as the cork was duly popped, more bubbles poured, and someone asked a question about Imogen's dress. Miranda didn't forget, though, and spent the rest of the weekend dreading a reprisal of the charge. She even felt as if she'd let her sister down, for not managing to hide her difficult feelings about Felix. She of all people should have been able to play the part convincingly.

Fast-forward a few weeks, and it was Imogen and Felix's wedding – a lovely ceremony, a sunny day, both bride and groom looking gorgeous and elated in the photos – and Miranda made sure to smile and look happy throughout too. Even when the photographer urged them jokily to 'Come on, guys – squeeze up, pretend you like each other if you have to!' during one of the family photos, and she felt Felix's hand slide onto her bottom. It took every ounce of her drama school training to keep a smile on her face for the agonising seconds before the photographer pronounced himself satisfied. How dare he? she fumed, shaken and upset. On his *wedding day*! To her *sister*! It left her feeling as if he was mocking her *and* Imogen, and she was powerless to react. How could she say anything now? If only she had been more assertive from the get-go, she might have nipped this whole unsavoury side of him in the bud, established better boundaries. But now she wondered if he might have interpreted her silence to be acceptance. Encouragement, even. Was this actually her fault, for letting it carry on at all? How would she ever be able to stop him? She was only able to relax once the bride and groom finally left for their wedding night to a raucous round of cheers.

Two more years went by and she still didn't tell anyone, just tried her hardest to compartmentalise the situation by staying away. Imogen had enough to deal with anyway, what with trying (unsuccessfully) to get pregnant, plus the demands of her job as a mental health nurse. Miranda was busy too, with the *Amberley Emergency* job lifting her into the public glare and the resulting flurry of invitations to glitzy events. Men seemed more interested in her too, all of a sudden, and she enjoyed a series of flings with minor celebrities. Meanwhile, she resigned herself to the fact that she had basically lost her sister. It was awful, but on a practical level it was at least more straightforward than having to deal with her gaslighting brother-in-law.

Imogen didn't seem quite so willing to let her go, though. 'I miss you,' she wailed one Christmas when they'd both sunk quite a lot of Baileys. Everyone else had gone to bed, and it was just the two of them left standing – or rather, slumped into opposite corners of their parents' saggy red sofa. 'I never see you, Min. Don't you like me any more?'

The question had all but broken Miranda's heart. 'I *love* you,' she had said raggedly. 'It's just . . .' Then she'd shut her mouth, aware of the cliff-edge ahead.

'It's Felix, isn't it?' Imogen had persisted. 'I know you don't like him. But why? I can't bear it, my two favourite people in the world not adoring each other like I adore you both.'

Oh God. The big question, the one that she simply couldn't answer, not now. 'I'm going to bed,' she'd said in the end, because it seemed the only safe option.

Things came to a crunch in June. It was Imogen's thirty-fifth birthday and, because they'd had a tough time of it (still no pregnancy news, poor Imogen), Felix announced to the rest of the family that he was pushing the boat out for his beautiful wife and treating everyone to dinner at Le Manoir aux Quat'Saisons for the occasion. 'Isn't he wonderful?' Tracey had sighed down the phone to Miranda, and it had taken a moment for Miranda to reply, because the words were lodged in her throat. 'I'm glad he's doing this for Immie,' was what she managed eventually.

She should have known that Felix Anderssen would never do anything without his own agenda in play, though. And she should have borne this in mind on the night in question when she nipped out alone for a quick vape between courses.

Blame the champagne going to her head, she'd thought after-wards. That, and the fact that she was there with her latest beau, Maxim, a beautiful-but-dim footballer, and Felix had barely looked her way all evening. It was such a relief. Had he changed his ways, maybe? Got over his creepy little power play? Evidently not, she realised with dismay when he appeared behind her a whole two minutes later.

'Look at you, Sexy Miranda, star of the fucking show, as ever,' he'd said, putting a hand on her waist and speaking low-voiced into her ear. 'I can't take my eyes off you.'

She whirled round at once and stepped back from him, almost falling into the lavender in her haste. Rage roared up inside her. Enough was enough. 'Get off me,' she hissed. 'What the hell do you think you're doing?'

'Come on,' he said, his words slurring. He'd been drinking heavily all evening. 'You're not fooling anyone. We both know what's going on here.'

She took another step back, loathing that he had put her in this position. 'No,' she told him, glaring. 'You're so wrong. Because I'm with Maxim – and you're married. And if you ever dare touch me or speak to me like that again, I am going straight to Imogen, *your wife,* and I will tell her what you've been doing. Do you understand me?'

He gave a jeering laugh, his eyes gleaming with amusement. He was loving this, she realised. Euphoric that he'd finally provoked a reaction. 'What, and you think she'll believe you over me, do you? Dream on, Miranda. She's already told me how jealous you've always been of her. How you've never been able to stand it when she does things better than you.'

He winked, moving towards her. 'Still, I can think of a way you can get one over on her, can't you?'

It still makes her shudder, even now, months on from that night, to replay the nightmarish scene in her head. Talk about twisted. How ugly he really was beneath that handsome façade. How grotesque. 'I despise you,' she'd said, and barged past him to return to the restaurant. 'Babe, do you mind if we go now?' she'd asked Maxim in a low voice when she was back at the table, and he'd leapt up gratefully at once. ('Your family are, like, well intense,' he'd said later on in the cab.) 'So sorry, everyone, but I'm coming down with a migraine,' she'd told the others, putting the tips of her fingers to her temple and wincing. 'We're going to have to leave before it gets any worse, I'm afraid.' Then she had hugged Imogen, whispering 'Happy birthday, I love you,' into her ear, feeling like her heart was breaking. Especially when both Imogen and her mum looked disappointed in her for leaving so early, before they'd even had a chance to think about dessert. But how could she have stayed?

With a groan of regret, Miranda sits up in bed now, her head jangling with the movement and reminding her of all the wine she drank the night before. Evelyn is a surprisingly bad influence for an 82-year-old, she reflects as she reaches for the bottled water on her bedside table and drains it with a few parched gulps. Maybe she'll tell Evelyn about the Felix situation today, she thinks to herself. So far she has proved to be a really good person to talk to, when she's not trying to matchmake Miranda with this so-called godsend of hers, anyway.

She picks up her phone, squinting at the screen, to see that a message came in from her gramps in the early hours of the morning. He's a terrible insomniac, like her. She opens it and gives a little moan when she sees that he's sent a picture of her and Imogen as little girls, both with the same godawful Tracey-cut fringes, beaming as they stand with their arms round one another. *She'll always be your sister,* he's written, as if he can see into Miranda's mind. *I've told her as much too. By the way, between you and me, I never thought much of that Felix fella. Bit of a creep, in my opinion. And Jackie's! But don't tell anyone I said that. Hope you're having a lovely holiday. Love Gramps xx*

Miranda winces, imagining Imogen's response if he's sent her the same picture. She'll have deleted it with brutal speed if so, or printed it out and stuck it on the nearest dartboard. She rubs her eyes, knowing that dwelling on the situation is hopeless. Imogen has chosen to stick with Felix, and that's the end of it. She's made it quite clear that she never wants to see or hear from Miranda again. Then she remembers that, according to Tracey, Imogen is booked in for a difficult doctor's appointment today, about why she's been struggling to conceive. It's the sort of appointment that, in a parallel universe without Felix in their lives, Miranda might have accompanied her to; or at least she might have been waiting in the wings with sisterly support. She hesitates, knowing that Imogen won't welcome her contact but unable to resist reaching out anyway. They'll always be sisters, as their grandad just pointed out. *Hope it goes well today* she messages. *I miss you,* she wants to add but doesn't, loathe to reignite the argument. Mind you, she's pretty sure Imogen has blocked her number and hasn't received, let alone read, the many texts she's already sent. That's what you get for opening your big mouth.

She texts Evelyn next, focusing on the day in hand. *Morning!* she writes. *Last night was fun, I hope you're feeling better than I am right now. Still up for Argostoli later? Let me know when you want to go. M xx*

A message comes back a minute later. *So sorry,* Evelyn has written. *I'm not feeling great this morning. Can we go tomorrow instead? X*

Miranda slumps back in bed, actually rather disappointed. Selfishly, she would have liked to see Evelyn again today, if only to talk to her about Imogen and Felix, and have Evelyn's passionate condemnation of his awfulness. In the meantime, it looks as if she's got a day to herself. *Of course we can,* she replies. *Hope you feel better soon. X*

She'll miss her feisty travelling companion, she reflects, but the chat can keep until tomorrow. And at least this way she doesn't have to listen to any more bloody Bach in the car.

She's about to drag herself out of bed and into the shower when she remembers she hasn't yet replied to her grandad. Reading the message again, she frowns. Gramps' dementia means he sometimes gets muddled up, but she can't help wondering what he meant about Felix. Nobody in the family has ever said a bad word about him, to her knowledge. Why is Gramps calling him a creep? she wonders. And who the hell is Jackie?

Thanks, Gramps, she types. *Having a lovely time. Drove all over the island yesterday seeing the sights – photos attached!*

Then she hesitates. How does she ask what she wants to

ask? She knows that sometimes her mum reads Gramps his messages aloud when she pops in to see him; the last thing Miranda wants is for Tracey to see a message that could be construed as stirring the pot. But if Gramps knows something, then she damn well wants to find it out. *PS Who's Jackie?* she writes in the end, and presses Send before she can change her mind.

Chapter Twenty-Eight

The Cleaner

The cleaner knocks on the door, calls, 'Cleaning!' then waits for a few moments with her trolley. Nothing. A second knock, then she opens the door a crack, listening for any sounds of acknowledgement within. 'Cleaning!' Counts to five. Still nothing. Okay, in she goes, with her vacuum cleaner, her mop and her spray bottles, deliberately rattling around just in case somebody is still in the bathroom or bed, to give them a chance to make themselves decent.

The room is empty though and she glances around appraisingly. It's messy – the bed covers rumpled, room-service trays piled up on the floor, damp towels dumped on the bed. So now the sheets will be damp too, she thinks resignedly, snatching up the towels in one soggy armful.

An older couple are staying here, not generally the messiest kind of guest – it's the triple rooms of girls that she generally finds the most chaotic: beauty products littering the surfaces, hair straighteners and driers plugged into every socket, clothes scattered everywhere as if there has been an explosion in a textiles factory. Smears of make-up and fake tan streaking the bedlinen too, so that she has to do a full change of bedding every day. As for the empty alcohol bottles she finds rolling about the floor ... well. The cleaner clucks about them to her husband when she goes home, but secretly she has a soft spot for the holidaying girls and their excesses. You enjoy yourselves while you can, she thinks – although, admittedly, not so much on the days when she has to clear up vomit (or worse) in their bathrooms.

The cleaner strips the bed, bundling the sheets and covers along with the towels into the large, wheeled laundry bin. Then she deftly puts on a fresh set of linen, corners tucked in tight, creases smoothed out, just like her mother taught her so many years ago. Her eyes have been opened by a few discoveries within bedsheets over the years, by St Gerasimos, so they have. There's one young couple currently staying at the hotel and the smell of sex is so pungent each time the cleaner walks into their room she has to open every single window. Good for them though, she thinks, shaking her head as she remembers how, back in the day, she and her husband would fall on each other like animals given the slightest chance too. Now she counts herself lucky if he's having one of his lucid days, and remembers who she is; if he gives her one of his smiles, the sort that still makes her soften inside. Marriage is a journey, not a destination, as her priest is fond of saying.

The cleaner goes through to the bathroom, where a woman's nightie has been left neatly folded on the small cabinet there. It's a scrap of a thing, thin-strapped and gauzy with a print of rosebuds, the sort that a husband might buy for a wife as a ribbon-wrapped gift. Or so the cleaner imagines, anyway, experiencing a slight ache as she wonders what that must feel like. She holds the nightie up against herself, shaking her head at her reflection in the mirror, then laughs and folds it up again. It's not for the likes of her, of course. None of this hotel world is, other than the tabard she wears and the cleaning trolley she lugs around with her every day.

She sniffs the woman's perfume – light and floral, very nice – then sets to work cleaning the shower and bath, scrubbing the twin sinks. When she first started working here, she was initially taken aback to be coming face to face with the lavish lifestyles of the guests – apparent from their designer clothing, gleaming shoes, the casual leaving around of fancy watches and jewellery. It had fascinated and shocked and sickened her all at once, being so close to their lives – smelling their smells, handling their clothes, scrubbing the stains they leave behind. She's used to it now, of course, and views them as a visitor to a zoo might, peering with interest at this other species with their glossy façades hiding the real humans beneath.

'Don't you hate them a bit for it?' friends of hers have asked when she has described a beautiful dress or piece of jewellery she has seen when cleaning, an elegant bag or pair of shoes. 'It must be tempting, no?'

No, the cleaner can reply truthfully. She is an honest person, who goes to church every Sunday without fail, who prays on her knees each morning to her God. She is not tempted. The closest she ever came was the day after her husband's accident, when they were told that he would probably never work again.

216

That there was long-term damage. The shock had hit her like a fist; she was numb, uncomprehending, full of sorrow and tenderness towards her injured husband. Angry, too, that this could have happened to them. She had gone to work in a daze and found herself picking up a fine solid watch that had been left by one bedside, feeling its weight in her palm and wondering how much it was worth. Wondering how life could be so unfair as to give a fortune to some people but inflict challenge upon challenge on others. Her fingers had closed round that cold heavy watch for a brief moment, then she had put it down and burst into tears, upset that she could even have considered such a thing. Then she had gone to Dimitris, told him about her husband's accident and explained tearfully that she wasn't sure she could work that day after all. He has been very good to them, Dimitris. Very kind.

It's funny though, how, even when you never see the people staying in the rooms you clean, you come to form little narratives about them while you work, if only for your own amusement. The couple in this room, down whose toilet she currently has the scrubbing brush? Well, they are wealthy, obviously, because this is one of the best suites in the hotel. She knows they are not young from their clothes (sober, classy, good-quality – the sort the cleaner herself would like to wear, if she had a spare thousand euros). The thick moisturiser in the bathroom is a giveaway too, along with various medication bottles – those, in her experience, tend to accumulate once past the age of fifty. Is this a happy couple? she wonders. Still laughing, still looking at one another with a gleam in their eye? That's a harder one to call.

As she squirts bleach into the toilet, then crouches down to retrieve and empty the small bathroom bin, the cleaner weighs up the evidence. Well, she's noticed a huge stack of books by the woman's side of the bed, whereas there's merely a plugged-in phone charger by the man's side. Is the pile of reading because the wife doesn't want to talk to her husband? she muses. Or is she trying to escape the reality of her marriage by taking herself to fictional worlds?

She frowns as she suddenly notices the torn-up sheet of paper in the bin while she's emptying it. There's handwriting on the scraps – a note from one of them to the other, maybe? She only knows a few foreign phrases – *Guten Tag, Merci, You want cleaning?*, that sort of thing – so is unable to decipher what is written there, but she can't help wondering if the note was torn up in a moment of pique. The signs, she thinks, filling her mop bucket with hot water, are not promising.

There's an abrupt bang of the door – someone has returned to the room. She turns off the tap and leaves the bathroom, mop in hand, to find herself face to face with a tall man with grey hair and big eyebrows. He's red-faced and breathing heavily, dressed in running clothes and trainers, and doesn't look particularly happy to see her. She bites her lip as he rattles off something she doesn't understand.

'You want . . . I finish?' she tries uncertainly.

He thunders a reply and it's another cross-sounding torrent of nonsense to her ears, although she's pretty sure she hears the word 'No' in there. Yes, and he's actually making shooing motions at her, as if she's some kind of sheep he's trying to herd out of his space.

218

'Later?' she tries, because the last thing she wants is for a complaint to be made that she hasn't finished cleaning the room properly. Especially if his wife comes back and is cross that the floors haven't been mopped. (Where is the wife, anyway?)

He's shaking his head, and pointing at the door. No, he does not want her to come back later. She nods and puts up her free hand – okay, yes, message received – and retreats to the bathroom, trying not to take his curt dismissal personally as she silently gathers her cleaning things. As she wheels her trolley out of there a few moments later, she sees that the man is now sprawling on the freshly made bed, shoes still on, ignoring her in favour of his phone. No wonder his wife brought so many books with her on holiday, she thinks, pulling the door closed behind her.

The question rings around her head once more: does she hate the guests? Well – no, she doesn't. Not really. But every now and then she'll get a peek into their lives and it's enough to make her feel that, in comparison, despite everything that life has thrown at her and her husband, they are actually the richer ones. The happier ones. And the guests? She feels sorry for them. Truly, she does.

Chapter Twenty-Nine

Nelly

Standing on the deck of the ferry as it noses towards Ithaca, Nelly thinks back to the last time she was approaching this small island, full of hope and excitement, so happy to be there with Alexander, about to meet the rest of his family. 'They'll love you,' he'd pronounced confidently, slotting his arms round her and kissing her, once they'd moored the boat in Vathy. Little did they know that she'd be leaving again, all alone and utterly heartbroken, within the space of a few hours.

Alexander Nikolaou, the man, the legend, she thinks to herself, feeling a bittersweet tangle of emotions as his handsome rugged face rises into her mind once more, almost four decades later. Her first real love. How her heart had brimmed with joy as they'd disembarked the *Miaoulis* and proceeded to walk, hand in hand, up the steep hill to his parents' home. But far from Alexander's *They'll love you* assurances, his mother had looked positively stricken when she answered the door to see them standing there together. A small woman with a spotless white apron tied round a long grey dress, a black scarf holding back her shoulder-length grey hair, she had given Nelly a quick unhappy glance before reaching forward to enfold her son within a tight embrace.

Alexander began introducing her – 'Nelly, this is my mum, Irina,' and Nelly had smiled and put out her hand, saying '*Kalimera*,' only to be completely ignored by Irina, who launched into some sort of tirade before Alexander could say another word. His body had immediately stiffened, and his expression changed as the tirade went on. Eventually he had stammered a response, looking both grave and dumbfounded.

Oh dear, thought Nelly as Alexander's arm lifted away from her, and he and Irina continued to talk very quickly and seriously in Greek. Somebody's ill, she guessed, biting her lip as her gaze flicked between them, wishing one of them would pause and give her an explanation. Had somebody died, even? Clearly something was badly wrong.

'Alexander, what's going on?' Nelly asked when, at last, Irina gestured for them both to come inside. 'Are you okay?'

She had never seen his tanned face so ashen. 'Nelly,' he said heavily as he took her into the living room, which had roughly plastered whitewashed walls, a white tiled floor and a couple of shabby armchairs set before a television. 'I've just heard some news,' he went on, sitting down in one of them and motioning for Nelly to do likewise. 'My ex-girlfriend Sofia . . . She's . . . Apparently she's pregnant.'

'She's . . .' Nelly repeated dumbly as Irina's stricken expression and the sombre tone of their conversation fell into focus. 'She's *pregnant*?' She gulped a breath. 'And it – the baby – is *yours?'*

'Yes,' he said.

'And she's . . . keeping it?' she said, although she was pretty sure she already knew the answer. Indeed, he frowned at the question as if it was wrong of her even to ask.

'Of course she is,' he replied, and stared down at his knees. When he looked up again, his eyes glistened. There was a deep anguish in his face that was far from his usual sunny disposition. 'Nelly . . .' he began. 'I must . . . I will have to marry her. There is no choice. Not unless I want to bring shame on both of our families.'

Something in Nelly had known this was coming from the moment she heard the word 'pregnant', but nonetheless his announcement felt like a hammer-blow. 'I see,' she said numbly, wanting to comfort him but no longer sure it was even her place. She remembered the automatic lifting away of his arm as he'd spoken to Irina; was that the moment he had made his decision and subconsciously detached from her? But it was so unfair! So awful!

'Do you even love her, though?' she asked hoarsely, remembering what he'd told her about his ex: how she wanted him to get a sensible job with her father for the rest of his life. 'Will marrying her make you happy?'

He had shaken his head slowly, looking deeply miserable. Devastated. He spread his hands helplessly. 'But I must do it. I'm sorry, Nelly. I'm very, very sorry. But—'

'I get it,' she said tonelessly, because she couldn't bear to hear the defeated note in his voice. Except she *didn't* get why it had to be this way, not at all. She'd *never* get it! And she hated

222

Sofia for ruining everything, she realised, emotion surging inside her. How could this be happening? They'd barely had a whole day together as a couple, and already their romance had been blown apart. A sob convulsed her; her heart felt as if it was being ripped in two.

'I am so sorry,' Alexander said again, and then he got up to put his arms round her, but it was the hardest, most shattering embrace of Nelly's life. An embrace of sorrowful goodbye.

The sea breeze whips at Nelly's hair as she stands on the deck of the ferry, reliving that dreadful day, and she wipes her eyes before looking around at the other passengers to distract herself. There's a family nearby with young children, two adorable little girls playing peek-a-boo with their dad while the mum feeds a deliciously chunky baby. Elsewhere there's a middle-aged couple and a young man with long hair (their son?) drinking takeaway coffees as they chat. 'Mum, you say, "it's not rocket science" but rocket science is actually pretty basic,' the young man is saying, laughing. 'It's just: burn something really fast, to an extremely high temperature. Nothing more to it than that. The mechanics of a rocket, on the other hand ... *that's* the complicated bit.'

Nelly catches the mum's eye and smiles, thinking of Owen, her eldest, who did a chemistry degree, because it's exactly the sort of thing he would say too. Then the chunky baby gets the hiccups and looks so surprised that his parents laugh fondly. His dad leans over to kiss his soft dark hair. Oh, these happy families, she thinks yearningly, feeling very alone as she stares ahead to where Ithaca looms on the horizon.

After the bombshell of Sofia's pregnancy that day, everything had moved horribly fast. Alexander offered to see if he could help her find another boat to work on but Nelly knew that it would never be the same, she'd always compare any other job to being with him on the *Miaoulis*. It would have broken her heart, she thought, to be out there at sea every day without him there beside her. Weeping torrents, she said goodbye, wanting to get their parting over as quickly as possible. Alexander's brother, a priest at the nearby church, had given her a lift to some port or other, possibly the one she's about to arrive at now, although she was too distraught to take in the details at the time. From there she'd caught a boat to Kefalonia, then booked herself on the next flight back to Heathrow, the dream crushingly over.

The tears she had cried, all the way home! How it had tortured her to picture her beloved Alexander trapped in a loveless marriage, resenting having to work for his father-in-law, mourning life on the *Miaoulis* and – or so she dared to hope – a life with her, too. What had happened to him and Sofia, after the shock news of their expectant child? she wonders now. She imagines him older, with greying hair and perhaps a beard, thicker about the waist, maybe, but surely still with that twinkle in his eye, that lust for life. They're probably grandparents by now, he and Sofia – if they're still alive, anyway. Does he still love pottering about on a boat?

An announcement sounds in Greek, then English, that they are approaching Pisaetos, and that all passengers intending to leave the ferry at Ithaca are requested to head for their cars or the foot passenger exit. Still wrapped up in memories of

Alexander, Nelly follows the crowd of people as they start to descend to the lower deck. Wouldn't it be strange if she were to bump into him today, she thinks. Would they even recognise each other after so long? She's sure she would know him anywhere; she's never forgotten those mischievous brown eyes, the angle of his lovely big nose, the breadth of his shoulders.

Waiting for the ferry to dock, she puts a hand to her face, sure that her cheeks have bloomed with sudden colour as she imagines a chance reunion. Would she still feel it, she wonders, the magnetic pull towards him? Would her body respond to him in the same way, with a rush of blood, a jolt of attraction? Oh gosh, she thought she'd left hot flushes behind, but now it feels as if her blood is really thumping around her system. What's more, she realises, as two crew members start to winch down the large metal gangplank, now that she's entertained the possibility of glimpsing Alexander again she already knows that, if she gets on the return ferry later today and *hasn't* seen him, she'll be a tiny bit disappointed.

The gangplank is lowered into place and there's the island before her; they've arrived. The first car in line starts its engine and drives with a shuddering rattle over the gangplank. The foot passengers disembark too, wheeling cases behind them. There would be no harm in making inquiries, Nelly tells herself, say in the Vathy tavernas, or maybe at a post office if she can find one. Just as one old friend, curious about another. She strides off the ferry, feeling a new energy and purpose taking hold of her. Absolutely no harm at all, she decides as she steps into the sunshine.

Here she is, back at last, on the island where Alexander

grew up and maybe still lives today. The same island where her world was turned upside down all those years ago. The good thing about going back somewhere, though, is that you can reset a painful memory. Try a take-two.

'Hello again, Ithaca,' she murmurs aloud, as a sudden thrill travels round her body. 'What have you got for me this time, I wonder?'

Chapter Thirty

Evelyn

Evelyn is curled up on the sunlounger on her balcony, feeling wrung out. Yesterday was clearly more strenuous than she'd realised because today she feels absolutely dreadful, as if there's nothing left in the tank. Her body aches, her thoughts are slow-moving, and last night's wine has given her a splitting headache. She's just wondering if she has the energy to make herself another cup of tea when she hears a knock at the door. 'Coming,' she calls, rising stiffly to her feet with a little groan.

One of the cleaning ladies is at the door, a stout woman, in her late fifties, Evelyn estimates, with a pleasant face and chapped hands. 'Ahh,' she says when she sees Evelyn there. 'I come later? No clean?'

'Now is fine,' Evelyn tells her, gesturing for her to come in. 'Do you mind if I'm sitting out on the balcony? I won't be in your way.'

The woman looks nonplussed as she hovers in the

doorway. 'Sorry — no English,' she says haltingly after a moment. 'Later?'

'Just a minute,' Evelyn says, holding up her finger. She retrieves her phone and jabs at it to find Google, then searches for the translate function. 'There,' she says, showing the woman the screen, where it has translated, 'Yes please to having my room cleaned, but is it okay if I stay on the balcony? I am very tired today.'

The woman reads it and nods, then puts a hand briefly on Evelyn's arm — a gesture of kind understanding that needs no translation. 'Yes,' the cleaner says. 'Is okay. Thank you.'

Evelyn returns to her spot in the sunshine with a novel, her phone and a bottle of water as the cleaner quietly starts work on the other side of the sliding doors. She finds her place in the book but, as it turns out, she is just too weary to follow the words across the page, as if the short interaction has sapped her remaining energy.

She puts the book down, shuts her eyes and folds her hands in her lap, then dozes in and out for a while. It's silly of her to dwell on such things, but she keeps coming back to the small sting of shock she'd felt yesterday in Fiskardo, where she'd remembered the unhappy lunch she and Rose had had there on their honeymoon. You can lionise someone perhaps too much on their passing, you can revere them as a heroine, a saint, a goddess, airbrushing out their less splendid aspects, only for the rose-tinted filter to drop now and then. 'You? A wet lettuce? Never!' Miranda had cried disbelievingly on hearing Evelyn describe the scene.

It wasn't that Evelyn had completely forgotten how Rose's

sharp tongue had sometimes made her feel the lesser person in their relationship, more that she has always chosen to sweep those thoughts into a dusty, distant corner of her mind. Didn't everybody who had lost a loved one do the same? It was natural to want to reminisce about the great times they'd had, to wallow in fond nostalgia, assuring herself that theirs had been the best marriage ever. But . . . what if it hadn't been?

Last night in Miranda's lovely suite, sitting there companionably with their wine, they had begun planning their trip to Argostoli, and Miranda had repeated what she'd read earlier: that if you wanted to see the turtles you were advised to arrive early so as to coincide with the fishing boats returning. 'Are you all right with early starts on holiday, Evelyn?' she'd asked. 'Or does that sound too much like hard work?'

'Oh, I can do early starts,' Evelyn had replied. Mostly because of her poor sleep quality, admittedly; she's regularly awake by five these days. 'I've always been the annoying sort of person who'll be early for an early start, even.'

'I'd say that's impressive, not annoying,' Miranda had replied with a little laugh. 'I wish I was like that. The hair and make-up team on the show used to tease me when we had a crack-of-dawn shoot coming up on the schedule: *We're getting in extra concealer for you, Miranda, love, don't worry,* they'd joke, knowing that I'd arrive with massive bags under my eyes, completely dishevelled because I was so bad at getting up. I once turned up in my pyjamas when I'd overslept; they absolutely rinsed me for weeks on end about that.'

Evelyn had laughed too. It was nice to hear Miranda

speaking positively about her acting work rather than being despondent. 'Rose was a bit like that,' she'd said. 'She would calculate, to the last second, how long she could stay in bed before she had to drag herself out. I used to drive her mad, because I was the opposite – I'm that annoying person who likes to be at a station or an airport ages before my departure time. Back when I was still playing in the orchestra, I used to get in such a flap about being late for a performance, I'd be the first to arrive every time.'

'That's twice you've called yourself annoying,' Miranda pointed out, narrow-eyed. 'And I would call that being professional, actually. I bet we've both worked with those people who crash in seconds before they're meant to be on stage, and they're a massive liability, half the time.'

'Exactly! And yes, how can they bear it? But Rose would—' She broke off, feeling rather that she was being unfair, telling tales on her dead wife.

'Rose would what?'

'Oh, you know, tell me I was neurotic and uptight, that sort of thing.' She'd smiled, but it felt rather an effort. Meanwhile, Miranda was pulling a face.

'Was she the one who put it into your head that you were annoying too?' she'd asked, then glanced up at the ceiling. 'No offence, Rose, if you're listening, but that sounds a bit mean from where I'm sitting. Especially when Evelyn here is slogging around the world on your behalf now, like the most loyal, loving person in the world.'

'She wasn't mean,' Evelyn felt compelled to reply, waving a hand as if to dismiss the idea. 'It wasn't like that.'

Nonetheless, Miranda's indignant words have been circling around her head like sharks ever since. It's true, isn't it, that since Rose died she has rather glossed over some of the rows they had, some of the unkind things they'd said to one another during the course of their relationship. She has never, in fact, told another person how, in the last few days Rose was conscious, she had become unusually vicious to Evelyn, snapping at her and telling her to eff off. *It's not you, this sometimes happens towards the end,* the nurses had consoled her when Evelyn was left shaken by the outbursts. *They lose their real selves, the medication can make them behave out of character. Don't take it to heart.*

But she had taken it to heart all the same. It was impossible *not* to, hearing the love of her life hiss, 'Get off me' with real contempt when Evelyn tried to brush her hair or make her pillows more comfortable. And ever since then, she has boarded up those tarnished memories, not wishing to look at them for any length of time. *That sounds a bit mean,* Miranda had said and, although Evelyn isn't about to hold a dying woman's peevishness against her, it has tugged a loose thread inside her, nevertheless. Something has unravelled, leaving space for dark thoughts, difficult questions. What if Evelyn has been kidding herself this entire time about their relationship? Rose could be selfish and hot-headed, Evelyn always ending up the one who had to broker the peace. Had she been a pushover that whole time, the so-called wet lettuce, too weak to stand up to her partner? She has even started to wonder whether this whole pilgrimage of ashes-scattering has been a performative act of unnecessary exertion, designed to guilt-trip Rose in the afterlife. *See how devoted I have been to your last wish? See how I am dragging myself around the world for you, even when I'm dying? Bet you feel bad now, don't you, because we both know you wouldn't have done this for me!* Even Miranda had alluded to it in similar terms.

She claps a hand to her mouth as these thoughts tumble through her mind, and has to suppress a little cry of horror. That can't be true, can it? That *isn't* why she's spent so long undertaking these trips, surely. Is it?

'*Efcharisto!*' she hears the cleaner call just then, as she makes her exit, and Evelyn thankfully hauls herself up from the sunlounger, feeling too hot all of a sudden and in need of shade. After the bright sunlight outside, the relative dimness of the room prompts black spots before her eyes, making her head spin as she steps towards the freshly made bed. Sitting heavily on it, she feels overwhelmed by doubt, bilious with the sudden dread that she might have got everything wrong after all.

Lying back against the crisp white pillows, she picks up her phone and writes a message to Charles. *Having a wobble. Do you think Rose really loved me? Please be honest.* She presses Send before she can bottle out, then wraps her arms around herself while she waits for a reply.

In the next moment, she starts to feel most peculiar. As if something seismic is happening within her at a cellular level, something quite beyond her control or understanding. How is it that she can be so dizzy when she is lying down? Her head swims, her vision seems to swing in and out of focus, the world pixellating and freezing confusingly. Her body has become numb, as if it belongs to someone else entirely, when she tries to move. What is happening?

What is—?

What—?

Chapter Thirty-One

Nelly

Vathy seems bigger and busier than Nelly remembered, she thinks, paying the taxi driver and exiting the car. The harbour is horseshoe-shaped, with shops and cafés lining the top of the long, narrow bay, and verdant green mountains rising around it. Her gaze swings instinctively towards the boats on the water, and it's only after a moment that she realises she's looking for Alexander on one of them. What's more, she's foolishly looking for the man she knew back then – young, handsome and fit – and she drags her eyes away. Unless Vathy is some kind of time-travel portal, she won't see him again now.

Her phone buzzes in her bag as the taxi drives away and she pulls it out, to see Frank's name on the screen. Oh dear, and there's also a string of missed calls, she notices, where he's been trying to ring her. The reception must have been poor on the ferry crossing, she assumes, but now there's no stopping him. 'Hello?' she says, trying to sound calm. She's never done this sort of thing before, taken off on impulse without first seeking his approval. She's not sorry though.

'What are you doing? Is this some kind of punishment?' he blasts into her ear.

'Good morning to you too,' she replies drily. No, she's not sorry, she repeats in her head. 'Didn't you see my note? I just woke up early and thought I'd take myself off for a bit.'

'But why, though?' he asks. 'And when are you coming back?'

There's something about his vinegary tone that gets her hackles up, leaving her unwilling to fall into line. 'I'm just out and about, exploring,' is all she gives him. 'I'll be back this afternoon, I should think.' Then, rather more sharply, 'I'm allowed to go out by myself, aren't I? I didn't realise I needed your permission to leave the hotel.'

That pulls him up short. 'Well, no, of course you d—'

She cuts him off. 'Good,' she says. 'Glad we agree on that much at least.' She peers out across the harbour, watching as a boat full of holidaymakers begins to chug away from the quayside and down the long neck of the bay. For a wild moment she thinks it's the *Miaoulis*, but her memory is playing tricks on her, of course. 'I'll see you later, then, Frank,' she says, turning away again. 'Have a good day.'

She hangs up before he can start quibbling and drops the phone back into her bag, determined to enjoy her time away without being made to feel guilty. Let him stew in his bad mood alone; she refuses to let it infect her today. Then, glancing once more at the boat heading into the distance, she finds herself wondering what she would have done if it *had* been the *Miaoulis*, with Alexander at the helm. Would she have raced along, parallel with it, trying to catch his attention? Or would it have been enough for her just to know that he was still here?

It's a difficult question. And here's another: now that she's actually arrived on Ithaca, having made her daring escape, what next? There are only two return sailings to Kefalonia, both late afternoon, so she has a whole day here to do as she pleases. Putting Frank out of her mind, she decides to take a closer look at the rather beautiful cast-iron statue of Odysseus she can see at the harbour's edge. She's always loved the Greek myths and can still picture the battered paperback of retellings that she picked up from a second-hand bookstall when she was working at the Aphrodite in Corfu. The tales had captivated her, taking her away from the drudgery of her day job. As she stands before the statue now it's wonderful to imagine Penelope gazing out, perhaps from this very spot, as she waited for Odysseus to return from his adventures. The view can barely have changed since the story was first told. It's ironic, though, to think of Penelope yearning to be with her husband again when Nelly has just put the phone down on hers.

You'd understand if you knew the whole story, Penelope, she says in her head. In fact, brave, clever Penelope would probably have thought up her own, better course of action before now anyway. Nelly, meanwhile, still doesn't know what she is going to do about her husband, her marriage. For now, she takes a few photos of the statue and sends them to the boys. *Hanging out with Odysseus, like you do,* she writes.

She sets out to explore the little town, following the line

of the harbour, enjoying the sight of the sun twinkling on the water, and popping into shops to browse whenever something catches her eye. She buys a postcard each for the boys, miniature bottles of ouzo and souvenir shot glasses for them too, and a citronella candle for herself and Frank in the hope that it might keep the mosquitoes off them in the evening. There's a post office further along the street, and she queues up to buy stamps for the postcards, wondering whether or not to ask about Alexander's whereabouts. Is it silly of her, after so long, to have kept a tiny flame burning inside for him? Maybe. It's perhaps not the greatest timing either, seeking out The One Who Got Away as her marriage collapses in ruins. But if she doesn't ask, she'll only regret it, she decides while she's paying for her stamps.

'Um . . . I was wondering, do you know somebody in Vathy called Alexander Nikolaou?' she blurts out. 'Married to Sofia?'

As soon as she says the words, she cringes a bit inside. The woman serving her can only be in her early thirties; she's certainly not any kind of contemporary of his. She might not even have been born when Nelly and Alexander parted ways. 'No, sorry,' the woman says. 'Would you like a receipt?'

'No, thanks,' Nelly says, then hesitates, unable to walk away just yet. 'His brother was a priest here,' she goes on, wishing she could remember his name. 'The Nikolaou family? Alexander had a boat?'

But the woman is shaking her head, apologising again, and Nelly, after a quick glance behind her at the queue of people waiting to be served, has to leave it there. '*Efcharisto*,' she says, and beats a retreat.

Back on the street, she tries to remember which direction Alexander's house was in. All she knows is that it was up a steep hill – but with the mountains rising all around the main street, every road up from the water appears vertiginous. Shading her eyes with her hand, she gazes about, trying to find a landmark she might recognise, and her eyes alight on a church. After the bombshell of Sofia's pregnancy, she and Alexander had walked in miserable silence to his brother's church, she remembers, because his brother was the one member of the family who had a car and was able to drive Nelly to the ferry port. Might that be the same church?

There's no harm in looking, she decides, and doubles back on herself to take a side street up and away from the main road. Even though Alexander has barely crossed her mind in years, now that she's here again she realises she wants to hear the rest of the story. She wants to know whether or not his decision to marry Sofia was worth it.

It's a warm, windless day and, as she climbs the hill out of town, she feels sweat beading her hairline and armpits, her skin becoming unpleasantly clammy. If Alexander is still alive and if, by any chance, he is still on Vathy, she does not want to meet him red-faced and sweaty, she thinks, before coming to a halt and grimacing at her own vanity. Then her thoughts return to her book of Greek myths, and she's remembering the Fates; the idea that the actions of humans were predestined before they were even born. Maybe they've planned it this way, she thinks wryly, mopping her brow. Maybe it was in fact destiny that the nice receptionist back at the hotel suggested she came to Ithaca this morning, because her narrative is still intertwined with Alexander's after so many years?

She rounds a corner and – ahh, at last, the steps are coming to an end. The church is in front of her, painted a peachy shade, with a large square bell tower that reaches up into the sky. Pausing for breath, she turns round, to be rewarded by the most spectacular view down to the bay below, the sea a great bolt of rumpled azure fabric and the mountains thronging all about. But the splendour of the sight isn't quite enough to lessen the sharp disappointment she feels on having arrived at the church – because it's definitely not the same one she went to all those years before. Her memories of that day, post-bombshell, might feel as foxed and yellowed as her ancient book of Greek myths, with pages torn and missing here and there, but she knows in her bones that she has never been to this place before. Damn it. Perhaps she's been kidding herself about destiny, after all.

Reluctant to turn back immediately after her epic schlep up, she asks a man sweeping up a few fallen leaves in the courtyard if he knows anything of the Nikolaou family (no), and even scouts around the graves in the cemetery by the church, just in case she sees Alexander's name there. Again, no – and thank goodness too, she thinks, beginning the slow trudge back down to the harbour, and square one. How upsetting it would have been to find his gravestone today; a sad punctuation mark to end the story.

Maybe someone on one of the boats will know of him, though? She wanders along the harbour's edge, keeping an eye out for anyone on board. Her mouth twists as she remembers doing exactly this back in Corfu, the day she first met him. Was that Fate again, throwing them together? She wishes Fate would lend a hand here now, if so, because her first sweep of the boats is not promising. There's a large commercial yacht with banners adorning its sides advertising a company website, offering trips to a nearby beach, but otherwise the boats all look privately owned, or rented by holidaymakers. It might be many decades since she knew him but she just can't imagine Alexander working for a big operator, retracing the same trips out and back every day.

She pauses by the harbour wall to stroke a large black and white cat that's sprawled out in the sun. 'Any thoughts, puss?' she murmurs as it immediately rumbles with a throaty purr. 'Have you seen him anywhere? Am I wasting my time even looking for him, do you think?'

The cat purrs louder than ever, which is nice even if unhelpful. 'Okay, thanks,' she tells it with one last chin-scratch. 'I appreciate that.'

Wandering further along, she sees a taverna that looks more rustic than some of the tourist places, with sturdy wooden benches outside and an ageing painted sign advertising Mythos, the local beer. Might this be where the fishermen hang out? she wonders, approaching the door. Inside, it's dingy and there are shabby sofas and armchairs set round wooden tables. A man behind the bar is staring down at a folded newspaper in front of him, but glances up as she approaches and silently looks her over. A small brown dog rushes out, barking, and the man grunts an order, which the dog completely ignores.

'Um . . . *Kalimera*,' Nelly says over the high-pitched yapping. 'Do you speak English?'

The man shouts at the dog, which stops barking at last and lies down with a heavy sigh. The man turns back to Nelly. 'English? Small, small,' he replies, holding his thumb and forefinger a tiny distance apart.

She nods. 'Okay. Do you know someone called Alexander Nikolaou?'

His face does not take on the vacant look that others have so far adopted at the question. 'Katerina?' he asks, which confuses her. 'Katerina Nikolaou?' he says.

Who is Katerina Nikolaou? A second wife? A daughter? Or just someone with the same surname? She shakes her head. 'No, *Alexander* Nikolaou,' she says, enunciating clearly. Then she gestures above her head, trying to show that it's a man she's in search of, a big tall man. 'He has a boat?' she adds, miming – well, it's meant to be a mime of a boat on the waves, but she can tell from his eyes that he has no idea what she's doing.

He shrugs, then makes a reply, the only words of which she understands are 'Katerina Nikolaou', and what sounds like 'Penelope' (her again), followed by a thumb jerked towards the door – out, and then to the right.

'I need to go that way?' she asks, repeating the gesture. 'To find Katerina?'

He nods, stepping out from behind the bar. 'Come,' he says, beckoning her to follow. He leads her back out of the pub, the dog trotting after them, then points along the bay. 'Penelope,' he says again.

'Okay, thank you,' Nelly says, still none the wiser but fearing that they've reached the limits of their Greek–English chat range. '*Efcharisto*,' she adds and he smiles, making a little bow. '*Parakalo*,' he tells her, which she seems to remember means something like *You're welcome.*

She can feel him watching her as she sets off in the direction of his pointing finger, and she wonders what on earth he just told her to do. Nevertheless, she walks on obediently, hoping the answer will become clear in time. The road is quieter now, with only the occasional building on her right as she leaves the town behind. A couple of houses, a small hotel set back from the road, the sea glittering, wide and tranquil, in the bay to her left. She's just starting to suspect he's sent her on a wild goose chase for his own amusement when she spots a taverna ahead of her. Then she sees the name above it – Penelope's Taverna – and a smile breaks on her face. *Thank you, Penelope,* she says under her breath, her step quickening along with her heartbeat as she walks towards it. Is she about to meet someone who knows Alexander at last?

Chapter Thirty-Two

Miranda

Miranda has been driving her hire car rather aimlessly so far this morning, turning left or right at junctions as the mood takes her, but she seems to be nearing a town called Poros now. Already breakfast feels like ages ago, and she could do with stretching her legs, so she finds a spot to park. The heat wraps around her as soon as she steps out of the car, and as she wanders down to the waterfront she's grateful for the breeze that comes stroking in from the sea. The water is a perfect light blue – the exact shade of her favourite scarf back home – and there are a few people swimming beyond the waves, while others sunbathe on the beach. It's a picturesque spot, with a lush green mountain behind the bay and a briny tang coming from the sea. No doubt it's far busier here in the summer months but today, mid-September, there's a calm, unhurried atmosphere about the place, and her walking pace slows in response.

She passes a beachside taverna with cushioned wicker

armchairs and lanterns strung between poles, and it looks so inviting that she stops on impulse, takes a seat and orders herself a gyros and a Diet Coke. Evelyn would love this, she thinks, taking a photo of the view and sending it to her. *Poros is nice!* she writes. *Hope you're feeling a bit better.* Then she checks to see if her gramps has replied to her text, following his previous intriguing comment. Nope. Hopefully later.

'Oh my God, what are you going to *do*?' Bonnie had said, that fateful day when Miranda finally poured her heart out about the Felix situation. They'd been in her dressing room as usual, the site of most of their chats when they weren't needed on set. Miranda's dressing room was one of the larger ones, much coveted by other cast members for its size and comfortable sofa, on which Bonnie had become such a fixture that they had their own regular ends where they preferred to sit. This was where they'd been when Miranda had been dumped by Maxim over text ('I never thought he was good enough for you, Mims,' Bonnie had consoled her, busting out an emergency bottle of tequila); this was where they'd sat for numerous rounds of Shag, Marry, Kill featuring cast and crew members; this was where they'd read each other's horoscopes, tried face packs, eaten numerous Marks & Spencer prawn sandwiches. And there they were now, both still in full hair and make-up but with bare legs beneath their medical outfits, because it was so insanely hot that neither of them could bear to keep their tights on between scenes.

'Maybe you should call his bluff,' Bonnie went on, 'and tell your sister. She won't want to hear it – and yeah, maybe he's right, she won't believe you – but at least you won't feel like you're going mad, hiding it from her. It might put him off trying anything else, too.'

'I don't know,' Miranda had fretted, fiddling with a tassel on the cushion beside her. She had considered this already, of course, many times, but the fear of hurting Imogen had always stopped her.

'I think, if I was your sister, I would rather be told the truth than for this to keep happening in secrecy,' Bonnie had encouraged her. 'And stop looking like that, by the way, you've done nothing wrong! This is all on him.'

'I know,' Miranda said. 'But where do I begin? I know already she won't believe me.' She'd tipped her head backwards over the sofa's backrest and groaned. 'It's just so tacky, isn't it? Like one of those hideous stories you see on the front of magazines: *Seduced by my sister's husband.* What does he think I'm going to do, fall gratefully into his arms? I mean, I know I'm a slut,' she'd said, because she'd gone through so many boyfriends that year she'd started calling herself that ironically '– yeah, and proud of it too – but Jesus, I'm not a monster. What should I do?'

Bonnie must have been recording the conversation, Miranda assumes now, given the headlines that appeared the next day. Either that, or she'd made some lightning-quick notes on her phone the minute she had the chance, before breathlessly calling up the gossip columnists. The story had landed the following weekend, smashing a crater into Miranda's life, and nothing has been the same since.

Needless to say, Imogen went absolutely apeshit, slamming her front door in Miranda's face when she went straight round there to protest her innocence. It's uncertain whether even her own parents believe Miranda's passionate rebuttal of the story or her version of events. Two days later, she was papped going for a routine appointment at the sexual health clinic and a whole new rumour swirled up, this time even worse. For poor besieged Imogen, still longing for a baby, the insinuation that Miranda had been made pregnant by Felix must have been unbearable.

She is not proud of what happened next. How she had proceeded to drown her sorrows so thoroughly that it then seemed a reasonable idea to look up Bonnie's whereabouts on Snapchat and rage over there in order to publicly confront her. 'I swear, Miranda,' Bonnie kept bleating as Miranda loomed over her at the pub table, shouting incoherently, 'I'm as upset as you are about this . . .'

Shocked, angry and betrayed, Miranda was in no state to listen. She can't remember exactly what took place after that, only that Bonnie had followed her out of the pub, saying something about getting her into a taxi (the snake! Like Miranda wanted anything from her, ever again!) and Miranda had wheeled round in fury and . . .

Okay, so there had been some argy-bargy, as her dad would have put it. A shove. A slap. She's seen the photos of Bonnie with a black eye and a cut across her cheekbone where Miranda's ring must have broken her skin and, despite her anger, despite everything, the images filled her with shame. *Miranda Vallance went at her like an animal,* one eyewitness apparently said. SACKED! 'ANIMAL' MIRANDA THROWN OFF SHOW AFTER VICIOUS ASSAULT, the papers reported gleefully. Of course they did.

'Looking on the bright side,' Emma-Lou, the show's publicist, had said drily when Miranda dragged herself into work the next day for the emergency meeting called by Geoff, 'we're getting a lot of press about this.'

'Great,' Miranda had said bitterly. 'Glad to be of help.'

She bites into her gyros now, staring out at the tranquil view before her. For all Evelyn's talk of writing her 'karma report' yesterday, Miranda could seriously have done with some karmic intervention back then, namely horrible punishments being meted out to both Felix and Bonnie. Letting the world know that, actually, poor old Miranda has very much been given the shitty end of the stick here, and is entirely blameless. (Well . . . apart from the slapping incident anyway.)

Maybe she should get the karma ball rolling with a good deed, she thinks. Put some kindness out into the world herself in the hope of the universe noticing and returning the favour. Or, she amends hastily, recognising that her last sentiment might be a touch mercenary, because it would be a nice thing to do. She picks up her phone again and fires off another message to her octogenarian compadre. *Hi again, do let me know if you want anything picking up while I'm out and about. Hope you're having a good day. M x*

A response pings in almost immediately. *Skjf WOIH A;SOUIG* S. She reads it in surprise, then smiles to herself. Oh dear. That must be Evelyn sitting on the phone or something, she assumes.

Okay I'll see if I can pick one of those up for you, she replies, adding a winking emoji to show that she's joking.

But then comes another response, similarly cryptic – *Qlk23 ta76* – and Miranda's smile fades, replaced by a frown. Evelyn *is* all right, isn't she? This isn't some weird cry for help, is it?

She dials her number, and hears it ring once, twice, expecting to hear Evelyn's girlish laugh, an apology – she can't find her glasses, maybe, or she just dropped the phone. Or—

The phone is answered and Miranda can hear breathing, but nothing you'd call an ordinary response. 'Evelyn?' she says after a moment, her frown deepening. 'Are you all right?'

There's a faint sound – a crackle on the line maybe, or perhaps a croak, as if the older woman is trying to speak.

'Evelyn?' Miranda repeats but there's just that croak again, the rasp of a dry throat. Miranda's heart starts to pound. Something's wrong, she's sure of it. She knows it. 'Okay, I'm going to hang up and call the hotel reception,' she says, thinking rapidly. 'All right? I'll get someone to come and check on you, make sure you're okay. Are you in your room?' she asks, before remembering that Evelyn doesn't seem able to respond. 'I'll send them to your room,' she says, feeling increasingly desperate. 'Hang on, Evelyn, okay? You just hang on in there – and help will come, I promise.'

248

Chapter Thirty-Three

Duska

Duska has ten minutes left of her shift and she'll be glad to leave, she thinks, eyeing the clock. She's been here since six this morning, leaving the house while the baby was still asleep, and it's been an unusually testing time. First there was that awful Mr Neale shouting at her in front of a whole group of new arrivals, demanding to know the whereabouts of his wife, as if Duska was some kind of warden, responsible for everyone's movements. Duska, who had noted the rush of tears to Mrs Neale's eyes when she booked her impulsive ferry ticket to Ithaca first thing, didn't exactly feel inclined to help him. 'I'm sorry, this is a busy hotel, we can't keep track of everybody's comings and goings,' she had said, polite but firm.

'Oh!' Julia had piped up helpfully. 'Apologies for interrupting, but are you talking about Mrs Neale?' Julia is a kind person, always wanting to help the customers, but in this instance she had no idea that Duska was trying to protect another woman. Worse, she said this in English, in a misguided attempt to appease the famous Mr Neale. 'Didn't you sell her a ferry ticket this morning, Duska? I saw it on the booking sheet.'

Duska had widened her eyes in a not-now-Julia expression, but the damage was already done. 'Ah yes,' she had said through gritted teeth. 'So I did. I must have forgotten.'

'You forgot, did you? And now you've miraculously remembered?' The sarcasm in Frank Neale's voice could have curdled milk. 'That's convenient, isn't it? How am I going to get to Ithaca, then?'

Hot-cheeked, Duska had clenched her fists under the desk while she explained that the only other ferry of the day wasn't until late that afternoon – by which time Mrs Neale would probably be returning. He had banged a fist on the desk and told her that he was going to report her to the hotel manager for her impertinence. Duska had been so upset that she actually felt like crying, but instead was tasked with trying to look welcoming as she checked in a group of new arrivals, some of whom appeared quite disconcerted by all the shouting.

That was bad enough but now it sounds as if lovely Evelyn Chambers might have taken a bad turn. Hanging up the phone, Duska tells Julia that she needs to attend urgently to a guest, then grabs the universal room key and hurries towards Evelyn's suite. As she passes through the restaurant area she spots Zoe, one of the waitresses, who is halfway into a medicine degree at Patras University. 'Could you come with me, please?' she calls to her. 'I'm on my way to check on a guest, I've just been told that she may be unwell.' Duska will, of course, call the paramedics if Evelyn needs emergency assistance, but it doesn't hurt to have Zoe with her as a first responder now, she figures. Just in case.

'Of course,' says Zoe, falling quickly into step. 'What's the problem?'

'Well – I don't know,' Duska admits. 'It could be nothing, but Mrs Chambers is elderly, and the woman who just called said she couldn't get a response from her on the phone.'

They arrive at Mrs Chambers' suite and Duska knocks first, then unlocks the door and calls cautiously through the gap. 'Hello? Mrs Chambers?' There is a faint groan from within and Duska immediately pushes the door wide, both of them racing inside.

'Call an ambulance,' Zoe instructs her as they see the elderly woman's prone body on the floor. Her eyes are open and so is her mouth, a whimpering sound coming from her. Zoe races over, kneels on the floor beside her and takes her pulse, talking gently to her. 'Tell them it's a suspected stroke,' she tells Duska over her shoulder.

Duska calls the paramedics, her heart pounding. 'Elderly patient, in her eighties, we think she has had a stroke,' she gabbles into the phone. 'She is on the ground, I'm guessing she's fallen. Thank you.' She finds herself thinking of her grandad, who had a stroke in his seventies and was never the same again. She thinks too of her baby girl, the rounded curl of her cheek as she lay sleeping in her cot this morning; the precious gift of life. Then she dials through to reception and alerts Julia to the situation, asking her to direct the paramedics to Mrs Chambers' suite when they arrive. She puts her hands together momentarily, praying to God that the delightful Mrs

251

Chambers will be all right. *Please,* she adds fiercely, because all of the staff like her very much.

She props the door open so that the paramedics will be able to come straight in, then crosses the room back to Zoe and Mrs Chambers. Then she takes the older woman's hand in her own and they wait.

Chapter Thirty-Four

Nelly

Penelope's Taverna is a white-painted building that has mismatched chairs and tables in a front garden, and bright pelargoniums flourishing in pots. There's a large blackboard chalked up with the house specials – pork souvlaki, grilled sardines, rabbit stew – propped beside the front door.

Inside, a young woman whose long black hair is kept off her face by a red printed headscarf perches on one of the tables, her legs swinging as she reads a book. At Nelly's entrance, she leaps down at once, looking embarrassed. '*Kalispera*,' she says, putting the book behind her back, but not before Nelly has seen the picture on the cover of a man and woman kissing passionately. Ahh, a romantic, she thinks with a little smile.

'Please, have a seat,' the young woman says. 'Inside or outside?'

The inside dining area is light and airy, with whitewashed walls and huge windows, but Nelly would always rather have a sea view. 'Outside, please,' she says, then hesitates, wanting to ask her question about Alexander. There's no time though, because the young woman has grabbed a laminated menu and is already leading the way back out into the front garden and gesturing around at the tables.

'Thank you – *efcharisto*,' says Nelly, taking a seat at one. 'Um—'

'One moment, I get you water,' the woman says, and vanishes once more.

She might as well have lunch here, Nelly decides, as she looks at the menu and finds it to be full of delicious-sounding things. The woman comes back with a jug of water and a basket of fresh bread, and Nelly orders some tomato fritters, salad and tzatziki. 'And also,' she adds, as the woman nods and prepares to whirl away again, 'I was wondering . . . I am looking for Alexander Nikolaou. Do you know him?'

'Alexander? Hmm,' the waitress says thoughtfully. She has high cheekbones and magnificent eyebrows, one of those naturally beautiful women who don't need a scrap of make-up to look stunning. 'No, but my boss here, she is Katerina Nikolaou. I think she has two brothers – maybe one is Alexander? I will ask her for you?'

A bolt of electricity seems to rush through Nelly. Oh my goodness. Penelope's Taverna is run by Alexander's sister? That must have been what the guy in the bar was trying to tell her. 'And the brothers are still . . . alive?' she asks with a gulp.

'Oh yes,' the waitress replies. 'One brother, he is priest. Another brother, he has a boat.'

Nelly feels hot and cold all over. It must be him. It must be! 'Can I speak to Katerina, please?' she asks. 'Is she in today?' If

254

Katerina can get a message to Alexander, there might be time to see him while she is here, she thinks faintly. Her heart is pounding. He's still alive. Alive, and with a boat!

'She is working later,' the girl says. 'After six o'clock. You come back then, maybe?'

Disappointment crashes over Nelly, because she'll be long gone by six o'clock, back on Kefalonia, probably having to deal with her sulky husband. Wildly she wonders if she should just stay here, forget her return ferry ticket, see if she can find a guest-house to put her up for the night. Sod Frank! she thinks in a sudden burst, before loyalty tugs at her and she remembers the state he's been in all week, how paranoid he might be getting in her absence. Anyway, who knows if Alexander is even on Vathy right now? If he's anything like the young man she fell in love with, he'll be out at sea somewhere far away. Or, of course, busy with his wife and family.

'I can't come back later,' she replies regretfully. 'But if her brother *is* Alexander, perhaps she could say hello to him for me? I'm Nelly,' she goes on. 'Maybe she could tell him "Nelly says hi"?'

'Nelly says hi,' the waitress repeats, looking intrigued – and also rather elated, Nelly thinks, remembering the overtly romantic cover of the book she was reading. 'Yes, I can do that,' she says. 'Of course. But what if he wants to say hi back? You want to leave him your number, yes?'

'Oh! I . . .' The thought of Alexander calling her up is discombobulating. She can't imagine what it would be like to hear his voice again. Where would they begin after so long? 'Well . . . I suppose so,' she says uncertainly, and fishes in her bag for a piece of paper. She finds an old receipt from Peter Jones in London. It'll have to do. 'If he wants to, that is.'

'He is . . . an old friend, this Alexander?' the waitress asks as if she can't help herself.

Nelly writes her name and number on the receipt, then looks up and smiles at her. 'Yes,' she says. 'We were friends a long time ago.' *I was head over heels in love with him,* she thinks but doesn't say.

'And perhaps . . . *handsome* too, I think?' The girl's eyebrow is cocked hopefully.

Rumbled. 'Extremely handsome,' Nelly confirms, handing over the note.

The waitress presses it dreamily to her heart, gazing heavenwards, and they both laugh. 'I wish you luck,' she says with a happy sigh.

'Thank you,' says Nelly, and then holds up her crossed fingers. She still can't quite imagine this as-yet-fictional phone call taking place but she's definitely warming to the idea. Why not? Over to you, Fate, she thinks, as the waitress leaves her alone once more.

Chapter Thirty-Five

Miranda

As soon as Miranda receives the call from the hotel telling her that Evelyn has been rushed to hospital in Argostoli following a suspected stroke, she abandons her lunch and runs out of the taverna. Two seconds later she has to run back in again in a total fluster, having remembered that she needs to pay. Once she's belatedly settled up, she races to her hire car. Sorry, Poros, you look lovely, but not now, she thinks, her fingers shaking as she finds the hospital on her Maps app. She starts the engine, her mind taken up by thoughts of Evelyn, fragile and alone in a hospital bed. Is she going to be okay? Will she be well enough to finish her quest for Rose? Or, she wonders, her throat tightening, is that no longer an option?

'Don't you dare go and bloody *die* on me, Evelyn,' she says aloud, and the words are so awful, they're followed in the next second by an anguished sob. She won't really die, will she? Not yet? For all that Miranda might have found the older woman annoying and overbearing at first, she has come to

257

like her very much since then. Even yesterday, when Evelyn pushed her about Bonnie, it was the right thing, in hindsight; she was only trying to understand, to help.

'I didn't even get to give you the full story,' she says, her voice catching. 'I need you to stay alive so that you can tell me what to do. Please stay alive, Evelyn. I'll be there as soon as I can.'

When she reaches Argostoli, the hospital, thankfully, is well signposted and easy to find. The parking gods must be on her side again too because, just as she arrives, a battered white Volvo reverses out of a nice big parking space, leaving it free for Miranda to claim. 'Thanks, Tyche, thanks, Hermes,' she mutters under her breath as she leaps out and locks the car. 'Much obliged to you both.' She wonders who the god of health is, because she could really do with sending them a heartfelt prayer of their own right now.

Inside the hospital she is directed to a ward. Evelyn is lying in bed, hooked up to a monitor, her eyes closed. For a moment Miranda doesn't recognise her, because sleeping Evelyn is so different to the animated, vivacious woman of yesterday. Without her vibrant personality lighting up her face, she looks so small and weary. Old too. Miranda's heart breaks a little to see that one side of her face has sagged noticeably downwards as a result of the stroke. *Don't worry, I'll be dead soon,* she hears Evelyn saying, matter-of-fact, in her head, and the thought chokes her up.

'Well, not yet,' she says under her breath, sitting down in the chair beside the bed and taking Evelyn's gnarled hand in hers. 'Not on my watch you don't.'

She's already spoken to one of the nurses, with the help of Google Translate on her phone, and learned that Evelyn's stroke was a fairly sizeable one. 'But she can still recover, yes?' Miranda asked anxiously. The nurse, however, knew better than to give false hope. 'We are making her comfortable,' was the less-than-affirmative reply.

'Hi,' she says now, gently stroking the back of Evelyn's hand with her thumb. For all that she has played the character of a hospital doctor for the last few years, Miranda has been fortunate enough not to spend much time in any real hospitals herself. It is strange to be present in an actual, functioning medical setting that isn't merely a TV set filled with props. 'How are you doing?' she asks. 'I hope this isn't all an elaborate ploy to get out of tomorrow's road trip, Evelyn. You could have just said you were too busy or something.'

There's no response from the other woman, and Miranda tries to reconcile herself with the fact that a response might no longer even be possible after what has happened. She knows that a stroke can damage the brain and cause long-term disability to a person. Evelyn may not be able to understand what she's saying, even if she can hear her. If she comes round at all, she might not recognise Miranda – in fact, she might even feel alarmed to discover what she believes to be a stranger sitting beside her, holding her hand. Although – the words jog a memory from yesterday – she *had* said that she wanted someone to hold her hand as she died. Tears skid down Miranda's cheeks as she thinks back to that innocent conversation they'd had, only twenty-four hours ago, little realising where they'd find themselves today.

'Don't die, Evelyn,' she begs, clasping her fingers. 'I might be holding your hand but that's not because I'm expecting you to die, all right?' She swallows hard. 'Please not yet.'

She hears a beep from a phone in the vicinity and notices that Evelyn's handbag has been put in a nearby bedside cubby. Does that mean she was conscious when she was brought in and wanted her bag with her? Miranda frowns, worried about the safety of an elderly woman's personal possessions being left unattended while she's unconscious. The phone beeps again and she reaches down to retrieve it and sees a message from someone called Charles on the lock-screen. *Evie, are you there? Let us know you're okay, darling x*, it says.

Miranda bites her lip, wondering what to do. Charles – is that Evelyn's ex-husband? She's sure she heard his name mentioned in one conversation or another. The fact that he's calling Evelyn 'darling' and 'Evie', the fact that he sounds concerned about her, convinces Miranda that he's someone who ought to know what has happened. If she can get into Evelyn's phone, anyway. It's locked, just the last message visible on screen, but she suddenly remembers Evelyn's rubbish passcode – one-two-three-four – and types it in. She's doing this for Evelyn's sake, only, she tells herself as she opens the message thread between Evelyn and this Charles person. She's not snooping, she's merely—

Oh gosh. The thread consists of many photos, sent by Charles today, of Evelyn with another woman who Miranda is guessing must be Rose. Evelyn and Rose caught laughing at a private joke in someone's sunny garden, their faces luminous with affection and humour. Evelyn and Rose, much younger,

260

in bikinis on a beach – a British beach that is not super-hot by the looks of things, Miranda thinks with a smile, because Rose appears to be brandishing a Thermos flask like a trophy, and Evelyn has a tartan picnic blanket round her shoulders as a shawl. Ah, and there they are on their wedding day, or civil partnership, whatever it was called back then – the two of them in white dresses, flowers in their hair, looking at one another as if there is nobody else in the world.

By now Miranda has scrolled back far enough to see the message from Evelyn that must have prompted these pictures. *Having a wobble. Do you think Rose really loved me? Please be honest.* 'Oh, Evelyn,' she says aloud, devastated that the sleeping woman beside her could have wondered such a thing. 'She *adored* you! I never met her but I can see it in every picture. She loved you so much. You two looked great together!' Her voice trembles – she has perfected that voice-quaver as an actress, wheeling it out with ease for many emotional scenes over the years. She's not acting now though.

She makes a note of Charles's number, then calls him from her own phone. 'Hello, Charles?' she says when he answers. 'My name's Miranda. I'm sitting with your friend Evelyn in hospital – I saw your name come up on her phone and thought—'

'Good God,' he interrupts. 'Is she all right?'

'She ...' How she would love to soften the truth, but she mustn't. 'No,' she says after a moment. 'I don't think she is. She's had a stroke, and ...' She realises, too late, that she doesn't have much factual knowledge she can give him. 'I'm with her, but she's asleep at the moment.' Asleep or unconscious? She isn't sure, but 'asleep' is definitely nicer to hear. 'I just thought I should tell someone who knows her. I wasn't sure if she has any close family members who'd want to be informed, or . . .'

'Couple of nephews,' he says. 'I'll let them know. Thank you. This is very kind of you. You know, I thought something odd was going on because she sent me the most peculiar message about – Well, it doesn't matter. But it was very unlike her.'

'I was with her all of yesterday – I was driving her around the island because she wanted to find somewhere to scatter what's left of Rose's ashes,' Miranda tells him, the words pouring out. 'She seemed absolutely fine then. I mean – a bit tired, and a wee bit emotional, but . . .'

'Are you—' He breaks off. 'Sorry, I don't understand. Do you work at the hotel where she's staying or are you a friend from London?'

'Neither. I'm staying at the same hotel as Evelyn and . . .' Miranda glances over at her, feeling a rush of affection. 'She was kind to me. Befriended me. Sweet-talked me into being her chauffeur for yesterday, too. Not that I minded.' She dashes the tears away with the back of her hand. 'I've only just met her really, but already I feel like I'd do anything for her, if you know what I mean.'

'I do know what you mean.' She hears the emotion in his gruff voice, then; the reality is catching up on him. 'Well – leave it with me. I'll contact the nephews in case they want to fly out there. I would come over myself but I'm recovering from an op, unfortunately. Hip replacement last week. But tell her we all love her, won't you? Me, Hazel and the boys – we all think the world of her. And we hope she's going to be okay. But ...' His voice really cracks then. 'But if she's not, would you be so kind as to let me know?'

'Of course I will,' Miranda says. 'Whatever happens, I'll keep you posted.'

She hangs up and, as she slides Evelyn's phone back into her bag, she hears a rustle and feels a plastic bag against her fingers. 'Rose, is that you?' she finds herself asking, then shakes her head at her own question. Talking to a plastic bag is possibly a new low. But then a whole other question occurs to her. What will become of Rose's ashes if Evelyn ... if Evelyn is unable to scatter them? Should Miranda do that for her? 'I will, if it's going to be too much for you,' she whispers. 'A promise is a promise, right? I'll find the perfect spot for her, don't you worry about that.'

Evelyn lets out a little moan, smacking her lips together, then moves her head on the pillow. 'Are you okay?' Miranda asks her. 'It's me, Miranda. I'm right here with you, Evelyn.' In the next moment, she remembers what Evelyn had said about her basic death list; that she had wanted to hear a particular piece of music playing as she slipped away. Was it Bach? Whether she's dying or not, maybe Miranda should put it on for her anyway; it might be soothing. She remembers hearing a radio programme about the astonishing effects music can have on people with damaged cognitive function, how it can reach a part of them when language has become unavailable.

Miranda doesn't know anything about classical music; she's the sort of pleb who only recognises famous pieces if they've been on adverts. But Evelyn definitely mentioned a specific piece – a concerto, Miranda thinks – and, although she can't remember it off the top of her head, she might do, given a prompt. She quickly Googles 'Bach concerto' on her phone and scans the results that appear. Concerto For Two Violins, no, it wasn't that. Concerto in A Minor – nope. Harpsichord Concerto in D – definitely not. Bloody hell, how many did he write? Brandenburg Concerto, she reads next, and a tiny synapse flashes in her brain. That was it. Although – oh, help – there are loads of Brandenburg Concertos, she realises. Typical. 'Which one do you like best, Evelyn?' she asks. 'Send me a telepathic message if you can.' No telepathic message comes but she goes for number three. They might be here long enough that they get to hear all of them, let's face it, she figures, setting the music playing quietly from her phone.

It's like magic. Barely have the first few notes sounded than Evelyn's eyelashes flicker as if she's surfacing from a dream, and then her eyes open fully. She stares at Miranda, looking bewildered.

'Hi,' Miranda says softly. 'Hi, Evelyn. You're in hospital. You've had a stroke.' There's no immediate response. Is Evelyn making *any* sense of this? she wonders dolefully. She gives her hand the tiniest of squeezes. 'I'm Miranda, I'm staying at the same hotel as you. In Kefalonia. And—' Her voice cracks a little. 'And it's nice to see you awake again.' She presses her lips together, trying to regain control of herself. 'Although – well, I turn my back on you for five minutes, and you go and end up in here.' She's trying to be light-hearted but Evelyn still just looks confused. 'I'm joking,' she says. 'Sorry. How are you feeling?'

Evelyn's mouth scrunches up as if she's trying to say

something. Her eyes flick to Miranda's phone on the bedside table, playing Bach, and then back up to Miranda.

'I hope I got the right one,' Miranda says. 'I couldn't remember exactly what you said, so I went for number three. But I can put on a different one if you …'

A rusty sound comes from Evelyn's mouth. Her whole face is screwed up with the effort. 'Vi …' she says after a moment. 'Dar …'

Miranda has absolutely no idea what she's saying but doesn't want to discourage her. 'Are you trying to say "five"?' she wonders aloud. 'You want Concerto Number Five?'

A tiny shake of the head. Evelyn gives it another go. '*Vi*,' she says again, 'DAR.' There's frustration in her eyes that it's so difficult to communicate. 'Car-uh. Re-or.'

Car-uh. Re-or. Miranda's brain works frantically. She's desperate to understand. 'Karma?' she guesses, taking a leap into the darkness. 'Are we talking about karma again?'

Evelyn nods. *Yes!* her eyes say, the relief of connection apparent. 'Vi dar,' she repeats.

Then Miranda gets it. 'Five stars,' she says, not sure whether she's closer to laughing or crying. How she loves this woman. 'Five stars on my karma report – is that what you're saying? You're signing me off, are you? I've passed?'

Evelyn nods again. 'Passed,' she agrees, her voice thick and sibilant. Then she shuts her eyes, breathing heavily as if the exertion has worn her out.

Tears roll down Miranda's cheeks. 'Thank you, Evelyn,' she says. 'You're a legend. You're the absolute best.'

Chapter Thirty-Six

Nelly

Frank has form when it comes to going on benders, of course. Back in the nineties, giddily riding a crest of fame, he'd taken to partying with some of the Britpop bands who were enjoying a similarly heady period of notoriety. A large amount of coke went up his nose during this decade, gallons of booze down his throat too, and there were days when he would simply vanish from sight because he'd got caught up in a session at some celebrity or other's luxury Primrose Hill mansion that could last the better part of a week. The number of times Nelly's hand had hovered over the telephone, wondering if it was too soon to call the emergency services, uncertain how long you should leave it before you put in a missing person report. But up he'd bob eventually, baggy around the eyes, skin pallid, voice hoarse because he'd been shouting over loud music for hours on end. And somehow, even though she'd been by turns frightened, worried and pissed off the whole time he'd been AWOL, he would always manage to sweet-talk her into forgiveness, laying it on good and thick that this was definitely the last time, he knew he was a dreadful husband, he was absolutely going to make it up to her, don't you worry.

He was good at the latter, at least, lavishing her with jewellery so expensive she was scared to wear it, armfuls of flowers, and extravagant trips to New York, Tokyo, Puglia. Nonetheless, such largesse was never enough to completely seal up the fissures his disappearances created between them, fractures that left the surface of their relationship feeling eggshell-thin, liable to disintegrate under the slightest force.

Then everything changed. It was his fortieth birthday and the party Nelly threw for him degenerated into chaos just after midnight when he suffered a minor heart attack, caused, she later discovered, by the vast amount of stimulants he'd hoovered up his nostrils. 'This has got to stop,' she'd told him the next day when he was discharged from the hospital with the worst hangover of his life, their ears still ringing with the doctors' stern-faced warnings. 'Do you hear me? This ends now – for me, for the kids, for your career. We need you to stay alive, Frank. And that means getting a grip on the partying.'

To everyone's surprise, Frank had cleaned up in rehab, having frightened himself with the episode, and turned the ship round. No more drink, no more drugs. Clean, sober Frank went on to garner a second Michelin star, successfully pitched and presented a new Channel 4 cookery show, and had another number one bestselling cookery book the following Christmas. Their lives were back on track and he'd never vanished on her again. Until now, it seems. Because however spotless a person's new start, it's hard to completely eradicate all the temptations of the past. And so, when Nelly arrives back at the hotel and finds their room deserted, with no note regarding his whereabouts, the old dread rushes right back in there. Hello darkness, my old friend.

Yes, she had taken off herself that day, but she'd made sure to keep Frank updated about her return journey, texting him the time of the ferry she was catching, messaging again when she was in a taxi back to the hotel. She tries calling him but there's no answer. She leaves voicemails asking him to get in touch – still nothing. It's unnerving. Has he relapsed, unable to cope any more following the media storm? Or is this a petty way to punish her for leaving him alone this morning? It's working, if so. The tranquillity she felt on Ithaca, gazing out to sea, has evaporated. Is he alive? Dead? Drunk? High? With another woman? There are so many siren calls out there in the world for a man with an addictive personality. Which one in particular might have enticed him this time?

Don't suppose you've heard anything from Dad, have you? she writes in a message to the boys, before immediately deleting it. No need to panic them before she's looked for him down at the pool or at the beach, she reasons. Or at the bar, for that matter. Maybe he's gone for a walk and mislaid his phone, or the battery's dead. Maybe he's fallen asleep on a sunbed, lost track of time.

She writes him a quick note – *Hi! I'm back – gone looking for you! N x* – then exits the room once more, trudging back down the stairs on tired legs. She'd been looking forward to a cool drink, maybe sitting out on the balcony with her feet up after her long day, but she won't be able to relax until she's found him.

The pool, when she gets there, is half empty, only the last few sunbathers still out enjoying the early evening sun. She wanders round to the bar, braced for the unpleasant sight of her husband half-cut and falling off a bar stool, but – thank goodness – he's nowhere to be seen. The beach, then, she decides with a little sigh, and retraces her steps back through the main hotel building and out onto the street. But when she eventually reaches the stretch of golden sand, she can't see him either on a lounger or in the sea, despite walking quite far in both directions. By now the drumbeat of worry is starting to thud to a crescendo, dread curdling her stomach. *Don't do this to me, Frank,* she thinks with a sigh of both concern and exasperation.

It's embarrassing to do so but she grits her teeth and asks at reception if, by any chance, they might know where her husband is. Has he booked himself onto a trip, or ordered a taxi, or . . . ? The man on duty is unable to help. 'Do you want us to contact the police?' he asks, taking in Nelly's worried expression. 'Or the hospital?'

Nelly gulps, hoping it won't come to either of those options. 'I'm sure he'll turn up soon,' she lies. 'Thanks anyway.'

There follows the most awful evening and then night when Frank still doesn't reappear or get in touch to let her know where he is. She can't sleep, instead lying in bed listening out for sounds that might presage his return, trying him periodically on his phone and cursing his name aloud. 'There had better be a damn good excuse for this, Frank Neale,' she mutters as she wrangles the pillow into a more comfortable position and tries to block out visions of her husband in various states of disarray. She eventually drifts off around five, only to be woken at seven-thirty by the sound of him crashing in through the door. He stumbles across the room, doesn't quite make it to the loo before pissing himself, then passes out on the bathroom floor, snoring loudly.

She doesn't quite know how to respond at first. A whole volcano of emotions is bubbling and spurting inside her. For crying out loud, Frank! Why can't he do anything by half measures? Why has it always been this way? She actually hates him for doing this to her again. She truly hates him. Where has he been all night, and why did it not occur to him to call her, even once, to let her know what he was doing? There must have come a point as he sank a beer – or whatever else he's ingested – when he thought, *I should really let Nelly know where I am, otherwise she'll be worrying.* It *must* have occurred to him. But how long did it take him to overrule that thought with a shrug and a decision of *Nah, I won't bother* – a few seconds? A whole minute? Whatever, he'd clearly carried on with the easier task of hurling himself into oblivion, all the way down into the black hole of unconsciousness. The selfish, stupid, thoughtless bastard.

All the same, she knows, even through the mist of her rage, that of course there's a whole lot more to the situation than one bad decision. It's impossible to ignore the groundswell of deep, terrible sadness for him that surges beneath her anger. She's heartbroken for him, in truth, knowing that his sobriety has been a daily struggle, one he has worked so hard at, with all those AA meetings, week after week, month after month, keeping him on track. Facing down the demons. Later today, when he comes round, he'll surely have the most almighty reckoning with himself. He'll be devastated that he's slipped back down the ladder, he'll hate himself for it. Oh God, and the boys will be gutted too, she realises in despair.

With some difficulty, she peels his wet trousers and pants off his heavy, unyielding body and dumps them in the bathtub, then gingerly sponges him down. It's like trying to clean up a great big helpless baby that you love but also detest and feel repulsed by. Tears course down her face as she thinks about their marriage vows: *In sickness and in health;* how she'd promised to care for him that day in church, their faces shining with joy for one another. Well, he's cashing that one in this morning, all right.

Having found some clean pants, she wrangles them onto him. 'Frank,' she says, shaking him. 'Get up, Frank. Get in the bed.' He's spark out though, completely unresponsive. He isn't going anywhere. He'll be stiff as a board when he wakes up, aching all over, after hours spent sleeping on a cold tiled floor, she thinks, pulling a face. But if she can't physically move him, that's where he'll have to stay. She brings a pillow in from the bedroom and makes up a little bed for him with a blanket she locates in the wardrobe.

It's as she's kneeling beside him, manoeuvring his head onto the pillow, that she smells it: an unfamiliar woman's perfume. It stops her short, and her heart knocks a tattoo in her chest. No, Frank. You didn't. Tell me you didn't, she thinks, bending over him to sniff his neck. There's a sour stench, quite possibly

271

neat alcohol, seeping from his pores – a horrible smell that flashes her right back to the nineties – but along with that there's also a musky sandalwood scent detectable that definitely isn't hers. Unless he's splashed out on some new aftershave in the last twenty-four hours, it's not his either.

She jerks away from him in disgust. 'You pig,' she hisses, tears pricking her eyes. It feels very much like a last straw. However sorry she is for him about his falling off the wagon, however dreadful she knows he'll be feeling when he comes round later on, this is something she cannot, will not, overlook. Because every woman has their bottom line, and every woman knows when it has been crossed.

She heaves him onto his side so that if he's sick in his sleep he won't choke on his own puke. Then she steps away from him, potentially for the final time, contempt, sorrow and hurt all mingling inside her. 'You blew it,' she says under her breath, then goes to pack her case.

Chapter Thirty-Seven

Claudia

They had been half-expecting the news after the ambulance call, but nonetheless the hotel staff have all been saddened to hear that the nice lady from room seven, Evelyn Chambers, has passed away, following a stroke. According to Yiorgos, who was on night porter duty, another guest, Miranda Vallance, was with her at the end, and had returned to the hotel at around two in the morning, very distressed.

'I hope he poured her a brandy,' Dimitris said at the morning meeting, when they heard what had happened. He'd glanced over at Claudia. 'We should make sure she's okay today. She might want to talk about it.' Then he ran a hand over his head, looking pained. 'Unfortunately, this is the same woman who had somebody trying to film her when she was by the pool the other day.'

'What, phone-gate?' Claudia asked. 'Oh dear. She's not having the greatest holiday so far, is she? I'll get in touch with her, don't worry.' Since then, she has left a little note under

Ms Vallance's door, and emailed her a message of condolence, saying that if there's anything the hotel can do she only has to ask. Ms Vallance might want to talk about it, she might not, but it's only courteous to offer her the option, she feels.

Dimitris has been in touch with the hospital about next-of-kin details so that they can send on Ms Chambers' suitcase and personal effects. Decisions will have to be made about whether or not the body is to be repatriated. For the time being, though, Claudia is in Ms Chambers' suite, packing up her belongings. To say that this is a sobering experience is a complete understatement. There's something extremely poignant about carefully folding and packing another person's clothes into their suitcase, knowing it's for a different kind of journey than a simple flight home. Everything has been cast in a new, mournful light. The mere sight of Ms Chambers' book left on the bed half-read, a bookmark in its pages, was enough to make Claudia feel emotional.

She takes a long dove-grey cotton dress from its hanger and neatly folds it. A light floral fragrance drifts from the fabric and the scent makes Claudia think of garden parties, croquet on a lawn, tea and scones. (She's never been to England herself, admittedly; perhaps she's watched too much *Downton Abbey*.) Did Evelyn Chambers go to garden parties? she wonders, placing the dress in the suitcase. Did she enjoy her life? Was she fulfilled, was she loved?

It's all over for her now, either way. And it's such an obvious thing to think but, truly, death is so final. You're there one moment, gone the next – leaving unread books, unused plane tickets, unfinished conversations adrift in your departure. Had

Evelyn known the end was coming? Claudia wonders, bagging up a pair of white trainers, then a pair of well-worn Birkenstocks. Did she manage to achieve everything she wanted before her last breath, or did she die with regrets? Claudia loves a ticked-off daily to-do list as much as the next person but she has a bigger list at the back of her mind, what you might call a bucket list, that she hasn't considered for a long time. She still hasn't seen the Parthenon, even though she's been in Greece for three years. There are so many other European countries she'd like to visit too – Italy, Germany, Sweden, Scotland, for starters. She wants to have children one day. A big exuberant dog. And most of all, she wants to experience love – real, romantic love. The forever kind.

She pulls out a drawer and stuffs neatly balled socks into a bag along with some sturdy bras and underwear. Yes, she wants love, she acknowledges, lifting a pile of folded tops from another drawer and placing them in the suitcase. The thought gives her pause, so much so that she has to stop and sit on the bed for a moment, her head full of difficult feelings. Ever since she came to Greece she has spent her life like a plane in a holding pattern, she reflects. Up in the air, circling around, without ever landing. She has assured herself repeatedly that she'll make proper plans again one day, but that, in the meantime, this is what's best. She has felt safe circling up there, continually putting off the moment when she has to take any decisions about landing again. But if today ended up being her last, if she were to suffer a sudden death herself ... Her hands clench and unclench in her lap. If that were to happen, she admits, her final moments would be full of regrets for the life not lived. She would wish that she had been bolder about life, about love; that she had plucked up the courage to try again, and opened her heart, however daunting the prospect.

This isn't getting Ms Chambers' room packed up though, is it? She rises to her feet and picks up a pretty rose-pink blouse to fold. She thinks about the woman's friends and family back in the UK who are presumably hearing the news about her passing this morning. 'She was such a lovely woman,' Duska had said. 'Really warm and sincere from the very first moment – the sort of person who actually *sees* you when they look at you, rather than just speaking to you like you're an ornament behind the desk.'

Claudia places the blouse in the suitcase, then notices a framed photograph on the bedside table. It's a black and white picture of two silver-haired women in what look like wedding dresses, holding hands and both roaring with laughter, their heads tilted back, mirroring one another. Oh gosh, it's beautiful in its depiction of rapture. It's obvious that the women in the frame adore each other. If Evelyn Chambers was one of those two women, then clearly she was loved and gave love in return. *That must be nice, mustn't it, Claudia?* a voice in her head says pointedly.

She wraps the photograph in a thin cotton jumper and sets it in the middle of the case, finding herself reminded of her own wedding day with a small automatic shudder. What happened to the album of photographs left behind in her marital home? she wonders. It's odd to think of those pictures still existing in the world, ironically lasting longer than the marriage itself. Something else odd, she realises in the next moment, is that she's starting to feel differently about that time, about him. Since the discovery that the mystery hotel emailer was *not* her ex-husband after her fearful paranoia, she has noticed a marked upswing in her own sense of wellbeing. It's as if . . . Well, to say that it feels as if a curse has lifted is perhaps a bit hokey. But something has shifted within her, the tension replaced by a new sense of acceptance. Of calm, even. Maybe, just maybe, she's letting that whole episode go. Moving on. She doesn't have to be scared of him any longer. Why should she be? She's got her whole life left to live! If she can just land her own damn plane, anyway.

The wardrobe and drawers are now empty, so she heads into the bathroom to start gathering together Evelyn Chambers' toiletries. Then comes a knock at the door. 'Claudia?' she hears as it opens. 'Are you still in here?'

There's an immediate rush of blood around her body in response. Here he is. The best person in her life. The most decent, funny, handsome man she's ever met. Not that she's ever dared tell anyone how she feels, obviously. She's hardly dared even admit it to herself. He is her boss, after all, and he has never shown any kind of romantic interest in her. Never. There's being brave and opening your heart, and there's humiliating yourself and jeopardising your job. Her fingers reach for the reassurance of her gold evil eye charm round her neck, and close around it briefly. 'Coming,' she says, without actually moving.

Standing there with the contents of Evelyn Chambers' washbag – the perfume she'll never wear again, the lipstick left unfinished – is pretty galvanising. You've got one life,

Claudia, she reminds herself. She could ask him for a drink, couldn't she? Test the water, see what happens to his face when she suggests it. It's going to be scary as hell but it'll feel as if she's living, at least, she figures. Breaking out of that holding pattern at last.

'How's it going?' Dimitris asks when she steps into the bedroom a second or two later. His gaze sweeps around. 'Looks like you've nearly finished, well done. We've heard back from one of Ms Chambers' relatives now, a nephew, who—'

She can't pay attention to the details; she hopes it isn't unfeeling of her, but she doesn't know how long this sudden spurt of bravery will last. She's got to act on it right now. 'Listen, I was thinking,' she interrupts him, just as the door crashes open. In comes Aglaia, one of the cleaners, dragging a hoover behind her while simultaneously pushing her trolley, which rattles busily with cleaning sprays.

'Ahh, there you are,' says Dimitris. 'Thanks, Aglaia, Claudia's nearly finished in here.' Then he turns back to her. 'What were you about to say?'

She swallows, a rictus smile on her face. There's absolutely no way she's going to ask him out for a drink in front of an audience. Or worse, if Aglaia starts up the hoover and she ends up having to shout over its roar to make herself heard. Bravery has its limits. 'Nothing,' she says weakly. 'Carry on – you were telling me about the nephew who's been in touch?'

'Yes,' he says, as Aglaia closes the door behind her and starts stripping the bed, humming under her breath. 'So, here's the situation . . .'

Claudia listens and responds in all of the right places, and

278

then he goes away again. She returns to the bathroom to finish off packing up Ms Chambers' belongings, and catches her own eye in the mirror. Next time, she promises her reflection with a rueful shake of her head. Definitely next time.

Chapter Thirty-Eight

Miranda

Miranda programmes the destination into her phone, then finds one of the Bach concertos she'd downloaded last night for Evelyn and presses play. The music swells around the car, acting like a lightning rod for her emotions, and tears spurt almost immediately from her eyes. She still can't believe that Evelyn is dead; that she won't see her smiling face around the hotel again. That their conversation has now come to its final full stop.

Not that conversation was anything other than one-sided by the end, she thinks, as she starts the engine and reverses out of the hotel car park. Miranda had spent the last few hours of Evelyn's life describing aloud to her the photos on her phone, the ones that Charles had sent, in the hope that her words would somehow penetrate the older woman's consciousness. 'You were so loved,' she told her. 'You were treasured, Evelyn, anyone can see that. And deservedly so.'

She also took it upon herself to sneak the bag of ashes out

of Evelyn's handbag and sequester it within her own. It felt like the right thing to do. 'Don't worry about Rose now, I'll finish the job for you,' she promised her. 'I'll scatter the rest of her ashes in Argostoli, just as you wanted. Only – here's a suggestion. How about if I scatter *most* of them there, but keep the tiniest bit back – and then put that at *your* resting place, wherever that may be? So that you're together?' Her voice wavered but she pressed on. 'You did the most incredible job, taking Rose's ashes back to so many of her favourite places, but I think that, above anywhere else, she liked being with you most of all. And vice versa. What do you think, are you happy for me to do that?'

No reaction had been forthcoming, but Miranda thought she detected the faintest of squeezes from Evelyn's hand. She'd take that as a yes, she decided. 'That's a plan, then,' she assured her. 'You leave that with me now.'

They sat together and listened to the passages of the concerto rising and falling around them for a while, and Miranda found herself imagining a much younger Evelyn at her cello, bow flashing across the strings, her other hand coiled round the neck of the instrument. She wishes they could have talked more about all the many likenesses of their professions, how the work you individually produced was amplified to another level by those around you, what a rush it was to be on a stage with your fellow performers, when you knew, collectively, that you were part of something really special, transcending the ordinary. She regretted not asking Evelyn more about her career when they were on their road trip; the older woman must have had so many great stories to tell.

'I'd have loved to have heard you play,' she had said last night. 'I bet you were amazing.' Evelyn would have been one of those generous ensemble players, she reckoned, who didn't try to make it all about them but was in it for the love of the music, the performance. It gave Miranda a wrench of nostalgia for those pre-curtain moments backstage with a cast, back in her theatre days, and the jag of adrenalin that would electrify your entire body the moment you heard your cue. Nothing like it. The thrill of experiencing a hush drop across the auditorium, knowing that you were taking everyone in there on an emotional journey. The jolt of excitement when you connected with another actor in a single, skin-prickling moment; the chemistry between you a force of its own. As for the exhilaration of the applause at the end . . . ! 'We're the lucky ones, aren't we, to have been there and done that,' she'd said wistfully, still holding Evelyn's hand.

No answer came, of course, and she was just wondering if she would ever hear Evelyn's voice again, or whether her friend had already slid deep into a permanent state of unconsciousness, when all of a sudden Evelyn's eyelids fluttered, then opened. The most radiant smile appeared on her face. An indistinct sound came from her throat as she stared beyond Miranda, her gaze one of sheer joy. She made the sound again and Miranda realised what she was saying: 'Rose! Rose!'

Foolishly, Miranda had swung round as if she too might see a vision of Rose, but of course there were only the hospital curtains surrounding the bed. By the time she turned back, Evelyn was resting against the pillow once more, eyes closed, still smiling. 'Evelyn?' Miranda whispered, her heart in her mouth. 'Can you hear me?'

Before this morning, she had never actually seen anyone die for real. Oh, she's acted in death scenes galore – as her *Amberley Emergency* character, of course, in a bedside role, as well as plenty of others where she has been the person gulping their last breath. She thought she knew what to expect when it came to the real thing but now she's experienced a genuine moment of passing, she can see that she totally underestimated the magnitude of the event. How huge a deal it turned out to be.

Is it melodramatic to say that it felt like a privilege to be with Evelyn, holding her hand, Bach playing, as she breathed her last? There was a moment of true serenity, when the world seemed to hold its breath to mark her departure, before the monitors attached to Evelyn started beeping in shrill chorus. Then, as if on cue, a woman in the next bed let out a great cough, with an accompanying fart for good measure, and the concerto playing from Miranda's phone came to a sudden end, followed by a ripple of audience applause. 'Oh, Evelyn,' Miranda had said, not sure whether to laugh or cry at this mixed fanfare for her friend. Seconds later, a nurse rushed in and took Evelyn's pulse before glancing at Miranda with a sorrowful expression.

'I know,' Miranda said, still clutching Evelyn's hand. 'She's gone, hasn't she?'

Yes, the nurse confirmed. She had gone.

Even though she'd already felt it in her heart, Miranda still crumpled instantaneously at the nurse's nod. The enormity of the situation almost didn't seem real. The nurse patted her shoulder, asked in broken English if she could get her anything (no, thank you), then set about quietly unplugging Evelyn from the monitors. So this was death, then, this strange subdued silence. The stillness of an absence.

Miranda gave Evelyn's hand one last squeeze while it was still warm within hers, before gently setting it down beside her inert body. 'Goodbye, dear Evelyn,' she said, tears falling. Her voice shook. 'Thank you for making me laugh again. Rest in peace, you truly wonderful person.'

There's a crumb of comfort to be had, she reminds herself, slowing at a junction, to imagine that, in her dying moments, Evelyn seemed to be back with her beloved Rose. Are they together now? Miranda isn't sure she believes in an afterlife, but she likes to picture Evelyn and Rose pain-free and reunited, perhaps in some beautiful garden like the one in her photo. Laughing together. Full of happiness. Making up for lost time.

She had left a message for Charles – *I'm so sorry, but she's gone. It was peaceful. She just slipped away when I was holding her hand* – and he rang her this morning, his voice gruff with sadness, thanking her for being there at the end. The hotel staff have been lovely too – when she arrived back there in the early hours, shattered and upset, the young man behind the desk had been kind and solicitous, asking if he could get her anything to eat or drink, despite the hour. This morning, she found a note had been pushed under her door from someone called Claudia, checking in on her. *If there's anything we can do for you, please just say*, it read. *Even if it's just to talk about what happened, I'm here and I'll listen.*

People were nice, weren't they? she found herself reflecting as she sat on the edge of the bed reading the note. When they weren't being arseholes, complete strangers could be surprisingly kind. Even when Evelyn was so weak at the end, she had reached out to Miranda, awarding her five stars on her so-called karma report. It was enough to make her cry all over again, remembering the enormous effort it took the older woman to say the words, how she'd battled to get her meaning across. Five stars indeed.

'You legend,' she says aloud now, feeling emotional at the thought. 'Well, I'm looking forward to the people on the Big Karma board processing your report any minute now and dishing out some karmic justice on my behalf. Whenever you're ready, guys!'

Or not, obviously, she concedes with a small eye-roll. And maybe that's the real point to be grasped: that, pleasing as the concept of karma might be, it's pretty basic, really, isn't it? Demanding retribution for those who have crossed you, like a child stamping their foot and shouting, *But that's not fair!* Also, let's face it, what a cop-out, expecting some great hand of God to reach down and move the chess pieces around on your behalf, rather than doing anything about it yourself.

Bollocks. Why does it always come down to having to tackle the difficult stuff oneself? How annoying is that? Nobody else is going to make things right between her and Imogen, she accepts, huffing a sigh. Nobody else can apologise to Bonnie bloody Beresford for the slap. It's up to her, and her alone, to sort out her anger issues, her trust issues, to go crawling back to her team at Guy Drewers in the hope that Helen will find her more work. 'All right, all right,' she mutters under her breath, feeling sick at all of these awful tasks ahead of her. This must have been how Hercules felt, faced with the Hydra and his other labours. Possibly even worse.

She's coming in to Argostoli now, the biggest town on the island. Other than last night's visit to the hospital and what Evelyn said about the sea turtles here, she doesn't know anything about the place. Hopefully she can find a suitably lovely site to scatter Rose's ashes though. As she parks up in a side street a few minutes later, she realises that she is feeling under a certain amount of pressure about the task ahead, especially as Evelyn had prevaricated about where that place should be. Perhaps she should have left the responsibility to Evelyn's descendants to figure out after all, rather than presumptuously taking it upon herself to finish the job, she frets in a moment of doubt, before rallying. She's here now, she should at least try.

The warmth of the day hits her as she gets out of the car: it's muggy and close, the sort of weather that preludes a booming thunderstorm. She would quite like that, she decides, heading down to the waterfront. Something powerful and awesome to mark Evelyn's passing – yes, that would be appropriate. Bring it on.

Argostoli seems busy, with tourists strolling along the harbourfront, and traffic backed up the length of the main road. She notices a few people wearing identical branded T-shirts and bags, and is confused until she works out that they must be passengers from the great hulking cruise ship visible at the far end of the harbour. Closer by, there are plenty of tourist boats offering chartered day trips around the island, as well as more modest fishing boats, with nets and lobster pots, left there for tomorrow's catches. Miranda remembers her conversation with Evelyn about the sea turtles coming to feed on scraps of fish hurled overboard from the boats, but assumes she has arrived too late to see this phenomenon, because they're all empty now, the day's catches long since brought to shore. She peers into the water just in case, but there's nothing to be seen other than dark reflections from the boats above.

Argostoli is on one side of an inlet, with an opposing bank of land visible as she looks straight ahead. A main road runs all the way round the inlet, but there's also a long stone footbridge, punctuated by lampposts, that crosses the water. As her eye follows it over to the other side, she feels herself brighten. Surely when Evelyn and Rose came to Argostoli they would have strolled across this same bridge, she thinks, picking up her pace and walking up to the start of it. She'll follow their footsteps, she decides, and see if it feels like the right place to leave Rose.

The bridge is wide and low, practically on a level with the water it spans, and there are only a few other people wandering along it. It must look beautiful at night, when the lampposts are lit, Miranda imagines. The noise of the town recedes as she walks on; there's something very tranquil about having sea either side of you. Reaching the middle point, she leans against the wall, gazing out to sea, appreciating the faint breeze as it ruffles the water and strokes her sun-warmed skin. The water is a clear, light blue, the atmosphere serene. 'What do you think, Evelyn?' she murmurs under her breath. 'This seems like a pretty good spot to me.' She waits for a moment, just in case there's some sort of a sign that her words have been heard – a sudden rainbow, perhaps, a feather falling from a seagull overhead – but nothing comes. Which is fine, because Miranda doesn't believe in that kind of thing anyway.

She retrieves the plastic bag and unseals the top. She's been so preoccupied by the need to find the right place that she hasn't given any thought to what she'll do once she's there. Should she say a few words before the actual scattering? She doesn't know the protocol. 'Rest in peace, Rose,' she says quietly in the end. 'You were loved.' Then, pinching the bottom corner of the bag so that a tiny amount will be held back, she tips it over the bridge. The grey dust swirls briefly in the warm air before falling to the surface of the water. 'Goodbye,' she whispers, watching as the dust motes disperse, some sinking, some floating; all of them becoming part of the sea. There she goes.

Carefully resealing the sandwich bag, she tucks it back into her handbag, a lump in her throat. She's always prided herself on being such a tough bird – you have to be in her profession – but coming to Kefalonia has profoundly changed her, she thinks, staring blindly across the water. Peeled off a layer or two, chipped away at her blackened old heart. Arriving here at the weekend, stewing with bad temper, she could not have dreamed that she'd end up befriending Evelyn, still less that she would be sitting with her as she died, and then be scattering her late wife's ashes a day later. But that's exactly what's happened, and she feels a different person for it, as if she's been recalibrated, softened. All of those aggy things that previously incensed her so greatly have silently fallen away.

Stopped mattering quite so much. A deep quiet calmness settles upon her, instilling her with a new confidence that she's going to be okay. Whatever happens, she'll manage, she'll make things right.

She starts walking back across the bridge and, although she knows rationally that it's impossible for her bag to feel noticeably lighter on her shoulder, somehow it does. Everything feels lighter. *It's going to be okay,* she thinks again, with increasing conviction.

That's when she sees it – the large oval body of a sea turtle swimming majestically through the water alongside her. She holds her breath and stares down at it, awestruck. 'Hello,' she says, watching in delight as its great flippers carve through the water, noticing its beady dark eyes, its patterned shell. There's something so ancient about it, so timeless. She feels a true sense of wonder to have seen it in its element. What's more, she knows that none of this would have happened if she hadn't been here with Rose's ashes, if she hadn't accepted that initial Diet Coke – and ouzo – from Evelyn, if they hadn't opened up to one another. If she hadn't let somebody in. Maybe karma exists after all, she thinks, watching the sea turtle until it eventually swims out of sight.

Chapter Thirty-Nine

Nelly

Having screwed up her previous friendly-sounding note and thrown it in the bin, Nelly has left a new one for Frank. *I can't go on like this,* it says. *I know you're hurting but you need help, and I'm not the person who can give you that. Not when you've come back smelling of another woman on top of everything else. I've asked the hotel to move me into a different room here and I'd like to get an earlier flight home.*

Frank, I've loved you so much. We had so many good times together. But I think we've both got to face up to the fact that this marriage has broken beyond repair. Let's talk when you are up and about today, and discuss where we go from here. Nelly x

It's almost one o'clock now, and she still hasn't heard anything from him. She doesn't know what to do with herself. The thought of going down to the pool or beach, or enjoying any normal holiday activities, seems impossible while the mother of all difficult conversations hangs over her head. Still, as luck would have it, with the summer season being over there

are a few empty rooms at the hotel, and when Nelly asked
to move into a different one the young man on reception
merely nodded and began tapping on the keyboard. 'But is
everything all right? Mr Neale – he moves as well, or ...?'
he had asked a moment later, looking confused.

Oh Lord. It's awful having everyone know your business.
First the sweet woman Duska yesterday, now this dark-eyed
man in his slightly too large suit jacket. 'Everything is fine
with the room, thank you. Mr Neale will not be moving,' she
had said crisply. 'Only me.'

'Okay. And this is for how many nights?' he wanted to
know next, before he took in her stricken expression. 'I mean,
we are not full, you can have the room for as long as you
want, but ...'

'I don't know,' she had said, feeling tired and flustered. 'Can
I get back to you on that?'

'Of course,' he told her, handing over her new key.

It has taken all her willpower not to go and check on
Frank while she's been waiting for him to get in touch. She
did leave him safely in the recovery position, as comfortable
as she could make him, she keeps reassuring herself. The 'Do
Not Disturb' sign is on the door, so the cleaner won't find
him lying on the bathroom floor and freak out. Hopefully
he's come round by now anyway, at least enough to relocate
to the bed and sleep off his hangover in greater comfort. She's
so used to caring for him, used to fitting her life around his,
that it's hard not to keep wondering what he might be doing
every minute.

Marriage is a deep river, with subcurrents and countercurrents, she thinks to herself, lying on the bed and staring up at the ceiling. The problem is, marriage to Frank has often been so turbulent, she has felt on occasion as if she might be dragged under. As if he might not even notice her drowning. It's exhausting, frankly, and it's been lonely at times, too. She's not sure she has the energy to carry on like this any more.

Her stomach rumbles, reminding her that she hasn't eaten anything for a while. She leaves the room and seeks out a quiet table on the restaurant terrace beneath a big patio umbrella, where she orders herself a salad and some iced water. The salad, when it arrives, is huge and delicious-looking, full of the ripest tomatoes, plump kalamata olives and piquant crumbly feta, but she feels too agitated to eat more than a few bites. She hides behind a book, but the words keep jumbling before her eyes whenever she tries to read a sentence. Besides, her own life feels far more volatile and urgent than any fictitious plot.

She's about to venture back upstairs when she sees a woman in a big hat and sunglasses walking across the terrace to the bar area. It's the actress, she realises, remembering Frank pointing her out the other morning at breakfast, although she must be wearing a wig, because she's now sporting a dark brown pixie cut. She's with the Guy Drewers agency, like he is, apparently. (The agency that – sidenote – is headed up by Nelly's former fashionista colleague Cath these days. Go, Cath!). 'And we saw her in a play, remember,' Frank had said. 'Years ago, at that place in Islington, you know the one.'

She does know the one – the Almeida – because being in a long-running marriage means the sharing of thousands, millions of shorthand memories between them. All the plays they have seen, the dinners they have eaten. Concerts at the Barbican and the Albert Hall. She couldn't remember precisely the play Frank meant at the time he was pointing out the actress, but seeing her now in that wig is ringing a faint bell in Nelly's memory. It'll come to her. Meanwhile, the bartender has rushed out from behind the bar to put his arms round the actress, who appears to have burst into tears. Oh dear.

In the next moment, though, she forgets the scene entirely, because her phone buzzes with a notification: a text from Frank. Her heart seems to stall, her fingers feeling stiff and clumsy as she unlocks the phone. Here we go, she thinks. What does he have to say for himself?

Nelly, I'm sorry. Where are you? Let's talk. X

A pent-up breath sighs out of her as she reads the words. He's alive, then, she thinks numbly. What next?

I'm down in the restaurant, outside, she replies. *Are you up to a walk?* Better to be out in the warm benevolent September sunshine, she thinks, than back in the same room where she knelt earlier this morning to peel off his sodden, stinking underpants. No doubt he'd rather avoid that indignity too, because his response is almost immediate: *I'll come down and meet you,* he writes.

Now she feels so jittery she can hardly sit still. Adrenalin fires in bursts around her body, her senses heightened and on alert. Her mind turns to that dashing, cheeky young man she first met back in her Soho temping job and it's hard to believe that the years between them have now taken them to this precarious place. It feels as if someone has pressed fast-forward on their relationship in the last fortnight and they are currently hurtling towards the final denouement. The endgame.

Here he comes, loping towards her with his old easy grace, smartly dressed in pale trousers and a loose white shirt, every inch the gentleman abroad. You'd never know to look at him the state he was in a few hours earlier. She stands to greet him as he approaches, fumbling her phone and book into her bag, her pulse racing. 'Hi,' she says, taking in his freshly shaven jaw, the clean scent of him. She feels as if her heart is shattering.

'Hi,' he says, and puts his arms round her. For a moment she wants to protest – no, you can't just do that any more – but she knows, as she thinks he does, that this is the end. She could scream and shout at him, she could push him away, but they've almost gone beyond that now, to a new place of uncertainty, where they have to figure out how the future will look without one another. It's because of this that she leans against him, as she has done so many times before. They stand there together for a moment and it's so easy, so natural, it's a wrench when they eventually pull apart. 'Shall we wander down to the beach?' he suggests.

'Good idea,' she replies.

They are both silent as they walk back through the hotel and out onto the beach road. The air is still and very humid, with only an occasional breeze to rustle the silver-grey leaves of the olive trees. 'I'm sorry,' he says, once they are quite alone, without anyone in earshot. His voice is low and husky, a far cry from the booming confidence of what she thinks of as his Showbiz Frank voice. 'I know this is all my fault.'

He's wearing sunglasses, so she can't see his eyes, but she

imagines they must be pretty bloodshot after the excesses of the night before. Repentant too, judging by his wretched tone. 'I wish you had told me where you were,' she says quietly. 'You scared me, Frank.'

Two young men zoom by on a moped, both of them with brightly coloured shirts open to their bare chests, and she thinks of her sons with a pain in her heart. 'I'm sorry,' he says again.

'If I'd known, I could have come and rescued you from yourself, before—' She breaks off, not wanting to go any further. 'I could have come and intervened,' she says instead. 'Put a stop to ... everything.'

He hangs his head and she hears his weary exhale. 'You could have done, Nell, but ... Well, you shouldn't have to,' he says. 'It's not fair on you.'

'No, but ... ' She would have gone to his rescue, regardless of whether or not it was fair, she wants to say. It isn't simply about fairness when someone you love is repeatedly pressing self-destruct buttons. You can't help but want to protect them.

'I've let you down,' he says baldly before she can find the right words. 'And – as my old mum would have said – I've let myself down too. I've messed up, and it's not right that I keep involving you in my mess.'

'But ...' *But I'm your wife*; it's there, right on the tip of her tongue. *For better or worse*, she thinks. *In sickness and in health.* The words are too hard to say today, though, when she remembers how he smelled this morning, of this mysterious other woman. When she thinks about all of the other women he has hurt as well.

295

'Everything got to me yesterday,' he says when it becomes obvious that she can't finish her sentence. They've reached the edge of the beach by now, and they make their way carefully down the rocky slope. The sand stretches ahead, soft and golden, giving way to the sea, where the waves are rolling in like long white ruffles. There are two rows of rustic-looking beach umbrellas with a pair of sunloungers beneath each one, but very few takers for them today; a sunburnt couple here and there, a family with two toddlers in brightly coloured sunsuits, both digging intently with plastic spades. She thinks again of their sons, who also loved digging beach moats and trenches as little boys, how Frank would help them construct enormous turreted castles, big enough for them all to stand on together as the tide gradually came in. They've ended up on a lot of beaches together over the decades, she reflects; in Devon and Cornwall back in the early days, and then a whirl of others around the world during the giddy rise of his fame: Australia, Thailand, Mexico, California. She's always associated the feeling of sand beneath her feet, the sound of waves rushing into shore, with good times. Happy times. She knows that this particular beach will snag like a thorn in her memory for all the wrong reasons though.

'I'm not making excuses for myself, but it was the pressure from the last fortnight, the accusations, the speculation,' he goes on. 'It all just reached a peak. I boiled over. I couldn't cope any more.'

She says nothing in response, merely stares out at the horizon as they walk along the shoreline. Call her disloyal but she's always found it incredibly graceless when someone facing very serious charges positions *themselves* as the victim of the piece, the one who has *really* suffered. It feels even worse when that person is your own husband, someone you once idolised.

He starts telling her about the bar he ended up in, how he'd had an out-of-body experience standing there, ordering himself a vodka and then hesitating for a moment before recklessly throwing it down his gullet. How hard it had been to stop after that first shot, how easy, after all, it had been to relinquish everything to the drink. 'I know I'm a bad person, Nelly,' he says, voice shaking. 'I know I'm not a good man.'

'Frank—' If she's supposed to contradict him here, she's not entirely sure she can.

'But I'm going to sort myself out,' he goes on. 'I'm flying back to London this evening, and I've booked myself into rehab again. I've been speaking to my agent about making a new statement on the allegations and ...' His voice, which has been getting progressively lower, is barely audible over the crashing waves now. 'I think ... I mean ...' He takes a deep breath, tries again. 'The thing is, I do ... recognise myself in those stories. The bad behaviour. I mean, a lot of those nights, I honestly can't remember what I did.' He clutches a hand to the side of his face, a gesture of agony, before forcing the next words out. 'But the things that have been said ... I can't dispute them out of hand. Because ... Because I might have done them. I might have been that person. And I think ... I fear ... I probably was.'

He breaks down then, his hands coming up to cover his face in his distress. Nelly steers him to the nearest empty pair of sunloungers, where nobody is within earshot. 'Come on,' she says, positioning him so that he can sit with his back to the other beachgoers. She can't see anyone nearby who looks like a citizen journalist or an amateur photographer, but you can never be too careful. She sits opposite him, their knees almost touching, and puts her hand on his arm. This is a big deal, him finally dropping his defences and admitting that there may have been wrongdoing. She can respect his honesty far more than his previous brick-wall defence, denying everything as malicious lies. All the same, it's pretty devastating to hear the confessional note in his voice. Despite everything, there was a part of her that longed for the claims to be untrue as he'd initially professed. She looks away, her stomach turning. 'Rehab sounds like a good idea,' she says after a moment. 'So does apologising in this new statement of yours, if that's what you were thinking of doing.' She hesitates, then forces herself to ask. 'You *are* sorry, aren't you?'

'I am,' he says miserably, taking off his sunglasses and wiping his eyes with the back of his hand. His fingers are shaking, she notices, and he can't look at her. 'I know it's over, me and you,' he adds. 'I accept that this has been my doing, and I don't expect you to stay with me.'

'Frank—'

'I mean it. It's going to take me a while to get my act together and I don't want you to have to put your life on hold while I do that. I think we should split up. You can be free of me. You deserve better.' He lifts his chin and finally looks at her properly. 'This is not me being self-pitying, by the way. I'm not saying it because I want you to argue that we should stay together. I just think it's the right thing to say. The right thing to do.'

She doesn't reply for a moment. Even though she agrees with what he's saying, it's still a jolt to hear the words out loud. Again, though, this is new, she reflects, glancing at his stricken face. For once he's putting her first, rather than himself. Saying that he's setting her free is a bit on the dramatic side but … well, there's a truth there too. She feels like a caged bird whose door has swung open. Dare she fly out alone, now that they have reached this point?

'I mean it,' he says again, voice soft. 'You are the most wonderful woman, Nelly. A brilliant, kind, funny, gorgeous wife. A fantastic mother. But being with me … I'm causing you pain – I know I am.' He starts to cry again and she reaches forward, puts a hand on his knee. 'I have been lucky to have you in my corner for all these years,' he says brokenly. 'But it would be wrong of me to keep you there any longer.'

Her eyes sting with tears. She feels too numb to speak. The world outside the cage looks so big, so unknown, she thinks. What will being free even look like for her without having Frank to fuss around? Then she remembers Melissani the nymph plunging into the cave in sacrifice to Pan, no longer able to bear living. She will not be like Melissani, she vows.

'The boys agree with me,' Frank says with a hitch in his voice. He's trying to laugh but it doesn't quite land. 'Well, not in so many words, but they've both let me know, in their own ways, that they think I've been pretty selfish. That I should be very sorry about the way I've treated you – and I am. And obviously you can have the house, you can have … Well, anything. And don't feel you have to rush back to London with me either – you can stay on here at the hotel, have yourself a proper holiday. Whatever you want, Nell.'

She still hasn't said anything and has to clear her throat because her mouth is so dry. 'I'm glad you're going to get some help,' she says carefully after a moment. There's a bit of her that wants to dismiss his suggestions of splitting up, a bit that's scared of such a change. She's managed this long, hasn't she? And she does still love him – or at least she loves the Frank of her many happy memories. Is it enough for her to stick by him while he gets himself well again? She exhales, forcing herself to dig deep into her own feelings. Would she ever, truly, feel relaxed and carefree around him again, after everything that has come out? Whatever marital loyalties still exist, she has to consider herself too. Plus 'free' is a lovely word, isn't it? A glorious, boundless word; one that spins a globe in front of a person and says, *Where next?*

When, she wonders, did she last feel free?

She takes his hand in hers. 'Thank you,' she says eventually. 'There's a lot to think about. But . . . yes. That sounds . . .' How does it sound? Overwhelming, heartbreaking, terrifying, a little bit exciting, the saddest thing to do, or possibly the best. No one phrase or word can sum up her turmoil. 'Thank you,' she repeats, in the end. 'I think you've said what I couldn't bring myself to. And I think you might be right.'

'Nelly Neale,' he says to her, and there's a glint of the old Frank still visible as he smiles. No longer quite so cocky, though. A little bit more self-aware. 'When have I ever been wrong?'

300

The sea rushes in and the sea rushes out. A husband and wife stand up from their sunloungers and embrace one another tightly. The wife, practical as ever, is the first one to let go. 'Come on,' she says. 'You've got a flight to catch. And I bet you haven't even started packing, have you?'

Chapter Forty

Miranda

Miranda thought she had it all figured out. She would leave Argostoli, drive back to the hotel, then order herself a cocktail at the bar and quietly drink it in Evelyn's honour. It seemed a fitting tribute after the ashes-scattering, and she was pretty sure Evelyn would have approved. So much for the best-laid plans, though – because as soon as she reaches the bar, the bartender puts down the glass he's holding and says sincerely how sorry he was to hear that Ms Chambers had died, which prompts Miranda to instantly burst into tears. Talk about embarrassing. Talk about making a show of yourself. The one single consolation is that the annoying young blonde woman who'd filmed her by the pool the other day isn't on the scene, attempting to make a follow-up viral sensation.

The bartender – and obviously it's the same guy she drunkenly flirted with that time – is absolutely lovely, thank goodness. Wiping his hands on his apron, he rushes round from behind the bar to hug her. It's so nice to have a gorgeous young man put his arms round her that she does feel better pretty quickly. 'Thank you,' she says, as he releases her. 'Oh dear, I've made a wet patch on your shirt now,' she adds apologetically, seeing the damp splodge she's left, but he waves away her concern and asks what he can get her to drink.

'I was actually going to have a cocktail in salute to Evelyn – Ms Chambers,' she tells him, perching on one of the high bar stools. The day is still humid and feels airless; she picks up a menu and fans herself. 'I don't suppose you can remember what she liked to drink, can you?'

He tilts his head, considering. He's *very* attractive, she thinks again, with those soulful brown eyes and the angled planes of his cheekbones. Then she notices his perfectly bladed eyebrows, and belatedly registers how nice he smelled when he was hugging her. Oh, she thinks, her gaydar finally catching up. Perhaps it's not all that surprising that he resisted her flirting if her hunch is correct.

'I definitely mixed her a Greek Mimosa one evening,' he replies. 'It's made with tsipouro, a Greek spirit, as well as lemon juice, cinnamon syrup and Greek sparkling rosé. Would you like to try one?'

'Sounds delicious,' Miranda replies. 'Yes, please.' She watches him as he sets to work, his hands deftly straining the lemon juice into a gleaming silver cocktail shaker, measuring the tsipouro, adding syrup. 'Wow,' she says when he eventually pours the mixture into a champagne flute and tops it up with the rosé. 'That looks amazing. How much do I owe you?'

He waves a hand dismissively. 'For you, it's on the house,'

he tells her. 'I think your Ms Chambers would want me to say that, yes?'

Miranda smiles. 'She probably would,' she agrees. 'Thank you very much. Maybe I could buy you a drink then, instead?' Evelyn would have done so, she thinks. And a person could do a lot worse than modelling themselves on Evelyn Chambers. 'I'm Miranda, by the way,' she adds, with that in mind.

'Konstantinos,' he says, holding a hand over the bar. 'It's good to meet you, Miranda. And thank you for the drink. We can toast her, perhaps.' He mixes himself something fruity, with strawberries, cucumber and mint, and they clink their glasses together.

'To Evelyn,' Miranda says. 'Rest in peace.'

'Rest in peace,' he echoes, then holds his glass up. '*Yamas*.'

'*Yamas*,' she replies, sipping her Mimosa. It's delicious, cool and citrusy, the bubbles frothing on her tongue. 'Thank you, this is perfect.'

'My pleasure,' he says. It's quiet at the bar, with very few people around, and after a moment he asks, 'Do you want to talk about your friend? I only met her a few times but I liked her very much. She told me all about her wife, how happy they were together. It was nice.'

'I only met her a few times as well,' Miranda confesses. 'But she sort of barged her way into my life, in the best possible way. I can't believe I knew her less than a week, because she was so' – She tries to find a nicer way to say 'nosey' – 'so interested in other people,' she settles on eventually, 'and so open about her feelings. She was pretty good at telling me

304

to sort my life out, to be honest. I just wish she was still here to . . . to help me with that.' She laughs but it's somewhat shaky, the sort of laugh that could easily turn into a sob. 'Although I'm still hoping she'll pull a few strings for me on the karma front, so who knows?' He frowns as if he doesn't understand what she means, and she's just about to explain when her phone pings with a message.

'That'll be her now,' she jokes, ignoring it, only for it to ping again, and then again. She glances at the screen to see that a load of notifications have appeared, including, most recently, a message from a number she doesn't recognise, asking if she wants to comment on the story. Oh God. What story? What is this? *Ping.* Now there's one from Todd, her former co-star on *Amberley Emergency*, the preview reading: *FYI babe xxx*

'Something important?' she hears Konstantinos say.

'Um . . . I'm not sure. Excuse me a moment,' she says, then takes another gulp of her Mimosa, terrified that this 'story' might be some awful new scandal with her at the centre. Her brain whirls with possible disaster scenarios. What if Charles, Evelyn's ex-husband, has gone to the tabloids accusing her of killing his beloved ex-wife? Or she's been papped scattering Rose's ashes and talking to sea turtles? Oh Christ. She's not sure she can cope with another battering right now.

She opens Todd's message to see a link to his Instagram page. Okay, she thinks, none the wiser, as she clicks it. They've always got on well, so, unless he's randomly thrown her under the bus today, it's hopefully not a new worst-case-scenario situation after all. She scans his latest post, screenshots he's taken of his Notes, and gasps. 'Oh my God,' she says under her breath. 'No way.'

'Is everything all right?' Konstantinos asks, but it's impossible to drag her eyes from the screen long enough to even glance at him.

'I think . . . maybe . . . it might be?' she says uncertainly, then takes another glug of her drink and reads the words again.

Hi everyone, Todd's post begins. *Some of you may have noticed a few stories about me in the press over the past few months but what you might not know is that almost all of them have come from personal conversations I've had with friends. Believe me, it's a uniquely horrible thing, wondering if a close friend or family member has gone around sneaking stories to the press, and in the last few weeks I've felt myself becoming guarded – paranoid, even – about what I've said, and to whom. I even wondered if I was being spied on, or if my phone was tapped. But then a story appeared last week that confirmed my worst suspicions. Perhaps you saw this particular story? It was the one about me supposedly being scared that my studio dressing room was haunted, because the lights kept flickering on and off at strange times, and my sunglasses were never where I'd left them, that sort of thing. What was even more peculiar than a haunted dressing room was the fact that a) it wasn't true (shame on you, press, for printing absurd lies) and b) I had made the whole thing up, to see if I could get to the root of what was going on.*

I'd realised by now that all the stories that had ended up in print had been from conversations I'd had, either in person or on the phone, in the privacy of my own dressing room at work. (I say 'privacy' but please read that word with a heavy dose of sarcasm.) Was my phone bugged? I decided to do a little test by pretending to call my mum and tell her all about the (fictitious) haunting, only with my phone completely switched off. I felt a bit insane doing this but, then again, I've had to do crazier acting jobs over the years so gave it my all.

I wasn't paranoid, I quickly realised, when the story appeared in one of the tabloids the very next day. (SUCKERS. Do better research next time.) It looked as if my phone wasn't bugged – but now I strongly suspected that my dressing room was, and that somebody had been listening in on all my private conversations, then taking the recordings to the press. But now the joke was on them, because they had taken my lame, completely invented and not even very interesting story about the haunted dressing room, and it had ended up in print. I went straight to Geoff Underwood, the Amberley director, and presented him with my suspicions. (Move over, Jessica Fletcher, am I right?) Long story short, the person responsible has been rumbled – and fired. Similar recording devices have been found in other actors' dressing rooms, as well as the hair and make-up rooms, wardrobe etc. I am livid to think about how many secrets and confidential pieces of information this particular piece of shit listened to. What is wrong with people???? All I can say to the person who did this is – Karma is a bitch, and you're gonna get yours, honey.

'Oh my God,' Miranda says again, hardly able to believe what she has just read. Other actors' dressing rooms ... hers too, presumably. Does this mean ...? The penny drops and it feels like a lead weight. It's a warm day but she suddenly feels cold all over as the implications unfold in her head. She'd been so convinced that Bonnie was the one responsible for all the

307

smear stories about her, but ... what if she wasn't? What if, in fact, she had never betrayed Miranda at all?

Dazed by the bombshell, Miranda blindly reaches for her Mimosa and drains the rest of it in a single swallow, still unsure if this could really be true. Because if it is ...

'Can I have another drink please, Konstantinos?' she asks faintly.

'But of course,' he says, sounding not a little worried. 'What's happened? Are you okay?'

'I've just had some weird news. Sort of good but also sort of bad,' she says, biting her lip.

I'm in shock! WTAF??? she replies to Todd. *Who was it??*

'Another Greek Mimosa coming right up,' she hears Konstantinos say.

'Thank you,' she says distractedly, reading Todd's post for a third time. She's still trying to process everything, while simultaneously reliving the way she'd turned on Bonnie, screaming at her in public like a banshee. Slapping her so hard she'd broken the other woman's skin. A deep, deep shame envelops her and for a moment she has to grab the bar in front of her because she thinks she might topple off her stool. What has she done?

Then her phone pings again with a reply from Todd.

Emma-Lou, it says. *And if I ever see that rancid guttersnipe again, it'll be too soon. Apparently she thought it would be good PR for the show, having us dragged through the mud in the press every week. Can you believe the neck of the woman?? I bet she stirred things up for you too, M, the disgusting shit-hag.*

Miranda's mouth falls open. But of course it was Emma-Lou.

She's – or rather she *was* – the show's publicist, who'd made that glib remark about Miranda's awful sacking. *Looking on the bright side, we're getting a lot of press about this.* Yes, it all made sense now. How she must have laughed behind Miranda's back, rubbing her hands together in glee no doubt when the whole thing snowballed. The absolute – to steal Todd's phrase – disgusting shit-hag.

Miranda feels a pain in her chest, thinking of the unnecessary anguish her sister has gone through because of Emma-Lou's callous disregard for privacy, her desperation for column inches. The humiliation caused to Bonnie when Miranda went off on one. Sure, she appreciates now that slapping people is not the answer to anything, but my God, put her in a room with Emma-Lou and she'd be sorely tempted to ... well, kill her, the mood she's in right now.

Oh, shit. She also owes Bonnie the most gigantic apology. More grovelling than she's ever had to do before. *I'll tell you what really helps – saying sorry,* she hears Evelyn's voice in her head, and it's hard not to groan aloud. No kidding, Evelyn.

'Your Mimosa,' says Konstantinos, setting it down on the bar in front of her.

'Thank you,' she says grimly, getting out her debit card. 'Oh, Konstantinos, I've made such a bad mistake. Have you ever had that feeling where you just want to hide away from the world for the rest of your life and not come out again?'

'Of course,' he replies. 'And the worst thing is, you *will* have to come out again.' He pulls a funny face, pretends to flick lint from his shirt. 'Trust me, I know, coming out is not easy.'

'No,' she says, smiling ruefully at him.

Another two women have arrived at the bar and are waiting to be served. 'But I believe in you, Miranda,' Konstantinos tells her over his shoulder as he heads over towards them. 'You've got this!'

Chapter Forty-One

Claudia

It's Saturday morning, and when Claudia knocks on the door of room twenty-seven, she's a little apprehensive about how she'll be received. This will be twice in two days she's had to directly intervene with guests facing unexpected issues. Yesterday was the note of condolences to Miranda Vallance. Today she's checking in on Leonora Neale. According to Andreou on reception, Mrs Neale requested to have a separate room from her husband yesterday, and, as of last night, a certain Frank Neale is now out of the country. There's a fine line to be drawn between looking after one's guests and interfering in their business. Claudia hopes she isn't about to cross it.

'You're good at talking to people, Claud,' Dimitris encouraged her when he dropped by her office earlier on and she expressed her concerns. 'People like you.'

She's never been good at taking compliments gracefully – she's wondered before if it's a residual scar from her ex-marriage, that she doesn't have the confidence in herself to believe people's praise. Or maybe it's simply her Aussie tendency to shrug off any kind of fuss? 'People like you too,' she had countered, sitting back in her chair and folding her arms. *I* like you, she might have added, had she been braver.

'Yes, when I am at the bar, maybe, and telling funny stories, but not when they need to talk about difficult, emotional things,' he'd replied. 'In a language, that is not my own tongue, too.' He pantomimed squinting in miscomprehension, making himself look so ridiculously gormless that she snorted in amusement. He shook his head. 'No, you will do a better job, I think. You are a nice person, good at listening.'

Before she could react – more compliments! – he was talking again, as if giving her no room for deflection. 'By the way, did you hear that he complained about Duska? This Frank Neale?' he asked. 'Because she was kind to his wife and he didn't seem to like that. Yes, on Thursday, when you were off,' he added, as her eyebrows rose.

'No way,' Claudia said, horrified for poor Duska, who's still finding her feet after her return to work. 'I hope you told him where to go.'

Dimitris spread his hands. 'Alas, he was very drunk, he was not interested in what I had to say. Also I had no intention of sacking her, like he wanted, so we did not agree on much.'

'I can imagine,' said Claudia drily, checking to see which room Mrs Neale is in.

The door opens in front of her now and she sees a petite, slim woman in a short-sleeved coffee-coloured shirt dress, her silvery hair in a neat bob. She's probably about the same age as Claudia's mum, although far more crisp and put-together than jovial, slapdash Barb. 'Hello?' she says, her tone not exactly unfriendly, but verging on suspicious.

'Hi, I'm Claudia, one of the hotel managers,' she begins. 'I just wanted to check everything's all right for you in this room, or if you'd rather move back into the suite where you were before?'

'I'm fine here, thank you,' the woman replies, a little defensively. Understandably, really; she must have had her absolute fill of people poking their noses into her affairs. But then something in her face changes and she softens a touch. 'Well – okay, not *exactly* fine,' she concedes. 'But I'll survive. Worse things happen, don't they?'

'Yes,' Claudia agrees. 'Although, as my mum would say, misery's not a competition,' she ventures after a moment. 'You can still feel rotten, even if you're not experiencing the absolute number one worst thing in the world.'

She holds her breath afterwards because, while she's trying to show empathy, she doesn't want to come across as dismissing Leonora Neale's view out of hand, particularly when that woman happens to be a high-paying guest here. But to her relief Mrs Neale smiles. 'That's true, I suppose. Yes. Your mum's got a point.' She looks properly at Claudia for the first time. 'Is that an Australian accent? You're a long way from home.'

'Yes,' Claudia replies, slightly wrong-footed by having the focus redirected back to her. 'Um . . . So anyway,' she goes on, 'I just thought I'd check in and make sure everything's okay. And to let you know that if you need anything, then—'

'What brought you here to Kefalonia, Claudia? If you

don't mind me asking,' Mrs Neale interrupts, leaning against the door jamb. 'Sorry, I hope that's not terribly nosey of me,' she adds quickly. 'I've been doing a lot of thinking about the future recently, and ...' She bites her lip. 'I feel at something of a crossroads.'

In her professional role, this is where Claudia should trot out some sanitised line about wanting the experience of working abroad or challenging herself. She's never had much of a convincing poker face though. 'I came here because ... well, heartbreak, basically,' she says, with a self-conscious laugh. 'The end of a bad marriage, the need to get far away.' Too late, she hears her own words, and could bite off her tongue in embarrassment. Oh, God. This, to a woman whose own relationship doesn't appear to be in the greatest of shapes. Talk about tactless.

Leonora Neale nods, though, as if she understands perfectly. 'I don't suppose you have time for a quick coffee, by any chance?' she asks tentatively. 'It's just that ... I don't have anyone else to talk to right now, and I'd appreciate the company. Of course you must be very busy though, so ...'

'I've got time for a coffee,' Claudia replies. 'We could order room service if you'd prefer, or we could venture down to the terrace? It's not so muggy today, after last night's storm.'

'Let's go out,' Mrs Neale says. 'I've been cooped up indoors all morning with my own thoughts; I could do with a change of scenery.'

A few minutes later, the two of them sit down at an empty table on the terrace, and Claudia puts up the large umbrella there before waving to Zoe, one of the waitresses on duty.

'Zoe, could you bring us — what would you like?' she asks Mrs Neale, who is studying the drinks menu.

'An iced coffee would be lovely, please,' she replies.

'An iced coffee for Mrs Neale, and — yes, actually, I'll have the same, please,' Claudia decides. 'Thank you.'

'And thank *you*,' Mrs Neale says to Claudia when the waitress departs. 'This is very kind of you. Do call me Nelly, by the way.'

Nelly suits her far better than Leonora, Claudia thinks. 'Right you are, Nelly,' she replies. 'So . . .' She's not quite sure what to say next but thankfully Nelly plunges right in.

'I hope this isn't weird, me asking you for coffee,' she begins.

'Not at all!' Claudia assures her.

'But it was you saying about your marriage ending and wanting to get away . . . it struck a chord.' Nelly exhales, staring down at the table. 'I don't quite know what I'm going to do with myself.'

Claudia nods. 'It's difficult,' she says diplomatically. 'I remember feeling completely frozen, with no idea how I could possibly pick myself back up again. It takes time. I think it's perfectly natural that you feel uncertain at the moment.'

Nelly gives her a little smile, but she looks sad nonetheless. 'I've been with Frank for so many years that I can't quite imagine what my life will look like without him,' she says. 'But it's definitely over, our marriage. I know that much.'

'I'm sorry to hear that,' Claudia says. 'It is a bit Ground Zero at first, isn't it, coming out of a relationship. Nothing looks the same. But a new life will gradually take shape. You'll figure out what's important to you.' She blushes, feeling

315

something of a fraud to be playing agony aunt to this much older woman, when she definitely hasn't figured everything out for herself yet. Just then her eye falls on Dimitris, who is heading purposefully across the terrace carrying a toolbox. She still hasn't plucked up the courage to ask him for that drink. 'I only came here because my Uncle Kostas suggested getting away,' she confesses. 'It wasn't because I had some great plan up my sleeve. Although at the time I remember fretting to my mum that it felt as if I was running away, and do you know what she said?'

'Tell me,' says Nelly.

'She said, what if it's not running *away*, but running *towards*? Towards the next chapter, a new start, an adventure abroad.' She shrugs. 'I'm still here anyway, three and a half years later, so it worked out okay for me. The best thing I could have done, actually.'

'Good for you,' says Nelly. 'Oh, lovely, thank you,' she adds as Zoe sets down their iced coffees in tall glasses, each with an accompanying miniature honey biscuit in the saucer.

'Thanks, Zoe,' Claudia says too.

They're silent for a moment, sipping their coffees. 'Is it terrible to admit that I actually feel rather . . . not *relieved*,' Nelly goes on, 'but . . . well, certainly not as destroyed as I thought I would? Frank's gone back to the UK, as I'm sure you're aware, and for the first time in years it's not my job to look after him. And of course, I still care about him, and I hope he's going to be okay, but nonetheless it's as if a weight has been lifted from my shoulders.' She grimaces at her own words. 'Oh dear, that sounds callous, doesn't it? Really disloyal and heartless.'

'It doesn't,' Claudia tells her. 'Not at all. Sometimes you don't realise how much you've been carrying, emotionally, I mean, until it's gone.' Her mind has snagged on something, though, taking her momentarily out of the conversation. *As if a weight has been lifted from my shoulders.* Someone else has said this to her recently, but who?

'Exactly,' Nelly replies. 'Frank was always the star player in our relationship, and both of our lives revolved around him. And now . . . I feel a little bit at sea, to be honest, like I've lost my compass and don't know where I'm going.' She smiles to herself about something. 'Do you know, the last time I was in this part of the world, forty or so years ago, I actually *was* at sea, with a very handsome young Greek man, on his yacht.'

'Now you're talking,' Claudia says enthusiastically, and they both laugh.

'I was a lot bolder back then,' Nelly replies. 'Impulsive too. Left everything behind for the sake of adventure, followed my heart.'

'Oh *yes*,' Claudia says. 'Good for you, Nelly. So should we be on the lookout for another handsome Greek yacht-owner, perhaps . . . ?'

Nelly laughs again. It's nice to see her looking less drawn and anxious, even if only for a few moments. Claudia is glad she made the effort to knock on her door. 'I don't think so,' Nelly says, and her eyes crinkle as she adds, 'More's the pity, eh?' She smiles again, then drains her iced coffee and gets to her feet. 'I'd better let you get on,' she says, 'but thank you so much for giving me your time. Here's to running towards something new. Maybe even something better.'

317

'Absolutely,' says Claudia. 'Good luck, Nelly. If you ever need to talk again, you just let me know.'

Nelly walks away looking considerably less jaded than she did earlier. Her words about having a weight lifted from her shoulders come back to Claudia once more, and she frowns. It's really bugging her because she knows someone has used those words to her recently, and that there's a reason why her subconscious is prompting her to remember. Then the pieces click into place, and her eyes widen.

'Oh my God,' she mutters under her breath. Then she hurries towards her office.

Chapter Forty-Two

Miranda

To: Bonnie Mobile
From: Miranda's Phone
Hope you are okay. Todd told me the news about Emma-Lou today, and I am still in shock, but more than that, I am SO sorry for ever doubting you. I'm even more sorry for attacking you like that. I was totally out of order and I'm utterly ashamed of myself. You might not ever be able to forgive me but I hope you will accept my sincere apology. Miranda x

Following Todd's bombshell the day before, it had taken Miranda ages to find the words to write to Bonnie that night. Countless times she ended up groaning and deleting a half-written message or throwing the phone down in despair. She'd wondered about biting the bullet and just ringing her, but changed her mind each time, terrified of having to leave a grovelling voicemail and it coming out wrong. Even when she eventually pressed Send on her text, she still didn't know if it would reach its destination. Chances were, Bonnie had blocked her number weeks ago. Still, even if that was the case, it wouldn't stop her, she vowed. Now that she knows the truth, she urgently wants to make amends.

She has also tried, once again, to put things right with her sister, writing her a long, honest email, from the heart. *You are the last person I wanted to be hurt in this whole mess,* she wrote. *You deserve none of this. But please believe me, I never once encouraged Felix's behaviour or responded to it. I would never, never do that to you. I was talking to a friend about it in confidence because I didn't know how to deal with the situation, and, unknown to me, my dressing room was bugged, and the conversation ended up being twisted and leaked to the press. The reason I lost the plot was because I was so devastated to think that a friend could have gone behind my back like that and, worse, caused this rift between us. I know you might not believe me – you might not even have read this far – but I swear to you this is the truth. I love you and just want to be your sister again. M x*

Having taken a screenshot of Todd's Instagram post, she attached it to the email and sent it on, her heart in her mouth. Back when they were teenagers, she and Imogen would often try to send each other telepathic thoughts, repeating words over and over in their heads in the hope of trying to transmit them silently to one another. She finds herself doing the same thing now, years on. *Please read this,* she mentally begs her sister at intervals. *Please please believe me.*

As yet, though, she's had no response from either Imogen or Bonnie. Big fat zero. Even Gramps has gone quiet on her. You can go mad waiting around on your own for news, though – every actor in the business knows that to be a fact. Which is why she's ended up here today at stunning, unspoilt Kaminia Bay, having impulsively booked herself a paddleboarding lesson, if only to escape her own head for a few hours.

As far as impulse decisions go, coming to this beach, with its soft yellow sand and clear azure sea, is looking like a pretty good one, she decides as she locks the car and heads down to find her class. She's given the wigs a miss today – hopefully everyone will be too busy falling off their paddleboards to think about trying to take photos of her – and the sea breeze ruffles her hair as she steps onto the sand.

There's about twelve of them booked in for the lesson, a jolly group of young German women she recognises from the hotel (who seem completely uninterested in her, thankfully) as well as a friendly Danish couple and a Norwegian family with teenage sons. The surf instructor, Yiannis, issues them all with buoyancy vests, and shows them how to fasten a board leash to their ankles. Then, laying his own board down on the sand, he demonstrates how they are to find their balance on the water, first kneeling, then rising to a standing position.

'Okay? Give it a try!' he cries, leaping off again, and Miranda blinks somewhat uncertainly. Is that it? But everyone else is gamely picking up their boards and heading towards the sea, so she follows them. Here goes nothing, she tells herself, wading in, the board floating beside her.

There are quite a lot of ungainly attempts to scramble onto their boards, the group of women in particular screaming and giggling as they struggle initially even to kneel on the surface without overbalancing. Miranda isn't a natural athlete herself and it takes her a little while to get the hang of it, but the first time she manages to get up on her feet, swaying momentarily, before standing firm and then tentatively beginning to paddle, she hears herself giving a genuine, heartfelt whoop from the sheer gratification of achievement.

'*Ja! Suksess!*' cries the Norwegian woman, who has also just risen to her feet nearby.

'Go us!' calls Miranda to her, and they beam at each other. Then, mutually carried away with their own glory, they try to paddle closer, both with a hand outstretched in an attempt to high-five, only for their boards to collide with a *thunk*, which sends them tumbling back into the water. Up they pop again, laughing breathlessly at their own ineptitude.

'No more high-fives, I think,' the Norwegian woman gurgles, bright-eyed.

'Far too dangerous,' Miranda agrees with a grin, grabbing her board and propping her elbows on it. And then Yiannis the instructor comes skimming towards them, saying, 'Ladies, are we alive? This is not a swimming lesson, okay? We are trying to stay *out* of the water, today!'

'We're alive,' the Norwegian woman assures him, winking at Miranda, before they both do their best to clamber back onto their boards, neither of them with a scrap of grace. Miranda gets the worst wedgie of her life hauling herself onto hers with all the elegance of a beached whale, while the Norwegian woman's bikini bottoms go the other way entirely when she manages to catch the top of them on the lower rim of her board. The inadvertent baring of her bottom makes her shriek and plunge back into the water, while her teenage boys look as if they urgently want to drown themselves from sheer embarrassment.

Miranda and the Norwegian woman – Camilla – end up laughing so hard, it's impossible to attempt standing up again for a few minutes. Miranda actually finds herself clutching her stomach because it's aching from so much laughter. 'Poor Yiannis,' Camilla wheezes. 'He swam away *very* quickly, did you see? I think I frightened him.'

'Are you kidding? I think you made his day,' Miranda tells her. 'I'm not sure your boys were so happy though.'

'I just heard them calling the Norwegian Adoption Agency,' the woman replies, which cracks them both up again. 'Please help me. I need a different mother immediately!'

Eventually, everyone in the group masters the art of paddle-boarding and there are no longer so many dramatic plunges. As her confidence grows, Miranda paddles herself out across the bay, feeling a thrill to be standing proudly on her board, surrounded by the glittering blue water. The sun is warm against her body, her core muscles feel as if they're getting a good workout, and the burst of laughter she shared with Camilla has left her with a lingering sense of joy. Gazing back at the crescent of sand, she feels herself filling up with stillness, as if a pure, shining serenity is being poured straight into her. Everything back home – work, family, unanswered messages – seems far away, irrelevant. *I am happy,* she thinks to herself in surprise. *I am so happy!*

Something Evelyn said to her on that wine-fuelled evening comes back to her. 'Being alive is all about recognising those perfect moments when they come along,' she had opined, glass in hand. 'Those snapshots of pure contentment, whether you're with other people or quite alone. That's why we bother, don't you think?'

Yes, she agrees now, cruising across the blue. Absolutely yes. And she's recognising this perfect moment right here, right now, taking a mental snapshot so that she can keep it with her. It's funny, because she's been trying for weeks to enjoy life as a single person, after her disastrous dating record, but it's only today that she feels that she might just have cracked it. As if she's enough of a person to make herself happy, rather than looking for happiness from another. 'Maybe try to find someone who has at least *one* good personality trait going for them, instead of making decisions purely on their hotness?' Bonnie had once suggested, back when they were still friends. She'd been joking, admittedly, but all the same, with hindsight, Miranda can see now that her priorities – a six-pack or a sexy arse, rather than brain cells – have not exactly been on point.

'Personality *and* hotness, that's the dream, isn't it?' Evelyn had said, when Miranda raised this. This was towards the end of the evening, when they were both pretty drunk and it no longer seemed weird to be discussing her love life with an octogenarian. 'But don't forget what I said about my Godsend— I mean, my godson. He's a catch, Miranda, I'm telling you!'

Miranda had laughed, even though from what Evelyn had told her about the godson – Oliver, he's called – he sounds a massive nerd, and not her type at all. 'I'm sure he's wonderful,' she'd said diplomatically. 'What a shame I've retired from dating for the foreseeable future.'

'Well, I'll send him your way just as soon as you're ready, then,' Evelyn said, undeterred. 'Because we're friends now, aren't we? We're going to see each other again when we're back in London, I hope? I'll get front row tickets when you land the starring role in some marvellous new play in the West End, and we can catch up in your dressing room afterwards, with me telling you how wonderful you were.'

Miranda had felt absurdly cheered by this image. 'Oh, I would love that,' she'd said. 'And maybe you could educate me about classical music. We could go to a concert at the Barbican or something together, you can show off about how brilliant you were in your heyday.'

'It's a date,' Evelyn had said, clinking her glass against Miranda's, although of course that's never going to happen now.

Perfect moments – just like glorious evenings – must come to an end, sadly. All too soon, the lesson is up, and Miranda and the rest of the group reluctantly paddle back to shore. Nobody gets to exist in a permanent state of tranquillity, she reminds herself with a small sigh; presumably even Buddhist monks have to deal with life's small annoyances such as sand in one's crevices, bad traffic and mosquito bites. All the same, as she says goodbye to the Norwegian family and heads back to her car, she feels certain that she's going to remember the elation of being out there on the water, suspended in the scene, for a long time.

She's a few miles from the hotel when she hears her phone ringing from the glovebox, where she stashed it earlier. It might be a spam call or something dull like her accountant's office with a query, she reasons. But a sixth sense suddenly tells her to pull over and check, just in case. Having parked in a layby, she fumbles to retrieve her phone, almost dropping it when she sees Imogen's name on the screen. Her paddle-boarding chill vanishes instantly. Oh my God, she thinks, her finger skidding in her haste to answer, her heart banging in her chest.

'Hello?' she says.

Chapter Forty-Three

The Boss

Dimitris is at the top of a ladder, propped against the spa building, whistling between his teeth as he examines the damage caused by last night's thunderstorm. When Jasmine and Lucia, the beauticians, arrived for work this morning, it was to find water dripping from the ceiling in the main treatment room after hours of torrential rain. Since then, he's helped them move all their kit into an empty two-bedroom suite nearby, where they have now set up for today's bookings. There's always something when you run a hotel, he has discovered over the years here. No day is ever the same – but then again, he wouldn't have it any other way.

Still, he could have done without this happening on the rare occasion that both his groundsman and the head of maintenance are off the same weekend. Not least because Danilo and Antoni, two other members of their maintenance team, have called in sick today. Dimitris could have left this particular job until tomorrow in the hope that they'll be back then, but the forecast is for a further storm tonight, and he doesn't want to chance the damage getting even worse. Plus, although they were far too professional to complain to him, he could tell Jasmine and Lucia weren't happy about having to leave the cosy treatment rooms of the sanctuary shed for the makeshift space of a couple of impersonal hotel bedrooms. The sooner they can return here, the happier they and their customers will be — and therefore the happier Dimitris himself too. Staff welfare is paramount if you're going to run a successful business: something else he has learned.

So it's down to him, then, to put this right, but that's okay. He's not one to forget his tradesman roots, and hopes he'll never be too proud to climb a ladder and take care of a job himself if need be. It's not too onerous a task either — a couple of the wooden shingles have come away that need replacing — but now that he's up here, he can see that a few other roof shingles are split, and one looks a bit rotten, so perhaps it will take longer than he anticipated. Ahh well. It's a lovely day. He's got his hammer and flatbar, there's a box of nails jingling in his pocket, and he's found a stack of spare shingles in the maintenance shed, so he's all set. What's more, it's good to be out of the office, away from phone calls and emails for a change.

Unknown to Claudia, he's been keeping an eye on the general email inbox, ever since she became upset by that *malaka*'s aggressive email. The reply that Dimitris sent was, in hindsight, pretty fierce, threatening to forward their correspondence to the police with a note of the IP address, should there be any more abuse forthcoming. He'd hoped that would be the end of it, but when he had a look this morning he'd seen that a new message had arrived from the self-styled Ares. 'I curse you' was all it said, and Dimitris rolled his eyes, blocked the sender and moved the email into a folder where Claudia wouldn't have to see it. He'll deal with it properly later, follow through with his threats, he thinks, tutting under his breath. Honestly, some people are lunatics, simple as that.

His phone is propped up on the shelf of the guttering, the radio playing from it, and a song comes on that takes him straight back to when Andreas was a small baby. Dimitris was only twenty-four himself, full of energy, and liked to sing his infant son this particular song, whirling around the small apartment with him in his arms. 'Be careful with him,' Elena would snap, or 'You're getting him overexcited,' but the baby's eyes would always be wide and gleeful, and he would chortle at the thrill of being held by his big singing papa, and the way the world was spinning around them so. Oh, how Dimitris adores his children! Andreas, the greatest son, and Lili, his wonderful, talented daughter. His heart bursts with pride for them every time he thinks about them; he never knew a man could be capable of so much love!

'Eh, Papa,' Lili scolded him last time he dropped in at the bakery and said something along those lines. 'You need a woman in your life that isn't your daughter, you know. My staff are teasing me, calling me Daddy's Girl, because you come in here so often with all this love of yours.'

'Another woman? Ahh, no,' he told her. 'I have no time for that sort of thing now.'

She'd raised a disbelieving eyebrow at him. Even with flour

on her cheek, Lili is a force to be reckoned with. After school, she took an apprenticeship at one of the most famous bakeries in Argostoli (and aced it, let this proud father tell you) before setting up her own business selling Greek pastries and bread from a stall in the central market there. Since then she has expanded from her stall to an actual shop just off the high street, and has hired several apprentice bakers as well as shop assistants who serve at the counter. 'Papa, you do have time,' she'd told him firmly. 'You're just scared, yes? I understand. But you're a handsome man, you know. You've got a lot to offer. Let me sign you up to internet dating, I can do you a really good profile.'

Absolutely not, he'd told her, but all the same, her words nag away at him. He doesn't think of himself as the type to be scared of anything – spiders, sharks, snakes; none of those things faze him. Nor do macho arseholes, as a rule. When you're his size, with his muscles, he'd always back himself if it came to a fight. But love . . . Well, being married to Elena left its mark, put it that way. It knocked the stuffing out of him when she left him and the kids for a Portuguese musician, fifteen years ago; a man who drifted into town with his band, and left again with someone else's wife. He had done his best to wrap himself and the children in bombproof cladding, round and round and round, to protect them all through the fallout. From that day on, he has devoted himself to fatherhood and work, in that order. Nothing else has had a look-in.

He fits a new shingle into place, first trimming its width, then bashing it up into the felt with the hammer. He tacks a nail either side, *tap-tap-tap, tap-tap-tap*, enjoying the satisfaction that comes from repair, making good. These dating sites that Lili keeps threatening to sign him up with – mother of God, he looked at one of them the other evening and found it a disheartening prospect. The thought of having to package himself up like that – *tap-tap-tap* – a photograph, a description, aimed at attracting other people, scrolling through a list . . . no, thank you. Who wants to feel like an item on a supermarket shelf, to be examined, checked for bruises, rejected?

The other thing that kept coming back to him was that, following a cursory glance, he couldn't see that any of the women there were even half as good-looking or engaging or interesting or funny as – *tap-tap-tap* – well, in truth, as Claudia.

Okay, he allowed himself to go there. It's bad, isn't it, for him to have these feelings for someone who works for him? Yes, he tells himself miserably. Yes, it is. He prides himself on being a good man, an honourable man. He does not want to be that no-good boss who uses his power and position for his own gains. And yet, earlier this week when Claudia started to cry in fright because of the email that she thought was from her bad husband . . . well, something powerful had happened inside Dimitris, a bursting up of protective feelings, so strong he felt like killing this man for scaring her. In the same breath, he felt like putting his arms round her and making sure that nothing bad could ever happen to her again.

This, to put it mildly, was very disturbing to him. Obviously he has done nothing in response, nor will he. She is his employee, damn it, she is out of bounds! Isn't she?

Using the flatbar to start prying up a split shingle, he finds himself thinking about that email he saw this morning – *I curse you* – and rolls his eyes at the ridiculous melodrama of the sender. Then again, maybe it *is* something of a curse, to find himself with these feelings that he forbids himself to act upon. To find himself still so enmeshed with his self-constructed bombproof cladding that the notion of removing it and stepping out into the open unarmed is daunting.

'Screw you and screw your stupid curse,' he mutters under his breath, as the shingle refuses to budge. He works away at it with renewed energy – too much energy, as it turns out. Because as he leans back a little to get some extra purchase on the flatbar, his centre of gravity shifts, his foot skids an inch forward on the rung, and then he loses his balance entirely and falls backwards from the ladder with a yell. His body hits the ground with a horrible crack, the flatbar and hammer are sent whirling into the undergrowth, and everything goes black.

Chapter Forty-Four

Claudia

Ever since Dimitris' son Andreas traced the IP address of the hotel's aggressive emailer and discovered that it *wasn't* Marcus harassing her, but instead someone from a place called Leighton Buzzard, Claudia has been trying to remember where exactly she'd heard the name of that particular British town before. Then, over their iced coffees, Nelly had said something about Frank's departure having been a weight off her shoulders, and the cogs in Claudia's brain began whirring with greater intensity. Afterwards, she hurried back to her desk and opened up her 'Nice Emails' folder to see if she was right. Now, reading the email in question, her breath gusts out of her. Bingo. Connection made.

The Nice Emails folder is pretty self-explanatory. Bad working days at The Ionian Escape are rare but, very occasionally, there will be someone or something — say, a mean, unwarranted one-star review, or a drunk, angry guest shouting at her full in the face for some minor complaint — that leaves her questioning why she works here. That's where the file comes in: a reminder that a great holiday can change visitors' lives, that it's the best job in the world. Sure, not everybody follows up a wonderful getaway with an email of thanks, but occasionally people do. People like Katy Marksbury, for instance.

I've never emailed a hotel about this sort of thing before, she had written, *but after staying at the beautiful Ionian Escape recently, I wanted to get in touch to say how grateful I am for the experience.*

It was just meant to be a straightforward girls' holiday with my best friends to Kefalonia. We'd been planning it for ages and everyone was looking forward to escaping the daily grind. We're all from Cumbria, England, and have known each other since school, but I moved south about five years ago and have missed them so much. Two of my friends have had pretty tough times – one was going through a horrible divorce and another has undergone treatment for breast cancer. Another friend was pregnant for the first time and wanted to get away for some proper relaxation before the baby came along. Anyway, we all had the best holiday. We loved the beautiful rooms, the pool, the amazing breakfasts. Your staff were always so friendly and helpful whenever we wanted to book day trips or taxis. And being so happy with my best friends made me face up to a difficult truth – that I hadn't actually felt that way for a very long time.

Life is short, isn't it? It's too short to be constantly unhappy. Too precious to squander it on a husband who makes you feel small and worthless. Too full of great experiences and laughter to be stuck in a boring job you don't enjoy. Being in Kefalonia woke me up again to how wonderful life can be. I realised that The Ionian Escape had truly lived up to its name. But now that I'd escaped ... how could I go back?

Good question. And so, as I was packing my case on the last morning, ready to head for the airport and home, I made a few decisions. Somehow or other, I'd got into the bad habit of letting my husband make all my choices for me, rather than being my own woman. They say follow your dreams, don't they? I decided to follow mine for a change.

Since then, I've taken the plunge and left my bullying husband and my dreary office job in Leighton Buzzard, and have moved back north, where my heart is. It was terrifying at first but I don't regret it for a minute. I see my family and friends all the time now and have slotted right back into the community. I'm retraining to be an osteopath and love every minute of it. I can't tell you what a weight it is off my shoulders to have changed things around like this! I honestly don't know if I'd have done any of the above, had I not had such a great week on Kefalonia.

Sorry if this is all TMI but, for the first time in years, I feel excited about life again. Holidays really can change your life – thanks for inspiring me to change mine!

Katy Marksbury

Props to you, Katy Marksbury, Claudia thinks, rereading these upbeat words and mentally applauding the writer. Then she looks again at the messages from 'Ares', Leighton Buzzard's number one troll, and puts two and two together. Yes – it adds up. One jilted husband, angry at the world, taking it out on the staff of the hotel where his ex-wife had enjoyed such a life-changing holiday ... It's pathetic of him, it really is, but the pieces fit. Why take personal responsibility for what happened, Ares, when you can blame a whole other set of people for these events?

The question is, should Claudia alert Katy to her suspicions? Is it crossing a boundary for her to contact a former guest with what might be alarming or unwelcome information? Possibly. Given her own experiences, though, she feels that it's better to be forewarned about erratic, aggressive behaviour from an ex. If, after their break-up, Marcus had begun single-handedly terrorising the staff at her old marketing job, say, or waging a personal campaign against Elodie, damn right she would want to know. It's a risk she has to take.

She's already replied to the original email, but now she spends some time composing a second, more personal, reply, gently raising her concerns. *Of course, I could be completely wrong,* she writes, *in which case please do ignore this message! But on the off chance that your email and his are connected, then I thought you should be aware of it.*

I hope your new life is still going wonderfully well, and that you'll decide to return to The Ionian Escape for another holiday sometime in the future, she concludes the email. *Until then, yours in solidarity, Claudia.*

There. Done. A hand stretched out across the miles, woman to woman, that says, I've got your back. We're all in this together. Added to that, as she rereads Katy's email, it feels that the other woman is speaking directly to her. Prompting her. *Life is too short, isn't it? Too precious to squander.*

Yes, thinks Claudia, closing the Nice Emails folder. Yes, Katy, it bloody well is.

Chapter Forty-Five

Nelly

Nelly's on her way back from coffee with Claudia when she feels the vibration of her phone in her bag. It's probably one of her boys, she thinks. They have been solicitously calling and messaging every day to check in on her. So it comes as a surprise when she sees that it's a message from an unknown number. It's even more of a surprise when she actually reads what it says.

Nelly, is that really you? And you came to Ithaca? I could not believe it when Katarina gave me your message. I have often thought about you over the years. Can I see you? Are you still in Greece? Tell me where to meet you and I will be there. Your friend, always. Alexander

She stops dead, and has to read the message twice over before she actually believes the words are real. Oh my goodness. *Alexander!* Very much alive and wanting to see her! With everything that has happened recently, her trip to Ithaca has been sidelined in her thoughts, but now it races to the forefront of her mind, her nerve endings tingling to attention.

337

I'm staying on Kefalonia for another week, she writes back. *I would love to see you again! My hotel is called The Ionian Escape but I can meet you anywhere. How exciting!*

She adds a kiss, then deletes it. Then she adds a heart emoji but deletes that too. Her sons are always taking the mick out of her for it but she does enjoy an emoji or three. She settles in the end for a smiling face with sunglasses, crosses her fingers that he's not an emoji snob, then sends her message.

She's still standing exactly where she stopped, in the middle of the terrace, so she starts walking slowly back towards her room, smiling at the idea of their two lives converging once more. Who would have thought it? She's so glad she took herself off to Ithaca on a whim now, when this could so easily not be happening. In another world, where she hadn't sneaked out for a spontaneous day trip, she'd still be wondering about him, her questions forever unanswered. But now . . . well, now, it looks as if she'll be able to get all the answers she wants. Finally, she'll achieve some closure on that terrible, heart-breaking parting of theirs so many years earlier. If he's had a happy life in the meantime, she'll be glad for him. Maybe they'll even laugh affectionately about their passionate summer fling, toast their young, carefree selves of that time.

Her phone buzzes again just as she's letting herself back into her hotel room, and she kicks off her shoes and sinks onto the bed to read his new message.

Is tonight too early?? he has written, along with − yes! − a laughing emoji. *A friend of mine has a very good restaurant near your hotel. We could have a drink there, or even dinner? Of course you are welcome to bring your husband or family too. Let me know another day if that's no good.* He signs off with the champagne flutes emoji, and her stomach flips like a pancake inside her.

Tonight would be lovely, she types in reply. *My husband,* she continues, only to stop short. The situation with Frank is not something she can summarise in a few pithy words. Delete, delete.

I will be alone, she writes, *but I'd be delighted to meet your wife/family if they are coming too.* He must have beautiful children, she thinks to herself with a sudden pang, imagining strapping sons and a brown-eyed daughter. *How does 7.30 sound? Let me know the address and I'll see you there.* She copies his champagne flutes emoji, feeling a frisson inside as she imagines herself sitting opposite him at a restaurant table later on, clinking glasses. How will it be to see him again? Will he still be handsome? Will they still find one another good company?

She presses Send and lies back on the bed, smiling up at the ceiling. She's reacting as if she's still the same twenty-something Nelly who first met him, she realises, even though she's really in her sixties, she's got lines and liver spots, and she's just separated from her husband after a decades-long marriage. Calm down, you daft old bat, she tells herself, coming to her senses. All the same, it's impossible to completely snuff out her excitement. Now ... what is she going to wear?

Chapter Forty-Six

Miranda

'Hey. I got your email,' Imogen says, her voice so heartbreakingly small that Miranda has to press the phone right against her ear to hear her. 'And . . . And I believe you.'

Miranda's mouth opens, perhaps as a reflex because she was expecting to have to defend herself, but no sound comes out. Because she was not expecting *that*. 'You . . . you do?' she croaks after a moment.

'I went to the doctor,' Imogen goes on miserably. 'You know how we've been trying for a baby for, like, a gazillion years? I went for some tests to see if anyone could figure out what was wrong with me − or with him. Long story short, turns out I've got chlamydia.' She gives a sob. 'I've got fucking *chlamydia*, Min. The doctor thinks I might have had it for years.'

'What the . . . ?' Miranda can't take this in. She turns off the engine, because clearly this is not going to be a quick conversation. 'Chlamydia?' she repeats dumbly. Oh God. Where had *that* come from?

'It can bugger up your fertility, that's the thing,' Imogen continues. She's not a tall person, or large physically, but she's always had such a big personality, so vibrant with her blonde hair and colourful clothes, it's killing Miranda to hear her sound so broken. 'And not everyone has symptoms, so it can go undetected for ages. He must have caught it somewhere—' Her voice cracks. 'The fucking *bastard* – and had it treated on the quiet, thinking he'd got away with me not finding out. Except now I *have* found out, because he must have passed it on to me without realising.'

'Oh, Im,' Miranda sighs, feeling agony for her. Her heart aches as she remembers her sister's radiant face that first Christmas when she brought him home, the great love of her life. *Everyone, this is Felix!*

'But this is proof that he's been lying to me for years,' Imogen goes on. 'That he cheated on me with someone else. Maybe loads of someone elses for all I know. I can't bear it.' She breaks into sobs. 'I feel s-s-s-such an idiot. I hate him!'

Hearing her sister weeping hundreds of miles away, Miranda feels like driving straight to the nearest airport and jumping on the next plane home. 'That's so unspeakably grim,' she says vehemently. 'I hate him too, for doing this to you. Oh, Immie, I'm so sorry, this is unbearably shitty. What are you going to do?'

'I've already done it,' Imogen sobs. 'I've chucked him out. It's over. How can I stay married to someone who treats me like th-th-that?' Miranda hears her blowing her nose, a dismal honk. 'Oh God, and I haven't even told you the rest – Gramps sent me a weird message about someone called Jackie, one of

341

the care assistants at the care home. It turns out Felix even tried it on with *her*, squeezed her bum or something gross when I was looking the other way, talking to one of the nurses. I mean ...'

Miranda is still reeling. 'He doesn't deserve you,' she says, words that she has had to keep silent for so long. 'He's a fucking monster,' she adds, because it's liberating to be able to express herself freely at last. But slagging off Felix, however enjoyable, is probably not the vibe her sister needs from her now, she realises. 'What would help – do you want company?' she asks. 'I can come back and stay with you, if you want. Or ...' A better idea unfolds in her head. 'Or why don't you fly out to Kefalonia? My treat. It's beautiful here, there's loads of space in my suite, you can stay with me and get away from everything properly.' There's a lump in her throat suddenly. 'It would be like old times, us two sharing a bedroom again.'

The car engine ticks as it cools down, and she hears Imogen give a sniff, then blow her nose again. 'Are you serious? God, I might just do that,' she says. Then, 'I'm sorry I was so awful to you, by the way. I said some vile things.'

'Yeah, and you were justified in saying them, because I'd dragged you into a horrible publicity storm,' Miranda replies stoutly. 'So I'm sorry too.' A truck thunders past and her car rocks silently in the layby. 'Think about it anyway,' she urges. 'It might do you good if you can wangle the time off work, leave everything behind for a few days. I mean, your tan will never end up being as good as *mine*, but if you can get over that ...'

A laugh splutters down the phone and it warms her heart.

They've always been able to make each other laugh, even in the darkest of times. 'Thanks,' says Imogen. 'Are you okay, by the way? After all that shit in the papers?'

'Yeah,' Miranda replies, remembering her golden moment on the paddleboard earlier. 'Actually, I kind of *am* okay. Or at least I'm going to be, anyway.' Her thoughts spool like ticker-tape through the events of the last week: screaming at the woman trying to film her by the hotel pool, hurling her phone into the water. Her road trip with Evelyn, setting the world to rights. The sound of Bach in a too-warm hospital ward, the urgent beeping of monitors as Evelyn's heart stopped. The sea turtle paddling majestically through the blue. Laughing until she cried with a random Norwegian woman. 'It's been a funny old time, to be honest – but not all bad.'

'I'm glad,' says Imogen. There's a pause. 'Did you mean it, about me coming over there, by the way?'

Oh, she means it. So sincerely that, as soon as Miranda gets back to the hotel, she starts searching up the flight schedules for Kefalonia and sending screenshots to her sister, along with photos of the beach and pool. *Let me know which flight suits you and I'll book you a seat,* she messages. *Hang in there. Love you xxx*

Chapter Forty-Seven

Nelly

The spa team have had to relocate today because of last night's storm, but, when Nelly rings up to see if they could do her a last-minute manicure, they manage to squeeze her in that afternoon. In the eighties she loved a vampy red nail, with a slash of lipstick to match, but these days she leans more towards something pastel and pretty, so she picks a light pearlescent pink that really sets off her tanned hands. Afterwards, heading back towards her room, she bumps into Claudia, who has replaced her work shoes with trainers and is wheeling a bicycle along, presumably about to go home.

'Have you been treating yourself?' she asks, eyeing Nelly's gleaming nails. 'Good on you!'

'I have,' Nelly says, wiggling her fingers. Then she can't help herself. 'Because ... do you remember that handsome Greek man with a yacht that I mentioned earlier? You'll never guess who I'm meeting up with tonight.' She pulls a meaningful expression, and Claudia's jaw drops with gratifying astonishment.

'What? No way! Seriously? You *found* him?' Claudia clasps a hand to her heart. 'This is so exciting. How on earth did you manage that?'

Nelly explains, making a point of emphasising that her search had been for the sake of an old friendship rather than anything else. She doesn't want anyone to get the wrong impression and view her as some kind of scarlet woman when the truth is far less decadent.

'This is so exciting! I love that you went looking for him,' Claudia says, starry-eyed, and Nelly can't help but smile. Claudia, like the young woman she met in Penelope's, is clearly the romantic type. 'Well, I hope he's as divine as you remember him.'

'If he is, then his wife really did get all the luck,' Nelly says, and laughs as Claudia's expression immediately turns to one of disappointment. 'Oh, did I not tell you that bit of the story? Last time I saw him, he was about to get married, much to my heartbreak at the time. No, I'm afraid this is not going to be a love story for the ages. Not least because, until yesterday, I was here with my husband, so . . .'

'Of course,' Claudia says at once, chastened. 'Absolutely. I'm sorry if I spoke out of turn, or . . .'

'You didn't! Not at all. In fact, it's been really lovely to talk to you both times today,' Nelly tells her. 'Thank you for indulging me wittering on to you about my life.'

'No indulgence at all!' Claudia says, looking rather bashful. 'It's been great talking to you too. I hope you have a blast this evening, reminiscing about all the fun you got up to, back in the day. Now – can I order you a taxi for later or do anything else for you before I leave?'

'No, he's picking me up, I'm all set, but thank you. Have a good evening yourself.'

They say goodbye and Nelly heads back to her room, taking care not to smudge her nails as she lets herself in. Despite her deliberately pragmatic approach to tonight, Claudia's romantic comments have rubbed off on her. Butterflies start up in her stomach. Because . . . what if there's one more twist in their story yet to come?

Chapter Forty-Eight

Claudia

Seeing Nelly with her manicure and bright eyes, excited about being reunited with an old flame, coupled with Katy Marksbury's words about life being short, is enough to make Claudia feel that the universe is conspiring to galvanise her into action herself. Okay! Message received! Enough prevaricating, she decides. She's going to seize the moment, *this* moment, and ask Dimitris out for a drink tonight, before she loses her nerve. Just watch her.

After returning her bike to the rack — you can't have a big moment when you're holding on to a pushbike, she tells herself — she sets out to find him. She's finally doing this! No more holding back. *Life's too short,* Katy Marksbury repeats encouragingly in her head. Amen to that, sister! Time to tick off the most difficult task on her list once and for all. The only question is, where is he? He's not in his office, nor the staffroom.

'Have you seen Dimitris?' she asks Duska as she walks back through reception.

'Not for ages,' Duska replies. 'He was around first thing, wanting to know if we had an empty suite that Jasmine and Lucia could move their treatments into, but not since then, sorry.'

Ahh yes, the storm damage to the sanctuary shed, Claudia remembers. Hopefully Danilo or Antoni have sorted that out by now. She goes out to the bar but Dimitris is not there either. 'I saw him with a toolbox a while ago,' Konstantinos says with a shrug, 'although that was around lunchtime. After that – no.'

'Yes, I saw him then too,' Claudia replies. 'I wonder why he was carrying a toolbox,' she adds, frowning. 'You don't happen to know, do you?'

Konstantinos is wiping down the bar, the damp cloth turning circles along the wooden surface. 'Some of the guys are off sick,' he says. 'Maybe some emergency he needed to deal with?' The cloth squeaks a little under his vigorous rubbing. 'Or maybe he's gone home? It's pretty quiet today.'

'Maybe,' Claudia says, doubtfully, because Dimitris isn't usually one to slope off early without letting anyone know. Perhaps he's got caught up in whatever job he embarked on, she thinks. She thanks Konstantinos and walks towards the accommodation blocks, listening out for sounds of hammering or drilling. There's nothing, though; Konstantinos is right, it's very quiet. The hotel is running at half-capacity now, with dozens of guests having left yesterday and fewer arriving to fill their places. Staff are looking forward to holidays of their own as the season winds down. It's Zoe's last weekend here, before she returns to Patras to continue at university. A couple of the seasonal cleaners have already left as the work dries up. Kefalonia is beautiful year-round but Claudia particularly loves the shift into autumn, the cooler mornings and evenings, the slower pace.

Where is Dimitris? She texts him a quick *Are you around?* but receives no immediate reply. Might he be working on the damaged sanctuary shed? she wonders. She picks up her pace, setting off down the short winding path through the trees towards the building, smiling to herself as she hears the faint strains of music playing. Ahh – he *is* there. He'll be listening to the radio, unable to hear the sound of her message over the music, she figures. 'Dimitri?' she calls, as she rounds the corner and sees a ladder propped against the side of the building. Then she freezes as she realises there's a body on the ground at the foot of the ladder. A body that looks remarkably like—

'Dimitri!' she shouts, running towards him. A scream rises in her lungs as she sees the unnatural angle at which one of his legs is bent. Oh God, no. No! 'Dimitri, can you hear me?' she cries, dropping to her knees beside his body. His eyes are closed and her heart hammers as she puts her fingers on his wrist, searching for a pulse. There – very faint. He's alive at least. She fumbles her phone out of her pocket and calls an ambulance. 'Please hurry,' she says. 'Please, please hurry.'

Chapter Forty-Nine

Nelly

At twenty-five past seven that evening, Nelly sits down on the huge mustard sofa in reception wearing her favourite navy-blue maxi dress, a silver star necklace and a pair of white trainers. It's taken her ages to settle on the right outfit: she wants to look good without appearing too try-hard. Plus, she's got to feel comfortable, so that she's not fretting about a tight seam or a too-low neckline the whole time. She certainly doesn't want to give mutton vibes, nor does she want to tip too far the other way and look past it. *Past WHAT, exactly, darling?* she imagines Wayne, her hairdresser, intoning, one eyebrow camply lifted.

Well, Wayne, she imagines herself replying demurely. That's a very good question.

Heavens, she feels as giddy as a teenager going out on a first date. As tremulous as Juliet on her balcony, waiting for Romeo. Alexander is picking her up in a cab, which is nice, isn't it? Nelly's as feminist as the next woman but she does like some old-fashioned chivalry, now and then. Who doesn't like to be fussed over once in a while, made to feel special? She's used to doing that for Frank, of course — all the cossetting and pandering in an endless attempt to rearrange the world to his liking. It's actually quite a novelty to have someone go out of their way for her, for a change.

She glances at her watch again — twenty-eight minutes past — and wishes that her heart could stop racing so. She's being silly, she tells herself. Why is she getting so het up? They are simply two old friends who—

She doesn't manage to finish her own sentence because suddenly there he is, walking into the hotel, and her entire body seems to freeze as she takes in the sight. Alexander Nikolau, the man himself. Look at him with his thick white hair and the lines on his face, still cutting a commanding figure as he stops in the doorway and gazes around. She marvels at how dapper he is as an older man, in stone-coloured trousers with a white shirt and polished brown shoes. The influence of his wife, perhaps? He only ever wore faded T-shirts and shorts when she knew him, after all. Then his gaze alights on her and he breaks into a broad smile.

It's the same smile, she thinks, dazedly rising to her feet, unable to help smiling right back. The same smile that instantly reminds her of the connection that once fired between them, hot and true. Her lips form the shape of his name and she feels as if she's in a dream, a really good, joyful one. There he is, stepping out from the past, right into this moment. Her legs somehow carry her over towards him, and they're both still smiling.

351

'My little Nelly,' he says, his voice exactly as she remembers it. She would have known it anywhere. 'Look at you! Is this really happening?'

'Look at *you*,' she replies, intoxicated by the sight of him, her arms moving instinctively towards him and then stopping in mid-air. 'Are we – Should we ...?' She wants to embrace him but does he want that too?

He does. He steps towards her and clasps her firmly in his arms. Oh, the feeling of his chest against hers! He smells good too, of soap and an ironed shirt. It's really him, she thinks, astonished that time has flung them back together again. 'Hi,' she says, her voice muffled by the tightness of their embrace. 'It's been a while.'

He laughs, releasing her. 'It has certainly been a while, Nelly,' he agrees. 'But we have a whole evening together now, to catch up, yes?'

'Is that going to be long enough, do you think?' she asks, smiling up at him. Gosh, it's so lovely to be walking out of the hotel together, as if no time has passed at all. Surreal and utterly dreamlike but incredibly, wonderfully lovely too.

'Well, it'll do for a start,' he replies, gesturing to where a cab is waiting patiently outside, its light glowing against the dusky backdrop. He opens the car door for her. 'Let's see how far we get by the time the night is over, hey?' he says, as she ducks her head and steps inside.

Chapter Fifty

Miranda

'Settle into a comfortable position and close your eyes,' Tatiana the yoga instructor says, quietly closing the blinds so that the sunlight pouring through the windows of the fitness studio is temporarily dimmed. 'Let your breathing slow, let your mind become empty.'

It's Tuesday morning, sixteen hours since Imogen's flight landed and the sisters were reunited. Miranda can't remember a hug that has ever lasted longer than the one they shared in the arrivals area. It was the sort of hug that began tentatively, perhaps with the mutual acknowledgement of *Things have been shit, haven't they,* before tightening to incorporate the sentiment of, *I've missed you so much.* God, it had felt good; a real homecoming of a hug – right until the moment they drew apart and Imogen burst into tears anyway. 'My marriage is over,' she had sobbed, standing there in the echoing barn-like space of the airport, while irritated passengers swerved enormous brightly coloured suitcases around them. 'And I really, really loved him.'

Miranda had held her sister and rubbed her back, saying, 'I know you did' and 'You'll get through this' and 'You're going to be okay'. They'd eventually made it into a taxi for the hotel, where Miranda ordered them both room service and wine, there was a lot more crying and hugging, and then Imogen fell asleep for ten hours straight.

This morning, the two of them have come to a yoga class in the hotel's cool airy fitness studio, Imogen's suggestion. So far, they've both given it their all throughout the sun saluta- tions, warrior poses and grim-faced balances, but now they're lying down in savasana, which is always Miranda's favourite bit. Later on, she's booked them facials and massages at the spa, then they might get in the car and go sightseeing. Alter- natively, they might lie by the pool and soak up some rays. It's Imogen's call. Miranda wants her sister to find peace here, as she has done. To get away from everything.

Ting! Ting! At the front of the class, Tatiana is gently clinking two little brass cymbals together and telling everyone to wiggle their fingers and toes, open their eyes and move, slowly, slowly, back into a seated position.

'Thank you very much,' she says, once they've all intoned, 'Namaste' and the class is over. She has the body of an Olym- pian in a bright pink Lycra bralet and shorts, with her long black hair swept back in a ponytail. '*Efcharisto*. Hold on to the peace and serenity you have felt just now for as long as you can. Be grateful to your bodies for what they have done for you. Have a wonderful day.'

Miranda and Imogen smile at one another as they wipe down their yoga mats and return them to the pile at the back of the room. 'I needed that,' Imogen says. 'Can we do the same tomorrow, do you think?'

'Of course we can,' Miranda replies. 'Hey, and I'll take you paddleboarding too, one day, now that I'm such an expert. You'll love it.'

Before Imogen can answer, a middle-aged woman has appeared in front of them. 'Sorry to intrude,' she says. 'But . . . Are you Miranda Vallance?'

Miranda's serenity starts to dissipate immediately. She isn't wearing one of her wigs today, having imagined the embarrassment of it falling off during a downward dog pose, and she tucks a strand of her own hair behind one ear self-consciously. 'Um, yes,' she says guardedly.

Imogen cuts in, stepping forward so that she's marginally in front of Miranda, like a human shield. 'She is, but she's on holiday, so . . .' she says protectively, eyeing up the woman as if considering taking her down.

'Sorry — you're quite right, and you're probably sick of nosey parkers like me,' the woman replies, flushing and moving back. She's tall and dark-haired, a snake tattoo coiling around one arm. 'Just to say, I love *Amberly Emergency*, and I think you're really great in it. And I'm sorry that you've been so hounded lately. Including by me, right now.' She pulls an awkward face. 'Sorry,' she mumbles again.

'It's fine,' Miranda tells her. 'That's very nice of you. I appreciate it.' Gosh, check her out, being so magnanimous, she reflects, feeling amused. Perhaps it's because she won't have to put up with the dazzle of the spotlight for much longer, she thinks, as she and Imogen head back to the room to shower and change. Yesterday, while she was waiting for Imogen's plane to land, she had a call from Helen saying that the *Amberley* team were extremely sorry about what had happened, and, under the circumstances, they would be happy to have Miranda return to the show as soon as was convenient.

In reply, Miranda had taken a deep breath, and then said, that was nice of them but she'd decided to leave anyway. 'The break has made me realise that I'd rather do something different,' she told Helen. 'Maybe go back to the theatre for a while.'

'That was gutsy of you,' Imogen had commented when she mentioned it over dinner last night. 'Are you sure?'

'I'm sure,' Miranda said, knowing it was the right decision. The money won't be as good, nor will the certainty of having a role in a long-running series, but she's looking forward to that particular rush of adrenalin that comes from walking out onto a stage again. Playing to an audience every night, being there in the moment, fully alive. She can't wait.

She loops an arm through Imogen's as they walk towards the accommodation block. 'May I just remind you,' she says in a low voice, 'that you are in charge of a two-tonne killing machine: your butthole. I heard that downward dog fart in yoga, lady, and don't even think about denying it.'

Imogen bursts out laughing. 'That was not me,' she protests. 'It wasn't! That was probably your weird super-fan having some kind of orgasm over you.'

'Denial is a dreadful thing, Imogen,' Miranda teases, holding on to her sister a little tighter as Imogen tries to wrestle her arm away and push her. 'A dreadful, dreadful thing.'

Oh, but it's so nice, being under the warm Greek sunshine,

having a stupid play-fight with her sister again, after the bad times they've both gone through. She finds herself thinking of the two little girls on the beach in Assos, the bigger one hauling up the little one, the two of them holding hands as they rushed back to the safety of the sand. *She'll always be your sister,* she remembers Gramps saying in his text, and joy overwhelms her. Thank God, she thinks. Thank God for that.

Chapter Fifty-One

Nelly

Over dinner that first Saturday night, Nelly and Alexander had caught up on the intervening decades, and it was as if they'd never been apart. How could it be that two people were able to pick up the threads of a conversation put on hold over thirty years ago and resume it so seamlessly? But there were no awkward pauses or talking over one another whatsoever; they'd slotted back into their old rhythms of speech with ease.

She quickly learned that, soon after her departure, he had gone on to marry Sofia, and they'd had two sons and a daughter together. Their marriage, however, had never been strong. 'We were very different people,' he told Nelly diplomatically, 'who wanted different things. She wanted a big house, nice clothes, gadgets in the kitchen, a fancy car . . .' He spread his hands and shook his head. 'These things were not important to me.'

'No,' said Nelly, remembering him tanned and barefoot at

358

the wheel of his boat. How lightly he had moved through life with his few possessions back then.

'We had a small house in Vathy but it was not enough for her. She wanted us to move to Patras, so that I could work for her father's company and we would have more money. But my heart has always been with the sea. I am an islander, you know? Not a city person.' He shrugged, a movement that spoke of many arguments, a gradual grinding down of the soul. 'What can I say, we went to live in Patras because I wanted her to be happy, but then I was *un*happy. Me in an office ...' He ran a finger absent-mindedly around the collar of his shirt, as if remembering the constraints of the tie that had been knotted there, the suit he had worn. 'It was not a good fit, Nelly.'

'I can imagine,' she'd replied. 'Not much of a sea breeze in an office.'

'Exactly! And every day the same desk, the same telephone, the same papers to read and sign. No adventures, no horizon. I was like a dog chained up in a yard, I hated it.'

The evening was warm, the sun setting, syrupy and golden, into the sea, while melancholic guitar music played from a speaker above their heads. They were sitting out on the veranda of a fish restaurant Alexander claimed to be the best on the island, and it might well have been for all Nelly knew, but the food was wasted on her that night. Being with him was so absorbing, she barely tasted a single bite. What a pleasure it was to be able to gaze into that handsome face of his, to enjoy his deep, sudden laugh once more. What a thrill to be close enough that their feet occasionally met beneath the table, that their hands bumped against the other's reaching into the bread basket. Being able to smell the clean soapy scent of his skin, conscious of his knees mere centimetres from hers ... it was doing strange things to her body. Her breath felt a little shallow, her blood hot as it pumped through her veins; she found herself becoming aware of the space between her legs, remembering what it had felt like when ...

Stop it, Nelly, she had to tell herself. That was a long, long time ago, back when she was impressionable and wildly romantic. She had put that self away since then, turned the key. Was she imagining it, though, or was the lock now loosening, threatening to release with every passing minute? Or was that the wine going straight to her head? 'I can't bear to think of you feeling like a chained dog,' she blurted out. 'That's awful.'

He smiled at her but it was not a happy smile, more one of defeat. 'It was not a good time,' he said gruffly. 'I loved my children and tried to protect them, but Sofia and I argued every day. We never should have married in the first place.' He splashes more wine into her glass, then his. 'In fact ... we needn't have married at all.'

It took Nelly a moment to understand what he was implying. 'She was pregnant though, wasn't she? That was why you had to marry her?'

He stared into his glass, swirled the contents around. 'That was what she said,' he replied, and she could sense an anger in him beneath the surface. 'And we married very quickly. It was my duty, I thought. But no baby ever came. She said there had been a ... a ... I don't know the word in English.'

'A miscarriage? She lost the baby?'

'Yes, yes, that was what she said. Was it true? I don't know. Did she lie and trap me? I don't know.' There followed a bleak moment between them when Nelly remembered her agony at their enforced parting, how she'd wept for days on end. Had it really all been for nothing?

'Things could have been so different,' she said, emotions knotting inside her.

He looked her in the eye and her heart thumped. 'Yes,' he said. 'I would have married you instead, if you'd wanted that too.'

'Oh, Alexander,' she'd said, her voice somewhere between a laugh and a cry. Did he mean that? Because she'd have married him like a shot back then.

'In a different life, hey? In a different universe, we kept on sailing and we were together. Yes?' He crinkled his eyes at her; he was joking, she told herself, but she thought she could detect some regret there for him, as well. 'But in this universe ... it was not to be.'

She had to clutch the sides of the chair beneath the table to try to control her emotions. 'No,' she said quietly, reminding herself that in this universe she did at least have her two boys, and he had his three children, even if they hadn't had one another. His hands were clasped in front of him. She couldn't see if he was still wearing a wedding ring. 'But you and Sofia – you worked things out?' she ventured. 'You're still together?'

'No, no,' he said. 'We separated ... my God, a long time ago. Fifteen years ago? When our youngest son moved out and it was just the two of us. There was no longer a reason to be together. She stayed in Patras, I returned to Ithaca.'

'You left the office job?'

'Of course!' He laughed, his whole face lighting up. 'The shoes, the . . . what do you say, briefcase? Yes, the briefcase, the ties . . . I give to my sons. Take them. Have them. I go to Ithaca, I buy a boat. I am happy again, with my tours, my customers. It is a small life, but it is *my* life. And a good life.'

'I'm glad you got away,' she said. 'Really glad.'

'Yes, and me too,' he said. 'But that's enough talking about me. How are you? Tell me your story now. Have you been happy, my Nelly? Was the world kind to you?'

She told him about Frank, about the boys, keeping her voice bright and businesslike, and his eyebrows shot up as she mentioned Frank's celebrity status.

'I will ask my sister if she has heard of him,' he said with interest. 'What did you say his name was again?'

'Ahh – well . . .' Nelly faltered, wanting to skirt around the darker moments, the recent news stories that had exploded their marriage. 'I'm not sure his cookbooks were translated into Greek,' she went on after a moment, hating the thought of Alexander finding gossip about her husband – and her – online. 'Like the Greeks need anybody to teach *them* how to cook!'

He smiled. 'Still, a long marriage, good sons, success – that sounds perfect,' he responded. 'But your husband . . . Where is he tonight?'

'He . . . He has gone home,' she said after a moment. So much for keeping things light and cheery. Then again, why pretend? This time next week she'd be back in England, trying to navigate a new life there as a single woman; she needed to start adjusting to the situation, constructing a revised narrative. 'To be honest, I don't think we are going to be married any more,' she said bluntly. 'It's over.'

His gaze was compassionate. 'Ahh, I am sorry to hear that,' he said gently. 'And I am sorry if my question made you feel uncomfortable. Perhaps—'

Before he could get any further, the waiter came to take away their empty plates and asked if they would like to see the dessert menu.

'Yes, please,' Nelly replied, if only because she didn't want the evening to end just yet. 'What were you about to say when he interrupted?' she asked once they were alone once more. 'You said "Perhaps" . . .'

He smiled at her, his features softening in the dusky light. His eyes gleamed, dark and liquid, and she felt a quickening inside her, a deep magnetic attraction towards him. 'I was going to say, perhaps we should not speak of the people we married any more, yes?'

'It's okay,' she said. 'Really – I'm okay. Better for seeing you, anyway. Tell me about your new boat,' she went on, if only because it was so pleasant to hear him talk. 'Is it like the *Miaoulis*? Where have you been lately?'

They talked and talked, the conversation moving to happier times, the jigsaw pieces of their lives that they were most proud of (their children, his grandchildren), then they reminisced about some of the trips they'd taken together, although their one night of passion was carefully avoided. They ordered slices of honey cheesecake and more wine, both of which were delicious. It was only when one of the waiting staff began

363

sweeping up around the tables that she realised the restaurant had become empty, the other diners having long since
departed. The sky was inky black, with a cool breeze blowing
off the sea now, the moonlight catching the tops of the waves
so that they glinted a dark silver as they rushed into shore.

'What a perfect evening,' she said, as they set off in the taxi
that would drop her first at her hotel, then take him back to
his boat, moored at Poros. 'Thank you, Alexander. It has been
wonderful to see you again.'

And that might have been that, the end of the story, the
closing of the loop. Except that there was suddenly a new
charged silence between them in the back of the cab, as she
felt – and perhaps he did too – that the alternative universe,
where the two of them had sailed off together for a happy
ever after, was pressing meaningfully against their current
reality. Did this have to be the end already? All she knew was
that it was too soon, she wasn't ready to completely shut the
door. 'Well,' she went on, 'if you're ever over in England ...'

'How long are you here for?' he asked at the same moment,
the words rushing out of him. They turned towards one
another, the dark streets gliding by outside, Elton John
singing a ballad from the speaker. 'Maybe I could see you
tomorrow as well?' he suggested, his face intermittently
bathed in yellow from the streetlights they passed. 'If you are
not busy? Now that I have met you again, I ...' He trailed
off, but his hand found hers on the seat between them, his
fingers curling around hers.

Her heart seemed to stutter in her chest. No, she was not
busy, she managed to say, her hand still in his. Yes, she would

love to see him. He proposed dinner at the taverna nearest her hotel, and she agreed instantly. Well, why not? She was only here for a few days longer, she might as well make the most of her time. The taxi pulled up at the hotel and he let go of her hand and got out of the car so as to open her door. They hesitated, then embraced, and she walked through reception and back to her room feeling light as air.

That second night, the same thing. Another wonderful dinner, another long, enjoyable conversation, so engrossing in fact that, once again, the taverna staff were closing up around them before they knew it, and still they had so much to say. He'd walked her back up the hill to the hotel, accompanied by the soft hooting of owls somewhere in the darkness, and then, saying goodnight to her at the hotel reception, he took her hand and kissed it. Her skin had tingled all over, a great longing rising within her. 'I don't suppose,' she heard herself saying, 'you are free tomorrow as well? Now that we've found each other again, I . . .' She'd laughed self-consciously. 'I can't bear to say goodbye yet.'

He had pulled her in for an embrace and she closed her eyes, her head against his shoulder, breathing in his lovely, familiar scent. Oh, she still liked him so much. Yes, she was massively on the rebound, yes, this was the wrong time to start indulging in romantic feelings about another man and yes, she knew this was all a huge distraction, a smokescreen she was hiding behind, so as to avoid having to look at the mess of her real life, but . . . But . . .

'I have passengers booked for a trip tomorrow,' he said regretfully, releasing her from the embrace. 'But I could take you out on my boat on Tuesday? If you like? We can pretend we are young again, just for one day.'

It was the perfect answer. The best idea of all. 'I would love that,' she told him, smiling up at his dear face, still so handsome with his salt-and-pepper hair, the lines around his eyes. 'Let's do it.'

And so, this morning, it feels like old times as he holds out his hand to help her on board the *Anassa*, his yacht. 'Does *Anassa* mean anything?' Nelly asks curiously.

'It means "breath",' he tells her. 'And it is also an old word for "queen".' He grins, putting his hand to his heart. 'The perfect name for her, because sailing is my life, my breath — and this boat, she is a real queen, I think.'

The *Anassa* is way more modern than the *Miaoulis*, with its white painted deck and sleek white body, but there are a few home comforts too, that add character: the pictures of Alexander's children and grandchildren stuck to the fridge door in the small galley kitchen, the soft blue cushions on the benches, the battered leather binocular case slung from a peg in the cockpit. 'It's lovely,' she says, once he's given her the tour and they're up on deck. 'It's perfect, Alexander.'

He smiles at her, pride in his eyes. 'So. Where would you like to go to, Nelly?' he asks. 'Tell me, and I will take you there.'

'Will you take me back to Ithaca?' she says shyly. 'I'd love to see it properly. You must know all the best places.'

His smile only broadens. 'I do,' he says. 'And I would love to show you them. To Ithaca, then!'

She can't find the words that could possibly describe how

good it feels as he loosens the mooring rope, as he returns to the wheel and starts the engine – only that as they sail towards Ithaca, with a warm breeze tousling her hair, there is nowhere on earth she would rather be right now. The only danger, she thinks, is that it will be the most enormous wrench to have to leave him again, now that she has found him. Because when Alexander had asked her earlier where she would like to go, the very last place on her mind was 'back home'.

Chapter Fifty-Two

Claudia

There was a breathless wait at the hospital for Claudia, Andreas and Lili while Dimitris was examined by the doctors. By then, he had regained consciousness at least – in fact, he briefly came round in the ambulance, where Claudia was holding his hand, and he'd stared at her, bewildered, saying groggily, '*Agapi mou*,' before his eyes rolled back in his head and he was out again. The blood pounded in her ears at the endearment – 'my love', it means; 'my darling' – as the ambulance thundered on towards the hospital. *My love.* Had he actually seen *her* as he murmured those words, or was he confusing her with someone else entirely?

The bad news: his left fibula had snapped during the fall and needed surgery, plus he had the most enormous bump on his head, and severe bruising to his face, forearms and knees. The good news: after multiple scans, the doctors were able to confirm that there appeared to be no permanent damage to the brain, nor any bleeding there, as previously suspected. 'In other words,' Lili said to Claudia, as they sat beside Dimitris' bed, watching him sleep, 'he is the luckiest man on the island.'

Claudia, who'd been valiantly keeping it together until then, nodded, fighting back tears. 'I think we are pretty lucky too,' she said, gazing at Dimitris' poor battered face. His eyelids trembled briefly, perhaps with some vivid painkiller dream or other, and she found herself longing to soothe him, wanting to gently place her hand on his arm, murmur soft words of comfort. *I'm here. You're not alone.* She gripped her hands in her lap instead, too self-conscious in front of his son and daughter. Keep it together, she told herself.

It was still catching up with her, though, the awful shock of finding him that way, her mind repeatedly slamming back to the moment she'd first seen him on the ground. Imagine if she hadn't been inspired to seek him out after speaking to Nelly! She could so easily have cycled off home without knowing he had been injured. He could have lain there all night in the cold and dark. Her emotions swelled agonisingly at the image of him alone and in pain, and Lili caught her eye as if reading her mind.

'Thank you for finding him,' she said, her brown eyes steady on Claudia's. She's in her early twenties, with full lips and long dark hair scraped back from her face. A gold cross glimmered at her throat, a tattoo of a rose adorning her ankle. 'I am glad you did.'

'Why did he even go up the ladder at all?' Andreas wanted to know. As soon as the consultant had ruled out any significant brain injury, Andreas' relief had quickly turned to exasperation at his father's recklessness. 'Why does he always have to do everything himself?'

Lili had shot her brother a look. 'Because that's just Dad, right?' she'd said. 'He still thinks he is a superhero,' she added to Claudia. 'No problem too big! Except . . . for this roof, perhaps. His downfall.' She pulled a face at her own unintended pun. 'Sorry, Papa.'

It had been a strange, dreamlike Saturday night, the three of them at Dimitris' bedside. Claudia enjoyed getting to know Lili and Andreas though, and picked up that Lili had the same determined, practical nature as her father, while Andreas was more sensitive and emotional. They both adored him, clearly, fussing about him if he muttered or groaned in his sleep, their eyes constantly flicking over to him and back. Eventually the nurse came and told them that visiting hours were over. Someone would update them after his surgery in the morning, she said, but now they had to leave.

Andreas thanked Claudia and hugged his sister before heading off to meet friends, but Lili had lingered at the entrance to the hospital. 'You and my dad . . .' she said delicately, with a sidelong glance at Claudia. 'Is there anything I should know about?'

'No,' Claudia replied, perhaps a little too vehemently, hoping her face wasn't betraying her. A heavily pregnant woman accompanied by a terrified-looking man made their way past at that moment, the man shouting urgently for help, and Claudia stepped back, her cheeks still burning from Lili's question. 'No, we're just friends,' she said. 'Nothing more than that.'

Lili nodded, apparently satisfied with the answer, and they'd gone their separate ways, but as Claudia waited for a taxi to take her home, she had to acknowledge that she had totally downplayed her feelings to the younger woman. When she'd knelt beside Dimitris earlier, desperately trying to find a pulse, she had felt herself becoming swallowed up by a dark terror that she might have lost him. What she felt for him was far stronger than mere friendship, she knew that. But how could she have said as much to his daughter? She was nothing but a cliché, falling in love with her boss. She had to keep a lid on her feelings, try to play it cooler.

By Sunday evening, Dimitris was deemed fit to leave the hospital. The surgery had gone well and he was given a special boot to wear, plus crutches, although he'd been advised to rest as much as possible for the next week or two. His bruising appeared to be travelling through all the shades of the rainbow – currently yellow and green – and his head was tender and sore where it had hit the ground, so he'd been issued with some heavy-duty painkillers from the pharmacy to see him through the coming days. He would stay at Lili's ground-floor flat for the time being – 'No arguments,' she told him sternly. Claudia, Lili and Andreas were going to take it in turns to look after him until he was able to manage himself.

'Please, don't feel obliged,' Lili had said to Claudia privately. 'We know you have your job, and your own life – and that Dad is your manager! You might not want to look after him, we understand that.'

'He is also my friend,' Claudia had replied. There was that

blush again. 'And if I borrow a laptop from the hotel, I can work anywhere. If you don't mind me being in your flat, anyway.'

'Of course I don't! Thank you. And thanks again for being there for him,' Lili had said, giving her an impulsive hug. 'It's a big help for us.'

And so a routine has evolved where Lili sets out for the bakery at five in the morning, leaving her dad still asleep in her spare room. Andreas lets himself in around seven to help Dimitris up, then makes his breakfast, before he hands over to Claudia at nine. Andreas then goes to work, and Claudia keeps Dimitris company until Lili clocks off and comes home at three in the afternoon.

For the first few days, Claudia's involvement with her patient was pretty minimal. Plagued by headaches, Dimitris would stay in bed most of the morning while she worked quietly at the kitchen table, only stopping if he needed a drink or some lunch. But by Wednesday, he was already feeling much better, the bruising and swelling subsiding, and since then they've taken to sitting out in the small courtyard garden together, him hobbling out to sit with his healing leg raised up on a stool. In truth, Claudia enjoys fussing around him, tending to him. She likes rearranging cushions behind his back so that he's comfortable, she likes the appreciative exhalation he makes when she brings him a coffee. She definitely likes having the weight of his body against hers whenever she helps him get around, although she does her best to think chaste thoughts during those moments. He is usually so capable, so competent, that it feels like a privilege to be able to look after him for a change, especially when he has always been there for her. It's as if a new, more personal layer is being added to their relationship, a different kind of closeness, that comes from seeing someone you care about very much in new, more vulnerable lights: asleep, in discomfort, less able.

It's merely an interlude though, a brief bubble in time – and she's aware that he, for one, is struggling with the enforced limitations. The word 'patient' only really applies to him as a noun right now; Lili and Andreas complain frequently that he is dreadfully grumpy, although he seems to save his better behaviour for Claudia. 'Next time you find my dad unconscious on the ground?' Andreas growls in exasperation on Thursday morning as Claudia arrives for their handover. 'Feel free to leave him there. Did you hear that, Papa? I'm telling Claudia not to bother next time you fall off a roof!'

'Don't listen to him,' Dimitris tells Claudia as they take up their usual places in the courtyard – him in the sunshine, propped up by cushions, her in a shady corner, her laptop on a small patio table. The courtyard is full of fragrant shrubs in pots, a miniature haven for bees and butterflies. 'He and his sister like to say I am a bad patient, always moaning, but it is not true. Ungrateful, Andreas called me this morning. Too bossy, Lili said last night.' His lips twitch in a smile. 'Okay, so maybe they are a little bit right,' he concedes, holding up his thumb and forefinger a tiny distance apart. 'But it is very boring, waiting for your own body to heal itself. I don't like to wait, I like to *do*.'

'Yes,' says Claudia. 'I know. But that's why you were up on the spa roof, remember? Too much doing – and falling off – and not enough waiting.' *Don't ever scare me like that again,* she thinks, but arches an eyebrow teasingly to mask her true feelings. 'Do you think, just maybe, that there's a lesson to learn here?'

He laughs, looking rather shamefaced. 'Yes, all right,' he says. 'Perhaps.'

'No more roof-mending,' she tells him. 'And by the way, Danilo and Antoni finished the job for you. The roof is secure, they've dried out the plaster inside and will be repainting the ceiling next month. Jasmine and Lucia have moved back in – everything is just about back to normal.'

He nods, drinking his coffee. 'I *am* grateful,' he says after a moment. 'Whatever my son might say, however my daughter might scold me . . . I am grateful.' He frowns, running a finger round the rim of a large planter nearby, full of bushy lavender. 'And listen, you don't have to keep coming here every day. I know it is not really that convenient for you. I can probably manage on my own now, so—'

'It's fine,' she interrupts him, switching on her laptop and angling the screen to avoid the bright sunlight. 'Honestly. You're not *that* demanding, compared to some of the guests we've had. Besides, coming here to work . . . I like it. I'd miss having Lili's pastries and bread every day for lunch if I was at the hotel.'

He laughs. 'And that is all that you would miss?'

She stiffens in her seat, busying herself with her computer log-in. Of *course* she would miss him, she thinks, feeling her face flame. Ordinarily, when both of them are working at the hotel, their conversations tend to be small, businesslike slices, focusing on what needs doing in a particular situation. Spending so much time together in this way, they've been able to let conversations unroll at a leisurely pace, and open up about their lives rather than merely talking shop. She didn't know until yesterday, for instance, that he loves nature documentaries on TV. That he played bass guitar in a punk band that travelled all over Europe in the late nineties. That when he was fourteen, his little brother died in a car accident right beside him. She has also learned every detail of his face; the creases around his eyes, the faint silvery scar on his jaw, the distinct ways his mouth will twitch in amusement or disapproval or pain. It's like being given special access to a dossier of information about a person, and every single page only makes her like him even more.

Not that she's about to blurt out anything so personal, obviously. 'Yes,' she says, demurely. 'That is all I would miss. Why, have I forgotten something important?'

He lifts a shoulder, a strange half-smile on his face. Their eyes meet and hold there for a few heady seconds, a peculiar new silence descending. Claudia starts to feel flustered. What's happening between them? Is she imagining it, or . . . ?

She can't bear the tension for another second. 'Anyway, the season's coming to an end, so the hotel's pretty quiet,' she goes on, staring at her laptop and clicking busily between tabs, her heart pounding all the while. What did that smile mean? 'We've got . . . let's see . . . over thirty checkouts tomorrow, and after that we're down to minimum numbers. So you timed this little holiday of yours perfectly.'

She can feel his eyes still on her and it makes her skin prickle, but she daren't look at him again because she's not sure what she'll find in his face.

'I never thanked you,' he says after a moment, 'for finding me that day. What were you doing down there by the beauty shed anyway?'

'I was looking for you,' she says. *My love,* she hears him say in the ambulance again, and the memory of that startling moment paints her cheeks an even deeper red. He was probably hallucinating, wasn't he? He didn't know what he was saying. Why, then, has she been unable to forget it?

'Oh yeah?' he replies. If he's noticed her blushes, he's doing a good job of pretending he hasn't. 'What for? Was something wrong?'

She sighs, unable to meet his gaze. 'No, nothing was wrong,' she says, reaching down and fiddling with the strap of her sandal.

'Something good, then?' he prompts. 'Some news?'

'Not really *news,*' she says, feeling cornered, uncomfortable. Her heart thumps. *Do it,* she tells herself. *Come on.* 'Um ...' she adds, prevaricating desperately. Damn it, she can't think of a single plausible reason that she was going to find him, other than the truth. 'If you really must know, I wanted to ask you something.'

He sets his cup down on the table, suddenly serious. 'Claudia – are you leaving? You've found another job?'

She almost laughs at how wrong he is. 'No! I'm not going

anywhere,' she splutters. 'I love my job. I love – working at the hotel. It's nothing like that. I was actually—' She breaks off, losing her nerve, then catches his eye and feels that connection between them again. It's almost as if he's willing her on to say what she wants to. *Run towards the adventure,* she remembers Nelly advising.

'I was going to ask if you ...' She swallows. *Keep going.* 'If you maybe wanted to go for a drink some time.' Her heart thumps and she types hurriedly on the keyboard, absolute gibberish with spelling mistakes galore, but anything to cover up how awkward she feels.

'A drink?' he repeats. 'With you?'

Oh God. What has she done? Why didn't she keep her stupid mouth shut? 'I mean, not like *that,*' she blusters hurriedly, with a little laugh, but he's already speaking again and doesn't seem to hear her.

'You know,' he says, 'Lili, she was asking the other week: Papa, why don't you start dating again? She wanted me to sign up to some terrible *app,* to put my *photo* on there, to start meeting random women for *drinks* and *dinner ...*'

He looks so appalled she has to stifle a laugh, but in the next moment she turns cold inside because it's sounding very much as if he's about to give her the brush-off, to stamp his great plastic boot on her burgeoning hope. Has he been dating someone all along? 'Okay, it's fine if you don't want to,' she says quickly, mortified that she could have been so stupid. He's her boss, after all. What was she thinking?

'But the problem was, the person I would like to go out

for drinks and dinner with ... it's someone I work with,' he goes on. 'Which makes everything a lot more complicated.'

A rush of hope fires up inside her but she does her best to extinguish it. For all she knows, he's talking about someone else entirely. 'Right,' she says in a strangled-sounding voice. 'I see.'

'Because I don't ever want to be that man who puts a female employee in an uncomfortable position with that kind of attention. Those men who treat their staff like trinkets for them to pick up and put down ... that is not me!' He bangs his fist against his chest, possibly on a bruise, because he winces. 'Ow.'

Still none the wiser, Claudia stares at a pot of white star-shaped flowers nearby, which a couple of bees are bumbling around. Her head is jangling. 'Right,' she says again, wishing he would get to the point. *Does* he mean her? The longer this goes on, the more uncertain she's becoming.

'And therefore I am in this situation where I have to hope she feels the same way but I don't say anything,' he goes on. 'But now ...' He gives a sudden laugh and she glances warily at him. 'Now *you* ask *me,* and ...' He laughs again. 'This is a very long way of saying yes, Claudia. Yes, I would love to go for a drink with you. Maybe you can buy me a drink, I can buy you dinner? Then we are fair.'

This is all happening too fast for Claudia to unwind. Did she mishear, or ... ? 'Wait – so this woman at the hotel you like ... that's me?' she has to check, reverting to English in case she's having a severe translation malfunction.

'But of course!' he cries, apparently incredulous that she needs to ask. 'Of course it is you. Who else would it be?'

'I ...' They stare at one another. 'You like me,' she says, half-disbelievingly. 'Is that what you're saying? You like me?'

'Yes, Claudia! You! Why are you looking at me like that?'

She laughs too, feeling vaguely hysterical by now. 'Because you've got a head injury?' she says, joking to cover up her inner turmoil. 'And because I'm out of practice at ... well, at this sort of thing,' she admits. 'It's been a while.'

'For me too! Years. But by the way, I felt like this before I banged my head. Way before, Claudia.'

She swallows, trying to take in what he's saying, what this means. It feels as if a filter has swung across her vision, changing everything. 'Also,' she hears herself confess, 'because I like you too.' There. She's finally told him. Their eyes meet. 'I really like you,' she repeats, her voice thick with feeling.

The look between them is so intense, it's as if a whole other conversation is taking place. *I want this,* she tells him with her eyes. She's pretty sure he's saying it right back to her.

'We are both a bit ... what is the word in English? Rusty, I think,' he goes on. 'But we can try, can't we? We can figure this out between us, I'm sure. You, me, a nice bar, and—'

'Why wait until we're in a nice bar?' she interrupts, because suddenly it's impossible to hold back any more. And they have wasted so much time already! She smiles at him, a giddy recklessness surging through her. 'I'd hate to take advantage of someone with a broken ankle,' she goes on, rising from her chair before she can stop herself, 'but ...'

'Take advantage,' he commands, putting his hands up in surrender as she comes towards him. 'Right now. I insist. Boss's orders.'

She has never been happier to obey an instruction as she leans over him, her lips meet his and he puts his arms round her.

Making up for lost time, she thinks joyfully, as they begin kissing in earnest − tick, tick, tick.

Chapter Fifty-Three

The Troll

A few days later, two female detectives knock at the door of a small terraced house in Leighton Buzzard, England. From where they're standing, they see the curtain move at the front window, then the light from a TV screen go blank. They look at one another. 'Gary Blackmore?' one of them calls, knocking again. 'We know you're in there, Gary, we've just seen you switch your telly off. Open the door, please.'

There's no sound from within. 'Little toe-rag,' the second detective mutters. They're very keen to have a word with Gary Blackmore, even if the feeling doesn't seem to be mutual. A harassment issue with his ex-wife put him on their radar initially, earning him a warning, but from new evidence it now looks as if he has been conducting a widespread campaign of misogynistic attacks, online and in person, on various women he falsely believes to have wronged him. 'I'll bloody wrong him in a minute, if he doesn't answer this door,' says the second detective. She was once unlucky enough to have an abusive boyfriend herself; she has absolutely zero patience for Gary and his ilk.

The first detective knocks harder on the door, loud enough to get a few neighbours looking out of their windows. 'Let us in, Gary,' she shouts through the letter box. 'Otherwise, the whole street's going to hear what we've got to say to you, and trust me, mate – you don't want that.'

They hear footsteps, then the door opens. A sullen, piggy-eyed man stands there in tracksuit bottoms and a stained, baggy T-shirt. 'Gary Blackmore?' says the first detective with a steely expression. 'I'm DS Kumar and this is DS McLeish. We'd like a little chat.'

Chapter Fifty-Four

Everyone

'Dearly beloved,' says the funeral officiator, a petite woman in her forties with a yellow-blonde bob and large round glasses. 'We are gathered here today to pay tribute to our late friend, aunt, godmother and colleague, Evelyn Mary Chambers.'

It's twelve days later and Miranda is back in London, at a small Victorian church in Bloomsbury, for Evelyn's memorial service. It's the end of September now, and a coolness has set in across the country. The leaves are turning yellow and ochre on the trees, the evenings are becoming dark far too early, and the shops are filling up with winter coats and boots. September has been a pretty pivotal month this year, she thinks, as a matronly woman plays a sonorous chord on the church organ and the congregation rises to sing 'All Things Bright and Beautiful'.

This hymn always reminds her of primary school, sitting cross-legged in the hall for morning assembly, keeping an eye out for her siblings in the younger classes. It feels all the sweeter to sing it now, knowing that she has her sister back again, a restoration that is most definitely a bright and beautiful thing. Imogen has a tough road ahead for a while, as she, Felix and a bunch of lawyers begin the process of unpicking their relationship, but Miranda is determined to be a key player in her sister's support squad for as long as it takes. Their days on Kefalonia were healing: full of yoga, swimming, good food and long conversations into the night. Since they returned, other than going along to a few auditions for various plays (fingers crossed), Miranda's been camped out at Imogen's, keeping her company in the evenings. Whenever Imogen comes back from work, it's to a tidy flat, a box-set suggestion and plenty of wine in the fridge. Miranda has even cooked for them on occasion; a vertigo-inducing new height of domesticity for a person whose evening meals have previously been largely restaurant dinners, takeaways or microwave ready meals. 'Watch out, I'm getting used to this,' Imogen warned the other evening when Miranda produced a steaming dish of macaroni cheese from the oven like a conjuror. 'I might not let you leave again.'

Gosh, 'All Things Bright and Beautiful' is a long old song, Miranda thinks as they return to the chorus for the fourth time. She's seated towards the back of the church, the scent of lilies and lit candles hanging in the air, and you can tell that many of the mourners are trained musicians because there are a lot of very good singers around her, some even singing harmony parts.

A big screen has been rigged up at the front, with a slide-show of pictures of Evelyn that changes every few seconds. It's lovely to see the black and white images of her as a teenager with a great sheaf of dark hair tied back in a ponytail, her eyes mischievous. There she is on a bike with a university scarf around her neck; practising her cello, eyes closed, head tilted; at her graduation wearing a gown and mortarboard, a jubilant expression on her face. Now the pictures are proceeding through her career – professional photographs with an orchestra, some taken mid-performance, others during curtain calls. Evelyn is turning from a student into a young woman and on into middle age. Somebody has typed captions and added them to the images, and Miranda feels pride swelling inside for her talented friend, who played in so many cities and countries. Amsterdam . . . Vienna . . . Paris . . . Berlin. *And of course, the Barbican,* the last caption reads, showing a picture of her playing a solo on stage, bent over her cello as if completely at one with her instrument.

How wonderful it is to think of the many thousands of people who heard Evelyn play throughout her career, Miranda reflects as they reach the final line of the hymn and the organist thunders to a close. All the lives Evelyn touched with her music. She thinks back to the conversation they had on this subject – 'I bet loads of people have fallen in love, listening to you play,' she'd told her. 'Marriages proposed, babies conceived . . .'

Evelyn had seemed tickled by the idea, even if Miranda had been exaggerating for effect, but now, seeing so many photos of so many concerts, she can't help thinking she'd hit on something true.

The music ends and everyone sits down in their pews once

more. 'We're now going to hear a few words from Oliver Brewer, Evelyn's godson,' the officiator announces.

Ahh, the famous Godsend, Miranda thinks, peering with interest as a tall man in a good charcoal suit walks up to the front. The nerd himself. Except that when he turns at the lectern and she takes in his shock of dark brown hair and thick eyebrows, plus fantastic cheekbones, she has to admit that he's actually pretty good-looking. *Your star-crossed lover,* Evelyn pipes up in her head, just as a ray of sunshine beams directly through one of the stained-glass windows to his left, casting him in perfect golden light. It's enough to make Miranda think Evelyn's backstage somewhere, pulling a few spiritual strings. *Yes, all right, I see him,* she thinks in amusement. *You were right: very nice. Happy?*

The Godsend takes a moment to put on a pair of glasses, then gazes out at the congregation. 'Hello,' he says. 'Thank you all for coming today when I'm sure you're still feeling as devastated as I am. My godmother Evelyn – or Aunty Evil, as I called her; possibly the biggest misnomer ever – was truly one of a kind.' His voice is deep and rich, the sort that could make a killing in voiceover gigs, thinks Miranda, imagining him seductively reading advertising copy for ice cream and having half the female population rushing immediately to stock up.

'Evelyn took her godmotherly duties very seriously,' he goes on. 'Although "serious" is not really a word I associate with her, I have to say.' A small laugh ripples around the church. 'I always had the best fun with her. She took me ice-skating at Somerset House every Christmas, she talked my parents into letting me have a guinea pig, and frequently took me out for lunch or tea, kindly turning a blind eye when I inevitably ordered chips, followed by a knickerbocker glory, and never ate any vegetables.' Another laugh. 'In fact, we both loved knickerbocker glories. She used to pretend she thought they were called "knickerknocker glories" when she ordered them and we'd always corpse in giggles together.' He's smiling out at them all but you can see how sad he is to have lost his beloved godmother, Miranda notices, warming to him a little more. Okay, so he's not a total nerd, then.

'I could go on for hours listing memories about brilliant days out and treats and conversations I had with my glorious Aunty Evil,' continues the Godsend, 'but let me end by telling you about when I was being bullied at school in my teens, and feeling thoroughly miserable. I was in the middle of a French lesson when the school secretary came to the classroom and had a word with the teacher. Next thing I knew, the teacher was giving me a sympathetic look and telling me to pack up my things and leave with the secretary. All very mysterious until we got out into the corridor and the secretary said, in hushed tones, she was sorry to tell me that my Uncle Robert was in hospital, and that my godmother was going to take me to visit him.' A pause for comic effect. 'As I don't actually *have* an Uncle Robert, I was a bit confused – until I heard that Evie was involved, at which point I knew she had just cooked something up to get me out of there.' A big laugh now. 'Sure enough, there she was in her old Mini, and she proceeded to whisk me off to Brighton for the day. One of the best skives of my life.' Another laugh, everyone enjoying the story. 'We played on the Penny Falls, mooched around the Lanes together, and she bought me my first pair of Dr. Martens – good times. Then I told her about the latest bit of bullying,' he goes on, the entire congregation hanging on his every word. 'She was brilliant. Gave me a massive hug, bolstered me with a pep talk, and then the pair of us threw stones into the sea together, shouting . . . Well, I don't want to swear in church, but the ears of the boys who'd been giving me a hard time must really have been burning that day, put it like that.' More laughter. The audience loves him, Miranda thinks.

'She was there for me, that's what I'm saying. As I know she was there for so many other people here today. What an incredible, big-hearted, hilarious person she was. Thank you, Aunty Evil, for the knickerknocker glories, Snowy the guinea pig, poor old fictitious Uncle Robert, and everything else. I'm really going to miss you.'

Oh my God, thinks Miranda as he smiles rather self-consciously at everyone, removes his glasses and heads back to his seat. He is . . . He is pretty bloody great, on a first impression. *I've got to hand it to you, Evelyn,* she concedes. *Everything you said about him seems to stack up.*

An older woman is next to speak, a friend of Evelyn's who played first violin in the same London orchestra, and she gives a lovely speech about what a brilliant performer Evelyn was, as well as a dear, loyal friend. Miranda drifts off a little, distracted by thoughts of her own friendship with Bonnie, which she might just have resurrected. They had lunch together a week ago, and finally put Slap-gate to bed, before going on to the far more enjoyable business of slagging off Emma-Lou, the former *Amberley Emergency* publicist, as well as a proper gossip about the cast. 'I'm sorry,' Miranda said humbly once again as they eventually hugged goodbye. 'I've really missed you.'

'I've missed you too,' Bonnie replied. 'Sienna's got your old dressing room now and I can barely walk past the door without her pestering me with her thoughts on Uranus. Keep in touch, yeah?'

'You bet,' Miranda told her. She will, too. In the meantime, the newspapers seem to have lost interest in them both, thank goodness, and have moved on to a whole other scandal around a newsreader and his unusual peccadilloes. Maybe, just maybe, life can settle down again for a bit.

The funeral service – moving, uplifting and sincere – eventually comes to an end, and the church fills with the opening notes of some beautiful cello music that Miranda vaguely recognises. The members of the congregation wipe their eyes, some embracing each other as they start to make their way out into the autumn sunshine. Miranda stays seated for a minute longer, listening to the rise and fall of the cello, as people stream down the aisle. There's afternoon tea being served at some hall or other in St Pancras, and everyone seems quite keen to get over there in order to tuck in. Miranda is planning to drop by too, if only so that she can nobble one of the nephews and find out where Evelyn's ashes are to be scattered. *This might sound a bit odd,* she is planning to say, *but I did promise Evelyn something . . .*

'Hello,' says a voice, and she looks up to see that the Godsend is standing in the pew in front of hers, so tall and broad that it takes a moment for her gaze to travel up to his face. 'I'm Oliver,' he goes on, and all Miranda can think of is Evelyn twinkling at her and telling her, *I'll send him your way when you're ready.* 'You're Miranda, aren't you? Charles said you were with Evelyn at the end, and I just wanted to say thank you. That was so kind of you. We're all so glad that she wasn't alone.'

The lights overhead suddenly flicker in and out – faulty old wiring, perhaps? Or is that Evelyn meddling again? Whichever, the Godsend smells really good close up – peppery and masculine – and his skin is gorgeous. More pertinently, Miranda *does* actually feel ready to venture into a relationship again before long, funnily enough. All this time alone, and with Imogen, has given her a good new perspective about what's important.

She stands up, glad she is wearing her tailored black dress that cinches her in at all the right points. This feels like it might be a moment she will remember, as if life is about to make another of its switchback turns. She hopes so. She's up for this one. 'Hi,' she says. 'Yes, that's me. Good to meet you.'

They start walking out of the church together, out into the sunshine. 'By the way,' he says, clearing his throat, suddenly seeming bashful. 'Did she ever pass on a message from me? About seeing you in a Pinter play once?'

Many miles away from Bloomsbury, Nelly is gazing out at a different horizon: one that is wide, blue and seemingly endless. She and Alexander have embarked on a long trip together across the Ionian Sea towards Italy, where they plan to tour around the southern coastline, take in the sights of Sicily, and then – well, they haven't actually got as far as the 'and then', but she'd quite like to visit Sardinia or perhaps Sorrento or . . . 'Wherever you want,' Alexander keeps telling her. 'We're not in any hurry, are we?'

This is true. After so many years apart, they have come back together, found one another, and she feels as if she's come home, to this great pure love of theirs, in a way that has surpassed her wildest hopes. Is it terrible of her to feel this way so soon? It's not that the end of her marriage means nothing to her – it does, of course it does – but she has found herself swept up in the glory of being reunited with her first love, which turns out to be a miracle cure for sadness.

'It feels like we're in the most wonderful dream,' she had said to him, the first time the two of them went out on his boat together, when she could feel herself on the edge of possibly falling in love with him all over again. 'But we've got to be realistic, because this *is* going to come to an end, soon; we'll have to pick up our lives again, won't we?'

He had turned to her from where he stood at the wheel, steering them around the rocky coastline. 'Why must it come to an end though, Nelly?' was all he said. 'Give me one good reason.'

She'd looked at him, thinking about pedestrian things such as the plants that would need watering back home, the supermarket delivery she had booked to arrive the day after her flight, the post that would be piling up unanswered. All the silt of an ordinary life that can anchor you in a place. 'Because . . .' she'd said, her brain flashing up her diary where she'd pencilled in dinner with her sons next week, lunch with Lorraine and Jim the weekend after, her brother's sixty-fifth birthday party in October. The car needed its MOT, the utilities bills were due imminently, she'd had a text just yesterday about booking her flu jab sooner rather than later. 'Because ...' she began again, then shook her head. 'I can't.'

'I want to stay in the dream,' Alexander said. 'Me and you. Together again. Why not?'

The wind had dropped at that moment, with perfect timing, and as they looked at one another she could feel the old Nelly in her once more, the Nelly who had walked impulsively away from the check-in desk at Corfu airport, who yearned for adventures and the great unknown. 'I want that too,' she heard herself say. 'But—'

He did not allow the 'But' to proceed any further; he cut the boat's engine and pulled her towards him, his lips finding hers. And truly, time must have somehow flattened in on itself, because it felt exactly the same as their first kiss so many years earlier, her body pressing against his, an urgency overtaking them both. 'Stay with me, Nelly,' he beseeched her huskily. 'I can't bear to lose you again.'

Her sons, bless them, have been broadly supportive. Owen had some reservations – 'You will be careful, won't you, Mum? You're probably a bit fragile right now, after everything, to be making any huge life decisions' – but Cameron only encouraged her to have fun, to change her flight and extend her stay, promising he'd take care of all the domestic tasks that needed attention. They've both been in regular contact with Frank, who is back in rehab, and Owen apparently helped him find the words for his recent public statement, full of contrition. The *Panorama* documentary came out, and it was predictably awful by all accounts, but Frank's fulsome apology and admission of guilt have helped to lessen the storm. Cameron also persuaded him to make some sizeable charitable donations to women's shelters and addiction counselling organisations, which have been favourably received. Their father's misdeeds haven't totally dominated the boys' lives, though – Owen and his wife Polly are moving to a bigger house just outside Brighton, while Cameron and Nate are adopting a rescue puppy. They're doing just fine in Nelly's absence.

The women in her life have been far more enthusiastic about her decision to set sail with Alexander. *WOW!!!* Lorraine messaged, along with a boat emoji, sunshine emoji, dancing couple emoji and – Lorraine! – an aubergine emoji. *Can't BELIEVE you're turning down a stay in our static for this mad adventure, mind,* she'd added, along with a crying-laughing emoji. *You'd better send me more postcards this time. And photos! And all the juicy details please!!!!!*

Claudia gave her a hug when Nelly told her she was cancelling her flight home, and said this was the best news she'd heard all day. Even lovely Duska on reception had smiled and said she was very happy for her. Nelly has promised to give them a glowing review on some travel website they're all obsessed with but, in the meantime, she left three envelopes with generous tips for Claudia, Duska and whichever cleaner had had to contend with the state Frank had left their suite in.

On her final night at the hotel, she had got chatting to a pair of sisters at the bar while waiting for Alexander to pick her up for dinner. It was the actress and her sister, and the actress – Miranda – actually squealed and ordered Nelly a glass of champagne when she told her she'd seen her in a play at the Almeida, might it have been *The Seagull*? 'You'll never know how much this means to me!' she had cried, looking absolutely beside herself. 'Thank you! At last! Someone with a bit more culture than a yogurt!'

They had been such fun, the two of them, that when Alexander messaged with his apologies to say that he was running late Nelly had carried on chatting to them for quite a while. Towards the bottom of the champagne, she found herself confiding in them about her plans for travel, and they couldn't have been more delighted for her.

'I'm getting a divorce and I despise all men right now, but even *I'm* a bit in love with Alexander from what you've told us,' Imogen had declared. 'Sometimes you have to accept what the universe is offering you – especially if it's a gorgeous man with his own yacht.'

They'd all laughed, but the words have stuck with Nelly. The universe has given her so many things over the years – two wonderful sons, a mostly good marriage (until it wasn't), loyal friends – and now, yes, a gorgeous man with his own yacht. A gorgeous man who she adores, moreover, who she never wants to say goodbye to again.

She picks up Alexander's binoculars, peering through them to where she can just make out a lumpy shape on the horizon: Italy, presumably. What a thrill to arrive like this, by boat, as the mood takes them. 'Land ahoy!' she yells, feeling a sudden rush of exhilaration, and swings round to see Alexander smiling at her. Wherever it is they're going to next, she just knows they'll be happy there. She's sure of it.

★

Meanwhile, back on Kefalonia, The Ionian Escape has moved onto its low-season footing and a slower pace has descended. As the flight schedules are scaled back, so are the seasonal hospitality contracts, as most of the young staff members return to education or their home countries. Konstantinos has taken some time out to travel around mainland Europe with friends. So far they have seen the sights – all right, the bars and night-clubs – of Berlin, Hamburg and Amsterdam, and Konstantinos has found that there is something about dancing beneath the strobing lights in a new European city, catching the eye of one snake-hipped young man or another, that makes him feel truly alive. There's talk of them travelling to the Alps as the ski season starts, picking up some work there and enjoying the winter lifestyle while it lasts. Whenever he thinks about the village where he grew up, his father's small-minded ideas for him – building work, staying in his place – he is glad to have freed himself from the constraints of that world in favour of his own path, his own way to live.

Other staff members are feeling upbeat as the pace of work slows: Duska's baby has – praise be! – now started sleeping through the night, which is just as well, seeing as Duska woke up the other morning feeling bloated and hormonal. To her and her husband's great joy, it seems a new member of the family is on their way, a sibling for Anna, due in fact on what would have been Duska's grandmother's birthday. It's a good sign.

As for Claudia and Dimitris ... having set out trying to take their new relationship slowly, they've had to accept that that's just not possible. She's always liked him but now that they've spent so much time together, she has found herself falling for him, deeply and helplessly. Their radiant happiness, moreover, is apparently obvious to everyone. 'Wait ... something's different about you two,' Lili had said, eyeing them suspiciously, when she came back from work on the day when everything had changed. The two of them were in the garden, both sitting under the shade of the canopy, and their body language must have given them away. That, or the stubble rash all over Claudia's face, from when Dimitris had claimed he never wanted to stop kissing her. 'What's going on?' Lili had asked, one hand on her hip.

Dimitris and Claudia had looked at one another, smiling. 'We cleared up a mutual misunderstanding,' he told his daughter. 'We have both been kind of shy and stupid—'

'Speak for yourself!' Claudia interjected.

'But now we ...' Another look from one to the other, a bashful smile between them. 'But now we have said it – we like each other. And so we are ... Well, I hope we are ... going to give this a try?'

Lili had thrown her hands up, groaning. 'Papa, these are not romantic words,' she laughed. 'You might need to work on that a bit.' But she was smiling nonetheless, her face open and warm to Claudia. 'I am happy for you both. You two are good together!'

It's early days, but Claudia thinks Lili is right: they *are* good together. They've each chalked up a bad marriage in the past and so neither of them have delusions about what can go wrong, but she instinctively feels that the footings of this relationship are on far firmer ground than her previous marriage ever was. Dimitris is in a different league to Marcus; he is kind and funny and – who knew? – extremely sexy too. She feels safe with him. Safe, and happy, and excited about how the relationship might deepen further.

Barb, her mum, is already petitioning hard for them to take a holiday in Australia just as soon as Dimitris' ankle is completely healed. 'Or maybe your dad and I will have to take a little trip over there to see you,' she'd said on a video call the other day.

'Mum, why are you making that sound like it's a threat?' Claudia had laughed. 'Don't worry, you won't need to stage an intervention and rescue me from this one.'

Not least, she reflects afterwards, because she has learned how to rescue *herself* since then – and make a good life for herself too. The future, she thinks, is gleaming.

Epilogue

The Mother

It's November, and Tracey Vallance is washing up after a very jolly Sunday lunch, humming along to Classic FM on her phone. It's many years since her offspring flew the nest, one by one, for university and jobs and life in different cities, so it's always a treat when they find their way back home again. Today, both daughters are here, as well as her dad, and everyone is on good form. Paul excelled himself with the roast, her dad seemed to remember who everybody was and is now contentedly sleeping off the effort, and the girls ... Tears fill Tracey's eyes as she replays the evident closeness between them that is back; the good humour and affectionate teasing. She's even put up with being called one of their silly nicknames all day; anything to make them happy.

The first bars of 'The Swan' by Saint-Säens drift out from the speaker and she immediately dries her soapy hands on her jeans in order to turn up the volume, letting the plangent melody pour into her. Goodness, this takes her back, she thinks with a happy sigh. All the way back to the eighties, in fact, and her very first date with Paul, back when they both lived in London.

Miranda comes into the kitchen at that moment with a stack of dessert bowls, which she begins loading into the dishwasher. There's a difference about Miranda these days, Tracey thinks, eyeing her eldest daughter fondly. Since coming back from her holiday, she's seemed much happier. Easier in herself. Of course, that's probably helped by the fact that she's just picked up a cracking part for herself in *Penelope*, a new play ('a feminist retelling of the *Odyssey*' apparently), which she is buzzing about. The cast is all female, as is the director, and they seem to have bonded tremendously in rehearsals. 'I absolutely love them,' Miranda said over lunch just now, her face luminous with excitement as she described their days spent rehearsing, their frequent evenings out together, how the director has her sights on Broadway next and is promising to take them all over there if she can swing it.

Tracey is so glad for her; it's all you ever want for your children, isn't it, to see that light in their eyes, the enthusiasm shining out of them? Yes, and of course there was that intriguing moment earlier when Imogen started teasing Miranda about some man they're referring to as 'the Godsend', don't think Tracey didn't notice it. Miranda had turned very pink in the cheeks and looked down into her apple crumble with a secret smile. Well! What was all that about? She'll winkle it out of them later, she vows, when the men aren't around.

'This again!' Miranda says suddenly, gesturing to Tracey's

phone. 'You know when you keep hearing a piece of music all the time? I swear this one is following me around.'

'"The Swan"?' Tracey says. 'It's one of mine and your dad's favourites. You must have heard us playing it a million times.'

'They played it at Evelyn's funeral,' Miranda says, slotting spoons into the cutlery holder. 'Then I heard it in some advert or other on telly. Then it popped up on my Spotify even though I never listen to any classical music. Don't you think that's weird?'

Tracey shrugs as she rinses a saucepan and puts it in the drying rack. 'It's a very famous piece,' she says. 'It's special to a lot of people, I bet. I was just thinking before you came in, actually, about hearing it, the very first time I went out with your dad.' She feels herself soften all over again, remembering that night.

'Ahh, that's nice,' Miranda says, then goes to the kettle. 'Gramps is awake, by the way; I said I'd make him a cup of tea. Mind if I just … ?'

Tracey steps aside, leaving space at the sink for her to come in and fill the kettle.

'I didn't know that about your first date with Dad,' Miranda continues. 'That's very posh, going to a classical concert together. Was he a bit slick, then, back in the day?'

Tracey smiles. 'Not really. One of his friends worked at the Barbican, he was always getting free tickets for things,' she says. 'All the same, it was very ro—'

'The Barbican, did you say?' Miranda is giving her a funny look, for some reason, standing there with the kettle in her hand. 'And you heard this piece there? When was this, anyway?'

'Turn the tap off, love, it's full, look,' Tracey says as water begins pouring out of the kettle's spout. 'Gosh, let me think. The late eighties? Nineteen eighty-eight possibly?'

Miranda is still looking weird. 'Oh my God. Do you remember what the cellist looked like, by any chance?'

'The cellist? No! How could I? I was too busy falling in love with your dad,' Tracey says, steeped in nostalgia. Before that point in the evening, she had enjoyed watching the musicians concentrating so intently and the spectacle of the conductor, and the music had been wonderful too, swelling around the auditorium. But it was during this piece, 'The Swan', played only by the cellist and the pianist, that Tracey found herself unexpectedly moved. More than that, actually; she felt utterly overcome, as if the music was speaking directly to a part of her that she didn't even know was there before. It was only as the piece ended that she realised she had reached for Paul's hand at some point during it, as if the romance of the music had taken her over completely. Then she'd glanced at him to see that he was smiling back at her, shiny-eyed, and he'd squeezed her hand in his. It felt nice, she realised. Right. Certainly enough to sweep her through the rest of the concert, and all the way back to his small flat in Tooting, and his creaking double bed.

'There's a reason that your dad's always joking we nearly called you Swanhilda, you know,' she blurts out suddenly. Oh dear, that's lunchtime wine for you. 'Sorry, forget I said that. TMI, or whatever you and Imogen say.'

But to her surprise, Miranda's laughing as if something has delighted her. 'Oh, Mum,' she says, putting the kettle down and suddenly hugging her. 'That's just made my day. That makes me so, so happy.'

Tracey hugs her back, a little taken aback, not quite sure what's going on but glad for her daughter's professed happiness all the same. The piece comes to an end – beautiful as ever – and Tracey sends up a silent prayer of gratitude to its composer, and also the cellist they saw that night. They'll never know the seismic part they played in Tracey's life, she thinks, as she gives her daughter a final squeeze and lets go. 'Well, if you're happy, I'm happy,' she tells her. 'Aren't we the lucky ones?'

Acknowledgements

The Ionian Escape is (sadly) a fictitious hotel, although many of the places on Kefalonia and Ithaca that feature in this book are real – I hope I have done them justice! The aim of this novel was very much to recreate a holiday flavour within the pages, and take my readers away with me, and if you are now feeling remotely inspired to explore these beautiful islands yourself, I can heartily recommend visiting them both.

Closer to home, I would like to thank the many people who helped during the writing of this novel – it's always a huge team effort with a lot of heroic work behind the scenes. My editor Cassie Browne has done a brilliant job, as ever, in steering this book from when it first began as a few character scribbles on a page, through rounds of editing and many conversations, to the finished novel you have just read. Thank you, Cassie, for your fantastic creative input and for the thought and care you have contributed; I appreciate it all so much. Thanks also to Kat Burdon, editorial eagle-eye, as well as Ella Patel, Dave Murphy and Katy Blott at Quercus.

Hooray for the David Higham squad, especially super-agent Lizzy Kremer; thank you for your insight, wisdom, encouragement and sense of humour. Thanks also to Orli Vogt-Vincent, Maddalena Cavaciuti, Rachael Sharples, Alice Howe, Rhian Kane and Ilaria Albani.

Thank you, wonderful Ruth O'Shea, for answering my cello-playing questions! It goes without saying that any mistakes are mine, all mine.

Lots of love to my excellent author friends, especially Ronnie Henry, Harriet Evans, Rachel Delahaye, Milly Johnson, Cally Taylor, Jo Nadin, Jill Mansell, Mimi Hall, Kirsty Crawford, Rosie Walsh, Emma Stonex and Kate Riordan. You're the best (all of you) and I love hanging out with you.

Thanks as always to Martin − not least for our wonderful Greek trip together and (hopefully) not minding too much whenever I kept talking about the characters of this book while we were there. You are the greatest, funniest and kindest sounding-board, cheerleader, tea-maker, brainstormer and first reader an author could ever wish for − I know how lucky I am! Big love to Hannah, Tom and Holly too − you've made my life so much happier and better simply for being your gorgeous selves.

Finally, the biggest thank you of all has to go to *you*, and my other readers − I wouldn't be able to do this without you. Thank you, if you've ever sent me a nice message, come to an event, recommended my books to a friend − I appreciate you all enormously. It's truly an honour and a privilege to be a published author, and whether you're new to my work or you've read all twenty novels, then thank you for coming on this journey with me. I sincerely hope you enjoyed your island getaway!

Discover more from *Sunday Times*
bestselling author

Lucy
Diamond

Visit www.lucydiamond.co.uk for:

About Lucy

★

FAQs for Aspiring Writers

★

And to contact Lucy

To sign up to Lucy's newsletter
scan the QR code here:

Follow Lucy on social media:

 @LucyDiamondAuthor

 @lucydiamondwrites